LENIN LIVES NEXT DOOR

JENNIFER EREMEEVA

SMALL
BATCH
BOOKS

LENIN LIVES NEXT DOOR

JENNIFER EREMEEVA

MARRIAGE, MARTINIS, AND MAYHEM IN MOSCOW

Book and jacket designed by Carolyn Eckert

ISBN: 978-1-937650-31-5
Library of Congress Control Number: 2014930128

SMALL
BATCH
BOOKS

493 SOUTH PLEASANT STREET
AMHERST, MASSACHUSETTS 01002
413.230.3943
SMALLBATCHBOOKS.COM

For HRH, who promised to read it
when it was finished

ACKNOWLEDGMENTS

IN MOSCOW, DEAR friends encouraged and educated me, patiently read through blog posts, gave thoughtful feedback on the work in progress, and provided much of the inspiration and a good deal of the material upon which *Lenin Lives Next Door* is based. My heartfelt thanks go to Guy Archer, Henrietta Challinor, Torrey Clark, Katherine Dovlatov, Elizabeth Buchanan Elford, Alexandra Glebovskaya, Beth Knobel, Irina Korneva, Carole Lawlor, Teri Lindeberg, Annette Loftus, Marina Malakhova, Heidi McCormack, Elizabeth Messud, Michelle Michalenko, Holly Nielsen, Michael Pugh, Justine Seepers, Asiya Sharafoutdinova, Lisa Shukov, Alla Solovieva, Carol Sorrenti, Tess Stobie, Elizabeth Sullivan, Mike White, and Mikhail Yudin.

It proved a lot easier to write about Russia once I spent some time away from it, and Western Massachusetts is a wonderful place to write and live. Thanks go out for the friendship, support, and encouragement provided in generous Pioneer Valley helpings by Ted Giles, Kris McCue, Susie Miller, Regina Mooney, Lisa Papademetriou, Ben and Julie Quick, Lorraine Sahagian, Kevin Sprague, Anja and Marie Waechter, Ben Zackheim, and all the wonderful writers associated with Nerissa Nields's Big Yellow House writing workshops, particularly Elaine Apthorp, Melissa Carter Miller, and the incomparable Nerissa herself, who provided coaching and encouragement throughout the entire process.

To all my friends in cyberspace, whom I don't yet know in

person, thank you too. Your comments, feedback, tweets, and outreach across the Internet has been a big part of growing as a writer.

Bob Drumm, a great boss, veteran eggnog maker, and travel enthusiast made multiple trips to Russia possible, for which I will always be grateful.

Eugene Abov, Elena Bobrova, Nora Fitzgerald, and Artem Zagorodnov of *Russia Beyond the Headlines* gave me the invaluable opportunities and deadlines as a columnist that were crucial to honing my voice. Doug Grad pointed the way toward blogging, helpfully explaining what a "platform" was and how to build it.

I find it difficult to craft a sentence that conveys sufficient gratitude to my friend and fellow writer Liz Bedell, whose patient and skillful first edit of *Lenin Lives Next Door* helped turn a manuscript into a book. Thank you.

Trisha Thompson, Fred Levine, Carolyn Eckert, and the entire team at Small Batch Books got *Lenin Lives Next Door* ready to face the world with masterful editing, creative input, a new name, and a winning cover. Thanks to all for your patience, cooperation, and ability to get the job done!

Lenin Lives Next Door would not have been possible without the support of my family. My mother, Frances, an accomplished writer herself, was steadfast in her encouragement, always the first to respond to a new post or a completed chapter. With her in the front row of the cheering section was my father, Peter Buttenheim, who tackled the Augean Stables of my eclectic spelling and grammar in early drafts. My niece Claire Saint Amour provided enthusiastic but critical feedback on early drafts. Thanks as well to my brother-in-law Paul, sister Alison, and my niece Julia.

My mercurial daughter, Francesca, dazzles me every day with her graceful and joyful progress through this world, garnering friends and fans wherever she goes. She kept my spirits up throughout the writing of this book, ever optimistic about its ultimate success.

Finally, my particular gratitude goes to my Handsome Russian Husband, to whom this book is dedicated. You make me laugh and love every single day. Спасибо!

Entertaining vodka drinkers
Is a job they give to me.
Making nice guys out of stinkers
Seems to be my cup of tea.
What they really need behind the iron wall
Is the hostess with the mostes' on the ball!

—"The Hostess with the Mostes' on the Ball,"
from *Call Me Madam* (music and lyrics by Irving Berlin)

CONTENTS

CHAPTER 1

FINDING COMRADE RIGHT

YOU HAVE TO really want to go to Russia. The briefest of visits involves a lot of paperwork, and if you want to hang around for any length of time, they make you take a leprosy test.

Russians pride themselves on their legendary hospitality, but whenever I stagger off the ten-hour flight from New York, I never seem to see the smiling, flaxen-haired Slavic beauty in national dress offering me the traditional symbol of welcome: a round loaf of bread topped with a small container of salt. Instead, a thirteen-year-old passport-control guy with pitted acne and a dull green uniform scrutinizes me unsmilingly from behind a smeared bulletproof window just long enough to make me feel like I actually might *have* leprosy.

I pilot my rickety cart, stacked high with luggage, through a phalanx of the world's most aggressively unpleasant taxi drivers. Once outside the terminal there are the titanic statues of Russian military types who, "with conquering limbs astride," guard the gateway to every major Russian city. Some are dressed as medieval warriors, others in the high helmets of nineteenth-century hussars, but most, like the ones who guard the road to downtown Moscow, are clearly those who defended Russia from the Nazis. Huge and menacing, they loom up, their arms firmly extended, palms held out in warning. You do not need to speak a word of Russian to interpret their message: "Halt and go no further!" they say, and I never feel that this is madly welcoming.

If you ask me (and no one ever, ever does), the Russians should rethink the statuary. When you are all about turning Moscow into a global financial hub or transforming Sochi, a sleepy, subtropical backwater, into the venue for the 2014 Winter Olympics, the menacing Red Army dudes on steroids just send the wrong message.

None of this mattered to me in the beginning, because I really wanted to go to Russia. I had wanted to go since I was thirteen and stood on tiptoes to slide *Nicholas and Alexandra,* by Robert Massie, down off the school library shelves. That thick black tome became, as the best books do, a portal to another world. I didn't read *Nicholas and Alexandra*—I inhaled it. I devoured it. In fact, I think I eventually stole it from the library. I couldn't help myself. I spent hours poring over the sepia photos of the last tsar and his attractive, tragically doomed family, and I became determined to go to Russia. Who wouldn't want to go to that vast, distant, secret, snowbound country of Firebirds and onion domes, where beautiful, sepia-skinned grand duchesses had names like Tatiana and Anastasia? At this point in stories like these, there is always a kindly librarian to point the way, so I'll include one here: she pointed me further down the rabbit hole, and I discovered lusty Catherine the Great and lunatic Peter the Great. I met Prince Andrei Bolkonsky, Anna Karenina and Vronsky, and Yuri Zhivago and his muse, Lara; and of course I wanted to go to Russia even more. I wanted to drink tea out of a glass from a hissing samovar, I wanted to stay up all night for the Easter vigil, I wanted to ride in a troika and take a brocade-upholstered train through a blizzard, the obligatory handsome army officer at my side. I wrapped my head in woolen scarves like Julie Christie and Diane Keaton and imagined myself triumphing over adversity in the midst of war and revolution, though to be honest, my interest in Russian history ran out of gas at the logical stopping point of 1917.

Though later the grittier, grimmer, gray Soviet stuff came to interest me in an academic way, it never drew me in on a visceral level the way imperial Russia did. *Nicholas and Alexandra* left me with the unshakable conviction that Lenin and his cronies were the villains of the piece, and long after I was old enough to know better I nurtured a naive but heartfelt vision that one day, the sepia-colored Russian people would rise up, throw off the Soviet yoke, outlaw Marxism-Leninism, and bring back the sepia-colored tsar. Russia would live happily ever after. By happy coincidence, in the autumn of 1985, when I walked into my freshman-year Russian language class, the Russians seemed to be on the verge of doing just that.

Russians say of their native tongue that it is *bogatiy*, or "rich." By this they mean that Russian words and phrases can have multiple meanings and convey such universal truth that translation is often impossible. In my college years I associated "rich" with the considerable financial aid available from the US government if you were willing to take a crack at learning Russian—another happy coincidence. I spent tortured hours with flash cards and learned to use a different part of my mouth, forcing my tongue and teeth to pair unlikely consonants that have no truck with one another in Romance languages. *Z* and *h* tell the names of heroes: Zhukov and Zhdanov. *K* and *v* together herald two incredibly important Russian words: *kvartira* (apartment) and *kvitansiya* (receipt), and the lack of either can lead to epic Russian stalemate. *T* and *s* form one letter, crucial if, like me, one was interested in the last tsar, or the "*Tsentralniy Komityet*," of the Communist Party. See what I mean? I spent months figuring out the difference between two remarkably similar letters—*sch* and *sh*—through endless repetitions of a popular Russian tongue twister. Translated, it ominously warns that the Russian diet is relentlessly monotonous; it reads: "cabbage soup and porridge are our staple foods."

I learned that this is no mere folklore when I took a ten-day student trip to Leningrad, Pskov, Tver, and Moscow, during which time we consumed a great deal of both cabbage soup and buckwheat porridge and not a lot else. The USSR in February 1987 was gritty, grim, and gray, but the good news was that it looked like Team Lenin was losing the struggle for global Communism. Within six minutes of checking in at the shabby Hotel October on the wrong end of Nevsky Prospekt, my fellow travelers and I were deluged with offers from the chambermaids to buy our blue jeans, cigarettes, sneakers, and, in one case, our actual suitcases. Could we blame them? There was nothing in the stores, and Gorbachev's career-destroying "dry law" was in effect. Everyone looked positively miserable. This did nothing to dull my passion for Russia, however, as is evident in one particular photograph from that trip. We have just stepped off the tour bus in Palace Square in Leningrad. I am in the foreground, and the magnificent mint-green Winter Palace, which today houses the Hermitage Museum, takes up all of the background. The photographer catches the moment when I turn around to my fellow travelers with a look of pure rapture and triumph.

Readers, do not confuse a passion for Russia with a passion for one single Russian. The former involves a lot of great literature, the growing understanding that you should never ask a question beginning with *why*, and a certain amount of time poring over *501 Russian Verbs*. The latter means regular leprosy tests. I knew from an early age that I really wanted to go to Russia, but I never planned to stay there. Certainly not for twenty years. I never planned to start buying toothpaste there (a certain sign that you've committed to living in a country). A Russian husband formed no part of my vague "when I grow up" plans, although I was given fair warning that one was in my future.

A Georgian sightseeing guide spotted him in my coffee grounds about a year and a half before he showed up. Her name was Dzidzia, and by the time I met her, in 1990, I was pretty good at moving my mouth around those unlikely consonant pairings. I knew that Russian swear words packed forty times the amount of lewdness as their English counterparts, and thanks to a language lab staffed with a legion of Jewish émigrés from the Soviet Union, I had an adroit little rasp to my *r*'s, which made everyone think I came from Odessa. I had graduated from Columbia the year before, and instead of sensibly parlaying my Russian Area Studies diploma into a grown-up job, I had gone into the tourism racket, guiding American tourists around what would soon be known as the former Soviet Union. I met Dzidzia in yet another unpronounceable city, Tbilisi, the capital of Soviet Georgia. We shared the sacrosanct guides' table one day at lunch, and she offered to tell my fortune, which she said would be clearly written in my coffee cup.

"Take the cup," she commanded, "and swirl it around the way a clock goes, then, how do you say in English, upend it—"

"Turn it upside down, you mean?" I asked.

"Exactly so!"

I gave the cup a clockwise swirl and in one firm gesture flipped it onto the saucer. "Now what?"

"Now we see," said Dzidzia, gingerly picking up the cup with her index finger and thumb. She peered inside, silently evaluated the contents for a few minutes, then set the cup down carefully at the side of the now dirty saucer, brushed a few grains of coffee off of her hands, and smiled.

"Interesting," she pronounced.

"Interesting good, or interesting bad?" I asked.

"Let me see . . . you wander," she began, and then laughed. "Well, we don't need the coffee to show us that, do we?"

"Not really," I agreed.

"But soon, yes, quite soon, you will settle," she continued, "and far from your own home, for a long time, with a . . . with a man who is coming—you do not know him yet, but you will soon. Do you see him right here?" She pointed to a V-shaped smear that didn't look like much of anything, let alone a life partner.

"What kind of a man?" I asked.

"He's a military man, that much is very clear from the V— those are the, how you say, the epaulettes. This man, you don't know him yet . . . see how the V is on the other side of the cup? He's a strong man. Yes, I see that you will work hard and have . . . I see houses, yes, and I see one child." She flipped her hands up in a celebratory gesture. "Happy evermore!"

"Happily ever after, you mean," I said, laughing. "Okay, so where do I find this Comrade Right?"

"I think he is not so far from here . . . ," said Dzidzia, turning the cup thoughtfully.

"How not so far?" I asked.

"Perhaps it is our country," she said slowly, squinting back into the cup, then making a sound that was much more snort than laugh. "In which case, good luck with the happy ever after . . . you are going to need it. Our Soviet men are impossible."

So I set out to discover just how impossible Soviet men were. I herded my group up to Kiev, where I met Pasha, who had chiseled cheekbones and an arrangement with the door attendant of the shabby Hotel Rus. He later married a French countess— of course he did. Then on to dazzling Leningrad, where the sun never sets in June, and there I ricocheted from dates with Yuri, a sophisticated maître d'hôtel, to riding out to watch Leningrad's stately drawbridges go up at 2:00 a.m. with Stass, a black-market currency trader with Windex-colored eyes and a brand-new Lada. These encounters were mildly satisfying in the way a tepid Fanta can be at the lone café on the road from Samarkand to Bukhara, but like the Fanta they left an unpleasant aftertaste, did not slake my thirst, and left me craving something more authentic, something simpler and more straightforward. Something served at the right temperature.

I still really wanted to be in Russia, and by 1991 it was exploding with opportunity. The tourists were flooding in, and I spent the entire boom summer of 1991 running back-to-back tours and hosting trade show delegations. In 1991, it seemed, everyone wanted to go to Russia. I met more *Nicholas and Alexandra* fans than I ever imagined existed. They trooped, footsore but obedient, through the Kremlin, Peterhof, and Tsarskoye Selo.

"Can we spend six days in the Hermitage?" they would plead on day one, to which I would smile enigmatically and say sure, then watch with private satisfaction as they limped out of the world's largest museum, defeated after only three hours. I was still pining for my sepia-colored Russia, but I was distracted by the more garish celluloid-and-neon Russia that was steadily replacing the infinite shades of Soviet gray. The long-dormant Russian economy was sputtering and chugging slowly into first gear. There were the executives, who came to uncover a virgin market of 150 million people who had never known a reliable supply of toilet paper. Just opposite the seedy Hotel Cosmos, where we stayed with large groups, was VDNKh, the All-Russia Exhibition Center. This vast park opened in 1958 to glorify the triumph of the planned communist economy; in 1991 it played host to nonstop capitalist trade shows: furniture, mobile phones, agricultural machinery, office supplies, leisure and hospitality, oil and gas—you name it, it was at VDNKh.

That summer flew by, and my confidence soared. In my mind I had mastered all the complicated rules of perestroika Russia. There were two exchange rates: the official rate and the black-market rate, and I knew how to work them both. There were hard-currency stores and bars where you could purchase recognizable commodities such as Cadbury chocolate, Marlboro cigarettes, and Gordon's gin. I doled these out to oil the wheels that needed to turn flawlessly. Everyone wanted something I had, so I was popular. I knew exactly how to snag the only air-conditioned bus in Bukhara and where to score last-minute orchestra seats to *Swan Lake* at the Bolshoi. I was the best in the business at organizing shiftless porters to move 150 suitcases out of the bowels of a bus, onto a railway station platform, and into individual couchettes in under twenty minutes. At midnight. In the winter of 1990 I did it in a blizzard. Three times.

My packed schedule had one week free in July, and I knew exactly what I wanted to do with it: explore Leningrad on my own, unencumbered by a busload of weary American tourists. Friends eagerly offered sofas, and these off-piste arrangements, par for the course in New York and London, made me feel deliciously naughty. They further underscored, I felt, my total mastery of the establishment regulations. The only real problem was how to get from Moscow to Leningrad. My visa permitted me to stay in Moscow only. That in itself was no problem; I knew at least three train conductors on the midnight *Red Arrow* train between Moscow and Leningrad who, for a small fee or bottle of something from the hard-currency store, would forget to check my passport. The big question was how to buy a ticket. Soviet citizens had to show their internal passports to go to the bathroom, much less travel from one city to another, and I was clearly not a Soviet citizen, so I couldn't go to the train station and try to purchase a ticket. I could go to any state tourism committee office and purchase a "hard-currency" ticket, but they would definitely check my passport, see that I had no visa, and flatly refuse to sell me anything. No matter. I was, I fancied, really becoming quite Soviet in my thinking, and when presented with a regulatory roadblock, I immediately began to scheme a way around it. I deployed my *blat*.

Blat is one of those words you absolutely have to learn if you intend to hang around Russia long enough to need the leprosy test. Because Russian is such a rich language, it's hard to define *blat* in just one English word, but it means "connections," as in "I know someone who knows someone whose uncle has what you need." It connotes the valuable currency of influence in a country where the coin of the realm is about as useful as the stuff in the Monopoly box. Someone who is "*blatnoi*" or "*blatnaya*" (the feminine version) is blessed with these essential ties to decision makers who help them get through the day and inch up the greasy pole of Soviet life.

Outside the Tchaikovsky Concert Hall earlier that summer, waiting for clients to stream out of another folklore performance, I stood with my fellow guides at the feet of the monolithic statue of Vladimir Mayakovsky, tribune of the Russian Revolution, depicted striding purposefully toward a brighter future (which included suicide). If you had told me then that in fifteen years I'd live two blocks up the road and that the bard of the revolution would soon be striding purposefully toward Moscow's largest KFC, I'd have told you hell would freeze over first. I chatted with the other guides, making sure to pass around my Marlboro Lights. Someone went to the concert hall's buffet for a bottle of Armenian cognac, which we drank from the bottom halves of a wooden matryoshka doll. I made discreet inquiries and was surprised and pleased to discover I was only one degree of separation from what I needed. Congratulating myself that I was very *blatnaya* indeed, I went to wake up Volodia.

Volodia Stepanov was an Arabic-speaking guide with a lot of time on his hands. All of his clients were Syrians who purchased package tours from the state tourism committee for seven nights in Moscow with the full complement of meals and excursions. Instead of going to the Kremlin or the Pushkin Museum, however, they went shopping for refrigerators and other electrical appliances. I had a vague idea why there was such a dearth of electrical appliances in Syria, but why the USSR was considered a consumer goods mecca I never understood. Volodia had to be at the hotel to sign for their meals, but apart from doing that, he spent most days flat on his back on the couches of the state tourism committee's large office at the Hotel Cosmos, sleeping off long nights of hard drinking.

I treated Volodia to a strong cup of Italian coffee from the hard-currency bar, and we began the delicate pavane of a transaction executed *po blatu* (by means of connections). Volodia told me to leave the ticket issue and a twenty-dollar bill or a carton of American Marlboro cigarettes with him. Preferably, he said, the cigarettes. Yes, he knew someone. No, it was no trouble. In the essential step of underscoring to one another that our relationship was in no way limited to the mercantile, Volodia pressed upon me a warm invitation to his birthday party the following week, which I enthusiastically accepted. He gave me directions to his apartment and warned me it was a little bit out of the way but accessible by taxi.

"Just don't tell the taxi driver you are American," he warned, "or they will charge you a fortune."

"I know that!" I said defensively, priding myself on the finely honed taxi-haggling skills my friends had taught me. We agreed to the handoff in three days' time, and I left for the airport to meet a busload of cellular telephone sales guys.

However, when the night of the birthday party rolled around, I almost didn't go. I had a bottle of gin in my room, and I was sorely tempted to slip Maxim the bartender a pack of Marlboro Reds in exchange for a bag of ice, buy three bottles of tonic, and call it a night. But my hotel room, which faced east and baked all day in the sun, was an oven, and the thought of letting Volodia down seemed churlish. Russians put great store in both *blat* and birthday parties. I had to go. So I took a hot shower, sprayed on some duty-free Chanel, and stashed the bottle of Scotch I'd purchased at the hard-currency store in my knapsack. I left the hotel and walked down the long driveway, specially designed to keep the hotel guests separate from the people in the street. I walked past the official taxi rank and took the underpass below Prospekt Mira to find a gypsy cab driver who would take me to the wrong end of the ominous-sounding Highway of the Enthusiasts for a price I could afford.

I pretended to be from Ljubljana, the most European part of crumbling Yugoslavia, a ruse I kept up for the entire fifty-minute journey as the driver of the beat-up Zhiguli sliced through the concentric circles of Moscow. We rattled past the monumental postwar Stalin buildings, which tapered off into the shabby five-story "Khrushchev slums" of the 1960s, then out to the grimy prefab high-rises of the 1970s, and finally to Collective Farm Workers' Street.

The party was in full swing when I arrived, everyone squeezed around a long table crowded with half-eaten mayonnaise-based salads and a jungle of sticky glasses. Volodia could barely stand but politely asked about my journey.

"I told the driver I was a Yugoslavian and only paid thirty rubles," I informed him proudly, as I struggled into a space between him and a girl called Lena.

"Our Yugoslavka," slurred Volodia, ". . . brilliant!" He made brief introductions of the other people around the table: his younger brother, Sasha; Sasha's girlfriend, who was confusingly also called Sasha; other colleagues; relatives; and then a guy sitting almost directly opposite me, who appeared to be one of the few people at the party still sober enough to carry on a conversation.

And you know what, reader? It really is a truth universally acknowledged: the minute you stop looking for Mr. Right, just look up, and there he will be.

Smashing looking, I thought, as I realized he was regarding me with equal interest. He had a smile that started in his warm brown eyes and ended at my curled-up toes.

"And this is our comrade who organized your train ticket," finished Volodia.

"Gosh," I said, and instantly mentally kicked myself. Who the hell says "gosh" anymore? Certainly not savvy Yugoslavians from Ljubljana. I switched back to Russian. "Well, thanks so much. They are hard to get. . . . Do you work at the train station?"

"Something like that," he said, adroitly avoiding answering.

There was a badly dubbed, grainy version of *Top Gun* on the TV—which back then they couldn't get enough of. Eventually everyone else evaporated in different directions to either pass out or pair up, leaving just Comrade Smashing and me. He opened one of the remaining bottles of sweet Russian champagne and sat down next to me to watch the film.

"Those aren't our pilots," he said presently, as Tom Cruise was being aerodynamically haggled by MiGs, whose pilots' faces were fully covered with sinister Darth Vader–type headgear.

"Aren't they?" I asked, not caring one way or another, just hoping he'd stay right where he was.

"Those are our planes, certainly," he explained. "Not our pilots."

"Oh," I said, thinking that, for someone who worked at a railway station, he seemed to know a lot about naval aviation. I said as much.

"I'm a military officer," he said, looking at the bottle of champagne to see if I'd had too much.

"I see," I said as we watched Tom take out another MiG.

"Our planes," Smashing said again, "but not our pilots."

"Are you sure?" I asked, wondering where military officers lived and worked.

"But you should know that," he said, looking confused. "You're from Yugoslavia."

"No," I said, "I'm American. I just said I was Yugoslavian to keep the taxi fare down."

"But Volodia called you 'Evgenia Petrovna.'"

"Oh," I explained, "that's just his joke. That's what the Russian guides call me. My name is Jennifer—they call me that because Zhenya, short for Evgenia, is the closest thing to it."

"But Petrovna—you have a patronymic?" he asked, referring to the universal Russian middle name consisting of the father's name and a gender-specific ending.

"No, but my father is called Peter."

"Duh-geen-ee-feyer . . ." He struggled over the unfamiliar syllables of my name.

"Good," I said, smiling.

"I'm going to call you Petrovna," he declared. My stomach flip-flopped. This was seriously encouraging. Russians use the patronymic together with the full formal name to show respect, but the patronymic alone, as my Russian teachers had explained back in college, denotes warm intimacy.

Warm intimacy duly followed.

The next day I went to wake Volodia from an epic after-party slumber. He was a mess, sprawled on the state tourism committee couch, snoring audibly.

"Tell me more about your friend from last night," I demanded, nudging him up and handing him a shot glass of brandy, then a double coffee.

Volodia sat up gingerly, holding his arm against his eyes to block the light streaming in the windows, and gratefully downed the brandy in one swallow.

"Come on, Volodia," I pleaded, "tell me everything!"

"*Bozhe moi*, my god, I've never seen you like this. Hang on a moment, let me just breathe for a moment," he moaned, massaging his temples. "Well, there isn't much to tell, really. We grew up with him in East Berlin. His dad was in the army, and his mother was our history teacher at the diplomatic school. Is there maybe a younger sister? Or is it a brother? Well, that hardly matters. Anyway, he was more Sasha's friend than mine—they called them the Berlin hooligans. They sold Western comic books and gum when they were fourteen and made a lot of money, I remember that. In fact, that's probably how Sasha got his seed money." Sasha Stepanov, Volodia's brother, was making a tidy sum as a "shuttle trader" going to Turkey and the Far East to buy everything from cheap leather jackets to refrigerators, which I suppose he sold to Syrian tourists. It was a funny time.

"And now he's in the army," I prompted.

"That's right. He left Berlin around the time I did. Well, we were both doing the hostage thing." I looked blank.

Maria Ivanovna, the state tourism committee's officious hotel representative, click-clacked her way into the guides' lounge on her metal-heeled stilettos.

"You aren't supposed to be here," she informed me curtly.

"I know. . . . I'm just going," I said, hastily scrambling to my feet.

"Please go now," insisted Maria Ivanovna, sniffing to show the magnitude of my impropriety.

"Come on, Evgenia Petrovna," said Volodia, hauling himself to his feet. "Let's get another coffee, and you can buy me another brandy while you are at it, and I'll explain it all to you. *Bozhe moi*, my god, I'm a physical wreck." Volodia exhaled, and I reeled from morning-after fumes. I helped him shuffle to a table at the hard-currency bar. He slumped over in a chair and buried his head in his arms. I went up to the bar.

"Maxim, can we have one brandy, two coffees, and . . ." I fished around in my backpack and found no cigarettes. "Give me a pack of Marlboro Reds for the birthday boy."

"Dunhill," grunted Volodia.

"Picky, picky," I said, carrying the brandy to the table.

"The hostage thing," I prompted.

"The hostage thing," said Volodia, gulping down the brandy and shuddering as it hit his system.

"When a family goes abroad to work, they can take any children with them who are under sixteen, but they have to have a parent or a sibling back in the Soviet Union. Once the oldest child is sixteen, he has to return to the Soviet Union as a sort of hostage. If that child wants to visit the family abroad, then the other child, or one of the parents, has to fly in to take their place."

"God, that's awful!" I blurted out. That kind of thing would never happen in my sepia-colored Russia, I thought.

"Not really," said Volodia, sliding a Dunhill out of the pack Maxim had brought to the table. "I lived with my grandparents, and they let me do whatever I wanted. Sasha stayed with our parents and finished school in Berlin. It's why younger children in families like ours are so goddamned spoiled. Probably it's why I drink so much," he added matter-of-factly.

"Why do they have a rule like that?" I asked.

Volodia looked surprised. "*Duritchka* . . . little fool," he said tenderly, "it's to keep the family from defecting to the West."

"Oh," I said. "Right. But they don't have that rule anymore, do they?"

"Who knows?" Volodia shrugged. "Everything is changing now. They say they are going to get rid of exit visas, but I'll believe that when I see it. As to your latest conquest: well, unlike me, who hung around Moscow State University doing not much of anything, he went to the military school in Leningrad, and he's an officer now, though for the life of me I don't know how he managed to get to Moscow. His family is from Ukraine, so how he didn't end up getting assigned to Dnepropetrovsk or some backwater like that is beyond me."

"Are the family still in Berlin?" I asked.

"No, I think they are in Lviv, in Ukraine."

"Ugh," I said, recalling the rubbery chicken and the watery borscht.

"But he's here. I'm guessing he got here because he plays volleyball really well—*really* well."

"How does that work?"

"Honestly," said Volodia, lighting another cigarette, "for someone so smart, you aren't very well informed. Some general or colonel or someone like that would have wanted him to play for the garrison team."

"Oh," I said. "And he's not married?"

"No," said Volodia, "not that I know of, anyway."

"Where does he live?"

"In a dormitory for single officers, which is not a place you can go, dear one, and he can hardly come here," said Volodia, waving his arm toward the entrance of the hotel, where guards were energetically checking visitors for hotel passes.

"No, I suppose not," I agreed glumly.

"Well, you can always meet at my apartment."

"I'm not sure we're at that stage after only four hours," I reflected, "but thank you, Volodia, that's very kind of you."

"He's a nice guy," Volodia said, pushing his coffee cup away and signaling the end of the conversation.

"You like him?"

"I'll tell you this," mused Volodia. "I've known the guy for about twelve years, and in all that time I've never heard anyone say one bad thing about him."

"Is that a good thing?" I pressed.

"Who knows?" Volodia moved his shoulders in an enigmatic Slavic shrug.

I decided the situation called for decisive action. I took a shower, dried myself as best I could with my damp towel, and sprayed on my Chanel. I went to the hotel's hard-currency grocery store, where I bought a six-pack of chilled Heineken beer, wrapped it up in my windbreaker, and stuffed it inside my backpack. I coaxed sketchy instructions from Volodia, who begged me to leave him alone for four consecutive hours. I took an official cab from the rank to the railway station and found the building Volodia described without a hitch. After a few wrong turns, I made my way through a long corridor adorned with scary-looking hammers and sickles and gray photos of old-fashioned people with lots of medals, all of whom looked clinically depressed. I ignored the funny looks I got from passing uniformed *apparatchiki* until I found the door I was looking for. I took a deep breath and knocked. When I heard a grunt, I pushed the door open. Apparently I am the first and last person to ever knock on that door.

He was sitting at a desk in an olive green uniform, playing Pac-Man on a computer.

"Hi," I said.

"Hi, Petrovna," he said, rearranging his features from surprise back into business as usual.

"I've brought you some beer," I said.

"You don't have to do that," he assured me.

"I know," I said, "but I wanted to."

He smiled the smile that went all the way down to my toes.

And that was HRH. My Handsome Russian Husband, although there are days when I silently think of him as my Horrible Russian Husband.

No one seems to "date" anymore, but I suppose that's what HRH and I did the summer of 1991. Exactly what we shouldn't have been doing. Even in 1991 there were strict rules for both of us about fraternizing with foreigners. But the old rules were fraying at the edges. If you pulled at a thread of a rule with enough resolve, you usually found it began to unravel.

"Do you see any scenario where we could possibly be together in a normal way?" I asked in late July.

"Of course," said HRH, for whom the possibilities of the future always seem limitless. "Maybe not now, but definitely later—*potom.* You'll see."

Then came a weekend in August when a military junta seized power for a few days. Gorbachev and his family were placed under house arrest in Sochi, and the world held its breath to see if this meant a return to the repressive regime or a new era for Russia. I was on the last plane out of Russia before things went postal, which enraged me and set a pattern for the next twenty years. I always miss the dramatic stuff—those windows of opportunity to do my Julie Christie/Diane Keaton head scarf thing. It's seriously annoying. I sat by the TV biting my nails, as much about HRH as about my livelihood, but I needn't have worried. We were back to work in three weeks.

After August, with the Wall well and truly down, life in the Soviet Union started to change. For one thing, very soon after that we started to call it "Russia," as the USSR broke up into independent nations. Traditionally safe careers like the army suddenly became professional dead ends. HRH weighed his options, then took a leap in the dark—he left the army with a few of his more adventurous classmates from military school and joined the ranks of fledgling entrepreneurs. At first they sold cigarettes and soft drinks out of a badly constructed kiosk, constantly at risk of attack from rival factions. Then they opened a small store, and then another one.

Contrary to my hopes (and those, no doubt, of Princess Michael of Kent), the hastily reorganized Russian government did not ask Prince Michael of Kent (who I felt had a lot going for him as a Romanov claimant) to come and be crowned Michael III, Emperor and Autocrat of all the Russias. More fool them. Instead we embarked upon the "roller-coaster years": that messy, wildly optimistic, helter-skelter Yeltsin era in "the Wild East." Anything and everything was for sale—these were the days when, down in the bowels of the Moscow Metro, you could buy shares of what would become major oil or metals

★

companies through the controversial "voucher" program, in which the state gave each citizen a portion of the state economy. A plate of Italian pasta cost sixty dollars, but vodka was still forty cents a liter.

As the Soviet system teetered on its fulcrum, the floodgates heaved open, and in rushed the latter-day carpetbaggers: oilmen, grain traders, European bankers, Dutch publishers, and a group of smarmy twentysomethings who thought they were invincible, brandishing newly minted INSEAD and Harvard MBAs, a smattering of Russian, and a very dubious understanding of the difference between right and wrong. They began to consult the Russian government on privatization auctions and the emerging business-savvy wheeler-dealers on how to turn the vouchers into major companies. Dazed-looking executives from places like Ohio stumbled off planes, under strict orders to supply the insatiable Russian demand for Tampax, Coke, diapers, face cream, and toilet paper; many fell prey to Russian girls with creamy skin and hard, calculating eyes looking for an expat husband and a one-way ticket out of Russia.

HRH moved his one suitcase from his military dormitory to a one-room apartment he received from the army in a sprawling urban jungle called Northern Butovo. Northern Butovo was—and occasional trips through it on my way to the airport suggest still is—a scale model of hell: an inelegant, sloppily thrown together cluster of prefab buildings painted in what must have seemed like optimistic shades of garish pastel blue, yellow, and green but which instantly faded into depressingly dingy versions of the original hues. No sepia tones in Butovo; more like pig-swill beige. Butovo and its ilk sprang up so quickly to meet the incessant demand of the post-perestroika housing boom that it took the public transportation system a decade to catch up. To reach Butovo in my day you took the distinctly proletarian orange line to its southernmost end and then waited way too long for bus number 835 (a number engraved on my heart). Then, hopefully, you crammed into it with three hundred other people and rattled and bounced until the end of its route, some thirty-five minutes later. Butovo made me understand that I had barely scratched the surface of what went on in Soviet life.

For HRH, this was a wild Soviet fantasy come true: an apartment of his very own at age twenty-four, in Moscow no less! Okay, the very messy edge of Moscow, but Moscow nevertheless, and with it came the all-important, highly sought after Moscow certificate of residence, the *propiska*. None of it was lost on me, although I was more focused on the fact that his new apartment and new civilian status meant we could not only live together, which seemed incredible, but also that I could finally unpack my suitcase completely and experiment with housekeeping, about which I knew nothing. I got a job in executive recruitment, about which I also knew nothing, but in those days you didn't have to be an expert in anything.

The apartment consisted of one long, narrow room, into which HRH had crammed a *stenka*, the ubiquitous oversize, top-heavy wall unit without which no Russian home is complete. The *stenka* featured a narrow closet in which you hung clothes one in front of the other for maximum inconvenience. Some of the shelves were protected by sliding glass panels, making both easy access and thorough cleaning impossible. The top was decorated with touches of Baroque carving as interpreted by a Slovakian factory in the mid-1980s, but it was the dernier cri in home furnishings for the period, and HRH was so proud of it that I didn't have the heart to complain. We slept on a divan— a couch that folded out into a flat surface rather like a glasses case. Hard as a rock, upholstered in faux brocade in contrasting shades of pink and beige baby vomit, it was five feet wide and featured a deep gully in the middle where the hinges opened. I saw it recently out at a friend's dacha, and I wondered aloud how on earth we ever got any sleep.

In the area of the long, narrow room designated as the living room there were two giant, clunky Turkish chairs shaped like oversize mushroom caps in a depressing shade of beige, surprisingly comfortable for something so hideous. We pulled them up to the TV, which didn't get great reception since the signal wasn't strong enough to reach Northern Butovo, but on a good night we could tune in to the latest innovations on the new commercial channels. There were game shows like *The Field of Miracles* and two cheesy Mexican soap operas called *The Rich Also Cry* and *Simply Maria*, which held the nation—the female part of it anyway—enthralled. We even watched the news, which in those days was enjoying a brief but exciting renaissance of hard-hitting journalistic grit. And commercials, which were a completely new thing.

"I form the impression," HRH called to me as he watched TV and I prepared dinner in the winter of 1993, "that America consists entirely of toothpaste, cat food, and feminine hygiene products. Does it?"

"Certainly not! We also have dishwashing liquid, diapers, fast food, and soft drinks!" I called from the kitchen, where I was experimenting with a marinade for two "Bush legs." This was the most popular type of meat available at the time: chicken legs and thighs named after President George H. W. Bush. Bush legs were sold as cheap surplus to the developing world by an America obsessed with boneless, skinless chicken breasts.

We got married in city hall, then got married again in a church, with a white dress and a big party, and then we even got married a third time on the beach in California to satisfy our need for all kinds of documentation. Neither of us can remember any of these dates, but I take comfort in the fact that getting divorced would be a bureaucratic impossibility. We changed jobs and moved apartments every three years or so, finally buying one when our daughter, Velvet, was born.

As the "wild nineties" gave way to the more "restrained oughts," HRH and I kept pace, and our life focused more on the minutiae of living it rather than the tectonic socioeconomic shifts that were rearranging life in Russia. Velvet developed a passion for horses, and all attempts to steer her toward other interests fell flat. A group of diverse Russian and expatriate friends gelled into what I called "the urban family." HRH continued up the ladder of corporate success as I cycled through jobs in tourism, hotel management, and airlines until finally stumbling into a wonderful job as the head of PR and marketing at a bank I called "The Firm." *Nicholas and Alexandra* gathered dust on the upper shelves of the *stenka*. After three enjoyable and mildly lucrative years, something I thought of as "Multinational" bought out "The Firm." I pondered my next move.

"Do you want to work for Multinational?" asked HRH.

"Not really," I mused. "I'm a strategic advisor at The Firm, but at Multinational I get the sense that I'd be just a canapé counter."

"What do you want to do?"

"I think I want to write," I said, voicing aloud for the first time an idea that had been gently percolating for months.

"Write what?"

"A book about Russia? Maybe a funny book; there aren't so many funny books about Russia out there," I ventured.

"Sounds good," said HRH, who has yet to experience the challenge of courting the capricious muse.

We moved again, to a new apartment located in one of Moscow's eclectic neighborhoods—and I use eclectic in its most negative connotation. Our building marked the crossroads of two completely different communities. Due east was a modern high-rise office building made of glass and steel, home to multinational banks and law firms. To the southwest lay the typically shabby and dusty dwellings of the middle class and the disappointing retail outlets that serviced them. The one exception was a long, low four-story gray building exactly like the hundreds of other long, low four-story buildings in Moscow that house research institutes or minor municipal government offices. This one looked so neglected and dejected that at first I worried it would be razed to the ground to make way for another glass and metal high-rise office space, which would block our view of the Moscow skyline and much of the lovely light that streamed into our apartment. Fear was replaced with intense interest when HRH told me what actually went on there. Our neighbor was a research institute devoted to one single task: maintaining and preserving Vladimir Lenin's embalmed corpse. Lenin, for all intents and purposes, lived next door.

I had visited Lenin many times in his mausoleum on Red Square: there was always one in my group I knew would find the stairs challenging, so I always went down with them and listened to the official spiel. So I knew very well that several times a year Lenin's body was removed from the mausoleum and brought to a special institute to take a bath in embalming fluids, get a clean white shirt, and be changed into his other black suit. I assumed they touched up the body makeup and maybe pumped something into him to keep him going for another three months, and I reeled at the idea that this was all taking place across the courtyard. I yearned to take a casserole over and try to make friends, but of course that kind of thing is not encouraged in Russia. So I contented myself with spying on them, which is very much encouraged in Russia. My tiny home office looked out on our courtyard and across a high metal fence onto the roof of The Institute. During my frequent breaks I would lean over the balcony railing to see if I could detect any interesting activity across the way. I pretended to be taking pictures of the Moscow skyline with my long telephoto lens, but I was really trying to sneak a peek into the windows of The Institute.

"Put that camera away," commanded HRH. "People are beginning to talk."

"What do you think really goes on in there?" I asked, perching on the deep window ledge and reluctantly unscrewing the lens from the camera body.

HRH shrugged. He's not into historical hypotheses or embalming, having real-world problems to solve. I put the camera away, but I kept up my surveillance of The Institute's courtyard from my balcony.

What was I looking for? A turn-of-the-century claw-foot bathtub, I imagined, or mysterious trucks delivering economy-size bottles of embalming fluid. Maybe I would get to see a covert 2:00 a.m. arrival of the architect of the Russian Revolution himself (I assumed they did it in the middle of the night—Russians are very into doing things in the middle of the night). I wondered how many people worked there and what they did all day between Lenin's baths. Alas, I never saw anyone or anything go in or out of what I came to think of as "Lenin's Bathtub." I knew that there was some life in there, since I could just make out, through the annoyingly tinted and smeared windows, the standard-issue dusty ficus plants that grace every mid-level Russian office building, but they seemed to be the only living organisms inside the building.

There were so many things about Russia in that post-perestroika era that made me think that Lenin would turn in his mausoleum. Living next door to Lenin provided me with a very tangible link to Russian history, and that somehow kept everything in perspective. It reminded me of the Soviet mantra "Lenin lived, Lenin lives, Lenin will live," which sounds far more assertive in Russian. There was a reassuring permanence about The Institute: no one was going to raze Lenin's Bathtub to the ground to make way for another Allied Municipal ("Ally-

Muni") Bank branch, and I liked that. But I was truly thrilled the day I walked past Ally-Muni and saw a group of Tadzhik migrant workers in orange and navy blue uniforms hefting a large sign into place on the ground floor. I stopped to watch them peel off the bubble wrap and canvas to reveal a familiar green and white logo with a smiling mermaid.

"I don't believe it," I breathed. A Starbucks . . . next door! "Take that, Sarah Palin!" I shouted, punching my fist in the air in triumph. "I can see Starbucks from my house!"

The Starbucks was—and still is—an absolute godsend. In fact, more than half of this book was written there. In the frigid winter months, HRH and I toss a coin; the loser has to escort Velvet to Starbucks for hot chocolate on the way to the school bus stop and bring a latte back for the winner. HRH almost always wins, which I found suspicious enough to insist we use an American quarter. He protested, and we compromised on a one-euro coin, but still he wins most of the time. One wet March morning, however, I won the toss, and I got to snuggle back under the covers while HRH took Velvet to the bus stop.

"Come on, Papa!" she enjoined him. "'*Ziegel, Ziegel, ay-lyu-lyu!*' We have to make time for Starbucks!"

HRH returned thirty minutes later. He placed a cardboard cup holder on the bedside table, shucked off his jeans and sweater, and climbed back in bed with me, invading my warm patch with his icy nose and hands.

"Hey, Petrovna," he said, "look at this." He pointed to a white paper cup on which Larissa the barista had written, in Russian, "Velvet's Papa."

"Oh, that is a keeper," I said, smiling. "Very sweet."

"It is," HRH agreed, and handed me a cup. "Here's yours."

"Helpful Russian Husband," I said appreciatively, "thank you!"

I stuffed some pillows behind my back, pried the lid off the cup, and stirred the contents to mix in the grains of chocolate sprinkled on top. I took a sip, automatically using my tongue muscles to filter the liquid from the foam. I stopped in mid-sip. I looked down into that coffee and then over to HRH, who was already burrowing his head into the pillow; his dark hair is now salt and pepper, but he still cuts it as short as a recruit's. I'm not saying it was like Proust and his cookie thing, because how pretentious would that be? But seriously, in that instant

★

I remembered something half forgotten for sixteen years: the mountaintop restaurant, the warm sun, Dzidzia, and the man she'd seen in the coffee grounds, the man I'd flippantly referred to as "Comrade Right."

So yes, I had really wanted to go to Russia. And I did go. And no, I never meant to stay so long, but there you go, reader: that's what happens when you marry him.

CHAPTER 2

ALONG WITH THE RED QUEEN, THE WHITE QUEEN, AND ME

UPSCALE TV IN Britain and the USA does a great job depicting expatriate life as drop-dead glamorous. Everything is hot sunshine and crisp linen for those sybarites in Kenya's Happy Valley or soigné, Vaseline-on-the-lens romantic and foggy for Hem and Fitz getting blotto down at Les Deux Magots. Alas, the real world of expat Moscow is far less elegant: there wasn't a *sola topee* in sight on the day I donned my unfashionable but serviceable calf-length North Face parka and slogged across Mayakovskaya Square to have lunch with Joe Kelly at the Starlite Diner.

Joe was in an uncharacteristic lather. "Babycakes," he said, "we need to get our fucking act together for the Tartan Ball. Radio Magellan Dude came in earlier and asked me if we had any spare seats at our table."

"Ew," I said, shuddering. "What did you tell him?"

"I said I'd get back to him later, after I'd spoken to you."

"We are not having Radio Magellan Dude at our table," I said with emphasis.

Joe and I were in charge of what we called the "mixed marriage" table for the annual Tartan Ball. It wouldn't be the only table featuring foreigners in meaningful relationships with Russians, but it would, Joe insisted, be the most entertaining table of foreigners in meaningful relationships with Russians.

"So let me be clear, babycakes," Joe drawled for emphasis, "that does not include Radio Magellan Dweeb with his fucking tongue down Miss Teenage Tomsk's throat all night."

ALONG WITH THE RED QUEEN, THE WHITE QUEEN, AND ME

★

23

"So unusually prudish of you, Joe," I said with a smile. "Are you feeling okay?"

"Listen," he said, "I'm prepared to spend an evening with some fucking Brits in skirts dancing on top of swords all night, and, okay, I'm prepared to eat sheep's intestines, but I draw the line at paying one hundred and twenty-five bucks—"

"Times two," I reminded him.

Joe inclined his head in acknowledgment. "Thank you," he said. "Two hundred and fifty bucks, then, to spend the evening with some fiftysomething, overaged, and oversexed hack doing a job designed for recent graduates of some online journalism school. That tool *schtups* anything that isn't nailed down."

"*Schtups?*" I asked. "Where'd a nice Irish boy from Ohio learn a word like *schtups?*"

"It isn't Russian?" he asked, perplexed.

"No, Joe," I said patiently, "it's not."

"No shit," he said, shaking his head. "That's a good word."

Joe's phone began to buzz and crawl diagonally across the Formica table that separated us. He scooped it up and planted it to his ear. A shapely waitress, whose name tag in English identified her as Masha, swished toward our corner booth clad in a 1950s miniskirt and bearing a large tray aloft. They choose the staff more for their shapely body types than for their waitressing skills at the diner, but Masha was that rare Starlite waitress who combined both. She slid an oval-shaped platter deftly onto Joe's place mat. I shifted the copies of *The Moscow Times* littering the table to make room for mine. Two large frosted glasses of Pepsi Light completed the order. The worst cheeseburgers east of Berlin lay apologetically on our plates, mounds of greasy French fries alongside them. As I said, it's not Les Deux Magots. Joe made a squeezing gesture at Masha as he continued his conversation. She nodded in understanding and silently added a bright red ketchup dispenser to the table. Joe gave her a thumbs-up. Turning, she gave her skirt an extra flip, revealing her bright red bikini briefs. Joe smiled appreciatively. I snapped my fingers over his cheeseburger to grab his attention.

"Okay, buddy, I'll call you." He finished up his call and began diligently decorating his mound of fries with a crosshatch of gooey red ketchup.

"Right," he said, "Radio Magellan Dude and the table?"

"Well," I said, spearing a fry and inserting it into my mouth, "I'm certainly not prepared to spend any more time than I have to with Radio Magellan Dude, period."

"He's a fucking tool," said Joe. "I heard he only took that job because it came with an apartment."

"That's right," I confirmed. "I'll tell you this," I added, pointing another fry in his direction for emphasis, "Tancy will refuse to come if she gets even a hint he'll be there. She got stuck sitting next to him at some dinner party and said it was a totally toxic evening. So forget Radio Magellan Dude. We have you and Tanya, me and HRH, Holt, Tancy, and Lucy, so that's seven and the table seats ten. We need two more guys and one girl."

"We need any warm body that isn't Radio Magellan Dude." Joe pressed his point home.

"No argument, Joe," I said, pulling out my phone to scroll through the contact list.

Joe Kelly and I seldom argue. He's one of my favorite people in Moscow, and indeed the whole world. A six-foot-four, three-hundred-pound Irish-American former Ohio State linebacker, he was a Moscow legend. Joe came to Moscow in 1991 on a hunch. He spoke no Russian and knew exactly one person, a friend of a cousin. He spent two days walking around, decided Russia was a potential gold mine, rented an apartment, and has been here ever since. Joe did a number of jobs before settling down to a lucrative fusion of real estate management, start-up investment, and project management coaching. He lives with his stunning Russian girlfriend, Tanya, who is fiercely organized and resolutely eschews all domestic tasks. Tanya works from dawn until midnight at something incredibly stressful that has to do with logistics, where she is the boss of everyone.

Joe runs his own empire efficiently, half of the time from his beat-up Nissan SUV and half the time from the hexagonal corner booth at the Starlite Diner on Mayakovskaya Square, in which we were now seated. His urban family nickname is "Mr. Mayor" because, one rainy Friday afternoon, having nothing better to do, a bunch of us exchanged hilarious emails pretending to urge Joe to run against Moscow's pint-size mayor, Yuri Luzhkov. Our feeling was that Joe could win it on height and personality alone. Joe and I share a passion for liberal American politics in general, and President Josiah Bartlet in particular. We split the cost of each new season of *The West Wing* when it came out on DVD and often pulled all-nighters, since as everyone knows, you can't watch just one episode of *The West Wing*. We were die-hard binge watchers before Netflix was even invented. HRH found this obsession slightly off-putting.

"Let me get this straight," he said, finding me in tears over Mrs. Landingham's untimely death in her brand-new car, "this is a fictional presidency?"

"Yes," I sobbed, indicating with hand gestures he should pour me a glass of wine and hand me more Kleenex. I sent HRH out bowling with his buddies so that Joe and I could watch the one where Leo dies uninterrupted. We cried like babies.

Joe's mind was still trained on the Tartan Ball.

"Will Lucy have some exotic yogi guru type in tow?"

"I'll find out," I said. "Here's an idea: I met a very nice woman who just moved to town called DeeDee. She's something impressive in executive headhunting, and she's married to one of those guys who is Russian but left when he was seven or something and grew up in the US—a repat. He works for one of those huge accounting firms—I don't remember which one. They live out at Bald Hills."

At the mention of the stuffy gated community on the outskirts of Moscow, Joe made a face. His business interests stop just south of Bald Hills.

"I know," I acknowledged, "but DeeDee seems nice. Bees Rees asked me to show her around."

Joe shook his head in mock sorrow.

"Babycakes, for fuck's sake! You quit your job like, what—five seconds ago? Bees Rees has already got you in her clutches? What the fuck?"

"I know . . . ," I said. "I know . . ."

Beatrice "Bees" Rees is one of expat Moscow's two queens. We have many, many princesses but only two queens. I think of Bees as the White Queen because she isn't nearly as sinister as Dragana Galveston, whom I think of as the Red Queen (about whom, much more very soon). Bees is the self-appointed welcome wagon of the two expatriate gated communities, over which she reigns, happy and glorious. She is an indefatigable putter-in-place of all the things that didn't used to exist in Moscow but which Bees felt should: trick-or-treating, the Girl

Scouts, and youth league soccer. Bees is in charge of anything referred to by an acronym: MWC (Multicultural Women's Club), USWC (United States Women's Club), IES (International Embassy School, which Bees and her court always refer to as just "school," suggesting that there aren't any others), and probably lots more I know nothing about. She raises millions—literally millions—of rubles for charities benefiting Russia's less fortunate citizens. She does this by commanding any expat princess not nailed down to buy mind-bogglingly expensive tickets to swanky events. Once captive in the ballroom, Bees then guilts them out of even more money to buy chances at winning a whole bunch of things that no one in their right mind would ever want or need, like a weekend in the Moscow Marriott Grand Hotel. No one wants that. Bees is a guided missile. Her husband, Hank, runs the Moscow office of one of those large American companies you think does one thing but actually does quite another. He is possibly the most boring man east of Paris, though competition is pretty stiff.

Most of us use the time we are stuck in Moscow traffic jams to telephone each other and have long chats. Not Bees. She's far too busy to just chat. When I saw her name on my caller ID I didn't even consider letting it go to voice mail. Bees has an uncanny way of running one to ground. I knew she wanted something, and I held my breath and hoped it wasn't a request to help her unwrap her collection of fourteen thousand Russian Christmas tree ornaments. These go on display each November through January at a museum. Bees corrals her court of princesses and ladies-in-waiting into spending two days unwrapping the entire collection, which she arranges on an enormous fake Christmas tree, and she hosts several parties on either side of New Year's so we can all come and ooh and aah over them. Once I dared my fellow expat enfant terrible, Holt Fairfax, to ask Bees how she intended to eventually get the ornaments out of Russia.

"Oh, Holt," she cooed, "I plan to leave them to the nation."

This has become a euphemism in our close circle to refer to anything one might leave behind during the final move from Russia.

"What will you do with your cleaning lady?" I said to Posey Farquarshon as she waited, knee-deep in packed boxes, for the moving company to arrive.

"Oh, I'm leaving her to the nation," she quipped.

Bees got right down to business.

"How *are* you?" she trilled down the line.

"Oh . . . Bees," I fumbled, "hectic, you know . . . just insanely hectic—"

"Oh, I know," she agreed, placing heavy emphasis on the word *I.* "But listen, I want to introduce you to someone who has just arrived from the States—moved into the townhouse next door to us . . ."

I grimaced. Like Joe, I'm not crazy about the Bald Hills crowd.

Bald Hills looks exactly like what it is: an American suburban housing development as interpreted by a Russian architect and built by a Turkish contractor. HRH calls it "Pleasantville," which is pretty apt. It takes fifty minutes to get there when there is no traffic and more than three hours if there is. The minute you get there you start worrying about how to get back into town. The women who live there, Bees's princesses and ladies-in-waiting, are all like Bees only not quite so energetic, which makes it easy for Bees to bend them to her will in all sorts of ways.

Once upon a time, I suppose, some of these women had real jobs and pumped their own gas, but then their husbands got posted to Moscow, and, whether they liked it or not, their lives became very different. They walk their kids over to school, hit the gym, then get together for no-fat lattes and a spirited round of "Whose nanny is the most annoying?" until it is time to pick up the children again. The appeal of Bald Hills is that it is self-contained, clean, safe, and it's right next door to school, so you really never have to leave. Halloween out there, thanks in large part to Bees, is amazing, but they make you audition for the school's PTA. On the weekends, the Bald Hills crowd either goes to Bees's charity balls or to dinner parties at each other's homes. On the rare occasion the need to leave Bald Hills arises (like to buy Betty Crocker brownie mix for fourteen dollars a box at the Finnish grocery store, Stockmann), the wives are driven into town by their husbands' drivers, with whom they communicate by means of sign language and speaking slightly louder than they normally would. If this fails, they call up their husbands' secretaries and have them interpret.

Slightly to the north of Bald Hills is its rival gated community, Otradnoe, which means "daydream." Bees rules Otradnoe as well, though from a distance. Not quite as antiseptic as Bald Hills, there are rumors of swingers parties and naked trampoline sex, but these, I feel, need to be taken with a huge chunk of salt. I don't get out much, but surely gravity makes sex on a trampoline challenging. And "naked" doesn't ring true either: there are only about eight evenings a year when you can be naked outside in Moscow, except for in the summer, but all the expats leave in the summer. The "swinger" thing also sounds fishy. In Moscow, when expat men are inclined to cheat, they need look no further than the office typing pool and then blame it on the traffic.

"Lovely girl," continued Bees. "She has two little boys at school, first and second grade, and I thought they must be just the age of your daughter—what's her name again?"

"Velvet," I said patiently. Bees doesn't know the name of any child who doesn't go to school, which Velvet doesn't. "But you know, Bees, Velvet is actually nine, and she's in—"

"Right," she said, barreling ahead heedless of the fact that nine-year-old girls avoid seven- and eight-year-old boys like the plague. "But the thing is, her husband was born in Russia, although, well, his English is so good, I guess he left here fairly early. So of course I thought you would like to get to know her."

I wondered for a moment what Bees would do if she were tasked with introducing Oprah Winfrey to Barack Obama. This is about as likely as naked trampoline sex at Otradnoe, since Bees and most of the Bald Hills crowd are rabid Republicans.

"They just moved here from Chicago, and he joined Hank's legal team. He's a little quiet—" Anyone within a fifty-mile radius of Bees, I thought, would seem quiet "—but terribly nice. She was something quite serious in executive recruitment back in Chicago. She talks about getting back to work once they get settled. So she's not going to be working, and I heard you aren't working either—"

"Well," I tried to squeeze in, "I'm actually writing a—"

"So you two could have some fun . . . show her around the center, that kind of thing."

"So," I recapped to Joe, "I called the woman, and, actually, she is very nice. I mentioned Bees had asked me to be in touch, and later, over coffee, she said she'd been terrified I'd be a drone."

"A what?" asked Joe.

ALONG WITH THE RED QUEEN, THE WHITE QUEEN, AND ME

29

"You know, like a bee that follows the queen," I explained. Joe smirked in acknowledgment. "I thought she should meet some people who don't live in Bald Hills. You'll like her; she's called DeeDee. Her husband is Marat."

"Babycakes, don't get sucked into the Bald Hills scene," pleaded Joe. "Don't go and get a whole bunch of newbie friends."

"So likely," I said, motioning to Masha for a refill of Pepsi Light.

What the glitzy TV series fail to adequately cover about expatriate life is that if you don't work in what they call the "formal economy" you risk getting sucked into a very odd sort of social vortex. It took me a little while to realize the thing all expats come to understand eventually, even if they don't ever admit it: locals are all very well and good, and a certain amount of going native is advisable (for example, learning a little of the local language), but you still need your own tribe.

Running compatriots to ground in a foreign country is harder than you might think. Sure, you can hang out at the obvious places, but winnowing out the like-minded ones is difficult, and along the way you end up meeting all kinds of people you would never encounter at home. In my search I met people with goatee beards, Republican people, Mormon people, and people who used "scrapbook" as a verb. I found myself getting involved in a range of bizarre organizations that would never have occurred to me stateside: the Girl Scouts, for example, and Nordic walking. At one point I was so desperate that I even seriously considered attending some form of divine service. Eventually, however, the universe cut me some slack, and I was invited to join a really cool book club, where I met Posey Farquarshon, and she introduced me to Tancy, and it was then that the urban family began to take shape.

That was a good book club for a while, but of course we inevitably had to kill it off. This is the ultimate fate of most expatriate book clubs that are brought into the world with lofty aspirations: a carefully considered, handpicked list of participants, a firm commitment fixture on the calendar, and rarified guidelines—"focusing on native English-language fiction currently enjoying critical acclaim." With time, however, along with the lack of a reliable source of books and the general ebb and flow of expat life, the rules soften, then rot. Blink and your book club is poised on the brink of chaos: Stephanie and Verity move back home, so you let Stacy—who isn't, let's face it, the sharpest tack in the box—join. It proves impossible to find a date that works for anyone, so you skip March. Since no one's husband went to London on business, there aren't any copies of April's book, but when you do get around to reading it the following September, the only "critical" material is something Amy copied and pasted from Amazon.com. Then comes the real death rattle: Becca, who hasn't been in Moscow long enough to know better, invites her new Russian friend Olga to join, and unless some decisive action is taken you'll all be stuck reading the goddamn *Master and Margarita*. Again. So another book club is dissolved and reconstituted. I performed a lot of book club euthanasia, or at least I used to until I ended up on the receiving end of a particularly nasty book club cull.

My good friend Tancy O'Reilly phoned me when I returned from a summer in the United States. It was early autumn, about four months after I'd left The Firm. I was trying to establish a disciplined stay-at-home-writer routine, but it was proving elusive. Tancy completely derailed me.

"Hey, girlfriend," Tancy sang out. "Got a minute?"

Is it just in Moscow or is it everywhere that, when someone asks you if you've got a minute, it is always bad news?

Tancy is a tough, cigarette-smoking corporate lioness. She runs an immense office for a Fortune 100 company. Legend has it she came to Russia with two No. 2 pencils and a fax machine and built the whole thing up from scratch, and most of that legend is true. Her industry is a very masculine one, so her spine is made of titanium and she has ice water in her veins. She does not believe in sugarcoating anything.

"Wanted to give you a heads-up. Dragana culled you from the reading circle," she said matter-of-factly.

"She did what?"

"She culled you. There was a major bloodletting over the summer because Dragana felt the group was getting too large, so she culled a whole bunch of people."

"Was it a culling or a bloodletting?" I asked, confused.

"I guess it was a cull," said Tancy. "Dragana called it a cull. Rufus called it a bloodletting."

"Tancy, *culling* is a horrible word—it's what cowboys do to herds of animals."

"Well, that's the word she used. Don't feel too bad; she culled the oligarch's daughter and the oligarch's daughter's stupid husband who never said anything . . . but of course in their case, there wasn't much evidence that either one of them could read."

This was too much.

"Tancy," I said through gritted teeth, "I can read. I do read. I read every single book, I always brought wine, and I always sent a thank-you note. Do you—do you remember how I lugged thirty copies of that out-of-print Wilfred what's-his-face book back from London—"

"I know, I know," said Tancy, taking a long drag of her ever-present cigarette, "but she culled a lot of people. She even culled Rufus, but of course he's never here. . . ."

"I can't think why you don't resign in protest," I grumbled.

"I'll be really honest with you, sweetie—I can't afford to alienate Dragana's husband," said Tancy sheepishly. "They are hosting a party when the assistant secretary of state comes over, and if I miss that I can kiss 30 percent of my bonus goodbye."

"Tancy, you are so fucking mercantile," I screamed.

"I'm afraid I am," she admitted. "Dragana is uphill work, I agree, but I'd much rather have her inside my tent pissing out than outside the tent pissing in."

"You didn't make that up," I grumbled. "Winston Churchill said that."

"Him and my direct report," she said. "It's a well-known management principle."

"Well, if that is the cornerstone of corporate business, then I'm very glad I've left it. I warn you, Tance—this is all going in my book."

"Yeah, what's going on with that, anyway? I thought you'd be done by now. So this is all for the good. You'll have tons of time now that you aren't in the reading circle. You should be thanking Dragana."

"So likely." I slammed the phone down. My blood was boiling. Culled by Dragana Galveston—the Red Queen!

I bet you have a Dragana Galveston in your life. Everyone does—the kind of woman who behaves heinously most of the time, insults everybody, but somehow never gets called on it because no one has the guts to do it. Unlike Bees, the admittedly annoying, but basically benevolent, White Queen, who kept busy all day doing good for others, Dragana the Red Queen never left the elite geographical downtown boundary of the Boulevard Ring and certainly never moved a finger to put anything in place that wasn't designed specifically for her own comfort and enjoyment.

Dragana was married to Sunter Galveston, a dull WASP with an excellent, if exhausted, pedigree. No one knew exactly how Dragana had got her talons into Sunter, and many marveled that she had not ruined his career through her abject rudeness. I never figured out if he was a lawyer or a banker—I assumed he had to be one or the other—but it didn't matter, since he spent most of his time schmoozing with the ambassador and playing golf with his cronies from a lobbying group of foreign companies, which had a complicated name but was always referred to as "BIZ4."

I normally would have given Dragana Galveston a wide berth, and that would not have been difficult, since I was way too low down the food chain for her to notice me. I had no currency in her realm—I did not run Google Russia, I was not married to the country head of a large oil company, nor was I the daughter of a billionaire Russian banker. But Tancy, regional grand pooh-bah of a Fortune 100 company, was very much on Dragana's radar screen. Tancy proposed me when Dragana's reading circle numbers slumped during a simultaneous rotation of top managers from Shell, Goldman Sachs, and Cargill and that awkward revoking of visa support from all of BP's senior management. I accepted with enthusiasm, since my own scruffier social circle had also been decimated by recent budget cuts in Moscow bureau chiefs.

I was a little daunted by the choice of book for my first reading circle visit; it wasn't really a book but a trilogy of plays by Tom Stoppard called *The Coast of Utopia*. Tancy briefed me that Dragana was flying especially to New York to see it when it opened on Broadway, which is why the circle was reading it. That was exactly the sort of thing Dragana loved to do and loved even more to talk about.

"This thing makes no sense to me," Tancy said cheerfully, as she handed me the three volumes over a large boat of sushi

★

we were sharing. "It's more your sort of thing—you have a go."

The Coast of Utopia focused on several generations of nineteenth-century Russian intellectuals in self-imposed exile in Europe. It had about seventy-five roles in it and covered three decades of complicated Russian political thought; Alexander Herzen, Vissarion Belinsky, and Mikhail Bakunin were major characters. Not the most dynamic figures in Russian history, I thought as I waded into Act One. On the day of reading circle I wore my best suit to work and slipped out at lunchtime to have my hair blown dry and my manicure refreshed. A bottle of Giscours and the three volumes tucked into my bag, I met Tancy with every hope for a successful debut at the reading circle.

The Red Queen lived in a palatial flat at a great address on fashionable Prechistinka Street. The first time I walked in, all of my senses were bombarded. The large room where we assembled pulsated with color—the walls were painted a bright orange-yellow on which the occupants had layered pictures, pieces of old fabric, and icons. Every conceivable horizontal surface was covered with objets d'art: knickknacks, icons, old china, and (bizarrely, I thought) a pyramid of bright orange Hermès cardboard boxes.

The Red Queen was enthroned in the largest and most comfortable chair opposite the entrance. She wore heavy necklaces and oversize, bright red "statement" glasses; behind these her rather cold black eyes surveyed the room. She had good hair and bad skin, and she clearly spent a fortune on both. Dragana did not rise to greet us, so I took my cue from Tancy and followed her across the cluttered room to make my obeisance. Subsequent visits taught me that if one were important enough Dragana might announce, with a wave of her hand, "This is so-and-so who runs such-and-such," but in my case no introductions were ever made. We formed a wide circle around the large room, with Dragana at twelve o'clock, flanked by her favorites, a chummy duo called Penny and Lenny, each of whom was married to someone who didn't come to the reading circle. They sat in the entitled slots of eleven and one o'clock, respectively, and the rest of us ranged in order of importance. I was at about five-thirty, Tancy at three o'clock.

I knew general book club form from my years in Moscow, so I tried to keep my mouth shut during the first meeting, though if called upon I was prepared to make four or five well-thought-out comments. I had colored Post-its stuck in the relevant pages. I was eager for some lively back-and-forth.

Dragana brought the room to order and opened the discussion.

"Well," she said, lighting another pink cigarette and blowing a cloud of silver smoke into the room, "I could not get past page two. It was way too boring." She waved her hand, dismissing one of the leading playwrights of our generation.

I wondered what would happen next. Would we all go home? I cast a covert glance around the room and saw that everyone was nodding in agreement.

"And what did you think, Lenny?" asked Dragana, turning to the nattily dressed guy on her right who did something for the UN.

"Well," he said, nimbly crossing his legs and cupping his chin thoughtfully in his hand. "I did manage to work my way through the first play . . . what was it called?"

"*Voyage*," I said to myself. *Voyage* was the first play, followed by *Shipwreck* and then *Salvage*. Cheerful stuff, Stoppard.

"Well, whatever it was called," continued Lenny, "what I was really struck by, actually, was the remarkable similarity to . . ." and he was off on a completely unrelated riff about Evelyn Waugh.

This was the amazing thing about the group, which Dragana called a "reading circle" but which I imagined she thought of as her "salon." Those who spoke the most (usually Penny and Lenny) were the least likely to have actually cracked open the book under discussion. It was fascinating to witness their adroit shifting of the conversation to something they wanted to—or could—discuss. Lenny tended to bring any conversation around to some esoteric Anglo-Catholic trope no one had heard of, while Penny, a nasty piece of work from a Republican red state, would draw a dubious comparison between the book we were supposed to have read and some cheesy self-help book she'd bought at the Atlanta airport. Dragana made a token effort to go around the circle, but she never got much past three or nine o'clock before she let Lenny or Penny take over. I would slip my copy of the book, with its carefully highlighted passages marked with Post-its, back into my bag and let my eyes wander around the room. Sometimes I mentally composed a grocery list.

I'll say this for Dragana: she wasn't stingy with the food or drink, and though unkind people suggested it was all expensed to Sunter's company, I didn't believe it. Reading circle started at 7:00 p.m., and by 9:00 p.m., when the discussion was over, everyone was well and truly lubricated. We then repaired to the dining room (also crammed with objets d'art) for a buffet supper and general chitchat. I enjoyed this part—I met interesting people and was able to actually discuss the book we'd read.

So though I loved to deride the reading circle (and for that I perhaps deserved to be culled), I found myself surprisingly downcast when Tancy lowered the boom. I wondered if leaving The Firm meant I was no longer a person in the eyes of Moscow expatriate society. It was a worrying thought and one that made me feel, I reflected, sort of like the seventy-five characters in *The Coast of Utopia*: exiled, adrift, and rudderless. I was mildly, but not sufficiently, comforted by the fact that this was a parallel that few in the reading circle could actually draw. To further cheer myself up I started to tell the story, emailing Posey Farquarshon, who had moved back to London.

"You won't believe this," I typed. "I've been culled from the Red Queen's reading circle."

"Darling," she typed back, "I'm stunned you put up with it as long as you did. I went to her place once—*ugh!* You could not move for all the debris. That woman is the exact opposite of feng shui! I'll tell you something else. Those ridiculous Hermès boxes? She got those on eBay."

HRH was less sympathetic.

"Dragana Galveston has axed me from her reading circle," I told him.

"What's a reading circle?" he asked distractedly, as he searched for a shoehorn.

"Like a book club."

"You are in about four hundred book clubs. Which one is this?"

"The depressing-books one on Prechistinka," I explained. "I'm very upset about it. I think leaving The Firm may have been an awful mistake. I think everyone is going to cross me off their lists."

"Don't be ridiculous," said HRH, tugging on his shoes. "Joe and Tancy and that crowd haven't crossed you off their lists, have they?"

"That reminds me. Keep next Saturday free—we are going to the Tartan Ball."

"Which one is that?" asked HRH. "Is that the Book Club Ball?"

"You mean the Broomball Ball?" I corrected him, laughing. "No, this is the one with the men in skirts and all the whisky you can drink."

"Oh, good," said HRH. "I like that one."

HRH is a very good sport about climbing into black tie, which he calls his "smoking," and accompanying me to charity dos. It's not his favorite thing, but of all the balls he likes the Tartan Ball best because of the whisky. His least favorite is the Broomball Ball, which marks the end of the broomball season and the ceremonial awarding of the broomball champion trophy, a large brass samovar, to the league's winning team.

"But what is broomball?" asked DeeDee when we gathered for cocktails in the foyer of the Renaissance Hotel before proceeding into the ballroom. The late-Soviet-era architecture, with its terrible acoustics, was slightly mitigated by swaths of tartan bunting. Bare shoulders and black ties added an air of glamour. It wasn't The Plaza in New York, but there was an unmistakably festive air about it.

"It's sort of like a cross between curling and hockey," explained Joe. "You play it on ice with sticks made of brooms."

"Except you wear rubber-soled shoes, not skates," I added, "and protective gear, sort of like football pads."

"Contact sport," said Joe, nodding. "You need to see it to understand."

Tancy joined us, for once not in her signature navy blue executive suit. She had on a red ball gown and pearls. Her brown hair had been coaxed into an updo by one of the stylists at the Expat Salon, and she'd put on mascara, eye shadow, and bright red lipstick that matched her gown. Joe whistled in appreciation, as she teetered unsteadily on heels across the foyer to join us. She laughed her deep cigarette-smoker's laugh and planted a cherry-red kiss on his cheek.

"Tancy played broomball," I said, introducing her. "She was captain of Frozen Assets one year."

"I don't play anymore," said Tancy, leaning in to light her cigarette from HRH's proffered Zippo. "I fucked up my knee in the quarterfinals when one of those mutant Finns barreled into me." She sucked the smoke greedily and offered her cigarette pack around. HRH slid a Parliament Light out of Tancy's pack and lit up, ignoring my disapproving look. I suspect another reason HRH enjoys balls is the opportunity to smoke, which he officially gave up ten years ago, when I did. I haven't had one since. He's had several, and I could see that he was warming up to the cigars that accompanied the whisky in Act Three of tonight's lineup.

"Do you play?" Marat, DeeDee's husband, asked HRH in Russian.

"They don't allow Russians," he said, shrugging. "I play hockey." And they were launched on a discussion of Russia's chances in the world championship.

"He's not a morning person anyway," I added, trying and failing to picture HRH getting up on weekend mornings, suiting up to slip and slide and slam on the ice at the German or Finnish embassy. So likely. HRH likes to sleep until 2:00 p.m. on the weekends, go to hockey practice, then watch crap Russian television until bedtime.

"They don't let Russians play because they would beat everyone," said Joe's girlfriend, Tanya, stylish in a silver-gray chiffon gown and sparkly sandals. There was truth in what she said. The camaraderie and informality of broomball, with its beer drinking and team brunches at the Starlite, could easily be derailed by beefy NHL rejects.

"That's not true," protested Tancy. "The leagues have always been foreigners-only because they date back to the Cold War, when Russians couldn't go inside embassies."

"They still can't," HRH growled at her playfully.

"Well, it sounds like fun," said DeeDee.

"Good way to meet people," said Tancy.

"Their ball isn't as fun as this one, though," said HRH, downing his whisky on cue in one long swallow, as the wheezing moan and groan of bagpipes shifted into the piercing notes of "Scotland the Brave." We lined up to process behind the kilted pipers into the ballroom for dinner and dancing.

I sat next to Holt Fairfax, which I always enjoy. Over the first course of Kamchatkan crab and smoked salmon croquettes, he suggested we pick up the thread of an ongoing discussion.

"Before we get completely shitfaced," he said, filling my wineglass up to the brim.

"I'm not planning on getting shitfaced," I informed him, as I slurped the glass's tide down to a manageable level.

"Well, I am," said Holt. "So where did we leave it?"

"I had suggested a flash yoga mob at 7:35 a.m. at Kazansky railway station," I said.

"Is that the one where the trans-Siberian comes in?" Holt pursed his lips, confused.

"No, that one is right across the street. Kazansky railway station is the one where the trains come up from the Caucasus . . . and yes, I think from Central Asia as well," I said.

"Outstanding! So, what, at a certain time everyone just gets into downward-facing thingy on the main concourse?"

"To get the full effect," I mused, "you'd have to do it in the middle of winter and have everyone shuck off their heavy coats and boots, and then, all together, get immediately into downward-facing dog." Holt nodded thoughtfully.

Holt and I like to dream up grandiose plans for screwball stunts. We executed a quite spectacular one in 2003: a cocktail party at Moscow's horribly dingy international airport on Bastille Day. A cleverly worded email, with an embedded picture of *Liberty Leading the People*, had run through the expat community with the speed of summer lightning; the number three at the French embassy had been hauled onto the carpet to explain himself to the number two, and everyone had had a fantastic time. It was high time, we felt, for a reprise.

"And I think that we'd have to do an entire sun salutation," I said.

"I can do a sun salutation," said Joe, leaning across Lucy Milne's empty seat to join the conversation.

"Can you really?" I asked, surprised. "That seems wildly unlikely, Joe."

"I did yoga in Thailand," he said, sticking out his tongue. I stuck mine out in response.

"Do you know a good yoga studio here?" asked DeeDee. "I want to join one downtown."

"We're actually planning a flash yoga mob at 7:35 a.m. at the Kazansky railway station, which is right downtown," said Holt, deadpan.

✦

"You are?" asked DeeDee, seemingly unfazed by our statement. "Are flash mobs huge here?"

"They are not," said Joe. "Those two are just insane."

"I still like the idea of Dickensian Christmas caroling and the mulled wine in the Kremlin," Holt continued. "I'm not sure we've developed that idea fully."

"The problem with that is we'd get arrested in about three seconds," I responded, gathering the flesh of my lower lip between my teeth to keep from laughing. "You remember what happened to the Yale Russian chorus when they tried to sing Mass in Old Church Slavonic in Cathedral Square? They were literally manhandled by the security and escorted to the gate."

"That's true," agreed Holt, rising to greet Lucy. She was flushed and breathless, her phone held to one ear and the forefinger of her other hand stuffed in the other. She exchanged kisses on each cheek with Holt, then fished three phones out of her evening bag and thunked them onto the table before sinking gratefully into the chair Holt held out. Holt is from Virginia and full of old-world courtesies. A stringer for a Midwestern media company, he claims he was sent over by one of the wire services to cover the 1993 coup and then forgotten—except that a check arrives once a month and his visa is automatically renewed each year. Holt feels it is better not to ask too many questions. HRH says Holt is definitely in the pay of the CIA, but if you ask me, the government that pays Holt to spy for them needs its head examined. He carves out a decent living by filing the occasional news story, freelancing for the glossies, and editing for big companies. He talks about starting his own cultural magazine, and periodically he gets up a head of steam, claims Russia is a lost cause, and threatens to move to the Near Abroad, which is how the Russians now refer to the Warsaw Pact countries.

"Bucharest?" I said in 2005. "Really?"

"Very civilized," Holt drawled.

"Holt, please don't tell me you are going to say Bucharest is the Paris of the East, because that may have been true back in the 1920s but not today."

"Lots of culture," he insisted.

He was back in three months. Bucharest, it seemed, was not the Paris of the East. It was full, Holt said, of Romanians, who were even more depressing than the Russians but with none of the Russian bravado or love of the grand gesture. The only foreigners were Republican State Department types who had not seen the appeal of Holt's eccentricities. They invited him to play golf one Friday afternoon and didn't even crack a smile when Holt refused politely, claiming, "Croquet's my game."

"Hey, how about the Moscow croquet league?" I asked. "That one had legs."

"You need a lawn for croquet," said Holt.

"How is it there are five broomball rinks and no croquet lawns in Moscow?" wondered Joe aloud.

"What are you talking about?" asked DeeDee, who was watching our exchange like a tennis match.

"They come up with these very silly ideas for . . . what are they? They aren't parties," Tancy tried to explain.

"Stunts," I said.

"Stunts?" asked DeeDee.

"They had a cocktail party at the airport," said Tanya, who regards us all as endearing, but mentally deficient, aliens from a different galaxy. "And not, you understand, the nice airport either."

"Why?" persisted DeeDee, perplexed.

"Honey," said Tancy, "we've known them for about ten years, and we are still wondering."

"Haven't you people ever heard of Scott and Zelda Fitzgerald?" I asked. "Someone has to put the ex in expat. This town is a far cry from the glamorous expat life."

"I've got it!" said Holt.

"If you are thinking of that fountain outside the Bolshoi," I warned, "it's boarded up until 2011."

"So the flash yoga mob at Kazansky station?" Holt asked, resigned.

"I guess, if we've totally ruled out the poetry slam on the Aeroexpress train out to Domodedovo Airport," I suggested.

Bees Rees ascended the podium in a taffeta tartan ball gown. A reverent hush fell over the room. She began to thank an impossibly long list of people, mangling most of the Slavic surnames. My back was to her, so I leaned over Holt to Lucy, who was squinting at her Blackberry, thumbs flying over the tiny keyboard.

"Earth to Lucy," I coaxed. She held up the index finger of

★

one hand to indicate I needed to wait. Holt and I exchanged raised eyebrows.

"Sorry," she said, running her fingers through her blonde curls, "just had to charter a helicopter."

"Where's your own helicopter?" I asked.

"It went for its technical inspection," she said, "but this was for Myanmar, so a little complicated—they didn't want to take my Amex card."

DeeDee looked impressed, but the rest of us just went about our business, unfazed. Joe emptied half a bottle of red wine into Lucy's water goblet and set about catching the eye of a passing waitress to procure a replacement bottle. HRH was removing the import seal from one of the four bottles of The Famous Grouse that had greeted us when we sat down. I was pleased to see him conversing easily with Marat. The HRHs don't automatically become best friends just because the wives do. This seemed to bode well for my friendship with DeeDee.

"Are you in the airline business?" DeeDee asked Lucy.

"Not really," said Lucy. "I own an adventure travel agency."

"Wow," said DeeDee, "that sounds like a dream job."

"Sometimes," agreed Lucy, "but not today. My client is a big Russian banker—"

"Which one?" DeeDee leaned in eagerly. It wasn't hard to imagine her as a very successful headhunter.

"Don't even try," cautioned Joe with a world-weary air. "I've been trying to get her client list for about five years. Her motto is 'I don't name names.'"

Not naming names is a big part of what keeps Lucy so busy— and alive. Her small but select client list includes some of Russia's best-known oligarchs, or at least this is what we infer from her very subtle hints as to their identities. They pay her to meticulously research, plan, and execute their lavish vacations. She has four Rolodexes and legions of men on every continent—including a Norwegian naturalist who spends four months a year in Antarctica, so it really is every continent. A typical day for Lucy involves checking the thread count of sheets in treetop lodges in Tanzania and haggling with customs officials over the import of six Land Rovers to Mongolia for a billionaire's off-roading. She once said to me, and she meant it, "No, I'll definitely come to yoga with you, I just have to take a rhinoceros hide my client shot to the guy who makes the luggage, but after that I'm totally free."

"Anyway," continued Lucy after a restoring slug of wine, "I'd scouted the whole trip, and they insisted that they wanted to go by road, so we sent in a Bentley from Hong Kong and got a chauffeur and a translator and everything, but then they changed their plans last night and called me at 3:00 a.m. and told me to organize a helicopter. Well, all the helicopters there are military, so it was a little dicey. Thank god I'd met this Malaysian helicopter pilot. I don't really have enough contacts there—I've got to spend another month there before I send anyone else." Her Blackberry buzzed, and she picked it up again, then excused herself from the table.

"Yep," said Holt, "living the dream, that's Lucy."

I turned to Marat on my other side, feeling I'd neglected him. He looked like uphill work. Tancy was drawing out monosyllabic responses from him about his work at Hank Rees's Big American Company. Happily the bagpipes began to wheeze, signaling that we would soon be blasted again and it would be too loud to chat. Saved by the bagpipes. I wondered what DeeDee saw in Marat apart from his well-toned physique. She had told me over coffee that he had recently become very religious and forced the entire family to go to St. Catherine's Orthodox Church every Sunday morning.

Classic repat, I had said to myself.

Repats—or "repatriates"—had become quite the thing recently. These were the children of the emigrant wave of the 1970s, those who had left the Soviet Union because of its repressive politics and stagnant economy. These émigrés had turned their backs firmly on their native land, assuming they would never be able to return, and done their best to assimilate to their adopted countries. For many, giving their children a better future was a prime motivating factor, a future they never imagined would include a return to Vladimir Putin's Russia on fat expatriate packages as lawyers or accountants. The repats, on the other hand, were insatiably curious about their parents' native land. Although they spoke Russian fluently, they had no idea how to pay the electric bill and didn't quite understand how to deal with a domestic staff. In vain they searched for the romance of their parents' dissident youth. No one seemed to want to sit huddled in kitchens, pillows over phones, listening to scratchy eight-track tapes of the Beatles and exchanging grimy samizdat copies of Solzhenitsyn. The Russians they met at work were too busy racing from their spinning classes to their favorite sushi restaurants, where they shared pictures on their iPads of their latest trip to the Maldives. Repats were neither fish nor fowl, and they had a hard time fitting in. To the horror of their thoroughly assimilated parents back in Great Neck, repats did unforgivable things, like marry local girls or try to purchase real estate. Repats tended to go slightly overboard. In Marat's case, he had become passionate about the Russian Orthodox Church, and a little of that goes a long, long way.

Holt swiveled his chair around for a better view of the most ridiculous part of the evening. The Scottish country dancing was executed by this year's crop of comely and enterprising young Russian women who had answered the society's ad in *The Moscow Times* offering lessons in the esoteric jigs and reels. These young women went in for Scottish country dancing not to expand their dancing skills but rather as a fast track to finding an expatriate boyfriend from among Moscow's many single Scots. The girls made a pretty picture as they hopped, bobbed, and swung each other around, their tartan sashes flying but their eyes hard and calculating. I saw Radio Magellan Dude clapping in time to the music on the periphery. I dug my elbow into Holt's and indicated to him with my chin. Holt rolled his eyes. The girls executed their final steps and processed out, swishing their shiny skirts. The bagpipes blew another blast, and we were enjoined by the Tartan Society president to be upstanding for the haggis. More kilts and more bagpipes as the Dutch executive chef held the signature dish aloft and made a circle around the room to wild applause. The president, who had a thick Glaswegian accent, made a long and largely incomprehensible toast to the haggis, and we finally sat down to the main course.

"What is haggis?" asked Marat. Tancy and I exchanged glances over his plate.

"Well," I began, "in Scotland they use barley, but here they tend to make it with buckwheat."

"Is it vegetarian?" asked Marat. "I'm fasting at the moment."

"Noooo . . . ," I said carefully. "No, it's not vegetarian as such, but the interesting thing is that they used to have to fly it in from

Scotland for the ball, but then Sausage Guy started his company, and he made one—worked on it, apparently, for three weeks."

"Sausage Guy?" asked Marat.

Tancy and I both sighed audibly.

"Really cute English guy," said Tancy. "He was a bond trader or something like that—made a lot of money, but one day he was at Sainsbury's in London shopping for stuff to take back to Moscow. He was trying to fit an absurd number of sausages into his bag, and then he had a brain wave. Bought two books on sausage making, came back, and started his company. Fantastic sausages." She forked some haggis into her mouth and chewed appreciatively.

"Does he make money?" asked Marat skeptically.

"Well, he's a DJ as well," I explained, "and he's expanded beyond the sausages. He does steaks too. There is talk of a TV show."

"He's heavenly," sighed Tancy. Sausage Guy was just the sort of man that Tancy would have no trouble reeling in if she lived in a normal expat country like the United Arab Emirates or Germany. In Moscow, however, she faced stiff competition from the Scottish country dancers.

"I'll send you a link to his site," I said to Marat. "They deliver."

"We don't eat red meat," he said shortly and excused himself to the men's room.

Tancy and I watched him go.

"He may be even more tedious than Radio Magellan Dude," she whispered.

"Not sure he's going to solve our dancing problem," I agreed.

Dancing was always a problem with the urban family. Joe hijacked HRH and carried him over to the cigar bar, where they would spend most of the rest of the evening. Holt was not a great one for dancing until he put away far too much alcohol to make dancing with him fun. Lucy tended to drift off at this stage of the proceedings in search of someone who could, and would, stay upright and dance with her. She would then disappear with her partner into the bowels of Moscow's seamy nightlife, emerging the next day with only the vaguest recollection of the night's events and a very acute craving for a Quarter Pounder with Cheese and a large Coke. This left Tancy, Tanya, DeeDee, and me to watch the proceedings. We shifted chairs and claimed wineglasses, clustering at one end of the table, where we had an unobstructed view of the dance floor. Joe, HRH, and Holt eventually staggered back to the table smelling of cigars and Famous Grouse.

"We are going to start a book club," Joe announced with a grand gesture.

"That's right!" said HRH, twisting the cap off a fresh bottle of Grouse.

"But darling," I protested, holding out a moderately clean water goblet I was fairly sure was mine, "you don't read."

HRH laughed. "As far as I can see, all you ever do is drink wine at your book clubs."

Holt slumped into his seat. His tie was undone and his eyes were glittering. He would start dancing in about three minutes. "We're going to go to Night Flight to discuss our list," he said in mock seriousness. "Very important to get the list just right. It could take six or seven meetings just to get it right."

"Night Flight?" asked DeeDee. "Someone was talking about that the other day. Is that the club where they dance on the bar?"

Joe threw an arm around her. "No," he said. "Now, it's important you get these straight. The one where the girls dance on the bar is the late and much lamented Hungry Duck, which tragically closed in 1999."

Holt threw an arm around her other shoulder. "Whereas Night Flight—"

"Amazing food at Night Flight," said Tancy scornfully. "That's what he's going to tell you."

"The food is amazing," agreed Joe, "but Night Flight is the one where the prostitutes all hang out."

"One-stop shopping," I scoffed, then turned to HRH. "You are not going to Night Flight," I said sternly.

"We have to have our book club," HRH protested, filling Joe's glass with Grouse. "You have your book club—you have tons of book clubs! I want my book club! Then we can really have a Book Club Ball!"

"At Night Flight!" said Holt, raising his glass. I shuddered.

"I wouldn't worry about it," Tanya said stoically. "Joe never goes anywhere except the Diner and Rosie O'Grady's for darts on Friday. I can hardly get him to take me out to dinner any-where. And he doesn't read anything since *The eXile* went out of business."

"The Diner," suggested Tancy, "what a good idea."

We piled into two taxis and headed over to the diner for omelets, fatty Russian bacon, super strong Bloody Marys, and coffee. It was the perfect end to a long night, and when HRH and I left there was a pale pink smudge on the horizon. As the cold air hit me, my eyes teared up, and everything went fuzzy for a minute. Maybe it was the cold air, or fatigue, or all that Famous Grouse, but for a split second Mayakovskaya Square looked very picturesque in a Vaseline-on-the-lens sort of way. Kind of like Paris in the 1920s.

CHAPTER 3

THE
RED
HANDSHAKE

TANCY HAD TO cajole me into going to the reception at the US embassy. I'm not a great one for going to embassies at the best of times, and particularly not the US embassy in Moscow. Some expats think it is the the cat's meow; any excuse finds them lined up outside the heavily fortified entry, waiting docilely to be strip-searched and relieved of all communication devices until they can get inside, where, for some reason, it smells exactly like a middle school lunchroom. Bees Rees and that ilk go in heavily for embassy dos. They act like they've been invited to a White House state dinner instead of a Tuesday night scrum featuring really bad wine and stale peanuts organized by some just-arrived minister-counselor.

No, I've had my fill of the embassy. A few years back I went each Sunday for Velvet's renegade, breakaway Girl Scout troop, which met at her friend Savannah's house. Savannah's mother was in charge, which meant it was absolutely no fun at all. She was rather Puritan and a joyless hand-slapper, fond of reciting, "you get what you get, and you don't get upset" when the troop ran out of imported marshmallows or juice boxes mid-campout. She left a few months ago to take up the position of ambassador to Albania, where I fervently hope she likes what she got.

Embassy people are different from the rest of us. They don't stay very long, since the State Department likes to keep them cycling through posts at a brisk pace to be sure they don't pick up any foreign ideas. In the case of diplomats assigned to the Moscow station, it's frankly no great tragedy when they go. They all look like John Bolton knockoffs, that really unpleasant, überconservative Bush-era ambassador to the UN, and they dress like him too: shaggy heads in need of a haircut, badly fitting khakis, wrinkled blue blazers, and 50-percent-cotton, 50-percent-polyester striped shirts. This looks exceedingly frumpy in Moscow.

I'm never completely at ease with embassy people, which must be their issue and not mine, since I've certainly done nothing wrong. Right? I know that a good 30 percent of them have to be CIA plants (and now that I've become addicted to *Homeland* I suspect a much higher number). HRH says he knows that 30 percent is lowballing it, and we play a fun game where we try to decide which innocuous expat lawyer or airline executive is actually a deeply embedded agent. But as for the other 70 percent, what is it that they do all day? I know what their trailing spouses do: they complain. Unless, that is, they've just arrived from Lagos or Jeddah, in which case they ricochet around, soaking up alcohol and culture. But most just complain. They complain about the commissary, which seems like a treasure trove to me, filled as it is with impossible-to-score items such as Nestlé chocolate chips and vanilla extract. They complain about the embassy school and the Moscow weather, and what could they have been expecting, really? They moan about the container that hasn't arrived yet, the chlorine in the embassy pool, and the fecklessness and uselessness of their hapless Filipino servants. It's very tedious. In general they lack animation, the embassy crowd. There is no urgency to them; they just chug along until someone like Condoleezza Rice comes to town, and then it's all hands to the pump, bunting up, and blue blazers to the dry cleaners.

Part of Tancy's grown-up job with her big multinational company is being an A-lister at embassy events, and being single, she's in constant need of a "plus one." On the night in question she lured me out with the promise that not only were we going to have fun, but we also were going to have good drinks, because the Commerce Department was hosting an Association of California Wine Growers delegation in Moscow.

"Except they couldn't get the paperwork for their wine samples filed with Russian Customs in time," explained Tancy, dragging on a final cigarette before we entered the strictly no-smoking zone beyond the south gate. "Everything is sitting at Sheremetyevo Airport, waiting for them to pick it up on their way home tomorrow. They sent another batch via diplomatic pouch directly to the embassy, so this is the only actual tasting they will manage to have." She waved her hand toward the short line of would-be attendees, a typical embassy-do crowd: the NGO nerds (who always need feeding), unimportant journalists like Radio Magellan Dude (who still feels that an invitation from the embassy makes him important), and the predictable gaggle of overeager, clammy, gray, fourth-tier Russian academics of whom absolutely no one has ever heard. Not an A-list crowd, but what could you expect? It was Friday night in Moscow; the demimonde denizens like Xenia Sobchak and Arkady Novikov had better places to be.

Once inside, Tancy and I split up. She waded purposefully into the group of minister-counselors standing with their British and EU counterparts at one end of the room. Agendaless, I meandered around the periphery of the room, trying to grab a glass of Russian River Valley Chardonnay without getting trapped by Radio Magellan Dude. I felt a hand on my elbow.

"Hello there!" said Holt Fairfax, smiling broadly, his white teeth already stained a nice purple from Ravenswood Cabernet. He was clad in his usual natty blue suit, starched white shirt, and red bow tie, which made him easy to spot amid the John Bolton types. He was chatting with a fresh-faced preppy who looked like he had just come off the lacrosse field.

"This is Matt something," said Holt, "and you are just the person he needs to talk to. I'll snag you some more wine while you explain to him why he doesn't want to work at a Russian metals company. He is heading straight for a Red Handshake—talk him out of it."

"I'll certainly try," I said, surveying a tray of canapés a smiling Filipino waiter swung under my nose suggestively. I selected a mini popover with roast beef and horseradish sauce and regarded the young hopeful opposite me.

"Okay, Matt," I said. "Let's cut to the chase: you don't want to go and work for a Russian metals company."

"But I do—I do want to work for a Russian metals company," he protested.

"I'm sure you think you do," I said. "Why don't you tell me why?"

"Uh . . . ," he said in that annoying up-speak the twenty-somethings use these days. "I don't know. Maybe, uh, lots of money, career advancement, the opportunity to travel . . ." Holt reappeared, cradling three glasses carefully between his hands, which he distributed, and then he abruptly turned his back to block Radio Magellan Guy from joining our little klatch.

"How's it going?" Holt asked.

"Surprisingly badly," I said. "Where do you come from, Matt?"

"He came over here to intern with USAID," supplied Holt. "His contract is almost up, and he got headhunted by some Russian outfit to do some development gig at a scary metals company based in Tomsk."

"Ew!" I recoiled.

"It's a great opportunity," protested Matt. "I could never pull down this kind of salary back in the States. Anyway, I don't have to work in Tomsk, because corporate HQ is here in Moscow."

"Doesn't matter. Believe me, I would rather scrub toilets than work for a Russian metals company," I declared.

"I'd rather scrub the Russian metals company's factory toilets than ever set foot inside their corporate HQ," agreed Holt.

"Are you somebody's kid?" I asked bluntly. "Because if you are, there is no—"

"I'm not," insisted Matt. "I'm not somebody's kid. I have a BA from Duke and over sixty thousand dollars in student loans to pay back, and this seems like a fast track out of debt."

Holt and I exchanged knowing looks.

"Don't do it. Don't fall for the Red Handshake," said Holt mournfully. I nodded my head in agreement.

"What the hell is a Red Handshake?" asked Matt.

"You know what a golden handshake is, right?" I asked.

"Sure," said Matt. "It's the compensation package you get when you leave a company before your contract is up."

"Right. So a Red Handshake is the Soviet-style strategy of easing unwanted employees out of their jobs before their contracts are up without having to pay them any compensation."

"That's a thing?" asked Matt incredulously.

"Oh, yeah, that's a thing. Ask her—she knows all about it."

Holt tilted his head toward me in acknowledgment, and I tried to look modest.

A hedge-fund chum of mine once explained human nature very succinctly as being "fundamentally motivated by two emotions: greed and fear." These are exactly the emotions that lead to Red Handshakes. First, the greed. It begins with a seemingly harmless telephone call from Yuliya, a perky junior associate at a local headhunting firm. She lures you to a meeting at her office, where she sings the praises of a large, unwieldy former Soviet behemoth, typically a producer of some essential good or service such as metal, coal, oil, gas, or telephony. You know from a daily perusal of *The Moscow Times*'s business section that this company is currently run by a well-known and savvy oligarch who is very chummy with the Kremlin.

Yuliya gushes that the behemoth is undergoing a "dynamic redevelopment," which includes the creation of several company subsidiaries known as *torgoviy doms,* or trading houses. These subsidiaries will be run according to Western business practices and will gradually take on certain parts of the behemoth's activities to put them on a more commercial footing. There will be a lot of interface with foreign investors, and this is where you come in. It's an exciting time for the behemoth, Yuliya stresses, and they are looking for foreign expertise to help launch these significant subsidiaries, which will ultimately run the entire enterprise.

"Hey, I'm supposed to be employed by a *torgoviy dom,*" Matt interrupted. "I'm supposed to run the investor relations department."

"Seriously?" I asked, accepting another canapé.

"Dude, you are just toast," said Holt.

Your next interview takes place in the lobby of the Metropol Hotel with an enthusiastic, fortysomething, semi-Westernized Russian (he has an iPhone 5 but introduces himself by his formal name and patronymic: Igor Konstantinovich). He knows absolutely nothing about your industry but makes up for this with his unbridled enthusiasm for the "great potential" of the behemoth's restructuring plans. He confides that he went to school with the well-known and savvy oligarch and that they are next-door neighbors out at their dachas. On the basis of these qualifications, Igor Konstantinovich is going to run the *torgoviy dom,* and he would like you to be his deputy director. He mentions the magic word IPO several times and quotes a starting salary that is four times what you currently make. In your effort to look indifferent in the face of sudden financial windfall, you ignore two red flags that your more seasoned friends warned you about. The first: the *torgoviy dom* is not going to be located in the behemoth's newly renovated, sprawling corporate headquarters in downtown Moscow but rather in a separate office building on Taganka, which is currently being renovated by a very good team of construction workers Igor Konstantinovich knows personally. Why? Well, it's complicated, Igor Konstantinovich explains, but just better that way.

The second red flag: Igor Konstantinovich, who has shown himself to be the very model of a modern Russian businessman type, suddenly goes all clueless and Soviet about how to arrange international health insurance as part of your package. But he promises enthusiastically, if vaguely, to investigate all this in the near future. A minor detail, you think, and one that can easily be hashed out once you begin. Igor Konstantinovich is clearly one of the good guys—the kind that is putting Russia back on track, you think. He'll keep his word.

You race home with visions of villas in the Côte d'Azur and top-tier private schools for your children dancing in your head. You gush enthusiastically to your friends and family about how much you like Igor Konstantinovich and how this is just the sort of work you hoped you'd end up doing in eight or nine years, and here it is, fallen right in your lap. It's the opportunity of a lifetime. Secretly you think it is about bloody time the universe woke up to your talents.

You ignore the advice of more seasoned expats, who suggest you not rush into anything and take your time to hammer out the details. They also seem to think it's important to hire a shyster lawyer to represent your interests in the salary negotiations as well as get a myriad trivial details, such as reporting lines, bilingual secretaries, and guaranteed business class travel, written into your contract. They suggest the (surely excessive, you think) draconian measure of putting a copy of the signed contract in a safe-deposit box in the UK or Switzerland. They seem a little paranoid to you. Meanwhile, Igor Konstantinovich phones with the exciting news that someone who works part time as the behemoth's "authorized representative" in the UAE has set up some investor relations meetings in Dubai—and he wants you there at his side. You haven't seen the sun in four months, so it's a no-brainer, and besides, you can take the opportunity of having Igor Konstantinovich to yourself to thrash out all these minor contract details.

The trip to Dubai is great! It's not very productive in terms of meetings, but you bond with Igor Konstantinovich, who turns out to be great—boy, does he unwind as soon as you are out of Russian airspace! You thought you'd hash out the details of your contract and the still-unresolved health insurance during the comfortable business-class flight, but it's much more interesting to do shots of Emirates Airline's excellent Hennessy X.O with Igor Konstantinovich. As a result, when the contract is finally drafted, it doesn't include a stipulation that you always fly business class wherever you go. You regret this when you take your first Moscow-Khabarovsk overnight flight on Russia's national carrier in economy class, which is so not why you signed up for this job.

Back in Moscow, Igor Konstantinovich is apologetic that your work contract is held up in the behemoth's legal department. The chief lawyer is on sick leave, he explains, but once she gets back, he assures you, everything will be fine. There is also a little confusion over your title, about which Igor Konstantinov- ich seems embarrassed. Apparently the behemoth's company charter does not permit you to be "deputy director." Instead, you'll be Igor Konstantinovich's "first adviser" but, he's at pains to point out, with all the accompanying responsibilities and sal- ary you've agreed upon.

You tell Igor Konstantinovich that this is so not a problem, thinking to yourself that for a nation that pioneered the first so- cialist state, Russians are obsessed with titles, rank, and status. Igor Konstantinovich seems relieved, and speaking of salaries, he regrets it, but until the chief lawyer returns from sick leave and your contract is signed by the savvy oligarch, he'll have to pay your salary in cash, is that okay? He presses a thickish envelope at you, which contains the agreed-upon amount in cash. You take your girlfriend out for a five-figure dinner at Vanil to celebrate.

The renovations at Taganka take longer than you expect, but you and Igor Konstantinovich are given a small conference room at the behemoth's main office, and you both work from your Gmail accounts for the moment, which is a little awkward when setting up meetings with the venture capital crowd in London but a minor detail considering all you are juggling. A lot of your time seems to be taken up by the behemoth's "Red Directors," the fiftysomething executives from the Soviet era who run the behemoth's various divisions. They squint at you with suspicion, if indeed they acknowledge you at all, when you go to their large suite of offices with Igor Konstantinovich for exploratory meetings. Each Red Director's office has a large *priyomnaya*, or antechamber, outside with puffy window treatments and heavy cherry furniture. You are a little taken aback to hear the secretaries answer the phones in what seems to you a very unwieldy and somewhat old-fashioned manner: *"Priyomnaya* of Ivanov, Sergei Vassilievich, chief of engineering department, I am Siderova, Svetlana Petrovna, first assistant to the chief of the engineering department, Ivanov, Sergei Vassilievich."

It is interesting, you think, that these women, while deferential, don't ever ask a caller how they can help them. In the inner sanctum of the Red Director's office, you are seated at a large rectangular conference table set perpendicular to the Red Director's large desk. As you and Igor Konstantinovich work your way up the behemoth's hierarchy, the conference tables get longer and the desks get wider and emptier. Senior Red Directors have nothing on their large desks except large malachite and bronze double-headed eagles and banks of old-fashioned, cream-colored rotary phones with no dials or buttons. You note with interest the complete absence of any IT equipment in the offices: no computers, no monitors, no keyboards. It occurs to you that the large conference table is a rather cool, sort of phallic, symbol of power—and you wonder if your new office at Taganka will have one. For men with empty desks and no dials or buttons on their phones, the Red Directors sure do have a lot to say, mostly delivered in long diatribes concerning their own personal biography, all of which Igor Konstantinovich dutifully writes down in a leatherette A5 diary. You try to avoid the disturbingly knowing look in Vladimir Putin's eyes in the large portrait of the president hanging behind every Red Director's chair. You come prepared to each meeting but never get to do your PowerPoint presentation about the seven synergies, core functions, and overall future mission of the *torgoviy dom.*

The office at Taganka is finally completed, and you move in. You experience a frisson of disappointment when you discover that although you do have a conference table, it is small and round, not long and phallic. On the other hand, the state-of-the-art telephones do have buttons but curiously, no dial tones. Since everyone from Igor Konstantinovich down to the four tea ladies has a mobile phone, this turns out not to be such a big deal.

You start working on a website design with a marketing company run by someone with whom Igor Konstantinovich also went to school. You still don't have a Behemoth.ru email address, which strikes you as odd. No matter—the thick envelopes continue to appear promptly each month, even though your contract is still held up because the chief lawyer is still on sick leave. You put your head down in an impressive display of Western work ethic and complete the business plan in record time. About seven months into the project, Igor Konstantinovich is a few days late with the thick envelope. Four days later he takes you out to lunch at Yolky Palki. He apologizes profusely for any unpleasantness that may ensue, but he feels he should let you know that he is leaving the *torgoviy dom* and returning to the Ministry of Economic Development. He urges you to stay in touch. You call him three days later to follow up on the thick envelope only to discover that his mobile phone is, the disembodied voice informs you, "switched off or out of the coverage."

Igor Konstantinovich's place is taken by a cheerless battle-ax called Lyudmila Mikhailovna, who comes from the seamy bowels of the savvy oligarch's banking empire. She knows even less about your industry than Igor Konstantinovich did but makes it clear that she is not interested in any help or advice from you. You pluck up the courage to mention your contract, at which point she hints ominously of an impending "restructure."

Four days later she brings in a smarmy, ratlike man who also knows nothing about your industry. He will be her deputy director, she explains, and he needs your office and your bilingual secretary. Although he is four or five years younger than you, the smarmy, ratlike man asks that you call him Vyacheslav Vladislavevich, which strikes you as both awkward and impossible to pronounce. You visit his (formerly your) office the next day and feel a little twinge of jealousy while you watch a large, rectangular phallic conference table being delivered.

And so begins the fear part of the Red Handshake. You worry about leaving on vacation while all this change is going on, but your girlfriend is excited about skiing in Chamonix, and you could use a break. While you are away you discover that your Audi has been redistributed to a Red Director, and you are advised to apply to the general driver pool when you need to get somewhere. They never answer your calls or emails, so you end up getting around on the Metro. A chilly awareness that you are somehow out of the loop in terms of meetings and memos begins to creep over you, and Vyacheslav Vladislavevich chastises you in front of the rest of the staff for not adhering to *prikaz* #46/2007-03-18, a six-page company memorandum from Lyudmila Mikhailovna detailing necessary downsizing measures effective immediately.

Olga Konstantinovna, the bovine chief accountant you've managed to avoid until now, calls you in to discuss *prikaz* #46/2007-03-18. On page four it clearly outlines the norms of salary payments in the "cadre" (Russian for head count) for "advisers," although Olga Konstantinovna notes that you don't seem to be in the "cadre" list. She orders you to go and open a bank account at the National Savings Bank and advises you that your salary will now be paid into that account according to norms. You are horrified to learn that the monthly norm is one-tenth of your thick-envelope amount. You produce your draft contract to protest, thinking this might be a good moment to clear up the four-month arrears, to say nothing of the medical insurance, but Olga Konstantinovna just heaves a massive Slavic shrug and advises you that employment contracts are not in the framework of her competency. She advises you to apply to the chief lawyer when she returns from sick leave.

"She's been on sick leave for fifteen months!" you explode. "What the hell is wrong with her? How can it be legal to be on sick leave for fifteen months?"

Olga Konstantinovna's eyes gleam, and you realize too late that she was just waiting for you to lose it. She fixes you with an impenetrable stare and calmly says, "She's the chief lawyer, and she knows exactly how long she can be out on sick leave." Olga Konstantinovna also confiscates your mobile phone, advising you that, according to *prikaz* #46/2007-03-18, all mobile phone contracts need to be renegotiated with a new provider.

Enough is enough. You decide to take your grievances to the top, thinking that the savvy oligarch can resolve everything, cut you a check for your back salary, appoint a new chief lawyer, and get this train wreck back on track.

You somehow make your way through the stronghold of metal detectors and intimidating security staff to the savvy oligarch's *priyomnaya* to apply for a time slot to see him. The *priyomnaya* is the size of an airplane hangar and decorated with the mounted and stuffed heads of a number of large endangered species from Africa. Three Barbie doll secretaries are evasive, and one asks you to return the following week, but you aren't fooling around this time. You stubbornly plant yourself on the large white leather couch and advise them that you will stay there until you get to see the savvy oligarch. They shrug and refocus their blank stares on their computers. One speaks quietly into her phone. An awkward impasse ensues, during which you are not offered green tea. Eventually a man arrives in an ill-fitting gray suit gripping a walkie-talkie and flanked by two large men in black storm-trooper uniforms wearing bulletproof vests and toting semiautomatic rifles. The man in the gray suit silently gestures with his walkie-talkie for you to leave the *priyomnaya*. The Barbie dolls continue to stare at their monitors. You decide protesting is a bad idea and make your way to the Baroque double doors. The storm troopers take up positions immediately behind you and escort you all the way to the street.

While you were besieging the savvy oligarch's *priyomnaya*, Lyudmila Mikhailovna issued *prikaz* #47/2007-03-22, detailing the imminent move of the entire *torgoviy dom* staff from Taganka to a new suite of offices on Krasnaya Vorota. You overhear a particularly unpleasant woman called Natalya Nikolaevna tell one of her cronies that Lyudmila Mikhailovna is having the new space completely renovated by a team of construction workers she knows personally.

In record time the entire management team (except you) moves to the new office space. Alone in the old office space on Taganka, you are wondering what to do next, when four men in quasi army fatigues with buzz cuts and epaulets arrive, unplug your laptop, place it in a metal box, then put you on notice to quit the building or suffer the consequences. You retreat to the Starlite Diner for a cheeseburger to weigh your options. You

THE RED HANDSHAKE

★

consider taking your grievance to a lawyer or the US embassy, but then you spot an announcement in *The Moscow Times* for an English-language editor at a Western bank. You polish up your CV and email it through. And you don't look back.

"Oh, come on, you must be exaggerating," protested Matt.

"Nope," Holt chirped. "That is exactly what happened to a guy we know who worked for a pulp and paper company."

"That wasn't nearly as grisly as the Goldman Sachs dude who quit to join the steel company in Siberia," I added with relish. "A bunch of masked thugs roughed him up, then threw him in the back of—it was either a truck or a helicopter, he was never sure. But they dumped him in the middle of nowhere in some wooden lean-to and left him there for three whole days. He was almost eaten alive by mosquitoes."

"Are you talking about that Goldman guy?" asked Tancy, joining us. "Jesus, that was scary. Know what else? When he joined them he had to forgo two years of Goldman deferred bonus compensation, which they promised to pay him . . . and they never did." She shuddered at the thought of a loss of bonus compensation, which in Tancy's world ranks worse than death.

"And don't forget Repat Guy with the mobile phone company," I reminded them. "He fell very far, very fast."

"He was an asshole though," Holt said dismissively. "He said he went to Harvard Business School, when he'd just like audited one class there. They were right to fire him."

"Is there anything good about working for a Russian company?" cried Matt. We three looked at him in surprise.

"Of course there is," said Holt in an upbeat tone you could tell he didn't mean. "There's the 13-percent income tax rate."

"Thank you, President Putin." I toasted him with my glass. "And there is the twenty-eight-day vacation thing, and with all the public holidays you get off, it ends up being more like thirty-seven."

"And hey," added Tancy with a big smile, "it's practically impossible to be fired."

"Well," said Matt, who had paled somewhat under his preppy tan, "I'm going to give it a go. I need to pay down these student loans."

"It's your funeral," I started to say, but that seemed a little too much like tempting fate. "Good luck with it," I said instead and shook his hand warmly.

HRH, of course, has never been fired, and he's almost never had a Red Handshake. This is because he is extremely good at working for Russian companies. He doesn't let the Red Director types get to him; he lets them pass as light through his crystal, taking the long view that they have about another decade and they'll be done. He's worked for a few real doozies, but he's appropriately deferential to them and a real corporate badass to everyone else, and as a result he's enjoyed popularity and a steady climb through the ranks wherever he's worked. As the years have gone by he's got a bit grumpier and a whole lot bossier. His early training as a Red Army officer has stood him in good stead, and occasionally I have to remind him that I am his wife, not his corporal. Sometimes when I hear him barking into the phone "*Da?*" or "Not now, Volodya!" I wonder if he is the same sweet guy I married.

When I started my character-building two years at my first Red Handshake company (a large, blue-chip Russian firm you've definitely heard of), HRH urged me to acquire some new management techniques.

"Your problem, Petrovna, is that you aren't enough of a *zagadka*—an enigma," he said. "Make them wonder where you came from and what your connections might be. Leave things unsaid."

"But darling, how can I do that? Everyone knows where I come from."

"At least be a little tougher with everyone," he urged. "Make everyone come to you. . . . When you want someone, call them up on the telephone and be forceful. Say, 'Get up here!'"

"Get up here!" I tried to bark in Russian. It sounded ludicrous.

HRH maintains that no real manager would be caught dead walking the floor of a factory he's in charge of. A good manager sits several time zones away from the factory he's in charge of. Highly effective Russian managers, HRH says, also know how important it is to infringe on employees' personal time. They hold regular management meetings at awkward times, like 8:00 p.m. on a Friday night or 10:00 a.m. on Sunday mornings in the middle of summer, and they fail to appear at a random third of these, phoning in regrets ten minutes after the scheduled start. This keeps the employees where they belong: on their toes.

This cachet of workaholism in Russia is spiraling slightly out of control if you ask me (and no one ever, ever does). The new chic thing among senior Russian management is to be forced to interrupt a vacation to fly back to Russia (mind-numbingly expensive in August and January, as only seat 1A is ever available) to resolve some work-related crisis. You aren't anyone until you have to do this at least twice a year.

HRH was very scornful of the little notes I wrote to staff members to thank them for a job well done. These, he advised, would not get me anywhere, and he turned out to be right. No one in Russia ever writes a thank-you letter for anything. Much better to rant and rage and rake everyone over the coals during large staff meetings, then walk out with a disgusted sneer on your face as if you are personally insulted that everyone has wasted your time. Putin does this really well. HRH also suggested I was insane not to pack the organization-chart tiers directly below me with my own people. Real Russian managers, he explained, fill key positions immediately under them with friends from school, neighbors, relatives, or other cronies. It doesn't matter if they don't know anything about the job in question—the important thing is that they can be trusted to keep their mouths shut and get the job done. Throughout the late nineties I kept trying to get HRH to do things like learn to email on his own, but he refused, noting that he had become too senior to start communicating on his own. Even today he puts all his calls through via his *priyomnaya* secretary, who he has to take with him whenever he changes jobs, since she is the only one who keeps his address book up to date. This went a long way to explaining why the Red Directors have no dials or buttons on their phones. HRH has a finely honed sense of when it is time to jump ship—none of this company loyalty nonsense. He just grabs his Rolodex and is on to the next thing.

I didn't jump ship when I left my job at The Firm, though I was, I hoped, making a thoughtful disembarkation to the right port at an appropriate moment in the voyage. I finished up just before the ten-day May Day holiday break. Half of the office had already left for Turkey, Egypt, Greece, or their dachas. Alexei Soloviev pronounced this an excellent reason for us to go and have a three-martini lunch at Café Pushkin.

"It's going to rain," I warned, looking through the glass panel that separated Alexei's office from mine and out his window.

"All the more reason," he said, pulling on his regulation "casual day" tweed jacket and shooting his cuffs. "We can take my car."

"Well, perhaps one martini," I said, stuffing three outdated corporate Amex statements into the shredder. "I expect the traffic will be hell. . . ."

"One for sure," said Alexei. "Come on, then."

We left the office as the first raindrops plopped menacingly onto the windshield. We sat together in the humid backseat as Alexei's driver, Garik, swung the car out of the driveway, edged it into the bottleneck clogging the slip road onto the Garden Ring, and settled into the snail's pace that would deliver us a quarter of a mile in forty minutes.

"Would it be quicker to walk?" I wondered aloud, although I had no such intention. I stretched my legs out in the generous backseat, already nostalgic for The Firm's perks.

"Don't be ridiculous," Alexei retorted as he raised his buzzing BlackBerry to his ear.

I ran through my bureaucratic to-do list and found it satisfyingly complete. Leaving The Firm was a smooth, well-oiled procedure. I'd collected my *trudovaya knishka,* the passport-size record of my professional life in Russia, which bore fresh stamps and dates charting the three and a half years I'd worked as head of PR and marketing. In exchange, I had turned in the plastic key card that allowed me access to the building, the elevator, and some of the more restricted areas of the office. And that was it. I hadn't had to train my replacement, since she was utterly convinced that she knew my job much better than I did.

The Firm was a gutsy, homegrown outfit—founded and run by a group of expats and Russians, all brilliant, who had beaten the odds by remaining friends and not shooting one another. Their success ultimately led to the sale of The Firm to big Multinational. To my way of thinking, this was a transaction not unlike the one where I proffered my credit card and a salesperson handed me a bag of groceries, but somehow it took Multinational three whole years to purchase The Firm. I was hired to glam up the PR and marketing materials and establish good working relations with the press. This wasn't my dream job, of course, because I was neither in my pajamas nor aboard

*

a large oceangoing vessel, but after a few choppy years of Red Handshakes, The Firm turned out to be a very safe and happy place to be, filled with bright, hard-working types who all had computers on their desks and dials on their phones. Only one guy had a portrait of Putin behind his desk, but he was the company joke.

There was an inevitable learning curve: at first I giggled when I heard grown men speak in reverent tones about something I considered an inanimate noun as if it had feelings and emotions. "The market likes it," they would say about something, or "The market wasn't sure how to take it." The syntax initially worried me; this crowd used team as a verb and win as a noun. Never mind; the work was interesting, I liked the guys I worked for, I didn't have to terrorize my team to get them to work, and it paid well.

The only fly in the ointment was that Multinational had a Moscow office of its own. The 35,000-foot thinking on this (as they would say) was that Multinational would integrate The Firm's gutsy, homegrown talent and put them to work for Multinational, and everyone would live happily ever after. Down on the ground, however, Multinational's Moscow staff either hadn't gotten the memo or decided to pretend they hadn't. During the last months leading up to the buyout everyone suddenly realized that we were Noah's ark. We had two of everything: two COOs, two heads of this, vice presidents of that, and team coordinators of something called CEEMEEPEA, which geographically referred to the known world minus the United States and Hong Kong. I was the only one who ever noticed that it sounded like "see me pee."

We had twice the number of secretaries, god knows how many superfluous drivers, and a government relations guy no one had ever seen. Maybe it was deliberate: a survival-of-the-fittest exercise. Multinational's top management were from Middle Europe, and their corporate culture of procedure, detail, and order had fused in a grotesque way with that of the centuries-old Russian preoccupation with rank and privilege and the all-important point of making damn sure that if your own life wasn't ideal, your neighbor's was equally bad or, preferably, much worse. At The Firm we vied to see who could make the best Panzer tank joke, but underneath it was a disturbing illustration of what a lasting Nazi-Soviet pact might have looked like.

Multinational had its own director of PR and marketing. Of course they did, and when I found out her name was Olga, I immediately began packing the cardboard boxes. After fifteen years in Russia I knew a thing or two, and I knew nothing good ever came of an Olga. "The Olga factor," I called it, and I was planning to write something really scathing about Olgas in general, and a few things in specific, when I started to write full time. It was time to go. HRH was doing very well at his job, Velvet was outgrowing her nanny but still in need of supervision and math homework help, and I wanted to write a book. I negotiated a graceful exit, leaving Olga to count the canapés. I was feeling good about the decision, if a little sad to be leaving friends like Alexei.

Alexei's car pulled up in front of the ornate facade of Café Pushkin, one of Moscow's most popular restaurants. It looked like a lovingly restored nineteenth-century mansion but was actually a complete fake, down to the scratches in the gleaming oak bar on the first floor and the Dutch porcelain toilet in the ladies' powder room. Having dropped a small fortune at Café Pushkin on events, dinners, and Russian financial journalists' appetites, Alexei and I were immediately recognized by the uniformed doorman, who raced out to shield us from the rain with his umbrella. Once we were inside, the head waiter deferentially escorted us upstairs to the third floor, where Moscow's movers and shakers all dine, away from hoi polloi. A long-haired waiter dressed as an 1820s Russian dandy proffered the hefty wine list and, in an elaborately graceful flourish, placed a footstool next to my chair for my handbag.

"So your money won't run away," he advised me in English, flashing a smile as fake as the Dutch porcelain toilet. It's very silly, Café Pushkin, but it is fun.

Alexei asked for dry martinis, explaining in detail that he wanted gin, not vodka, and how to swish a splash of Martini & Rossi extra dry around the frosted glass and discard any that didn't cling to the sides. He then had a lengthy discussion as to the exact origin of the olives, ensuring that they'd be liberated from a jar and not a tin.

"The lady," he said, indicating me, "will have four, and I will have two. Have you got that?"

"*Razumeyetsiya gosudarin*" ("It goes without saying, master"), said the waiter, clicking his heels. I snorted at the pompous eighteenth-century language that had come boomeranging back into fashion. "I think he's heard your martini lecture before, Alexei," I teased.

Alexei shrugged. In Moscow, even at Café Pushkin, there was always the risk of being served a glass of Martini Bianco or Rosato rather than the world's most popular cocktail.

"If you ask me—and no one ever, ever does," I confided to Alexei, "the attitude toward martinis here is one of the things that will continue to keep Russia out of the WTO."

We leaned back against the plush, plum-colored velvet chairs and regarded one another with affection tinged with sadness. I considered making a short and heartfelt speech before the martinis arrived but was interrupted by a bright flash of purple and some commotion by the rickety, faux-nineteenth-century lift. The doors shuddered open and Jesus (pronounced, he'd be the first to tell you, as "Hey, Zeus!") sashayed out with all the panache an exotic, five-foot-three, coffee-skinned Venezuelan gay man can produce in a room full of thick-necked Russian bankers and oilmen. He sauntered toward our table, seemingly oblivious to the nervous stares of the other diners, who had momentarily lost the attention of their long-haired, long-nailed, and long-legged luncheon companions. The female stares at Jesus's bold ensemble—purple silk bomber jacket over skin-tight white jeans and hot pink Tod's driving moccasins—held more than a twinge of envy. A large diamond stud winked in his left ear, and Prada sunglasses were perched on top of his head.

"*Querida!*" Jesus sang out, deftly leaning over me to exchange three kisses, engulfing me in a cloud of Chanel Homme. "Surprised?"

"Pleasantly," I said, as the waiter put a large frosted martini glass in front of me.

"Alexei and me," said Jesus, easing himself gracefully into the third chair, "thought this would be a nice way to end djour brilliant career, didn't we, *cariño?*" He turned to Alexei and ran a proprietary hand down his tweed-clad shoulder, then leaned in to give him a peck on the cheek. Across the room came the sound of more than one heavy fork clattering against heavy china.

Alexei Soloviev was my first and best friend at The Firm. If I had survived and ultimately thrived in that alpha-male jungle, I had Alexei to thank for it. Conscious of its imminent absorption into Multinational, The Firm had allowed what it called the "head count" to exceed standard meters-per-person allotments, so we doubled up in the office pods, and Alexei, the COO, became my next-door neighbor. The glass panel separating us encouraged an early and lasting friendship. He patiently tutored me in just what The Firm did, explaining the difference between asset management and fixed income, which I tended to mix up.

We took to sharing a ritual Friday evening glass of good Scotch, and one night Alexei broke off during an explanation of how Chinese walls (in which he had a touchingly naive faith) worked to confess that he was in love with just about the most inappropriate person imaginable, but he couldn't help himself. Homosexuality was against the law in Russia during the Soviet period, and that feeling lingered in society long after the law was rewritten. He experienced, to his surprise and my relief, relatively little fallout. Things would later get nasty, when the church and the government got busy rewriting and reinterpreting the laws in 2012. In the early oughts, however, Alexei was able to come out with very little fallout.

"My mother was wonderful about it," he said, as he dusted off the two heavy-bottomed glasses we used on Fridays, held them up to the light, and squinted through them. "She thinks my boyfriend is the funniest person she has ever met. But it's probably a good thing my father is dead."

I thought that might well be the case.

When I met him, I agreed with Alexei's mother: Jesus was the funniest person I'd ever met too, and once launched in the Moscow social scene he effortlessly became its star. Everyone loved Jesus; even HRH, who had a textbook unease with homosexuality, laughed out loud at some of his antics. Jesus was irresistible. He was an eternal optimist, one of the world's great epicures, and legendarily generous.

"Here you go, *querida*, I bring djou a . . . 'ow you say, the going-away-from-the-work present." He proffered a shiny silver gift bag.

"Can I open it now?" I asked.

"Djes, *querida*," he purred. I tore open the tastefully wrapped box. It was a pink fur sleeping mask with satin ribbons and rhinestones that spelled out "Beauty Sleep."

"Because djou can, you know, now sleep all day long!" He clapped his hands.

"I love it! Where do you get these things, Jesus?" I asked, leaning over to kiss him.

Jesus put one well-manicured forefinger to his lips and said, "*Querida*, don't even ask. . . ."

One could only imagine.

Jesus Arismendi was born in El Limón, Venezuela, and as he would often tell me with emphatic South American gestures, when you are from El Limón, you have to do something. He had—from El Limón he'd made his way north to New York City, employing means, he later told me, "I just prefer to forget, okay, *querida*?" After a brief but intense period trying to make it as a special events flamenco dancer, and on the verge of getting fired from the Starbucks on 82nd Street, Jesus mercifully met Roland, a sixtysomething Upper East Side Brahmin who had popped in for a tall, skinny mochaccino.

"And that ees exactly what he got," Jesus would giggle, doing a little twirl.

After a whirlwind courtship of three weeks, Jesus moved into Roland's palatial inherited apartment at Madison and 86th. It was a match made in heaven. Roland sorted out Jesus's overdue chat with the INS and taught him all about design and decor, for which Jesus showed an instant and lasting passion. Roland's tutelage continued to fine cuisine, thank-you notes, wine, custom-made shoes, and the Mitfords. Jesus tended to the trendier side of life, but when Roland introduced him to Dominick Dunne in the men's room at The Four Seasons, Jesus knew enough to know it was a big deal. It was like a fairy tale, and it would have continued unabated but for the blood clot that felled Roland during a trip to St. Petersburg to see the "Hidden Treasures Revealed" exhibit at the Hermitage.

"But djou know, *querida*," Jesus would often say, licking his finger and smoothing one already perfect eyebrow, "thees was how ee want to go. One minute, ee look at a Cezanne no one see since 1943, and the next day, poof, ee's dead."

Since Jesus and Roland were not married in anyone's sense of that legal tie, the Russian paperwork proved a nightmare. The cruise ship, with its sympathetic blue-eyed Danish crew, headed back to Copenhagen, leaving Jesus holed up at the Grand Hotel Europe trying to do the right thing by Roland, aided only by an unsmiling translator called Svetlana, from the Ministry of Foreign Affairs, who was the only person in the galaxy Jesus ever failed to charm. The Russian police and the American consulate in St. Petersburg each blamed the other for holding up the death certificate, without which Jesus could not dispatch Roland's remains to Frank E. Campbell on Madison and 81st Street, which he knew was exactly what Roland would have expected him to do.

Days during which the sun never set, which had sounded so romantic in the "White Nights & Hidden Treasures" brochure, passed in a frustrating haze of bureaucracy. Jesus was getting fed up with Svetlana's annoying facial hair, St. Petersburg's nightmare traffic jams, and the increasingly hostile phone calls from Roland's niece and official next of kin, Honoria, in Sneden's Landing.

One evening Jesus returned to the hotel, laden with misery, a shocking to-do list, and more perspiration than he was comfortable with. Passing through the metal detector at the door, he felt revived by a cool blast of air-conditioning and the soothing strains of harp music mingled with the chink of good china and crystal.

"So I say, okay, one cocktail—I think I earn it," and just at this moment during the telling of this story, Jesus would twist his right wrist to rotate his palm up in a request for affirmation.

"I'd say so," I would agree.

"I order Tom Collins. Well, of course no one understand what eet ees . . . and I try to explain to the waiter, and before I know eet, there he was!" Jesus would yelp, fluttering his hands up and down.

And there he was. Alexei Soloviev—blond, blue-eyed, conservative investment banker, in a perfect summer-weight Savile Row suit. Alexei Soloviev, born in wild northern Petrozavodsk, who had chiseled cheekbones and useful relatives on the St. Petersburg city council. Alexei Soloviev, who had graduated top of his class at elite Leningrad State University and launched his career in the first generation of bankers, who now owned and ruled Russia. Alexei Soloviev, who during his time with J. P. Morgan in London, on the Russian utilities beat, had managed to organize for himself British residency, a tiny flat at an excellent address in Holland Park, and a bucolic farmhouse in the Languedoc, was now a partner and COO at The Firm and was on a quick overnight trip to St. Petersburg to negotiate a deal, which eventually netted Alexei enough money to buy a duplex on Ostozhenka—and the far more valuable opportunity to meet the duplex's eventual chatelaine.

Alexei Soloviev explained to the bartender exactly how to make a Tom Collins, sending him scurrying to the kitchen for powdered sugar, then slid onto the barstool next to Jesus and ordered two. On their second Tom Collins, Alexei Soloviev explained to Jesus that his last name meant "nightingale." When the two strolled up to the Caviar Bar for champagne and some light snacks, Alexei Soloviev told Jesus that he would call his Uncle Sergei, who was high up in the mayor's office and could sort out Roland's death certificate. And that is exactly what Alexei did the next morning as the two sipped coffee, tangled up in the expensive Egyptian cotton sheets the hotel imported from Sweden. They have been together ever since.

"And so there djou go," Jesus would say, shrugging his shoulders. "Roland ends up at Frank E. Campbell and me doing up the daydream house on the Ostozhenka. . . ."

"*Querida*," Jesus said, pulling me back from my fond recollections, "do djou know that Ostozhenka is the green property on the Russian Monopoly board? I just find this out!"

"I think I did know that," I said, smiling over at Alexei, who rolled his eyes.

The 1820s waiter reappeared to take our order. Jesus made a big to-do of not understanding the menu (which he knew by heart), so the 1820s waiter had to walk him through all fourteen stiff pages of it before Jesus finally announced he would have the sea bass, which is what he always had. Alexei, defiant after one martini, ordered another, and the beef stroganoff and potatoes.

"That," said Jesus, taking a delicate sip of his Kir Royale, "is going straight to djour hips, *cariño*."

"Special occasion," retorted Alexei, skewering an olive and popping it into his mouth. "It's not every day I get abandoned by my drinking buddy and wind up stuck with Olga Quelque

Chose." He raised his fresh martini glass at me in mock sorrow.

"Look at it this way," I said to Alexei. "You're not losing a corporate spouse; Jesus is gaining a lady who lunches."

"*Exactamente!*" trilled Jesus. "But I am putting djou to work, *querida* . . . djou are going to help me in the nasty Russian tile shop."

"How the mighty are fallen," said Alexei. "From strategic communications executive to lowly translator for a poofter interior designer."

"Moscow's leading poofter interior designer," I corrected, as the waiter put down an enormous dish in front of me, which had surprisingly little asparagus risotto in it. He messed about with some fresh Parmesan and left me to it.

"Actually, *querida*," said Jesus, "what djou can really do to help me . . . djou know all of your gorgeous husband's rich friends?"

"Don't call HRH gorgeous, Jesus," I said, shaking my head. "It makes him very nervous."

"Djou don' think he's gorgeous?" asked Jesus, surprised, as the long-haired waiter put an oval platter of sea bass and wilted spinach in front of him and lingered an extra moment to fuss with Jesus's lemon wedge. Alexei multitasked by keeping a sharp eye on the waiter and Jesus while piling his fork high with potatoes and glistening beef stroganoff, then stuffing it into his mouth in a silent but pointed protest.

"I do," I said emphatically, "but I don't think he appreciates the thought from other men."

"Ee's a real Russian bear, djour HRH," said Jesus, showing the long-haired waiter almost all of his dazzling white teeth, which were specially bleached in Bonn, Germany, every six weeks. "But now ee will be very happy—djou will be home to cook for him."

"He is," I agreed.

Alexei snorted.

"But it leaves my poor *cariño* with the . . . what djou call her . . . the 'Baba Yoga'?" Jesus quipped. I burst out laughing. Even Alexei smiled.

"Baba Yaga is the fairy tale witch in the Russian version of *Hansel and Gretel*," I explained. "No, Alexei is stuck with my replacement, who is, of course, called Olga."

"Olga!" Jesus slapped his hand down on the table for emphasis. "That's right! What djou do about the horrible Olga, *cariño*?"

"I'm the COO," Alexei reminded us haughtily. "We are moving offices in June, at which point Olga the Terrible will be a full four floors under me."

"Good for you!" I applauded. "You want to be as far away from her as possible when it comes time to plan the *korporatif*." We exchanged nostalgic smiles.

In addition to sharing the glass wall, which was ritually shuttered by venetian blinds during bonus season and the weekly whisky, Alexei and I also shared the responsibility for planning and executing the *korporatif*, The Firm's annual holiday party, a saturnalia whose direct target audience (as we say in the marketing biz) were the upwardly mobile youthful secretaries and downwardly mobile middle-age tea ladies. Once a year both groups emerged from marathon sessions at the hairdresser completely unrecognizable. The glut of drivers, released from their primary reason for existence on this one night, indulged in a senior-management-sanctioned orgy of drunken debauchery, which always seemed to feature a dance with me. Raising the bar each year for these employees was a matter of intense personal pride: the *korporatif*, I discovered to my horror, turned up shockingly often in the category of "reasons you want to stay at The Firm" on the tedious annual 360-degree review. Alexei and I were in agreement that the party was a hideous waste of time, energy, and money. It was, however, part of our jobs, and with the help of larger-than-usual glasses of whisky from late October to mid-December, we delivered extravaganzas of mammoth proportions.

"Alexei!" I shouted the first year, as we navigated a path through the hideous oversize statues in the Tseretelli Gallery while a band called Uma2Rman hit chords that made all my fillings rattle. A normally dour IT guy did a credible imitation of Mick Jagger, surrounded by admiring secretaries and tea ladies, their lacquered hair in various stages of wreckage. "Alexei, this is the tackiest thing I have seen since the *Sound of Music* bus tour in Salzburg."

"Isn't it awful?" he said, shaking his head. "I'm just sorry Jesus isn't here to see it."

"He'd love it," I agreed.

"Alexei," I wrote on a cocktail napkin the following year, after we groped our way to the bar in the murky darkness of a hotter-than-hot nightclub called Rasputin, "do this math: if you took what we are spending tonight and divided it evenly by the number of employees at The Firm, do you realize that every single person could go—air-inclusive—on a week's holiday to Turkey at a five-star hotel?"

"That's not the point," he shouted back, slipping the bartender a five-thousand-ruble note and pointing to the eighteen-year-old Glenlivet behind the bar, the one that wasn't on the open bar list.

"Remind me again, what is the point?" I asked, gratefully accepting my glass.

"The point," he said, "is that thanks to this crowd, you and I can afford something better than a five-star Turkish resort."

"Fair enough," I said, draining my glass and handing it back to him. "Then clearly we can afford another round."

The year it "inked the deal" (annoying phrase), Multinational arrived on the scene to take over the annual revels. Oblivious to our reservations and eager for a slam dunk, Olga found and retained a slimy event manager called Sergei (slime-bags are always called Sergei) and bought out the entire evening performance of *Cats*, which, like all musicals in Russia, was experiencing a lackluster run at the Komsomol theater. At great expense, a dinner theater was constructed and truly heinous catering was booked. I calculated on the back of another cocktail napkin that we could have chartered the *Queen Mary* for a day.

It was epic. Like *Schindler's List* is epic. Senior staff from Russia, Holland, Britain, Denmark, and the United States, beyond ready for the lengthy winter break, who had seen *Cats* back in the day in London, winced as the soundtrack, translated into incomprehensible Russian, ricocheted around the vaulted 1950s House of Culture ceiling. The tea ladies and drivers sat in their holiday finery, miserable and seriously confused, peering at the stage as they tried to figure out the gist of an incomprehensible plot, performed by actors dressed, for some reason, like cats. Alexei and I stood together at the back of the room.

"This is a fiasco," said Alexei, crossing his arms resignedly.

"I think," I said, "I think I'm going to write that book."

"Fiction or nonfiction?" Alexei asked.

"Creative nonfiction," I informed him. "You can't make this stuff up, but it lends itself to embellishment."

CHAPTER 4

THE PREEXISTING BIRKIN

MAKING THE CHANGE from high-flying PR executive to stay-at-home freelance writer had lots of consequences, and most of them were positive. My dry-cleaning bill, for example, went from overwhelming to nonexistent. I had plenty of time to devote to trolling the online news aggregators. I started Proust (again). I thought about taking up yoga in a systematic way and had lots more time for long, leisurely, and gossipy lunches with Jesus at Shatush. I even started outlining the book I was going to write. The months passed very pleasantly indeed, until I woke up to a postponed, but inevitable, reality of my new life: without the monthly direct deposit of a salary, I was going to have to reveal some illicit spending I'd kept secret from HRH for years. For a long time now I'd been stashing money away into retirement plans.

I hadn't deliberately set out to deceive HRH about my savings addiction. When I first started at The Firm, I set up 529s, 401(k)s, and a hybrid life insurance policy. It wasn't that I tried to be sneaky or anything; it was more that I just never mentioned the savings vehicles, and I didn't include the contributions in our very cursory, primarily cash-based monthly financial reckoning. I had the feeling he just wouldn't get it, especially the insurance.

HRH is generous to a fault about a lot of things that do matter. He is indulgent about semiannual visits to Eileen Fisher, and he encourages me to splash out on Australian lamb (which costs as much per ounce as titanium in Moscow), good wine, and the kind of face cream you can justify buying only at duty-free outlets. Like many Russians, however, HRH thinks insurance of any kind is a Ponzi scheme of such epic proportions that it drives him to drink to even talk about it. And drinking, of course, just drives those premiums up further, not to mention exacerbating certain preexisting conditions. The preexisting condition thing truly enrages him, and he went ballistic when he found out that I had been very thorough about his preexisting conditions when I applied for the five-figure single-payer policy with the dangerous-sports rider and full emergency medical evacuation. I'm the type that ticks all the insurance boxes on the rental car agreement. Medical insurance wasn't a couture gown, designer jewelry, or a luxury car, but I felt guilty about it all the same. Guilty enough to resort to a tactic known in the parenting biz as "redirection" when opportunity knocked. It went something like this.

"What do you want for Christmas?" asked HRH.

"An Hermès Birkin bag," I responded promptly.

"Fine," he said smoothly. "Whatever you want, darling. Where do I go?"

"Oh, you don't just go," I said, warming to my narrative. "You have to get in touch with some guy in London, and he puts you on a waiting list, and then you have to give him a five-thousand-USD deposit if you want it by Christmas." HRH looked a little shocked but gamely forged ahead.

"Okay," he said, successfully concealing his sticker shock, "you get in touch with the guy, and I'll wire the money."

"And then," I continued, "you have to pay the balance, which should be somewhere between seven and eight thousand dollars."

"For a *handbag*?" he roared.

"That's right," I said, confident I was in the home stretch of this negotiation.

He swallowed hard and then summoned up what the Russians call *koorazh*: a unique Slavic fusion of flair, stupidity, and moxie. It's what makes a Russian man light up a five-hundred-dollar Romeo y Julieta cigar with a hundred-dollar bill or, indeed, buy an English Premier League football club.

"Okay," HRH said, swallowing hard. "If that's what you want for Christmas, then that is what we will do. . . ."

"Or," I said, moving in for the kill, "you could spend half of that and get all three of us comprehensive international health insurance/medical evacuation with the dangerous-sports rider, bodily remains clause, and for only 10 percent on top, US-Canada coverage, which means we are good to go everywhere in the world except North Korea."

"No, no," he said, shaking his head. "No insurance. I'll do the bag."

"Are you on crack cocaine?" I exploded. "You are seriously prepared to buy an absurdly overpriced handbag before you would buy medical insurance for your family?"

"Insurance never works for me!" he fumed. "And anyway, you blew any chances of it ever working with your stupid 'pre-extinction close.' Are you going to tell me where the hell they sell these insane bags or not?"

"Here is the thing," I said. "The insurance policy is all ready to go. It just needs your Visa card to seal the deal."

"Incredible," he said. "How do you come up with these kinds of things?"

HRH then launched into a bossy diatribe I'd heard a number of times: life is short, and though, yes, lifestyle costs money, it will all be over soon enough, so why not enjoy ourselves? Wondering how in hell I'd ever become the fiscal conservative in the mix, I presented what I felt was a winning counter-argument: that comprehensive international health insurance/medical evacuation with the dangerous-sports rider, bodily remains clause, and US-Canada coverage can prolong life, whereas an Hermès Birkin bag certainly won't.

Russians, however, don't see it that way. The long-range plan for the distant-future option is never their default position except where root vegetables are concerned. I blame it on two things: the climate and the Russian Orthodox Church. Millennia of long winters and short, intense summers have conditioned the Russians to extremes of feast or famine. The church cleverly parlayed these straightforward natural realities into the mystery of religious obligation that is Great Lent. Like all Christian calendars, Lent in Russia lasts for forty days, but as the Russian Orthodox Church is wont to do, they go into hyperdrive with Lent. The Orthodox refer to this obligation as the "Great Fast" or "Great Lent" to distinguish it from the twenty-some other fasts of the year.

As Great Lent progresses, the list of permitted foods dwindles to starvation rations: no meat, no fish with backbones, no dairy, no oil, and no alcohol. On Easter night, Orthodox Christians prepare to greet the risen Lord by gorging on a menu that features a staggering amount of eggs, butter, cheese, and alcohol. I guess the rationale is that if you have to go via a cholesterol-induced heart attack, you may as well choose the most sacred night of the liturgical year.

When you have the constant expectation of imminent famine coded into your DNA, then you are automatically conditioned to gorge at the feast. For centuries this kind of thinking has permeated other, more pragmatic aspects of Russian life. Like money. For the moment, Russians have a lot money, and they have not been afraid to use it. This book isn't about the land grab of the 1990s or the complex question of the Russian oil industry, and hey, if I knew where the Russian economy was going next, I'd be a research analyst, not a stay-at-home, yoga-pants-clad humor columnist. But for the past two decades, observing Russians with a lot of money has frankly been a great ride for anyone with a sense of the absurd. After four generations of a state-planned economy, the tenacious Russian spirit of excess, which once inspired Fabergé eggs, the construction of St. Petersburg, and record consumption of Veuve Clicquot (1913), awoke with a mighty roar that echoed up and down East 57th Street. Suddenly the place was awash with a whole bunch of cash, which could buy a whole bunch of things that a whole bunch of people wanted and a few could even afford. *Ka-ching, ka-ching, ka-ching.*

Joe Kelly always has a good Russian excess story, and his latest was a doozy, related around the table at our favorite restaurant, Scandinavia.

"So this new lawyer at Leonard & Kane called . . . let's just call him Tom."

"Wasn't it Steve Kohn?" interrupted Tancy bluntly. "I'm sure I heard something awful about him."

"Thanks for that," said Joe, smacking his hand on hers playfully.

"So this new lawyer just arrived in Moscow, and he meets some *dyev* from Krasnodar at a Starbucks—really good legs, nice

English, super ass—"

"Honestly, Joe," I protested.

"What?" Joe spread his arms out innocently. "She does have a great ass."

"What's a *dyev*?" asked DeeDee, who was fast becoming one of the gang.

"A chick," translated Holt. "It's from the Russian word for 'girl,' *devushka*—a *dyev* is a bodacious young female from the regions."

"Can I get on with this story or what?" asked Joe.

"If you must," said Tancy, drawing heavily on her cigarette.

"So Steve has to go to Paris for business, and he invites Krasnodar *dyev* to come along with him. Like, as a big treat. Off they go and check in to the hotel, good dinner, hot sex, and the next morning Steve gets up and takes off for his meeting. Leaves her a note saying he'll meet her in the evening and also gives her fifty euros for museum tickets and the Metro and stuff."

Anticipatory laughter echoed around the table.

"So around 3:00 p.m. Steve gets a call on his mobile phone, and it's a store on the—what's that fancy store street?"

"The Faubourg Saint-Honoré," supplied Tancy.

"That's right—some designer shop on the Faubourg—and they want Steve to come down there because Krasnodar *dyev* is having some kind of trouble with payment. So he excuses himself and grabs a cab to the store. He gets there, and she is just standing at the counter looking pissed off, with about eight huge shopping bags all packed up and everything, and they hand him the bill for seven thousand euros."

"He never paid it," I said, horrified.

"No," said Joe, drawing out the drama by refilling his wineglass, "he didn't. But then Krasnodar *dyev* takes him back to the hotel, sits him down, and explains to him how it works."

"How *what* works?" asked DeeDee.

"She explains that she expects him to set her up in an apartment on either Ostozhenka or Kutuzovsky Prospekt, give her a car—she's very specific about the make and model, either an Audi or a Mercedes—"

"The way I heard it," interjected Tancy, "she wasn't old enough to drive."

"That's the reason it costs so much," said Holt, rolling his eyes. "That, or you have to buy your way out of some embarrassing situation, like when they chain you naked to the radiator like Radio Magellan Dude."

"Come on, you read that story six years ago in *The eXile*," Tancy said. "That never happened to Radio Magellan Dude."

"It will eventually," Holt predicted darkly. "That tool is living on borrowed time."

"Hey, can I please finish here?" demanded Joe, checking his watch and scanning the entrance of the patio. "Tanya will be here any minute, and she won't appreciate my telling this story. Anyway, Krasnodar *dyev* also says she needs ten thousand euros a month, which doesn't include clothing or accessories."

"Does that include grooming?" I asked.

"Grooming?" asked Holt.

"You know," said Tancy, "manicures, pedicures, haircuts—"

"Hair color," I added, "eyebrow threading, and of course all-over waxing."

"And bleaching the hoo-hah, teeth whitening, elective surgery, and of course the personal trainer at the gym," added Tancy.

"Give me a ballpark figure," said Holt, intrigued.

"Three grand a month," Tancy said.

"Euros," I added.

Even Joe looked stunned.

"I don't think Steve got into that much detail, but I remember he said she mentioned four foreign vacations a year, flying business class," he said eventually.

We all looked at Lucy, who shrugged.

"I do a lot of paperwork for that crowd," she said carefully. "They usually call it a business trip or a hiatus to learn English, so they can fold it into corporate expenses, but—"

"You're not naming any names," we chorused.

"Well, I'm not," said Lucy defensively, as Tanya made her way across the patio, stopping to chat with friends before she joined our table, where she exchanged greetings with everyone, then ruffled Joe's hair affectionately.

"*Privyet*," she said. "What are you talking about?"

"Politics," said Holt, quickly pulling out a chair for her. "French politics."

The story of hapless Steve Kohn and Krasnodar *dyev* was pretty typical of the stories of Russian excess when shopping abroad. Russians are giving the Asians and Arabs a run for their money in the global luxury-shopping world. You can always easily tell which nationality has the largest reserves of disposable income: simply wander Burberry's flagship store, in what young Westernized Russians working at foreign banks and law firms annoyingly call "Laaaandon," and clock the sales staff. The minute the Svetlanas began to outnumber the Fatimas and the Mitokos, you knew that Russia was on its way to becoming a global economic powerhouse.

My British friends are always surprised when I tell them that Moscow has luxury shopping and secondary schools. As far as they can tell, Russians outsource both to Britain. Moscow and St. Petersburg have everything from Armani to Zegna in terms of luxury shopping, but as everyone in Russia knows, shopping is much better done abroad: things are cheaper, the security guards are less menacing, and you get your VAT back so you can continue the shopping spree in the duty-free. Really, though, it's a snob thing; nothing beats the élan of saying "Yes, I got this in Laaaandon." These days I board planes back to Moscow as early as I can to be able to stow my carry-on before someone like Krasnodar *dyev* comes along, with her sixteen Jimmy Choo bags, and then just stands there looking petulant until some unfortunate British Air flight attendant has to help her stow them in the overhead compartment.

Non-Russians are often dazzled by the amount of cash Russian men carry around as well as the somewhat cheesy man-bags they carry it in. Credit and debit cards have been the norm for more than a decade, but there is a certain stratum of Russian society that has yet to be convinced that plastic is indeed fantastic. Banking behemoths have still not hit upon a piece of plastic (with the possible exception of a black, heavier-than-average one) that instills in a Russian the same kind of confidence as a nice, thick, reassuring stack of foreign currency. For one thing, there are all those pesky security blocks, to say nothing of those woefully inadequate ten-thousand-US-dollar-a-day limits. The idea of a salesperson tactfully (in Europe) or rudely (in Russia) saying, "Excuse me, your card has been declined" is beyond the pale to any Russian suiting up to impress the female element at La Perla.

Even elite credit cards have their limits, and this was driven home rather graphically one year to HRH's friend Sergei Bichiyuk. HRH, Sergei, and just about everyone else we knew were delegates at the year's biggest conference dedicated to Russian business, which of course took place in "Laaaandon." It did, that is, until the year Vladimir Putin raised a quizzical eyebrow and noted to no one in particular that business leaders and ministers should attend conferences in Russia, not abroad. Everyone turned their private jets around in midair. The Russian government now holds it in St. Petersburg, which is not nearly as much fun as "Laaaandon," but I relish the fact that the truly annoying organizers of the original clambake have had to move on to other regions.

The program never changed: a plenary session kicked off on a Thursday morning, which everyone and his cousin attended in order to see and be seen during the two coffee breaks. After that, anyone with an *-ov* at the end of his name took off in the general direction of Knightsbridge, leaving the also-rans and the geeky British media types to attend breakaway sessions on ancillary issues like prospects for the fertilizer industry or the tomblike session on human rights. Anyone whose name ended in *-ova*, of course, was already shopping in Knightsbridge. On Friday night a massive black-tie orgy called, if memory serves, "Russian Roulette" or something like that was held in some over-the-top venue such as the London Zoo.

I was never able to skip off to Knightsbridge. There was always an emergency dinner jacket to fetch from Moss Bros for one of the M & A guys or a knock-down, drag-out argument to have with the organizers of the conference about my boss's slot in the plenary panel. Still, it was a nice spring getaway. HRH used the time to hobnob with his industry cronies, and one year he persuaded his friend Sergei Bichiyuk to join him at the conference.

Sergei changes his job often, and each time he gets a new and better job he gets a newer, shinier car, a scarier driver who doubles as a bodyguard, and presumably a larger piece of the Moscow power pie. Sergei's father was something enormous and unspecified in the city's hierarchy, which I have to assume was the reason Sergei enjoys this particular brand of Russian job security. He's not the sharpest knife in the drawer.

I don't see much of Sergei, and I like it that way. HRH sees him a number of times during the week, but primarily in the boys-only world of Russian business circles. About once a month HRH staggers home at 3:00 a.m. smelling of premium whisky, cigars, and something else that doesn't bear thinking about. As I dole out the Advil and the prairie oyster the next morning, Sergei usually features heavily in the narrative. These evenings begin with what seems like an innocent evening's entertainment: box seats to a soccer game, a VIP room at the Sanduny baths, or a steak dinner at El Gaucho, but then they somehow spiral out of control.

"It's work," HRH would insist, clutching his head. "Petrovna, get me a cup of coffee, and then leave me alone!"

It was an action-packed week that year in Laaaandon. HRH and Sergei joined minor minigarchs, government ministers, and Roman Abramovich at a Chelsea versus Manchester United football match in a hospitality box sponsored by a Scottish whisky company. They reeled back to the hotel three sheets to the wind at about 2:00 a.m. HRH woke me from a sound slumber and begged me to come down to reception, where Sergei was having trouble with his key. I threw on some clothes and hurried down to the main entrance.

HRH was in better shape than Sergei, which wasn't saying much. Both swayed unsteadily on their feet. Sergei was looking particularly disheveled; his Russian national judo team tracksuit top (mandatory traveling clothes for a Russian man who thinks he's at all important) was unzipped to his navel, revealing a crumpled black T-shirt, a heavy gold medallion, and matted chest hair. In one hand he clutched the strap of his Prada man-bag. With the other he thrust a plastic card aggressively in the face of the hapless night clerk, who was clearly resisting the urge to swat him away like a pesky mosquito.

"What's wrong?" I asked in English.

"Ah, madam," said the night clerk, Clive. He backed away from the scene with practiced aplomb, gesturing elegantly for me to move in.

I placed my palm gently between Sergei's clammy shoulder blades to steady him. "Sergei," I said as calmly as I could, "what is the matter? Can I help?" Sergei shot his arms out and waved them like peripatetic helicopter blades. He spun around, teetered, and would have crashed to the floor had HRH and I not propped him up. His red face softened from scowl to leer.

"Ah . . . my beauty, my *krasavitsa*!" he cooed to me. "Let me give you a kiss." Not waiting for me to agree, he proceeded to place multiple wet, slimy kisses on each of my cheeks, insisting "Three times in Russia!" This engulfed me in a fug of unwashed minigarch, very good cigar smoke, and the fumes of a great deal of single-malt whisky. My eyes met Clive's from his safe vantage behind the massive reception desk. He regarded me with sympathy but stayed firmly where he was. Sergei pushed HRH aside and lunged at me.

"Lissen," he cried, rising on the balls of his feet, working up enough leverage to hurl his arm around my shoulder and grab me in a tight headlock, forcing my nose into his armpit. He sprayed my ear with saliva as he hissed in my ear, "I understand everything . . . but these idiots won't open my door!"

"His door won't open?" I asked HRH quietly. "Did you help him with the key card? You have to insert it and then push the door handle down pretty hard."

"Of course I did," insisted HRH. "But it won't open. We came down here—I thought we'd get a new key, but Seriyozha . . . oops, watch it, *druzhok*!" He caught Sergei in mid-stagger.

I slithered delicately out of Sergei's headlock. I turned to Clive, who sprang to attention. "Here is the problem, Clive," I said. "Perhaps you can help. The gentleman says his door won't open. Would you check his card, please?"

"Well of course, madam. We will replace it immediately, and I am so very sorry," said Clive, with all the deference of one who has sat through a "How Russians Paying Rack Rate Impacts Our Bottom Line" meeting. He took the proffered card and tapped efficiently on his keyboard.

"There we go," I said encouragingly in Russian to the Chelsea fans. "We'll get this sorted right out."

"My beauty!" Sergei cried, throwing his arms open expansively, causing him to lose his footing. Helicopter blades whirled again as Sergei headlocked HRH under one arm and stuffed me under the other. We regarded one another ruefully across Sergei's matted chest hair and gold medallion. "I love you guys!" Sergei gushed. "You can have anything . . . anything you want! Let's go up to my room . . . and you will have whatever you want!" He hiccuped, then giggled salaciously.

"Yep, we'll go to your room, *druzhok*," HRH agreed jovially. "We just need to get your key card sorted, and we'll go right up and have another drink."

"My card . . . shhhhhhh." Sergei thrust his face into mine, and after several unsuccessful attempts placed his index finger against his lips. "This card is magic. It opens any door you like— any door at all!"

A discreet cough.

"Madam?" said Clive quietly.

"Yes," I said, sidestepping a fresh onslaught of kisses. "There shouldn't be a problem. He's registered here, and his last name is—"

"Madam, this would appear to be the gentleman's Diners Club card."

"Sergei," I said in exasperation, "where is your key card? You can't open your hotel room door with a Diners Club card."

"Oh yes I can!" Sergei shook his index finger at both of us, suddenly sober enough to resort to the bizarre staccato speech popular with Soviet-era Red Directors. "I was told . . . by the private wealth guy . . . that this card . . . this is very special card. I was told . . . this card opens all doors!"

You will readily imagine what can happen with a Master-Card.

Like most Russians, HRH is faithful to the unofficial national motto: "In Cash We Trust." When traveling outside Russia, he only ever feels comfortable with a good chunk of it in the hotel safe, and so much of the holiday is taken up with finding the best exchange rate available in town.

"We have a lot of Swiss francs left," he commented to me with concern at the airport on our way home from a skiing trip.

"Waaaallll, yew know," I said, aping the young Westernized Russians who always seemed to need to draw out and flatten their vowels, "if we put them in a Ziploc and stick them in the freezer, they'll keep until the next trip."

"Ha-ha," he said. Sometimes he gets it.

"Or," I ventured, "if you are truly concerned, I will perform a 'flight to quality' right now and invest them conservatively and safely at the La Prairie counter."

"Waaaallll, yew know," said HRH, getting into the swing of things. "I'm not sure our position needs to be that risk averse."

"Waaaallll," I countered, "if you are feeling really bullish, go see what kind of 'dynamic' return you can get at the Ferragamo tie boutique."

I'm laid back about most things, but I do keep HRH on an intensely short sartorial leash. Fashion faux pas abound in Russia, and if unchecked he can veer dangerously toward the minigarch tendencies for pointed white alligator or snakeskin loafers, black silk T-shirts, or chinchilla-lined white suede jackets and . . . jewelry. Instead we save our hard-earned kopeks, and every other year we head to No. 1 Savile Row (which is in "Laaaandon"), where we order one very good, very conservative, and very classic suit, custom made for him. These have proved excellent investments, providing superior return in the sense that they don't wear out immediately and look great, even at the end of a long night out.

Our patronage of No. 1 Savile Row is a time-honored tradition dating back to our first trip to London together, in the mid-1990s. On that trip HRH purchased a Burberry raincoat, several Jermyn Street shirts with nice French cuffs, and some very solid brogues, after which he expressed interest in finding a suit to go with them.

"Suits . . . suits . . . let me see." I scoured my mental database. My only association with male tailoring had military associations from my misspent youth walking out with a British cavalry officer. He went to No. 1 Savile Row to get his uniform, which interestingly included chain mail. I recalled No. 1 fondly, remembering quiet stretches of unmolested time on a comfortable squishy sofa leafing through *Tatler* while the boyfriend got measured. So that's where we went.

The crowd who works at No. 1 Savile Row (which these days includes several Svetlanas, but didn't then) was—and remains—incredibly nice, very patient, and not at all pushy. They have to be, to alleviate the very scary prices they charge, even for items without chain mail. On our first visit we ordered one suit and bought a few jackets off the peg, a tie or two, and then it came time to pay. This was several years before the complete annexation of Mayfair by wealthy Russians, but it was sort of the twilight of the Arab invasion. The deferential and beautifully dressed salesman did not bat an eyelid as HRH pulled out his wad of cash and began expertly peeling off about two inches of fifty-pound notes.

Three or four seasons of attending Russian business conferences has made me immune to any awkwardness around large amounts of cash, but just then I experienced a twinge of vague discomfort. Perhaps I recalled that money never, ever changed hands for the chain mail. Or maybe there was some unwritten rule I'd absorbed through osmosis or *Masterpiece Theatre* or something that said it lacked taste to have that much cash on you when visiting the W1 or SW1 postcodes. I don't know, but I felt undeniably awkward, and so I turned discreetly to perch on the squishy sofa, still there, unchanged, after a decade. And you know that dream—the one when you are back at school and everything is just the same, only you are totally bare-assed naked? What happened next was like that. Only worse. Much, much, *much* worse.

As I lowered myself onto the squishy sofa, up to the counter of No. 1 Savile Row walked the headmaster of my boarding school. In his hand he held a single "reduced for final sale" button-cuff shirt and stood watching with horrified fascination as HRH peeled off the last three-quarters-inch of notes to add to the slithering pile on the mahogany counter. Though the head had adroitly presided over several capital campaigns of seven figures, you could tell that he had never—ever—seen that much cash money in one place in his entire life.

I ask you, what are the chances of that happening? What on earth was this man doing in Mayfair, to say nothing of No. 1 Savile Row? Brooks Brothers or J. Press—that's where he belonged! I considered fleeing to the lavender-scented WC, featuring antique prints of cavalry officers in chain mail, but it was far too late for such decisive action.

One of the reasons the head is so successful at raising the kind of money he does is because he has a photographic memory of four generations of alumni. It took him a mere thirty seconds to place me as a former student, another fifteen to come up with my last name, and an additional three to make a successful stab at my first name. There was nothing for it. I squared my shoulders and waded into the battle. The head and I exchanged pleasantries as he flicked his eyes from me to the Burberry-clad Russian hunched over the mahogany counter placing an eighth-inch stack of fifty-pound notes crosswise on top of another eighth-inch pile and counting under his breath. You could hear the wheels turning inside the head's head. He was running through the four-mile microfiche of alumni notes he keeps up there.

There had been a lot of bad press about Russian organized crime that year.

"I heard you've been living in . . . Russia," he said carefully, with another fearful glance at HRH.

"That is . . . uh . . . that is right," I said brightly, blushing furiously. Then I thought, oh, to hell with it—in for a penny, in for a fifty-pound note.

"And this is my husband," I said, tugging on HRH's arm ill-advisedly, as he was in mid-count. He uttered a violent expletive, which fortunately only I could understand, and began to count the final eighth-inch stack again. He triumphantly laid the final bill on the stack just as it was about to avalanche off the counter.

"Very good, sir," said the deferential salesman, scooping up the bills expertly and repeating, in English, the staggering number HRH had counted to in base fifty. "I will be right back with your receipt." He beat a hasty retreat behind the curtain of the fitting room.

I thought the head might very well pass out.

"Darling," I babbled, "please say hello to my old headmaster—well, not my old, because he's not old or anything, but what I mean is—"

Poor HRH, who had already put up with Sunday lunch in Fulham and a matinee of *Phantom of the Opera*, to say nothing of a lengthy and, to him, incomprehensible debate at No. 1 Savile Row on the difference between charcoal and dark gray, seemed unfazed by this latest bizarre manifestation of Western civilization.

"So are you in business in Russia?" asked the head.

"Yes," said HRH, smiling his fake-for-the-foreigners smile.

"I hear there are . . . ah . . . lots of problems with the Mafia in Russia," said the head as the deferential salesman returned with a receipt and a stack of elegant navy blue garment bags with all three Royal warrants.

"Here you are, sir," said the deferential salesman. "Your receipt, your jackets, and we'll expect you in about a month for the final fitting of your suit."

HRH pocketed the receipts, flipped up the collar of his new Burberry, and turned a genuine smile toward the head.

"No problems," he said. "No problems at all."

As a new century dawned, Russians peeling off four- to six-inch stacks of high-denomination bills became quite the norm. The Firm's business boomed, and my duties included regular forays out to procure "something tasteful" for "someone important." Happy days, wandering through metal detectors, annoying security guards, and torturing Barbie doll salesgirls in Moscow branches of luxury stores, seeking out Tiffany carriage clocks, Hermès scarves, gold-and-diamond cuff links from Links of London, and three-hundred-dollar bottles of Burgundy. The "Laaaandon" conference grew ever more lavish and ridiculous.

A Bentley dealership opened in Moscow, then a Ferrari showroom. Out-of-season raspberries and truffles became available at a newly opened Moscow franchise of Hediard for the equivalent of the down payment on a small house in Ohio. Each year the ludicrous Millionaire Fair, which everyone took very seriously, and which was held in a massive suburban shopping mall, featured diamond-studded Mercedes Benz cars and salivating estate agents from Belgravia and the Hamptons. Upscale jewelry stores boasted prominent signs: "24 hours a day!" A bunch of lunatic asset management types started a polo league, and landlocked Moscow now sported two yacht clubs and an annual regatta called the Captains of Industry. Excess reached a fever pitch, fueled by black gold and Russia's unlimited capacity for consumption. *Ka-ching, ka-ching, ka-ching.*

But as the Bible warns, "To everything there is a season—and a time to every purpose under heaven." And who knows that better than the Russians?

Having gorged themselves at the feast, Russians once again found themselves in the midst of famine in 2008 and then again in 2011.

"I like a crisis—gets my blood going," said Jasper, an entrepreneur, with that very plucky British "we will defend our island" attitude they adopt toward adversity. It was gutsy of him given that he owned an outsourcing-service business for large multinational corporations, which were downsizing faster than you could say "stabilization fund."

A less lovable acquaintance from the banking sector, a

veteran job hopper, curled his upper lip into an unattractive, self-satisfied sneer and said, "Waaaallll, yew know, I don't give a shit actually—I had a huge signing fee and a guaranteed bonus, and I made them pay me both," proving yet again the very real danger of fusing the twin toxins of alpha-male Russian and investment banking.

"*Kriyses*?" asked Sergei Bichiyuk, who, thanks to overt nepotism, had landed yet another very lucrative "senior advisor to the general director" position at a huge Russian state monopoly. "Whaddya mean?"

As oil prices slid steadily south, Russian *Cosmo* got noticeably slimmer, and denial seemed to be the watchword of the day. Russian politicians started vehemently to assure the Russian people that the fundamentals of the Russian economy were solid, alerting the populace to the fact that the economy was in very bad shape indeed. The ruble teetered and nose-dived. The coolheaded, financially savvy Russians responded with a sprint to quality: investing their under-the-mattress cash reserves in durable goods like luxury automobiles.

In the run-up to Christmas 2008 I was double booked for nightly going-away parties as foreign companies yanked their expensive expats home. English-language book clubs were decimated, and it got eerily easy to get a Friday afternoon appointment for a mani-pedi at the Expat Salon. It dawned on me in those months that I had more friends in Chiswick than in Moscow. HRH, who runs on pure adrenaline, announced he was fed up with his current employer (who at that stage did resemble a reptile more—in both physical appearance and business ethics—than any mammal I've ever met) and was thinking about striking out on his own.

"Fantastic!" I enthused, with what I hoped was a plausible imitation of *koorazh*.

Moscow, in the midst of financial crisis, was a quieter place. The construction cranes stood idle, and there was an odd silence where once the jackhammer had rattled. Signs screaming "70% Clearance Sale!" adorned the windows of the stores still open, while tattered "For Rent" signs slowly peeled off dusty, abandoned shop fronts. Sullen waitresses surveyed half-empty restaurants. "Anti-crisis" became a marketing buzzword for everything from mobile phone plans to striptease bars. Holt re-christened a vodka tonic "the anti-crisis gin and tonic." Things in Russia were subdued, but you could still find pockets of *koorazh* in Moscow. It takes more than economic Armageddon to defeat the Russians. They've withstood Hitler, Genghis Khan, Napoleon, and Allied Municipal Bank's annoying national tele-marketing campaign, and my money is on them coming out on top of this one too.

As I sat writing in Starbucks, every day a nice-looking, well-dressed guy sat opposite me. For most of the day he did a superb imitation of someone who is gainfully employed and just grabbing a latte between meetings, when in actual fact he was furiously networking and job hunting. It was a fine display of *koorazh*. My lawyer friends said it was a great time to be a law-yer, and my banking friends—those who still had jobs—told me they were "deeply involved in restructuring." My gutsy friend in the car biz assured me, with a brave but trembling smile, that Russia was "not the worst place to be producing luxury cars."

HRH found some Japanese investors in early 2009, a whole bunch of assets at bargain-basement prices, a very reasonably priced off-the-peg suit, and a new word: "upside." He used it rather relentlessly in the next months.

"There is a lot of upside to this crisis," he informed me.

I thought about what the upsides might be, and I jotted down some notes, which I stuck up on the wall of my study, the way we used to brainstorm about a marketing campaign.

HRH and I worked to rein in our spending and hone down our budget, but I still wanted the comprehensive international health insurance/medical evacuation with the dangerous-sports rider, bodily remains clause, and for only 10 percent on top, the optional US-Canada coverage, making it thus applicable everywhere in the world except North Korea. HRH remained implacable.

"Get this through your thick Slavic skull," I erupted. "I want the insurance—not the stupid bag!"

"You can have the bag—not the stupid insurance," HRH said with impeccable *koorazh*.

"That's just great," I said, preparing to march out of the room in a self-righteous huff. "That's just fan-flipping-tastic, because it will be the perfect accessory when I come to visit you

★

in the ICU after you break every single rib downhill skiing and we can't afford for you to have an operation."

"What color do you want?" he called after me.

I let the question hang in the air for just a second.

"Black!" I shouted back.

Upsides to the crisis:

✔ Fewer traffic jams/more parking spaces.

✔ Competent English-speaking secretary no longer holy grail.

✔ VIP status at bank now means something.

✔ Ally Muni called off its annoying national telemarketing campaign.

✔ "School" at Bald Hills has "sporadic availability."

✔ More space in overhead compartments coming back from Europe.

✔ Cheap assets.

✔ Russian TV ramping up its game. Why? Putin and Medvedev engaged in phony/entertaining power struggle.

✔ Putin killed off the Laaaandon conference by raising one eyebrow (on my birthday which I really appreciated).

✔ Jesus told me an Hermes Birkin bag is available at 20 percent discount. Jean-Claude: ♡33 34 55 71 98.

✳

CHAPTER 5

LENIN
LIVES
NEXT DOOR

PARENTING, NO MATTER where you live, is hard work, but raising a child in two very different—sometimes diametrically opposed—cultures is a real challenge. Velvet is a great kid, but I worry that when she is forty and in therapy she will say that her childhood was ". . . you know, basically really happy, but Mom and Papa didn't really speak the same language." I can only hope that she will then expand and explain just why that was.

Education experts agree that if you want to raise a child of a "mixed marriage," and if you want that child to be bilingual, then each parent must speak his or her native language to the child from the get-go. So that's what HRH and I did, and once Velvet started to talk she was indeed fluent in both Russian and English. We always stopped conversations to ask about words we didn't understand, and so, oddly, we all got better at both languages. By the time Velvet was five, HRH and I had grown so accustomed to each speaking our native language in conversation that we simply carried on doing it even if Velvet wasn't around. It became the norm, not the exception. I lob an English phrase at him, he responds in Russian, and I follow up in English. We don't even notice it anymore, though we get some funny looks if we do it in public.

I'm immune to funny looks at this point. I know I stick out in Moscow. I look different, I sound different, and I don't blend in. I'm an *inostranka*, a foreigner. I even think of myself as a foreigner, which, if you are from the United States, is pretty unusual.

"It's because we have to pay the admission price for foreigners," I explained to a visitor from the United States recently, justifying the eighteen-dollar discrepancy between the ticket prices for native Russians and foreigners at the Kremlin.

"Foreigner?" he said, genuinely perplexed. "But I'm not a foreigner—I'm an American!"

Being a foreigner never seemed to worry Velvet. In our circle of friends, being "something and Russian" is not the exception, it's the rule. Her classmates and friends are Russian, British, Dutch, Indian, Korean, and Italian, and this was about the only thing I liked about her international school, a badly managed joint venture between rejects from the UK teaching pool and some wily Russian entrepreneurs. Velvet didn't go to "school" at Bald Hills because all the places were taken up with the BIZ4 and embassy types. So we had to make do with our incredibly unsatisfactory alternative. HRH hated absolutely everything about it. Raised in the elite Soviet enclave of the East Berlin "station," his mind still had trouble getting used to the fact that schools could cost money. He often pointed out that the state had paid him to go to military school. He was disgusted with everything from the always-intoxicated headmaster to the shabby physical plant.

"This building is designed for kindergarten children," HRH murmured during one parent-teacher conference, as we perched on hard, undersize chairs waiting to talk to Velvet's teacher. "Not for nine-year-olds! And why are there so many Asians?"

"So many Asians is considered a plus," I hissed back. "They are very rigorous about academics." HRH snorted and checked his watch. He stopped going to parent events early on, which frankly was a relief to everyone concerned. Velvet struggled with the academic side of school, and HRH maintained that this was totally the school's fault, not ours and certainly not Velvet's. I worried in a vague sort of way about "learning different" issues and "the spectrum," but secretly I suspected she was just bored. Time not spent on the back of a horse has ever been time wasted for Velvet.

I tried hard to supplement the educational program with some stealth lessons. I lured her into the kitchen to bake chocolate chip cookies (made with M&M's because they don't sell chips in Russia), casually asking her to halve or double the recipe in an effort to review fractions. I supervised homework, which came in the form of printed sheets from the British National Curriculum downloaded from the Internet. The reading comprehension was okay, give or take a few odd *u*'s thrown in seemingly randomly, but neither HRH nor I could make head nor tail of the math sheets. They seemed to add and subtract using number lines instead of equations. I have no idea why. It was like that Tom Lehrer song "New Math," only not so witty because it was actually happening to us.

"What are all these lines for?" thundered HRH. "Where is the textbook? We pay that much money and we don't even get a textbook? When I was a boy—"

"When you were a boy, everyone in the entire Soviet Union used the same textbook and every student was on the same page on the same day of every week! I know, I know!" I bellowed back. "This is the same thing, only it's the British National Curriculum and it's digital! Don't you get that, you Luddite?"

"What's a Luddite?" asked HRH in a normal tone of voice, which instantly defused the tension. "I haven't heard that word before."

"Well," I began, and domestic harmony reigned once again.

HRH was particularly scornful of "life studies," the school's half-baked attempt to inject something into the curriculum apart from the three Rs—or rather the four Rs, as Russian language was a mandatory subject. Velvet's Russian teacher, a gorgon called Olga Mikhailovna, was one of the reasons I was grateful HRH stopped going to parents' events. She told me quite bluntly that Velvet showed "no talent whatsoever" for the rich Russian language. Velvet did like "life studies," which examined different aspects of the nonacademic world in easily digestible one- or two-month modules. In September and October of Velvet's fifth-grade year, they covered the depressing subject of "Our Global Environment," and HRH and I came in for a good deal of undeserved abuse because we don't recycle anything. In our defense, neither does anyone else in Russia.

"Listen," HRH protested, "don't talk to me about recycling. In the Soviet Union, we recycled everything. When I was a kid we recycled newspapers for wallpaper, and when the wallpaper started to peel off we used it as toilet paper."

"Seriously?" I asked, reminding myself to write that one

down and absolutely find a place for it in my book.

"And glass jars!" HRH thundered on, ignoring me. "If you were lucky enough to find a glass jar, you used it for decades! I didn't see a plastic bag until I was fourteen years old!"

"I know, I know," I soothed. "But don't worry, Our Global Environment ends in a week or so, and they'll be starting Adult Module."

"Adult Module?" sniffed HRH. "What the hell is that?"

Sex ed, I hoped silently. It was long past due. "Oh, you know," I said aloud, "money management, career choices—things like that."

"Sounds like pornography," grunted HRH. "I wouldn't put it past them either."

That year the fifth grade dedicated an entire trimester to Russian history, and I looked forward to it with fervent anticipation. Finally, one subject devoid of number lines and recycling awkwardness, in which I could confidently coach my only child to the top of the class! One cold winter afternoon I waited to collect Velvet from the school bus at a Plexiglas shelter; I huddled against a merciless combination of snow and sleet while my frozen earphone buds crackled with MSNBC's new firebrand, Rachel Maddow, my latest brain crush. Old-age pensioners, seated on the shelter's bench, kept turning around to shoot me looks that could kill, as Rachel made me chortle, guffaw, nod my head vigorously, and cry aloud in English, "Amen!" I ignored them.

The bus crawled down Tverskaya Street in the pre-rush-hour gridlock, and I surged gratefully toward it. Velvet waved goodbye to her friends and jumped off the bus, a messy after-school tangle of knapsack and lunchbox, with her coat unzipped and the Velcro tabs of her boots flapping open. She trailed her snow pants in the gray torrent of slush in the gutter. There was no sign of her hat.

"I didn't have time—" she began before I could begin my tirade. We both looked askance at the damp, dirty snow pants.

"I can't put them on now," she argued.

"Well, quickly, then," I said wearily, removing my own hat and tugging it down over Velvet's head. I zipped up her coat, fastened her bootstraps, and shouldered the knapsack, then gingerly took the sopping snow pants from her.

"Come on, let's get home before we get arrested by the babushka squad." This was only half a joke. Russian elderly women, the *babushki*, that legion of granite women who made Hitler cry, resolutely adhere to the Communist-era concept of communal parenthood. In their universe it doesn't just take a village to raise a child—it takes fifteen former republics stretched over nine time zones. Their particular pet peeve is the inadequately clad child, and unless Russia is in the throes of a freak heat wave in August, the *babushki* almost always think kids are inadequately clad, and they aren't afraid to march right up to you and tell you all about your pathetic parenting skills. Can you imagine that happening in Park Slope? It would cause a riot. But in Russia? Par for the course.

"What's new at school?" I asked as we picked our way through the iron-hard ice ruts frozen into the sidewalk.

"We started Russian history," said Velvet with a grimace, "and I have three whole sheets to do tonight."

"Fabulous!" I enthused. "I'll give you a hand."

A wizened old babushka in an ancient fur-trimmed coat and an itchy woolen scarf pushed her whiskery face between us.

"Woman," she shrieked, "woman, your child is completely underdressed for our Russian winter."

The Park Slope in me rose up.

"You know what, *Babuliya?*" I said, grasping Velvet by the shoulders and turning her around to face the crone. "You are absolutely right—she is completely underdressed, so I want you to tell her that. She speaks fluent Russian, despite what her horrible Russian teacher thinks. Go on! You let her have it! Maybe she'll listen to you!"

"Mommy!" screamed Velvet in protest.

"Seriously," I said, turning to Velvet and addressing her in English, "could you maybe just once put your snow pants on at school or on the bus, and maybe we could just, I don't know, perhaps not have to go through this kind of public humiliation every single day?"

Our English conversation stopped the old woman in her tracks. I smiled at her encouragingly, and she squinted suspiciously in response. All the hot indignation in her seemed to evaporate, and she collapsed into her matted fur collar, muttered something incomprehensible, and shuffled off in the opposite direction.

I turned to Velvet, smiled, and held up my fist for her to bump.

"Never underestimate Russian xenophobia," I commented as we resumed our walk home. "That is a cornerstone of Russian history."

"What's xeno—what is that?" asked Velvet.

"Fear of foreigners."

"But I'm not foreign," Velvet reminded me. "I'm Russian."

HRH came home from work as I was getting dinner on the table for Velvet, who was galloping around the living room on her hobbyhorse, leaping over piled-up cushions. She stopped long enough to give HRH a kiss. He scrutinized the photocopied maps of Russia strewn over Velvet's mound of schoolbooks.

"What's this? Are they learning spy craft?"

"No," I said, laughing, "they just started Russian history."

"Bor-ing," drawled Velvet, coming to the table.

"Come on! Russian history is great," I contradicted as I spooned mac and cheese onto Velvet's plate. "It's got very interesting people and battles and really nasty villains and gory stories. It's larger than life and very . . . well, it's very not boring."

"Is it more interesting than the Second World War?" interrupted Velvet. "Because we just did that, and it was very boring."

"The Great Patriotic War," corrected HRH, "and that is a big part of Russian history."

"I don't think so, Papa," said Velvet, between bites. "That war all happened in England. The German planes bombed London every night. All the children had to go away from their homes. It was very sad, but very boring."

I didn't dare look at HRH.

"Let's go to the Kremlin!" I suggested as brightly as I could. "We can see all kinds of things there: Peter the Great's boots, Fabergé eggs, Catherine the Great's imperial crown, and—oh, Velvet, they have a whole room full of horses with armor! And we could go to the history museum! You'd like that, wouldn't you? Velvet, get your elbows off the table."

"How about Lenin's Mausoleum?" asked HRH. "I haven't done that yet."

"Seriously?" I looked at him in astonishment. "Well, let's definitely put that one on the list. It's the Necropolis in the

Kremlin Wall that is the really interesting part—John Reed is buried there, and Voroshilov—"

"No!" shrieked Velvet, and we both turned to her, surprised. She was in a flood of tears and vehemently shaking her head. I pushed back my chair and gathered her up on my lap. I guessed that we had pushed it too far with the idea of going to see a mummified corpse, although Velvet loved the mummies in the National Museum in Cairo. Velvet liked gory stuff—at Halloween she became positively macabre. It seemed out of character.

"What is it?" I asked. "Why are you so upset?"

"I don't want to see the bullet hole!" she sobbed.

I couldn't think what she meant.

"But he wasn't shot," soothed HRH. "We don't have to go—"

"He was so shot—right there in New York!" Velvet insisted. I gently corrected her and told her that Lenin had died peacefully in 1924 in Sparrow Hills in Moscow.

"No! We just did this in school! He was shot by a crazy guy in New York, and his Japanese wife was standing right there!"

"Oh, dear," I said, exchanging looks with HRH over Velvet's head. "She means John Lennon." HRH made a tsk-tsk sound and shook his head.

"Okay, Velvet, enough!" I said. "Stop crying—we don't have to go to Lenin's Mausoleum. We'll go to the Kremlin and you can see Catherine the Great's carriage and her wedding dress. It weighed something like sixty pounds—you'll like that. Come and finish these maps."

While Velvet colored in the maps, I browsed through my collection of books about Russian history, all of which had dust jackets the color of congealed blood or dirty snow and depressing titles referring to Russia's least cheerful periods: GULAG (for some reason always written in all capital letters) or *Stalinism: A Memoir of Repression*. Then there were several quixotic titles such as *Whither Russia?* (Implication: nowhere good.) The newest batch of books about present-day Russia was devoted to critical analyses of the less-than-charming aspects of Vladimir Putin's rise to power, which to me seemed like it had happened yesterday. Was I now history?

"Are we history?" I asked HRH.

"Speak for yourself," he retorted. "I'm still very much in the game."

"Half the people working for you were born in the Yeltsin era—the Yeltsin era! That's an era now." I shook my head.

Living Russian history in my mind's eye was still a Julie Christie/Diane Keaton headscarf moment, while the sepia-colored Russia of *Nicholas and Alexandra* heaved and roiled in the background. Of course, nothing like that ever happened in my real life in Russia. But then again, Lenin still lived next door. All was silent at The Institute across the courtyard, and though I detected no motion behind the dusty ficus plants in the grimy windows, the lights still went on in the morning and were switched off in the evening. And there was Lenin, still in his mausoleum down on Red Square, though there was occasional talk about burying him in a St. Petersburg graveyard next to his mother and dismantling the mausoleum. I wondered if the government would use the marble to face the walls of a new church, reversing the Soviet practice of destroying churches and using the marble to build the sumptuous Moscow Metro. That idea had a tidy "whole circle" aspect to it and bolstered my theory that Russia's history was cyclical rather than linear, a recurring pattern of predictable cycles: repression and revolution, war and peace, famine and abundance, world dominance and—well, something that is slightly less than world dominance. There are a few really exhilarating moments every hundred years or so (1825, 1917, 1991, etc.) when Russia seems poised on the brink of something new and different, when society seems ready to break the mold and start all over again. But then centrifugal force takes over, and Russia is sucked back into predictable cycles. For some reason this theory enraged HRH.

"History is history," he argued. "How can our history be somehow different? This is just Western claptrap."

"Where are we now?" asked Alexei Soloviev, over for dinner one evening.

"In 1936," I responded, "sort of September."

"Oh, dear. That's a little disturbing," said Alexei.

"Western claptrap!" thundered HRH.

"And 1826," I added. "Late January, early February."

"I don't like where this is going," said Alexei.

Linear or cyclical, Russian history is hugely entertaining—the canvas is epic, the characters legendary, and the drama intense. If Russian history were a film, you wouldn't wait for it to come out on DVD—you'd insist on the full-on popcorn-and-blue-drink experience at the surround-sound IMAX 3-D. You'd go early to get a good seat. Since Russia is chock-full of great stories and memorable characters, it might take more than one film to do it justice. I see it as a series, like the *Harry Potteriad*.

I was certainly hoping Velvet would see it that way. I peered over her shoulder to admire her homework. The assignment was to color three maps, showing the historical borders of each period of the expanding Russian empire. "Bor-ing," she groaned, putting the markers back in their big plastic tub. "You said Russian history would be interesting, Mommy. This is geography, and I hate geography."

"But it is a good place to begin," I said. "Everything about Russian history always begins with geography!" I fetched a large and very tacky faux marble globe that HRH had received as a New Year's gift from a work colleague.

"Take a look at this—look how huge Russia is!" I turned the globe so that Russia was front and center, as it is in Russian-made maps. Russia sprawls over seventeen million square kilometers—almost twice the expanse of the second largest country in the world, Canada.

"Now look at where Russia is in comparison with the other countries. What do you see?" I asked. Velvet took a long look at the globe.

"It's in the middle."

"That's right!" I said. "See how many countries surround it?" Now we were getting somewhere. "But what if I turn it like this?"

I spun the globe so that North America was on one side and Russia on the other, the way maps of the world produced in the United States look.

"Oh," said Velvet, "that looks different."

Russia, though massive, is also vulnerable from just about every direction. Spin the globe so that Russia is front and center and you find her surrounded, with almost no natural boundary to protect her, between the Danube River and the Ural Mountains to the west and only a narrow strip of the Pacific separating eastern Russia from Japan and Sarah Palin. So it has ever been. We—Europe and North America—see Russia as this great looming hulky presence to the extreme right of the map.

★

But they see us as a menacing circle of nations poised in a ring around them, ready to pounce.

I turned the globe back so that Russia was front and center again.

"Can you show me where Russia touches the ocean?" I asked, and Velvet began to trace the borders with her fingers to find the intersection of terra cotta Russia and the blue oceans and seas.

With the country naturally landlocked, a big thread throughout the Russian narrative is all about getting some prime beachfront real estate into the mix. All of the tsars after Peter the Great pushed their borders to oceans and seas to the east, south, and north, and this turned Russia into a significant naval power. Following the collapse of the Soviet Union, Russian naval leaders stress about their strategic port cities, many of which are not, at this particular moment, located inside Russia's new borders, but rather in independent countries, some of which are now members of NATO or have put in their applications to become so. Awkward. Yet from a historical perspective, this is really just another installment of the ongoing soap opera that is Russia's shifting borders. Russians are very adept at taking the long view; right now is certainly no picnic, but hey, things have been worse. Much worse.

Velvet's interest was sufficiently piqued by the globe lesson that I was able to persuade her to visit the State Historical Museum with me the next Saturday afternoon, while HRH stayed home to catch up on some paperwork. We made our way down to Red Square and into the Russian neo-Gothic, blood-red building, which faces St. Basil's Cathedral, with Lenin's Mausoleum in the middle. We wandered through the exhibition rooms to the displays depicting life in pre-Christian and medieval Russia, which showed the interior of a typical peasant *izba*, or hut. Dominating a third of the one-room hovel was a large ceramic-tiled stove.

"See the stove?" I pointed. "That was the most important thing in the house. They believed that spirits lived in the stove. They did their cooking inside it, and in the winter, the family actually slept on top of the stove to keep warm."

"The house is so small!" said Velvet.

"Yes, and most of the population lived this way," I said. "You can see that they were farmers—see, there is a scythe, and look, this is a sickle. They still use something very similar in parts of Russia."

"I bet they had horses," said Velvet longingly.

"The very lucky ones," I acknowledged.

Russia has always been what today we diplomatically refer to as a "human-resources-rich" country. What this really means is that there has always been a surplus of human beings to plant and harvest crops, build cities and dams in inaccessible and hostile environments, man assembly lines in factories, and most important, hurl themselves at enemy invaders. These people are called the *narod*, or the "People" (with a capital P), and they have always made up an overwhelmingly huge percentage of the population. They account for a hefty portion of it today. This massive human stockpile is what makes Russia a force to be reckoned with. It is the *narod* who execute Russia's intermittent spurts of energetic activity: her wars, her pushes toward industrialization, and yes, the construction of her Winter Olympic Village in Sochi, a remote, hard-to-pronounce subtropical seaside town no one has ever heard of. The general feeling in Russia is that the *narod* have supernatural traits vastly superior to those of their counterparts elsewhere in the world. Some prerevolutionary thinkers saw them as holy, utterly lacking in guile, and the true embodiment of the pure Russian character. The Soviets, whom you can always count on to screw things up, put the *narod* in charge for much of the twentieth century, which didn't really work out. The current crop of Russian leaders has savvily reinvented the *narod* as extras in the reality TV show that is Russian electoral politics.

Velvet and I paused in the room dedicated to the Tatar Mongol yoke, the three-hundred-year occupation of Russia by the hordes of Genghis Khan, which cut Russia off from the West and all manner of useful things, like the Renaissance and the Reformation. I told Velvet how the Mongols swept up from the plains of Central Asia on their many horses and conquered everything from China to Poland, and how the Russians finally banded together to defeat the Mongols just outside Moscow.

"That's when Moscow became the most important principality," I explained. "After that, the prince of Moscow became so powerful that he gave himself a new title. He called himself

'Tsar of all the Russias.' *Tsar* comes from 'Caesar.'" I snuck a look at Velvet, who was still interested.

"Do you know who Caesar was?" I ventured.

"No," admitted Velvet.

"Well, he was a very important Roman general who was so good at what he did that they put him in charge of everything, and they let him stay in charge for the rest of his life."

"Oh, like Putin?" Velvet asked.

"Sort of like Putin," I said, crossing my fingers behind my back.

"So the Mongols were the bad guys," Velvet said, scowling at a Mongol helmet in the exhibit window.

"Yes and no. They may have been a little nasty, but they brought many ideas to Russia as well. In fact, the Russian word for 'money' is a Tatar word."

"What else?" asked Velvet.

"Taxes." I groped for something readily appreciated by the nine-year-old mind. "Well, economics in general."

"Okay." Velvet was clearly losing interest, and I didn't blame her. Russian economic history has always been like watching polyurethane dry.

Imperial Russian economics is pretty straightforward: a teeny tiny minority of the population owned a disproportionately humongous percentage of the wealth of the country, and up until 1861 actually owned the *narod* as well. The teeny tiny minority lived very well—their consumption of champagne alone was a major part of France's GDP. The *narod*? Not so much. In 1861 the government decreed that the teeny tiny minority no longer owned the *narod*, but not much changed until 1917, when a small group of revolutionaries led by my next-door neighbor with the bathtub got together and managed to annihilate the teeny tiny majority, seize their property, and start running things themselves. Their idea was that the economy would chug along fine on its own if each citizen contributed to it according to his ability and took from it only according to his needs. As if. The ability-needs idea, while compelling on paper, proved difficult to implement in real life. Soviet citizens perceived their own needs to be limitless but discovered that their own abilities were finite, a mind-set that largely lingers today. The state eventually proved incapable of providing its citizens with their

★

most basic needs, which when I first arrived in Russia, in 1987, seemed to consist entirely of panty hose, cigarettes, toilet paper, and blue jeans.

In 1991 the "each according to his ability" concept was finally scrapped; Russians reverted to a version of the earlier, clearly more efficient system. Today the wealth of Russia is once again tightly controlled by a handful of individuals who are called "The Oligarchs." This has worked better than the "each according to his ability" idea, although the real profits primarily nestle safely in the cash registers of East 57th Street, Rodeo Drive, and Bond Street. The Oligarchs divide their time between homes in Miami, Kensington, and Siberian penal colonies.

Velvet yanked my arm. She had had enough of the Tatar Mongol yoke, so we made our way through the fourteenth and fifteenth centuries. The pace picked up as we entered the halls devoted to Russia's military prowess. Here were the arms and armor, cannons, the battle scenes and banners. An enthusiastic middle-age tour guide energetically recounted stories of Napoleon's invasions and Catherine the Great's wars of expansion to rapt groups of angora-clad pensioners from the regions. I put my finger to my lips and eased Velvet in to have a listen. When the group moved on to the next room, we lingered to look at the exhibits.

"Russians are really brave," Velvet succinctly summed up the message of the hall. "Aren't they, Mommy?"

"Very brave indeed," I nodded. "Exactly the crowd you want on your side in the event of a military invasion."

Really, absolutely nothing gets the juices flowing in Russia like a full-scale outside threat. Preferably military, but in a pinch the Eurovision song contest works just as well. Produce some clear and present danger to perceived Russian supremacy, and suddenly Russians go all organized, united, and efficient. It's bizarre. Time and time again you think, here it is—this is the moment when the Tatar Mongols, the Teutonic Knights, the French, or the Nazis are about to just flatten the place, but wait! The Russians turn it around with a very impressive show of sacrifice, heroism, and often, it has to be said, real panache. Stalingrad? I ask you, who else but the Russians? Hitler was so confident about invading Russia that he issued printed invitations to a victory party in the Hotel Astoria in Leningrad and had tons of granite shipped to Moscow to build an enormous and, no doubt, hideously tacky swastika monument. The invitations? Today they take pride of place in Moscow's Armed Forces Museum. The granite? It faces the elegant buildings on Tverskaya Street, Moscow's main thoroughfare. Russians have learned that revenge is a very tasty dish, even at room temperature.

I used to think all the "defense of the fatherland" stuff was slightly antiquated, a lot overdone, and definitely irrelevant in our global, Facebook age, but I was recently forced to revise this opinion. I have yet to witness Russia being actually invaded, but I did live through the super tense period when Russia went up against England to host the 2018 World Cup, and I've never seen a bloodbath quite like it. Well-heeled Russians, who had fondly regarded England as a one-stop shopping destination for clothing, property, and secondary-school education, took to violent anti-British rhetoric, burning Union Jacks and effigies of Prince William in the street. They will regret that when it comes time to send their children to school in "Laaaandon."

In the absence of modern-day Mongols, Napoleon, or the Third Reich, Russia can always fall back on her steadfast enemy, the United States of America. Every Russian knows that the Americans are hell-bent on staging democratic revolutions in Russia's natural vassal states like Bosnia and Ukraine to ensure the continued global domination of its fast-food market. Even though "America!" said with awestruck reverence is a synonym in modern Russian slang for "cool" or "cutting-edge," the Russian media spends at least 48 percent of its nightly news broadcast churning out the somewhat confusing message that America is both rotten to its core and ever poised to bring Russia down.

If you ask me (and no one ever, ever does), Russians are nuts to think America is their biggest threat. To begin with, the vast majority of Americans can't accurately identify Russia on a map, and those who can don't know or care that Russia is hosting the Olympics in 2014. No, the real threat to Russia is China, the world's most populous nation—a tenacious race that needs creature comforts like fish need bicycles. With their relatively small and seriously overstretched landmass, the Chinese live smack up against Russia, the world's largest country and one richly endowed with natural resources, which are unfortunately locked under miles of stubborn permafrost. Russia, on the other hand, is populated by a race that, despite its proven track record of playing an admirable defensive game, is nevertheless genetically conditioned to spend nine months each year sleeping on top of a stove. This is a perfect recipe for cultural and economic osmosis, and I think physics is just going to take over at some point. In fact, it is already happening out in the Far East: Chinese workers and investors creep ever westward, although, unfortunately, you still can't get a decent bowl of hot and sour soup for love or money in Moscow.

"Are you hungry?" I asked Velvet.

"Kind of," she said. "Can we go to McDonald's?"

"You don't want to go to the National Hotel like *Eloise in Moscow*?" I suggested.

"No," said Velvet firmly. "I want a Big Mac."

"I don't see why not," I capitulated. "Enough Russian culture for the day. Let's go have some national American cuisine!"

We walked up Tverskaya Street, past the buildings faced with all of that granite Hitler left behind, to the McDonald's on Gazetny Pereulok. It was lunchtime, and the place was heaving with customers. Each of the fifteen tills was manned by three people, who jogged around their stations picking up burgers and fries, filling up beverages, swirling soft-serve ice cream into cups.

"Don't let go of my hand," I instructed Velvet as we waded into one of the eight-person-deep lines. Twenty minutes later we squeezed out of the line clutching a tray. Somehow we found a table for two and dug into our lunch.

"Mommy, who was the best tsar of all?" asked Velvet.

"Excellent question!" I said. "Who do you think?"

"Maybe Peter the Great? Was he 'the Great' because he was the best?"

"Or Catherine the Great," I suggested. "She was great too. And she loved horses."

"Then she's the best," concluded Velvet.

"She was a tough cookie, that's for sure."

"Like Miss Halliday?" I winced, remembering how Velvet had once asked her kindergarten teacher, "Miss Halliday, my mommy says you are one tough cookie. Are you?"

"Even tougher than Miss Halliday, if you can imagine that," I said.

"Is 'tough cookie' a good thing?" asked Velvet, squirting

★

ketchup from a plastic sachet onto her fries.

"It is if you are going to rule Russia," I told her.

Here's what works in Russia: an alpha-male ruler with at least one personality disorder. The true alpha-male rulers of Russia—Ivan the Terrible, Peter the Great, and Josef Stalin—all seem to have had multiple mental health issues, so perhaps a cocktail of paranoid, histrionic, and narcissistic personality disorders is optimal. These psychological imbalances ensure the ruler's ability to identify an ongoing threat, get everyone wound up about it, and remain supremely confident in his own unique and unrivaled ability to manage the system.

It is under just these kinds of wack-job rulers that Russia only ever achieves true greatness. These guys get what the half-baked also-rans like Dmitry Medvedev don't: it's all about them and not about anyone else. Alpha-male rulers never need to use Twitter, Facebook, or, god forbid, Instagram—as if. Alpha-male Russian rulers know the Russians are already following them. And "liking" them.

HRH was curled up on the sofa watching a hockey game on TV when we got home. Velvet dive-bombed onto the cushions piled up next to him.

"Hey there!" he cried. "How was the museum?"

"It was cool," said Velvet. "I liked it. Did you know that people used to sleep on stoves?"

"I did know that," said HRH. "My great-grandmother slept on a stove. So what do you think of our history, then?"

"Cool," said Velvet. "Can I sleep on the stove?"

"You can certainly try," I said, "but get your schoolbag organized before you bed down."

I poured myself a large and, I felt, much-deserved glass of wine and plopped down on the sofa with HRH to watch the news. The top story of the day featured the rollout of not one, not two, but *three* mascots for the 2014 Winter Olympics: a snow leopard (the choice of then–prime minister Vladimir Putin), a polar bear, and a rabbit. None of them would have made the cut for any self-respecting American breakfast cereal, but there they were, prancing around for the cameras. A self-important-looking official with a badge the size of Idaho around his neck explained that as China had had three mascots, it seemed only right that Russia should have at least that number. "В чем же мы хуже?" he asked the group. I rolled my eyes. Loosely translated, this means "What makes us inferior?" with an implied defensive "Huh?" at the end. You hear it all the time when Russians start comparing themselves with anyone who isn't them.

Russians have a complicated relationship with foreigners, whom they divide into two basic groups: those who come from once and/or future vassal states and those who do not. The former group comes from what the Russians call the "Near Abroad," and they are regarded with benign condescension, as if acknowledging a poorer or less attractive relative—the same product, just assembled with less expensive parts. The also-rans. Nations from the Near Abroad enjoy largesse from the benevolent Russians like gas subsidies, employment in blue-collar jobs, and other favored national perks as long as they follow Russia's lead in politics and don't try to sneak off and join NATO.

What I call the "Real Abroad" (North America and Western Europe), on the other hand, is something I believe Russians secretly admire and seek to emulate. The problem is that occasionally the Real Abroad types get called in to do that which Russia cannot do herself. A random example: Russian history begins with the pagan Slavic tribes inviting the Vikings to rule over them. "Our whole land is great and rich," they declared, "but there is no order in it. Come to rule and reign over us." The Real Abroad crowd have innovated, renovated, built, designed, and generally set up everything from the military to haute cuisine. Every now and then Russians take a look at this, find it disturbing, then go all "Russia for the Russians" and make laws to restrict foreigners from coming to live in Russia. The latest incarnation of this takes the form of an impossible visa application process. In addition to trying to find a lab that runs leprosy tests, foreigners are obliged to fill out a Byzantine form, which takes four days to complete and demands a list of the exact dates of each and every foreign trip taken in the last ten years. This has reduced the number of foreigners who come to Russia, but as I point out to HRH, this doesn't change the fact that just about everything in Russia comes from foreigners—yes, even vodka, which the Poles invented.

"The periodic table of elements," argued HRH, "and radio."

"The Italians invented radio," I protested, "but I'll give you the table."

"And fighter jets," continued HRH stubbornly.

"Maybe," I conceded, "but since Sikorsky did that in, like, New Jersey or something, it's kind of like saying Maria Sharapova is a Russian tennis player—"

"Maria Sharapova *is* a Russian tennis player!" bellowed HRH.

"Uh-huh," I said dismissively, "right. Of course she is. The ten years at the tennis school in Florida means nothing."

"When I'm in the Olympics, will I be on the Russian team or the US team?" asked Velvet.

"Let's not go there tonight," I said, wearily setting the table for dinner.

Later that evening I plucked my worn copy of *Nicholas and Alexandra* down off the shelf, the same thick black book that had got me hooked on Russian history all those years ago. I took it to bed with me and leafed through it. I read it several times a year, always hoping for an alternative happy ending like the Bolshoi Ballet does for *Romeo and Juliet.* Clad in her striped pajamas, Velvet snuggled in next to me in a well-practiced bid to postpone bedtime.

"Did the stove prove a little uncomfortable?" I asked as she burrowed down under the covers.

"What are you reading?" she asked, leaning her head against my arm.

"A book about Russian history," I said, showing her the sepia-colored tsar and his family.

"You make history really interesting, Mommy. Much better than Mr. Sturgis."

"Thanks, sweetie, but let's perhaps not share that with Mr. Sturgis."

"Maybe you could write us a history book—or write about this in your book!"

"I'm not really writing that kind of book," I said, turning the idea around in my head. "But you know, you make a very good point, Velvet. How can I expect people who don't know anything about Russia's history to understand what is funny about it? Maybe I should include a chapter."

"It would be a super-long chapter if it starts eight hundred years ago," observed Velvet.

"It starts even before that," I said.

"Starts before what?" HRH walked in from the bathroom,

brushing his teeth.

"Velvet thinks I should do a chapter on Russian history in the book."

"I thought your book was supposed to be funny."

"It was—no, it is—funny," I said. "Definitely going to be very funny, but how do you make people understand why things here are so funny if you don't put them into historical context?"

HRH shrugged. He's a real alpha-male Russian: never cares if people are following him or liking him. He doesn't even know what Twitter is.

"Write it, Mommy," urged Velvet, "because it will be way better than those stupid handouts Mr. Sturgis makes us read." She yawned.

"Okay," I agreed, "I'll write it, and we'll see. You know what? I can always stick it in the back or something. Like an appendix."*

"America!" said HRH with something approaching admiration in his voice.

---

*Well, Readers:

    You know, I did take about a month to write up an entire (condensed) history of Russia. And it turned out just as I'd hoped it would: entertaining. The problem is that there is a lot of it, so it became a companion piece. To receive your free digital copy of *Have Personality Disorder, Will Rule Russia*, email: jennifer.eremeeva@gmail.com.

CHAPTER 6

AND THIS IS MY CHARMING WIFE, NATASHA

THE LAST TWO weeks in May are my favorite time in Moscow. The lilacs are out and the outdoor café managers are finally confident that no more snow is expected until October. They set their tables and chairs out, hoist the awnings, and mix up the mojitos. The evenings are light and the air is soft. It's the perfect time to while away a Friday evening with friends, catch up on the gossip, and relax after a long, hard week. Jesus, Lucy, and I went early to stake out a table on the patio at Scandinavia.

"Joe and Holt have their darts game tonight, so they will be here but much later," I said, counting chairs.

"Tancy has to fire someone tonight," said Lucy, unfolding a Polartec blanket over the top of the chair and spreading it out on the seat to cushion the uncomfortable wood-and-metal slats.

"She said something about that," I concurred, "and DeeDee said she'd try to make it, but she has to go to tae kwon do with her son."

"All the women in the Bald Hills go nuts over thees tae kwon do," said Jesus, rolling his eyes, "and djou know, ees very boring. Kick, kick, kick, and that ugly kimono—eet look terrible on everyone who wears it. Me, I now make the Zumba at the Chilean embassy. Eet ees much better the workout."

"Is Alexei coming?" I asked.

Jesus's eyes widened for a moment, and he broke into a charmingly mischievous smile.

"*Chicas*, djou are not going to believe when I tell you where is Alexei!"

"The Central Bank," guessed Lucy, faking a yawn.

"On a Friday evening?" I said in mock horror. "In May? Who on earth would still be there?"

A dumpy waitress with bad skin and a sullen expression rattled off a scripted cordial greeting she did not mean, hurled three menus on the table, turned, and stalked away.

"What djou have, *querida*?" asked Jesus.

"I'm having the burger," I said firmly. "I'm having it without the bun and the sauce on the side, and don't give me a hard time about it."

"I'm having the same," said Lucy, tossing aside the menu. "And a mojito and then about a gallon of the bad Chardonnay, and I'm also having"—she leaned in toward Jesus for emphasis—"I'm also having . . . fries."

"Fries—what a good idea," I said, feeling relieved Lucy had done the heavy lifting. Jesus was on our back about getting ready for bikini season. We had both told him that the last bikini season we'd participated in was in 1984, but he still rode herd on us.

"Go ahead," said Jesus, folding his arms across his chest, "but djou will need more than the boring kick, kick, kick to make up for it."

"Lighten up," I said.

"I'm listening to you," said the waitress, which was a poor English translation for "What would you like?" She didn't introduce herself or explain that she'd be taking care of us that evening.

"I take the salmon," said Jesus, smoothing down his taut designer-jean-clad thighs, "with no rice or potatoes and no sauce at all."

"I'll have the burger, no bun, and please, could I have the sauce on the side?" I asked hopefully.

"No sauce?" barked the waitress.

"No," I said, enunciating every word with extra care. "I do want the sauce, I just want it on the side."

The waitress rolled her eyes.

"Same for me," said Lucy, "and a basket of fries."

"How to cook it?" asked the waitress, as if she could care less.

"Rare," I said. She shrugged and returned briefly to dump

a basket of condiments onto the table and shove a bottle of the restaurant's really mediocre Chilean Chardonnay into a bucket filled, in a typically miserly fashion, a third of the way with ice. Lucy felt the bottle's stem with a practiced hand.

"It's practically boiling," she spat. "So fucking typical."

"Ten minutes won't kill you, Lucy. Do you want people to think you have a drinking issue?" I admonished her. Then I turned to Jesus. "So what's up with Alexei?"

"Djes!" squealed Jesus, returning to the narrative. "Well, Alexei, he has one of those—how you call it?—regu- . . . regu-communism things?"

"Regulatory commission," I corrected. Alexei was The Firm's representative on a tedious regulatory commission made up of Duma deputies, bankers, fund managers, and the scary undead types from the Central Bank of Russia. They met monthly, usually on a Saturday, so that everyone concerned could communicate the all-important message that they were way too busy and far too important to meet during the working week. Meeting on a Friday evening, however, particularly during peak dacha season, was unheard of.

"What a drag," I ventured, laying the back of my hand on the bottle's neck. Still warm.

"Thees one, she ees a leetle more interesting. Eet ees a em-errrr-gency meeting." Jesus drew out the syllables for emphasis.

"Seriously?" I asked. This was a crowd that didn't go in for anything but the regularly scheduled.

"Djes . . . eef I tell djou, *chicas*, djou cannot tell a seengle person . . . not ever!"

"I promise," I said, nodding my head automatically.

"Oh, come on," snorted Lucy. "How much can a bunch of investment wankers get up to?"

"Well," said Jesus, leaning in. "Djou remember back in February, that *demente*—I mean really *demente*—woman from the Allied Municipal Bank, she suddenly step down after everyone think she never, ever leave?"

"Natasha Mountebank," I said, nodding. "She's, like, officially crazy—medically crazy. She is the one with OCD. She carries a packet of wet wipes everywhere she goes and disinfects the silver and glassware at restaurants. I've seen her do it at Claridges."

"Is that the same thing as a narcissistic personality disorder?"

asked Lucy. "I thought that was really the thing everyone has here."

"Certainly a lot of the expat guys I know have that," I said, "but Natasha Mountebank may well have both. She is truly crazy."

Jesus nodded. "Djes, that her," he agreed. "Her husband ees that old goat Sam Mountebank—the Canadian."

"I remember," said Lucy. "Isn't he the one who sailed his boat all the time so he was never in any one country long enough to have to pay taxes?"

"I loathe those kinds of people," I said.

"Maybe that was someone else," said Lucy, furrowing her brow.

"*Chicas!*" said Jesus sternly. "Djou want to hear this story or not?"

"Sorry, sorry," we chorused.

"Djes, ee ees the goat with the boat. Anyway, thees Natasha Mountebank, she work for him: and he, what, four hundred years older than she is? And for years and years, well, they pretend for lots of years not to be doing it like foxes, until he retire."

"Rabbits," I corrected, "doing it like rabbits."

"Really?" asked Jesus. "Rabbits? The foxes don't do it, *querida?*"

"Not like the rabbits," I assured him, feeling the bottle's neck again. It was getting colder.

"Listen, just get that waitress to open the bottle and we'll put some ice in the wine," said Lucy impatiently, scanning the patio. There was no sign of our waitress.

"Oh, for fuck's sake!" Lucy said and began rooting around in her bag. "I must have a corkscrew in here somewhere; I'll do it myself. That wine is so heinous, ice can only improve it." She pulled out a corkscrew engraved with the emblem of the George V in Paris and began to open the wine. As she did, she said to Jesus, "I still don't think much of this story. Everyone knows Natasha Mountebank married her boss so she could leapfrog into some big job at Ally-Muni in Geneva." She feigned a yawn. "Female Russian employee snags foreign boss, moves to Europe. Stop the presses!" She pulled the cork out of the bottle and held it up triumphantly.

"She's right, you have to do better than that, Jesus," I agreed.

"Well," said Jesus, "djou listen to this: turns out, way, way back when the perestroika just start, she ees, what, sixteen or something? Anyway, she go away to the Canada with those . . . djou know . . . the crazy monks with the singing tea?"

"The who?" Lucy and I exchanged glances. "Singing tea?"

"Djou know!" said Jesus, impatiently shaking his wrists as if to dry his hands. "The singing tea . . . there is the red singing tea and the yellow singing tea."

I looked at him more closely, wondering if Jesus wasn't losing it slightly. I couldn't see how the unwieldy and obnoxious Ally-Muni could have anything to do with singing tea.

"What is singing tea?" I asked.

"Come on, *querida*, djou know—they are the religious crazy people . . . they make the Time for Sleep tea."

I began to see through the fog, if only dimly.

"Do you mean Sleepytime?" I asked.

"Djes!" said Jesus, with an elaborate gesture of relief.

"Oh, I see," Lucy said, nodding her head. "You mean Red Zinger tea."

"Ees what I say, Red Singer tea . . . what they are called?"

"The Yunnies," Lucy sang out.

"*Exactamente!*" said Jesus. "So this *loca* with the wet napkins, when she ees sixteen, the Yunnies come to 'er school in Russia and invite all these cheeldren to go with them to the Canada for the visit."

"And she went?" I asked in horror. "What kind of mother lets her sixteen-year-old daughter get on a plane with religious nut bags?"

"They make like eet is English-language practice," he conceded. "I don' theenk they say it is religion."

"Still," I shuddered, thinking of Velvet, "right after the Cold War . . . off to Canada?"

"I'd have totally gone," said Lucy. "Do you remember how grim it was here then?"

"Still," I said, shaking my head. "Seriously bad mommy moment."

"Djes, so she go for three weeks . . . very murky, very unclear what happen there, but then she come back to the Russia and then, *poof*! Few years later, she get the starting job at—what djou call it—Ally-Muni. Alexei say she nobody—nobody at all—no connections, no family, and eet turn out she never go to the university or anything like that."

"No way!" I said. This was getting interesting.

"Djes way! So back in February, the FSB discover she really working for the Red Singer people—her husband, he ees with them since 1960s—thees is how they meet, and they get married secretly in the Red Singer church and they are part of an extenso—huge—group of people in all the beeg banks like Ally-Muni. Eets a *grandísimo* deal for the Russian government—djou know how much they hate the other religions." This was certainly true. The Seventh Day Adventists kept their bags packed, as did the Mormons.

"Didn't I hear she got airlifted out to run the Astana office or something equally unimportant?" Lucy asked.

"Minsk," I corrected.

"So," said Jesus, finishing up, "Alexei, ee ees part of the committee, they writing a . . . 'ow you say, *querida*, memorandum to the Interpol!" Jesus twirled his hands around his wrists as he served up his denouement. He sat back, arms crossed, triumphantly waiting for our reaction. We were both gobsmacked.

"Jesus!" I exclaimed, referring to the savior of mankind.

"Come on," said Lucy, who is far more cynical than I am. "You made that up!"

"Huh?" snorted Jesus. "'Ow I make something like that up, huh?"

"God, can you see the headlines in the tabloids?" I held out my glass to Lucy, who sloshed some more of the bad Chardonnay around. "What I don't get is how Sam Mountebank got away with it all those years. Apart from the nautical tax dodging, I never thought he was the sharpest knife in the drawer."

"Well, but do you have to be?" wondered Lucy. "If you are brainwashed by a cult—you just do what they tell you."

"But djou can't tell nobody at all," Jesus warned, "or Alexei, ee will be very angry. Look, here are the boys—don't tell Holt, *chicas*, djou know what ee is. Ee will have too much to drink and call through to the BBC or something."

Holt and Joe made their way across the patio of the restaurant slowly, stopping to shake hands and exchange pleasantries with people they knew at other tables. I noticed that they had Matt in tow, the kid we'd tried to talk out of going to work at the Russian metals company. As Tancy, Holt, and I had predicted, he'd lasted about six months at the Russian company and was now working as an English-language editor at an investment bank. All three pulled up chairs. Holt grabbed a handful of fries as Joe wiped his forehead with a stack of yellow paper napkins and surveyed the patio.

"Kick-ass evening," he commented. "Everyone is here. It's like a BIZ4 meeting."

"Much better than a BIZ4 meeting," contradicted Holt. "We can get as rowdy as we like."

"The food is better," observed Lucy. "Not sure about the service tonight though."

The sullen waitress appeared and wordlessly held up her order pad.

"I'll have the burger with extra sauce," said Joe, "but can you leave off the onions?"

"I'll have the same, only leave my onions on, and can I have extra pickles?" said Holt, diving into what was left of Lucy's fries. "And a basket of fries?"

"Djou might as well bring two baskets," said Jesus, with a dazzlingly sardonic smile. "Een fact, djou bring five, and these American piggies, they will eat them all, and they will blow up like big balloons and we can float them on the river—"

"Shut up, you anorexic queer, I'm hungry!" Joe thundered. "Been playing darts."

Jesus sent air kisses across the table to Joe.

"Holt, you've eaten all my fries, you bastard," Lucy said, pulling the basket toward her.

"I'm sure I couldn't have," drawled Holt, languidly dragging one through a puddle of ketchup. "I just got here."

"Ignore them," I said to Matt.

"I'll have the burger too," he said, smiling at the sullen waitress.

She waited, pen poised.

"That's it," he added.

"With the bun?" she asked sarcastically.

"Sure . . . yes, I mean, if that's okay?" asked Matt.

"Sauce?"

"Sauce . . . sure."

"On the burger?" she persisted.

"On the burger," confirmed Matt.

"It's a miracle," she said, and disappeared into the kitchen.

I asked Matt how he liked life at his investment bank.

"It's great!" he gushed. "They asked me if I wanted to interview for a job as junior research analyst—telecoms, so it's a great opportunity. You were so right about the Red Handshake. I told some of the guys at work about it, and almost all of them had the same experience! Thanks for the advice, by the way. I know I didn't take it right away, but thanks to you I could see where it was going, and I got out before it got ugly."

"You had to learn it for yourself, Dorothy," I acknowledged. "I'm glad it's working out, although if you get into the habit of playing darts with these reprobates on a regular basis you'll be back in trouble soon enough."

"He's already in trouble," said Joe. "He's dating some *dyev* called Natasha."

"We were just talking about a *dyev* called Natasha," said Lucy, and I felt Jesus kick her under the table.

"Oh, dear. You want to be careful with Natashas," I cautioned.

"Don't start this," said Holt, "please don't. I can't take this tonight."

"What is this?" asked Matt as the sullen waitress plopped a beer down in front of him.

Feeling very writerly, I rummaged through my bag and pulled out my battered Moleskine notebook. You don't absolutely have to have a battered Moleskine notebook to be a writer, but I was finding it helped. David Sedaris says writers should never set foot anywhere without a small notebook, and he was exactly the kind of writer I was trying to be.

"I'm thinking of doing a piece on this," I informed the table, flipping through the pages. "I made some notes yesterday."

Holt let out a loud groan.

"You can't write a piece on this," he said. "For a start, no one in their right mind will publish it."

"So what?" I responded. "I have a blog now—I can write and publish whatever I want. It's part of what this literary agent guy I spoke to called my *platform*. It's dead cool: I can't think why no one thought them up before."

"You won't have any Russian friends left if you do," Holt warned.

"Don't be ridiculous," I snorted, "all the Irinas in town will bend over backward to befriend me."

"They have this crackpot theory," Joe explained to Matt. "They think that you can tell what kind of personality you can expect from a Russian chick by what her name is."

"Seriously?" asked Matt.

"Of course. Look at this." I smoothed a page with the side of my hand. "There are only like seven or eight first names for each gender in Russian, so it's pretty foolproof, and that is why Holt doesn't want to talk about it. He leads this very sub rosa social life with all kinds of women whose names end in -*a*. We know they exist, but he never introduces them to us."

"What's the sub rosa?" asked Jesus.

"It's a Dan Brown thing," Lucy explained. "It means secret." Jesus shrugged with indifference.

"Well, it makes perfect sense to me," said Joe. "If Holt introduced these *dyevs* whose names end in -*a* to you, or brought them over to your house, and if, god forbid, they wore like, I don't know, babycakes, high heels or even—oh, no—a dress! A dress! You girls would eat them for breakfast."

"I would never eat a *dyev* for breakfast," I sniffed. "I'm all into organic and healthy these days."

"All that acrylic and silicone!" shuddered Lucy.

"But what's the theory?" asked Matt.

"It's bullshit," insisted Holt, "and what's more, it's racial profiling."

"Racial profiling?" I yelped. "This isn't racial profiling. How dare you!"

"It's ethnic stereotyping," said Lucy haughtily. "Highly subjective but incredibly accurate ethnic stereotyping."

"For example," I said to Matt, "who would you rather hire: Irina or Svetlana?"

"Whoever was best qualified?" hazarded Matt. "Is it a trick question?"

"Noooo!" cried Lucy.

I tapped the page where I had written a phrase and swiveled it around so Matt could read my notes.

Want something done right?
Get Irina to do it.

IRINA (from the Greek "goddess
of peace")

Diminutives: Ira, Iritchka

✔ The leader of the pack

✔ Great in the workforce

✔ Clever, driven, exacting, resourceful,
successful

✔ Well behaved/cool tempered

✔ Long on intellect/short on emotion

Irinas are good at the drier things like
money and law

✔ CFOs, general counsels, HR
directors

✔ Savvy, cool Russian Law & Order
detective is Irina

WHERE DO YOU FIND IRINA?

✔ Already pulled out in front of you, in
the fast lane

★

PERSONAL LIFE:

✓ Often single parents (because, I
   suspect, the partner can't take the
   pace!)

✓ Very strict mothers produce very
   capable children

✓ Very good at putting systems in place,
   imposing order where there is chaos

✓ Achieves financial independence early
   on and establishes own domicile

✓ Incredibly good at delegating routine
   domestic tasks

✓ Can change a tire but rarely needs to

PERSONAL APPEARANCE:

✓ Very well groomed

✓ Stays in good shape

✓ Tasteful, conservative, tailored
   clothing

✓ Shoes match bag

✓ Nothing too flashy — pearls, not diamonds

✓ NO BLING

The sullen waitress shuffled over to our table. Lucy grasped the neck of the second bottle we'd consumed that hour, waved it at her, and asked in Russian if we could have another. I scrutinized the waitress's frayed name tag and was not at all surprised to see that it read "Lena." Lena tugged on her greasy hair with stubby fingers as she took the bottle, heaved a new world-record Russian sigh, and then asked, "White or red?"

"Maybe white this time," said Holt, deadpan.

"Lena," I said to Lucy, who nodded.

"What you got on Lena?" asked Matt.

"Hang on; you won't believe how apt this is," I said, riffling through the pages for a pithy phrase I was very proud of.

"But isn't there a drop-dead gorgeous Lena in *War and Peace*?" asked Holt.

"Yeah, but she's a wench," I argued. "There is the Elena in *On the Eve* by Turgenev though. She's maybe an exception."

"I hated that book," said Lucy. "She is completely joyless. Sure, she's brave, smart, and principled and all that, and she falls in love and runs away with the Bulgarian revolutionary, which, okay, is romantic, but then he dies."

"Cheerful, right? And really, a Bulgarian?" Lucy and I nodded in agreement.

"You can sum up Lenas easily," I said. "They aren't the person you'd choose to drive cross-country with. They'd so run out of things to say, and they'd never want to go out or anything."

"That," said Jesus, who likes stimulation of all kinds, "ees my idea of the nightmare."

Lena: not the sharpest tack in the box.

ELENA (from the Greek "a ray of sunshine")

Diminutives: Lena, Lenichka

If Elena means "ray of sunshine" from the Greek word helios, the god of the sun, then something got lost in translation around about the fall of Constantinople.

Elenas, or "Lenas," are the Eeyores of Russian Women:

- ✔ They moan and they groan and they almost never stop complaining

- ✔ Tasks given to a Lena will be sloppy of unacceptable quality

- ✔ Lots of unsolicited (really tedious) litany of disasters

- ✔ Excuses, excuses, excuses

- ✔ Lenas feel the world owes them and has yet to pay up

WHERE DO YOU FIND LENA?

- ✔ World—weary waitress at the down—market sushi joint

- ✔ Coat-check woman in the theater

- ✔ Hostile/disinterested low-grade government flunky (Lenas very into government service)

- ✔ She's the nanny you just fired because her endless complaining and deep sighs from the minute she arrives to the minute she leaves are just getting you down

LENA'S PERSONAL LIFE:

- ✔ Most Lenas are married, but not to Prince Charming

- ✔ Lenas are those exhausted, slightly grimy women who are ferried out to the dachas at the beginning of May and left there by husbands who don't visit every weekend

- ✔ Lenas are often cast in the role of unpaid domestic slave.

LENAS ARE:

- ✔ Primary school teachers, not professors

- ✔ Nurses, not doctors

- ✔ Wives, not mistresses

"Oh, no," I cried. "You know this—the real nightmare is Olga."

"What's wrong with Olga?" asked Matt.

I shuddered.

"Olgas are awful. A guttural name for the battering ram of Russian womanhood."

"Kind of harsh, there, babycakes," Joe commented.

"I was going to say that," Matt chimed in.

I shook my head. "I know from what I speak, Dorothy. Nothing good in my life ever came of an Olga with the possible exception of one very cool Pilates instructor, and that was certainly not free of pain. Three out of the four jobs I've had in Russia have ended—some with a bang and some with a whimper—with an Olga. In the end it's ten times easier to cower at home blogging in my yoga pants than venture out with all those Olgas lurking outside."

"The Baba Yaga!" said Jesus, clapping his hands. "Djou do the Olga, *querida!*"

Olgas always make me nervous, but I turned to that section of the notebook where I had made copious notes. As the Reverend Mother in *The Sound of Music* tells Maria, who passes this excellent advice on to Liesl, you have to face your fears.

I squinted to make out the last line of my notes.

"Listen to this, guys: Churchill predicted that it would be the Russian women who would make Hitler cry. Don't you think they all had to be called Olga?"

Sullen Lena dumped our burgers and Jesus's salmon down, indifferent to who had ordered which dish. We played pass the plates for a minute until everyone had the right order. Lucy consolidated three baskets of fries into two, and Holt topped everyone's glass off with more bad Chardonnay.

There was silence as we all tucked into Moscow's best cheeseburger. It wouldn't win any contests in Seattle, but by Moscow standards it was manna from heaven.

OLGA (origins are Greek, meanings vary:
"prosperous," "holy," "successful")

Diminutives: Olya, Olitchka

When confronted with an Olga, turn
around, then run as fast as you can, for
as far as you can, in the opposite direction.
Or get a prescription for mood-enhancing
pharmaceuticals.

Olga is a peculiarly Russian primeval force
of nature over which no one has any
control:

✔ She is the impenetrable Russian
   permafrost

✔ The merciless Siberian mosquito

✔ The stolid Friday afternoon Moscow
   gridlock

✔ And the backbone of a merciless
   state machine

PERSONALITY:

✔ Joyless and heartless, stubborn and
   immutable

✔ She cannot be swayed

✔ No sense of urgency about anything

✔ Structure is king for Olga

WHERE DO YOU FIND OLGA?

✔ She's the accountant who won't reimburse your taxi or lunch expenses

✔ She's the airline check-in girl, who won't let you on the plane because you were one minute and thirty seconds late for check-in

✔ She's the tax inspector who comes for an "audit" and stays six months

✔ She's the woman who yells at you in July at the playground because your kid doesn't have a hat on.

✔ She's the museum lady who won't let you take your knapsack into the gallery

✔ She's the Moscow Metro ticket sales woman who doesn't have any change

HOW DOES RUSSIA USE ITS OLGAS?

✔ Deploys their considerable strength to dig potatoes and cabbages, pickle the cucumbers, and harvest the dill

✔ Olgas keep everyone in line on public transportation

✔ Almost every accountant is an Olga

✔ Olgas keep the Soviet flame alive by adhering to the letter, and not the spirit, of every single goddamn rule

✔ Olgas keep alive the eternal Russian sense of fair play: things may be bad, but it's okay provided they are much worse for the next guy

"Do Natasha," urged Matt.

Lucy's eyes twinkled, and I could not conceal a Cheshire cat smile as I turned to my notes on Natasha.

"You really want to change the subject," said Holt around a mouthful of burger. "Natasha is their particular pet peeve."

"Is it our fault," asked Lucy, "that 'Natasha' in Turkish means *prostitute*? Did I make that up?"

"No, you didn't make it up," qualified Joe, "but you seem pretty determined to keep it in circulation."

"What djou have, *querida*?" asked Jesus.

Natasha: It's all about me.

NATALYA (origins are Greek means "birthday child," "Christmas")

Diminutives: Natasha

Sources make mention of a Saint Natalya, an early Christian who was present at the martyrdom of a couple of other early Christians, though not herself martyred. EXACTLY!!!!

PERSONALITY:

✔ Manipulative, mercantile, self-centered, egotistical, sneaky, bitchy, and tricky

✔ Like poor Lena, the world owes Natasha a great deal, but unlike poor Lena, the world usually pays Natasha promptly and often with handsome dividends

✔ Natasha is an expert at extracting everything she needs and wants from those around her, suffering no pangs of guilt about doing so because, after all, it is all about Natasha

IN CHILDHOOD AND YOUTH:

✔ Natasha stands out because of her perceived attractiveness. Natasha makes good use of any and all tools available to enhance her mystique

✔ She's acquisitional: the girl in fourth grade with the newest Bratz doll, the sex kitten in junior high who is the first to get "those boots," the prom queen in high school

✔ She is neither intellectual nor a scholar & she does not need to be, relying instead on her native street smarts to cut corners and get good grades by charming her teachers

IN MIDDLE AGE, THE GLOVES COME OFF:

A Natalya Nikolaevna or Natalya Alexievna can become a formidable nightmare

✔ On the receiving end of a bribe

- ✔ When she's your mother-in-law

- ✔ When she's deputy head of an organization critical to your continued well-being, such as your kid's school, the tax inspectorate, or a potential client

Natalya Nikolaevna will make everything an uphill battle until you make it worth her while, at which point she will become monumentally charming in a very obvious cheesy and insincere way.

NB: You will never, ever get a thank-you note from Natasha

If she were an animal, she'd be a reptile

WHERE DO YOU FIND NATASHA?

- ✔ Ahead of you at the hairdresser, already thirty minutes into your time slot because she has decided, on a whim, to add some highlights

- ✔ In the front row of your Pilates class, blocking your view

- ✔ In "Laaaandon" at a large conference about the Russian economy, aggressively husband hunting

"It can't be that bad!" gulped Matt, who had become quite pale.

"You ever read *The Three Sisters*?" Lucy asked Matt.

"Which one is that?" asked Joe, who doesn't go to the theater much.

"It's the one with the gun on the mantelpiece," offered Holt, who goes more often than Joe does.

"No, no, no!" I interjected. "It's the one with 'a hundred and fifty different words for going, and those three dreary sisters still couldn't get up and go to Moscow.'"

"A. N. Wilson wrote that," Holt informed me.

"I know, but it is so good that I use it whenever I can," I admitted.

"What's Chekhov got to do with Natasha?" asked Matt.

"Sister-in-law from hell," said Lucy.

The natural prey of a Natasha is a vulnerable man, like Matt, who would do well to study both Tolstoy and Chekhov and their particularly potent cautionary tales on the dangers of Natashas.

With Chekhov, all the creepy-crawlies scamper out from under the rock he peels back in his portrait of Natasha Prozorova in *The Three Sisters*. This Natasha is not one of the three sisters herself but rather their vulgar and crass sister-in-law. She starts out as a figure lacking dignity and stature, but as the play progresses she parlays her child and her influence over her weak husband, Andrei, and ultimately wields all the control over the Prozorov family. To get what she wants, she sleeps with Andrei's boss. Of course she does.

"I thought Chekhov was in love with Olga somebody . . . the actress," argued Holt.

"Yeah, but don't you think that somewhere along the way he encountered a skanky Natasha?" I asked.

"Isn't Natasha the heroine of *War and Peace*?" asked Matt. Lucy and I rolled our eyes.

In Tolstoy's *War and Peace* we follow the roller-coaster fortunes of Natasha Rostova, an attractive and energetic coquette who is billed as embodying much of the elusive Russian soul. This, however, is a massive smoke screen, because what Natasha Rostova really does throughout the entirety of *War and Peace* is focus exclusively on her own agenda. Of course she does! Not

★

content with bagging Andrei Bolkonsky (who is right up there with Mr. Darcy in the Prince Charming league tables) about five minutes into her debut in high society, Natasha gives in to the attentions of a romantic cad while waiting for Andrei to return to Russia and marry her. When Natasha's plain cousin, the long-suffering Sonya, foils her plot to run away with the cad, Natasha goes into a histrionic and clearly anorexic (of course) decline, which is the focus of absolutely everyone until Napoleon invades Moscow. Tolstoy then rewards her by not only reuniting her, albeit briefly, with Prince Andrei in a touching nineteenth-century Kodak moment, but even more typically he then marries her off to the seriously wealthy Pierre Bezukhov, and yet another nice guy bites the dust.

Alexei now joined us, his classic Slavic good looks crumpled from a twenty-hour day at The Firm. He downed the half pint of beer and slowly seemed to come back to the land of the living, the way a neglected houseplant perks up after a thorough watering.

"That's better," he sighed. "What are we talking about?"

"That thing they do about the names," offered Holt, "but you are here now, so we can talk about something else."

"Oh, no, I love the name thing. Have you done Svetlana yet? No? Do Svetlana," said Alexei. "I had an awful time with a Svetlana today."

"Svetlana . . .," I mused. I'd thought about Svetlana a bit but hadn't made any notes. I pulled a pen out and turned to a fresh page in the Moleskine, but then everyone began talking at once, so I switched on the voice recorder on my iPhone to capture the rapid-fire exchange.

"First wives," said Joe, with conviction.

"No, no, that's not it," said Alexei, looking up from the menu. "Svetlana is that woman selling beets at the market with the bad peroxide-dyed hair and filthy fingernails with chipped nail polish. The one with gold teeth and felt boots who wears an apron over her coat."

"Dios," marveled Jesus, his hand fluttering on his chest. "How on earth you know that, cariño?"

"I grew up in Petrozavodsk," Alexei said. "There is a lot of that kind of thing up there. Can I get the burger without the lettuce?" he asked Sullen Lena, who rolled her eyes.

"*Cariño*, we have the wedding of Jean-Luc and Fabrice een Nice next month," Jesus reminded Alexei. "Don't djou want to get into the Dolce?"

"Okay, okay," said Alexei, "I'll take the burger without the bun and the sauce on the side."

"Eet doesn't matter to me," said Jesus, clearly miffed. "I can go with Olivier—ee already propose to me twice, and ee leeves in a country where I can marry a man, not like—"

"Enough!" barked Alexei.

We waited in the awkward silence.

Sullen Lena pursed her lips and broke it. "One girly burger," she said, scratching on her pad.

"Actually," said Holt, moving in adroitly to yank the conversation back from the woeful and worsening state of LGBT rights in Russia, "I have a sort of positive association with Svetlana—it makes me think of good, solid Russian food on a cold day, like *solyanka*, borscht, and pork dumplings; nothing fancy, but filling and satisfying."

"Like, with a thick film of grease," said Joe, licking his lips.

"I think all of those are spot on," I said, looking to Lucy for confirmation.

"Sounds right to me," she said.

"I think of Svetlanas as always being outraged by something and saying, 'Ну вообще!'" I said to Alexei, who nodded in agreement. This slightly baffling phrase is always drawn out, the vowels elongated for emphasis, so it sounds like "Nu . . . voooooooh-hob-sch-yeeeeeeeeeh!" It's the sort of thing a Svetlana would say to a Lena about something annoying or frustrating. A good translation would be "generally speaking," which to my mind doesn't make for a great closing argument, but then again, your average Svetlana will never be known for her soaring rhetoric.

Svetlana: long on function, short on form.

SVETLANA (origin is Slavic, meaning "Light")

Diminutives: Sveta, Lana

Svetlana is the name we most associate with the Soviet period of Russian history. The name enjoyed huge popularity in the Soviet era because of its atheistic bent, having as it does, a purely pagan association, without any reference to a Christian saint. Josef Stalin's daughter was Svetlana.

Svetlana means "Light," which is lovely, but the romance of being named after "Light," so extant in the aristocratic and sensitive "Lucia" and the artistic and emotional "Claire," for some reason doesn't infuse Russian Svetlana with the same glamour. Perhaps this is because Russia is so far north and there is so little direct Light?

Svetlana is a great wing girl but no leader

PERSONALITY:

- ✔ Good with tasks she can do with her hands not her head

- ✔ Can be pedantic

- ✔ Not glamorous at best, wholesome

- ✔ Practical and capable

- ✔ No outstanding politicians or celebrities (exception: Svetlana Zakharova, ballerina)

WHERE DO YOU FIND SVETLANA?

- ✔ Ironing your clothes

- ✔ Performing data entry

- ✔ Passing out leaflets for a jewelry store in really foul weather

- ✔ Giving you an anticellulite massage

- ✔ On the staff of your child's primary school

- ✔ At the farmers market selling beets

"Oh, but what about Sveta from Ivanovo?" asked Holt, raising his eyebrows suggestively. "She's a celebrity Svetlana."

"I thought Anna Chapman was the love of your life?" said Lucy.

"Well, she is," sighed Holt, who had once met the sultry redheaded spy for about seventeen seconds at a party. "But I'm intrigued by Sveta from Ivanovo."

"Sveta from Ivanovo has a fantastic rack," said Joe, wiping the foam from his beer off his upper lip. "You can say that about her."

"Yes, and that's about the only thing you can say about her," said Alexei, as Sullen Lena put a burger down in front of him.

"Who ees Svetlana from . . . where?" asked Jesus, who never pays attention to the Russian news.

"She's Russia's Honey Boo Boo," I explained.

"Oh," said Jesus, who does pay attention to American culture.

I thought the analogy of Svetlana Kuritsyna (better known in Russia as "Sveta from Ivanovo") to Honey Boo Boo was apt, although Svetlana lacks a lot of six-year-old Honey Boo Boo's natural finesse. This zaftig, twentysomething member of Nashi, Russia's version of the Hitler Youth, was a nobody from the Russian equivalent of Akron, Ohio, until she was randomly caught on camera in the Moscow Metro during a pro-Putin rally in December of 2011. Asked by a journalist why she supported Putin, Sveta stumbled over facts and grammar, groping for words and concepts, looking exactly like a female moose caught in the headlines. She finally managed to articulate that, under Putin, Russians had "more better clothes," which she felt was a big achievement.

The YouTube footage of Svetlana went viral, and like Honey Boo Boo, she was plucked from her regional obscurity and given her own TV show, called *Ray of Light*, in which Sveta interviews various people and shares vignettes from her incredibly pedestrian life with the viewers. It is not nearly as entertaining as *Here Comes Honey Boo Boo*, and were it not government funded, I doubt it would last more than one season.

Tancy arrived at the table just as we were wondering about another round of fries to accompany the round of drinks, which Sullen Lena had just delivered. Tancy looked even more Friday-evening disheveled and tired than Alexei: her black suit was crumpled, her black bob flattened, and there was makeup smudged under her eyes. She gave us each a hug and collapsed into the chair Holt held out for her.

"I'm exhausted," she said, kicking off her square-toed heels and pulling a pair of sheepskin-lined moccasins out of her battered briefcase. "Get me something to drink while I get these damn contacts out." She thunked a bottle of saline solution and a small case on the table and started rooting around in her left eye. Alexei looked away and Joe winced. Jesus showed no restraint.

"*Querida*, djou look terrible!" he chided Tancy, who was one of his closest friends. "Go to the bathroom and fix the mascara right thees very minute. Djou can't just do your lenses here! Eets deesgusting. And why djou no go home to change into that leather skirt I bring back from Milan for djou?" Jesus's mission to glam Tancy up dovetailed nicely with my own master plan to get her profile on some Ivy League Internet dating sites. We both felt she could make more of an effort, but then we didn't have to work twenty hours a day.

"No, I didn't go home, Jesus," she retorted, clawing out her right lens. "I came straight from the office, and anyway, this is Scandinavia on a Friday night. I'm invisible to any potential boyfriends." She waved a hand in the direction of two sleek, smooth-haired twentysomething Russian women undulating across the patio on four-inch heels with designer handbags dangling from their elbows. "That's the chef's special here, so cut me some slack and get me a Scotch with ice on the side." She stuffed the saline solution and heels into her bottomless briefcase and drew her chair up closer to the table.

"Rough day?" asked Alexei.

Tancy rested her head briefly on his shoulder.

"Get this," she said. "I've been in HR hell today since 1:30. I had to fire one of our top sales managers. Turns out she'd given half of the Far Eastern dealers her personal bank details—her Cyprus bank details, I'm happy to report—and was skimming, like, 3 percent off the top of every single transaction."

"Was her name Irina?" asked Matt.

"No," said Tancy, "but that's close. She was Marina. Why do you ask?"

Lucy and I exchanged nods.

"What have we got for Marina?" asked Matt. I skipped over the scanty notes I had on Katya (sweet and pretty and good) and Anastasia (on which, oddly, I had bubkes) to my copious notes on Marina.

Marina: the air is pretty thin up here, and the rules don't apply to me.

MARINA (origin: Greek)

Marina means "of the sea," very apt for women who feel they inhabit a separate realm from the rest of us mere mortals.

PERSONALITY:

✔ Feels things deeply & broadcasts about feeling things deeply

✔ Claims great spiritual and intuitive nature

✔ Often moody or melancholy in a very dramatic sort of way

✔ Bold dresser, with ethnic accents and statement jewelry

✔ Often gifted in the creative realm, artistic, literary

✔ Flashy cook, but someone else does the dishes

✔ Not entirely trustworthy

✔ Effusive manners mask hostility, indifference

✔ Focused on own agenda

✔ Fierce, single-minded mother

✔ Vigorous selfish streak

WHERE DO YOU FIND MARINA?

✔ Teaching your yogalates class

✔ She's your landlord who shows up early one Saturday morning without phoning first and wakes you from a profound post-Friday-night slumber

✔ On the other end of the phone, aggressively and inappropriately promoting her nephew's candidacy for a job for which he is woefully and hopelessly underqualified

✔ In the hair salon, talking you into some henna highlights that you will later deeply regret

✔ Guiding your tour of the Tretyakov Gallery's Masterpieces of Early Icon Painting department

✱

"Wasn't there a famous poet who was Marina something?" asked Tancy.

Indeed there was. Marina Tsvetaeva was one of Russia's most famous poets. Her life was played out against the tumultuous landscape of two world wars, the upheaval of Russia's revolution, and civil war. She experienced firsthand the devastation of famine and the despair of exile as well as the deaths of many of her nearest and dearest, including her younger daughter, who died of starvation. Tsvetaeva had an unhappy and dysfunctional childhood, countless affairs with literary luminaries of both sexes, and a stormy relationship with her husband. Her lyric verse captured universal themes of love, despair, longing, and want. She died in obscurity under murky circumstances, sure of only one thing: that her life and her verse would be remembered.

She was an über-Marina.

I am often impressed by Marinas, but I don't trust most of them as far as I can throw them. I am unnerved by their unique combination of genuine gregariousness and hardy selfish streak. You will never be able to know for sure what a Marina really thinks; her accomplished people skills are too complexly interwoven with her cunning acting ability. Just as the colorful ethnic tapestry in her living room masks the dry rot in the wall behind, her effusiveness and artistic musings can cloak everything from massive indifference to simmering hostility. Marina can be inspiring, but she is also sly. Marina is supremely charming, which helps her to be manipulative. Marina has genuine talent and ability, but somehow it is never put to use for the greater good of mankind. I suppose that some Marinas do live in a spiritual (read *flaky*) world of their own, but for most it's just a put-on.

"Excuse me, the kitchen will be closing in twenty minutes and the bar in forty minutes." We all looked up to see Valya, the restaurant manager, at our table. She tapped a well-manicured forefinger on her wristwatch. "If you need anything else, please order now." She smiled and made to go.

We all nodded. Scandinavia is located in a residential courtyard, so they are obliged to kick everyone out by midnight, which has probably lowered the rate of liver failure among expatriates by a whopping percentage.

"Valya," mused Alexei. "My mom is a Valentina."

"That explains a great deal," said Lucy.

"Oh, 'splain it to me," said Jesus, eagerly. "Alexei's mother, Valentina Borisovna, djou know, she is amazing! Very fierce!"

"Wait—order some more fries," said Joe, motioning Valya back over. She took the order, suggested another round of drinks, and managed to up-sell us on a different bad Chardonnay. She then snapped her fingers, and three waitresses, all of them smiling, appeared to whisk away dirty glasses and plates.

Valya confirmed all my thoughts on her name jotted down in the Moleskine. I swiveled the notebook around to show Lucy.

"Sounds right to me," said Joe. "I've got one client who is a

Valentina: on top of her game. At the top of the heap.

VALENTINA (origin: ancient Roman means "strong" "healthy")

Diminutive: Valya, Valitchka

I have yet to meet an underage, weak, or vulnerable Valentina. Do they spring from the heads of their fathers fully grown and completely locked and loaded?

✔ Valentina the Victorious

✔ Valentina the Valkyrie

✔ Valentina the Vanquisher

I have also yet to meet a Valentina whom I addressed in any way other than the formal name and patronymic combination, which conveys respect.

- ✔ Valentina commands genuine loyalty and respect.

- ✔ Like Irina, Valentina works hard but rises higher. Why? Inexplicable extra V factor.

- ✔ Name a child Valentina, and you arm her to take over the world.

- ✔ Whatever a Valentina decides to focus on, she will ultimately master and distinguish herself in—the arts, sports, sciences, and most particularly management.

- ✔ Valentina Tereshkova was the first woman in space.

- ✔ Valentina Matvieyenko was the iron lady of Russian politics—the best bet for Russia's first woman president.

Valentina is the matriarch of the family, effortlessly dominating other family members, particularly her less impressive husband. The domestic arena is seldom enough of a challenge for Valentina, who runs departments, corporations, ministries, and municipal governments—and she does it efficiently and well.

WHERE DO YOU FIND VALENTINA?

Quite simply in charge.

Valentina, and she never, ever lets up. She's on the phone with me every effing morning at, like, 8:00 a.m."

"Ew," I said.

"It's not my best time of the day," Joe agreed.

"Why didn't you give Velvet a Russian name?" asked Tancy.

"We thought about a few names," I said, "because I have to say, the thing that really drew me to Russian history in the first place was the names of the last tsar's daughters, Tatiana and Anastasia; I thought they were just beautiful. But then you get here and find that they are actually called 'Tanya,' which always reminds me of that Olympic trailer-trash skater, and 'Nastya,' which sounds way too much like 'nasty' to me."

"It's true," said Alexei. "I hate being called 'Lyosha.'"

"It never in a million years even occurs to me to call you Lyosha," said Tancy, lighting up another cigarette. "I wouldn't have the balls."

"Well, we have other names for djou, don't we, *cariño*?" said Jesus, who had stealthily downed six mojitos and was now quite tipsy. He ran a proprietary hand through Alexei's hair. "And for those *cojones* as well, eh?"

Alexei turned red, and Joe and Holt looked the other way in solidarity. I was very glad HRH was having a business *banya*. He can't really take Jesus's spicier moments.

"I liked Xenia as well," I said to fill the awkward silence. "And I thought it would be totally cool to have a name that started with X, but Xenias always end up being called 'Ksiusha,' which is awful, or 'Oksana,' which I don't love."

"I live with a Tanya," said Joe. "What you got to say about that name?"

Lucy and I exchanged glances.

"Sweet and pretty and good," I said firmly. No one messes with Joe's Tanya, who is not a trailer-trash anything.

"No," corrected Lucy after a careful minute. "That's Katya and Galina. Tanya is 'sugar and spice and everything nice.'"

"Well, I can take that home in a doggie bag," said Joe, and we dug into the last basket of fries as Sullen Lena tipped a final bottle of not-quite-as-bad-as-the-other-Chardonnay into the melted ice in the bucket.

CHAPTER 7

DACHAPHOBIA

BACK IN THE bad old days of the Soviet Union, my tourists complained a lot about the food. "It's terrible," they would say, "and there is so much of it." And this was exactly how I felt about Velvet's school. It was the only one to stretch the academic year well into the first week of July, more than a month after the Russian schools shut up shop and at least two weeks after all the other international schools gave up the ghost. These last two weeks were best described as high-end babysitting. Each day the number of children dwindled as exasperated parents simply yanked their children out to start their more exciting summer programs elsewhere. Each nationality blamed the overlong school year on the others.

"It's all these Koreans," a Dutch woman complained to me as we waited at the school gate. "They don't believe in any vacations for their kids."

"It's all those Europeans," sniffed Olga, the mother of Seraphima, Velvet's closest friend. "They don't want to pay their nannies anything extra . . . and they don't have dachas."

"Pull out Velvet early," proposed HRH. "Who gives a damn anyway?"

Pulling Velvet out of school early went against the grain, but when Seraphima's parents invited Velvet to join them for a long weekend in Nice, I jumped at the chance. Far better for her, I rationalized, to explore a new culture, even if I suspected that exploration might feature a skewed shopping-to-museum ratio. Better, anyway, than sitting in a stifling schoolroom doing silly art projects or watching *Chitty Chitty Bang Bang* for the four-hundredth time.

With Velvet away for five days, I had a huge chunk of unmolested time, and I promised myself that I would finally get down to writing the book. I'd made modest progress: one wall of my study was now completely covered in multicolored Post-it notes, each with an idea or concept written on it in bold Sharpie. I moved them around a lot and stared at them. With five days to myself, I thought optimistically, surely I could come up with an outline.

HRH stuck a pin in this halcyon balloon.

"Sveta and Ilya have invited us to their dacha for the long weekend," he announced.

"Oh," I said.

"They want to do something nice for us, since you helped organize everything for Petya to go to camp in the US."

"I was happy to help," I began, "but as for—"

"Petrovna!" warned HRH sharply.

"We've really got to go," I said in a hollow voice—a statement, not a question.

"We've really got to go," he affirmed.

"How many nights?" I ventured.

"Three," HRH stated, not quite meeting my eyes.

"No," I pleaded, "really, I can't do three. Three is way too much."

"All right," conceded HRH. "If we leave on Saturday morning instead of Friday night, then we can spend two. We can leave early morning on Monday."

"I was going to write this weekend," I said feebly. "I am just getting to a really good place."

"Dachas are great places to write," said HRH glibly. "Look at Tolstoy, look at Pasternak—Pasternak is famous for writing at a dacha."

"Pasternak didn't have a lot of choice, you know," I shouted after his retreating back. "Pasternak was under house arrest."

"He won a Nobel Prize writing at his dacha," HRH shot back. "Let's see what you can do!"

I will write about how much I hate dachas, I thought. And then they'll be sorry. Pasternak hadn't needed Post-its, and god knows, he didn't have to plug in a laptop, which would be almost as impossible at the Potapovs' present-day dacha as it was in Pasternak's Peredelkino in the 1950s.

I love the Potapovs—Sveta, Ilya, and their two children, angelic Petya and impish Xenia—but I do not love their dacha. Or any dacha, for that matter. I wanted to stay in the half-empty city, work on my outline, and maybe meet Joe or Tancy at Scandinavia for a burger and a few bottles of wine. I wanted a bug-free, air-conditioned space with access to the Internet, electricity, indoor plumbing, a refrigerator, and a reliable source of ice. The Potapovs' dacha does not meet any of these criteria. Nor, really, does any dacha I have ever encountered.

A dacha (which rhymes, so appropriately, with gotcha) in its most basic incarnation, is a country cottage plopped precariously on a postage-stamp-size plot of land. Forget that scene in the Hollywood version of Pasternak's *Dr. Zhivago*—the one where Omar Sharif, Geraldine Chaplin, and Ralph Richardson arrive off the train from Moscow and are met by the faithful retainer who drives them out in the pony trap to that very bizarre interpretation of Varykino. That is not a dacha. That's meant to be a country estate, and anyway it was filmed in Spain.

At a Russian dacha every available inch of the postage-stamp-size plot is given over to the cultivation of root vegetables by the *dachniki* (those who own and operate dachas). In hard times—during the long winters or times of political instability—Russians survive on those root vegetables, a strategy that Omar, Geraldine, and Ralph pursued successfully until Omar went off to the Yuriatin public library and ran into Julie Christie; things went downhill from there. And so it is today—with the vegetables, I mean, not the Yuriatin public library.

Before perestroika, a dacha, along with a Soviet-made car and a tiny two-room apartment, formed the holy trinity of "The Soviet Dream": the pinnacle of economic well-being in the Stagnation Era. Some jobs provided dachas as a workplace benefit, the location, level of luxury, and amenities always an accurate measurement of the grandeur of the job. Other dachas—or, more accurately, the deed to the house but not the land—were passed down through generations. The Great Russian Soul strives for many and varied things, but a dacha is universal. Russians love their dachas with the passion they

*

reserve for family, country, and their national drink. Tentative and complicated it may be, but owning a dacha means kinda-sorta owning land, and that is the one thing the Russian people have yearned for from the year dot.

To a Russian, dachas mean fresh air, nature, and a welcome respite from the cement jungle of the city. For a population only very recently allowed to travel more than fifty miles from their own domiciles, dachas represent a feasible change of scene. Dachas satisfy the visceral Russian urge to grow, harvest, and preserve nature's bounty against the coming rigors of the long winter. Dachas, in the scarier eras of Russian history, offered havens from listening devices and prying eyes. In happier times dachas always are associated with mushrooms and mushroom hunting, which for Russians is elevated to an almost religious experience.

True to Russian form, however, dachas are a lot more complicated and seriously less appealing than their obvious counterparts in the Hamptons, Sussex, or Aix-en-Provence. Forget *On Golden Pond,* that remote, idyllic, and nostalgic summer retreat complete with old games of Scrabble missing the X, Y, and J tiles, mismatched jelly glasses, and waterlogged Herman Wouk hardbacks. Russia is the largest country in the world, but most dachas are inexplicably built in tight clumps, one on top of the other. HRH tries to explain this awkward clumping by positing the theory that the electricity and water lines only go so far out of major urban centers. Ha-ha. This is surely a ludicrous suggestion for a country that sent the first man into space.

During the Putin petro boom, dachas and grander year-round country residences sprang up like mushrooms, with a vigorous disregard for consistency of style, size, and taste. I recently got hopelessly lost in Silver Bank, a hundred-year-old dacha settlement. Driving around, I was able to see some of the more recent edifices next to the traditional wooden cottages. I saw King Ludwig's Neuschwanstein Castle next to a marble Tuscan villa and, next door to that, a newly minted *Little House in the Big Woods* log cabin.

"Turrets," Jesus often moans, "these turrets are going to be the death of me. A round room? Where djou put sofa pairs—eh, *querida?*"

A few years ago HRH's friend Sergei Bichiyuk dragged him off to see a cluster of "cottage settlements." They were called

Sherwood Forest, Tivoli, and Green-vitch. They got a glossy brochure showing the choices for house design: (a) the Swiss chalet, (b) the olde English thatched cottage, (c) the Spanish hacienda, or (d) the Florentine villa. Sergei, HRH reported, had suggested we purchase adjacent homes. I offered a contested divorce as option (e).

"Down with dachas!" is my battle cry.

My dachaphobia, much like my passion for ice in my drinks, is a source of constant bafflement to my Russian acquaintances.

"The fresh air!" protests Raisa, our sturdy, fiftysomething cleaning lady, recently hospitalized for three weeks following a collapse that, I strongly suspect, was not unconnected to a marathon spring planting at her dacha.

"Oy . . . ," sighed my colleague Yuliya every Monday morning from May to September as she sank gratefully into her office chair and surveyed her scratched, sunburned hands in dismay. "I am beyond tired."

The fact of the matter is, and no amount of Chekhov will convince me otherwise, the whole dacha thing is a well-oiled machine designed to keep indentured service for females alive and well in twenty-first-century Russia.

On Saturday morning, instead of lingering in bed with hot tea and the AC, HRH and I faced off, hot and sweaty, in a spirited argument over the best way to cram everything we needed for a two-day trip to the Potapovs into the Discovery.

"I still think if you pack the square stuff first—those cases of juice and milk and beer—then you can put the vegetables and all that bedding in the backseat," I said.

"No," argued HRH. "We have to get those six 5-liter bottles of water in first and then Xenia's bike."

"Put Xenia's bike on the roof," I suggested. "That way we can get these in." I motioned to four large tote bags that held a range of clothing—from bathing suits to thick, long-sleeved fleece jackets—plus fifteen pairs of socks, a large bottle of Advil, Alka-Seltzer, Bengay, bug repellent, sunblock, Wellington boots, and three unread issues of the *New Yorker.*

Like all men, HRH does not like to be told how to load a car, and certainly not by a girl. He went into attack mode. "Do you have to pack everything in those weird bags?"

"Yes," I replied through clenched teeth. "I do."

"It looks like Chechen refugee luggage!" HRH fumed.

"They are from L.L. Bean!" I protested. "They are incredibly practical. I use them at the cash-and-carry. They lower our carbon footprint—"

"Our what?" HRH, like most Russians, believes that climate change was invented by Bill Clinton with the sole intention of ripping off the Russians.

"I use them at the cash-and-carry instead of those cruddy plastic bags. People in the parking lot come up to me all the time and ask me where I bought them!"

"They look like carry-on luggage from the last flight out of Grozny."

"And this is more tasteful, you think?" I snarled, kicking a glow-in-the-dark, made-in-China duffel bag that held HRH's all-important *banya*, or sauna, accessories: a ratty bathrobe, four felt hats, three sheets, and a bunch of eucalyptus branches. Across one side was a lurid logo: "TsCKA—The Red Army Sports Team!" HRH has a lot of these hideous bags, including one that says "Gazprom: 15 Years! From Victory to Victory!" My least favorite reads "Aeroflot—Welcome!" (This wins the coveted "best use of irony on a tacky Second-World promotional bag" title.)

HRH grunted in a noncommittal way that indicated the conversation was at an end. I leafed through a *New Yorker* and tried to ignore the group of Tadzhik courtyard custodians who had gathered to enjoy our little performance, squatting the way Central Asians seem to find so effortless and which we pay good money to learn how to do in yoga class.

A few more shoves and HRH squeezed in the cooler filled with four pounds of marinated pork, and we finally climbed into the car. It was 11:00 a.m. By leaving on Saturday morning we hoped to make much better time than if we left on Friday night, when traffic in all directions moves at a snail's pace from four to eleven. We had eighty miles to travel and hoped to get there in under five hours. Alas, we were not alone in our strategic planning. Although we sped through the center of town, once we turned onto Peace Avenue we slowed to a crawl, joining the immovable phalanx of traffic pushing westward out of Moscow, identical to the immovable phalanxes pushing east, north, and south. We passed rusty, rickety, box-shaped Ladas with far too many people in them. No one wore a seat belt. The smaller the car, the higher and more precarious the flotsam strapped helter-skelter to the roof: DIY supplies, old furniture, chicken coops, and boxes of groceries, all dragging the car's chassis perilously close to the asphalt. We fought unflinchingly for three feet of supremacy against the inaptly named Gazelle trucks. We were dwarfed by haughty, impeccably clean black BMW SUVs with tinted windows, piloted by square-headed men in mirrored aviator sunglasses. We were all wayfarers in the purgatory of summer weekend gridlock, all heading to the magic that never is: the dacha.

"Here we are," HRH sang out cheerfully. "Real *dachniki!*"

"Yeah," I said, taking a small sip of my coffee. Too much and I'd have to go in the bushes in front of all of Yaroslavskoye Shosse, since once we left the confines of the city the toilet opportunities would be few and far between.

How do people do this each week? I wondered.

Dachniki adhere to an exacting schedule. Over the long May Day weekend they load up the family car with everything from barbecue spears to economy-size packets of diapers. Thus provisioned, the man of the house ferries his wife, his parents, in-laws, and children out to the dacha for the entire summer. Russian men refer to this process as "I have sent my family out to the dacha" and accompany it with a vaudeville-style waggle of the eyebrows, a mischievous grin, and the brisk rubbing of hands. Translation: "I finally got the old ball-and-chain, me mum, and the brats the hell out of town for the summer."

Thus sounds the opening bell for a season of unchecked hedonism in urban centers from Brest to Ulan Bator. Dacha season kick-starts a mind-boggling transformation: bus drivers start to shave daily, cafés and bars extend their happy hours, restaurants offer asparagus and oyster and other aphrodisiacal food festivals, and hotels coyly advertise weeknight specials. Sales of condoms and nail polish reach annual spikes, and just you try to get a bikini wax on a Tuesday afternoon. I walk down the street, knocked for six by the scent of cheap cologne on beefy security guards and blinded by the metallic sheen of secretaries' regularly highlighted hair from May 1 to September 1.

I do not want a dacha of any kind: not an authentic wooden hovel nor a scale model of the Disney castle, complete with

★

drawbridges and a flat-screen TV. I don't want to spend all day breaking my back over the cucumber crop. HRH agrees; his intermittent twinges of dacha lust are easily squelched by reminding him that he would have to forgo his marathon six-hour weekend naps. Sometimes, however, his innate Slavic desire for a wooden roof and too many potato plants gets the better of him, and that is when we get sucked into visiting the Potapovs.

I may hate their dacha, but I love the Potapovs, who might have stepped out of the frame of an ideal 1970s Soviet-era film armed with every virtue that idealized genre espouses: a lyrical love of culture, expansive traditional hospitality, saucy wit, strong moral compasses, and an unwavering devotion to family and country.

Ilya Potapov, despite growing up in a closed military city deep in the heart of Siberia, where distrust of foreigners is a given, has never once, in all the twenty years I've known him, made me feel awkward, out of place, or different. If he doesn't understand something I say, he just leans in a bit closer and asks me to explain it again. He and HRH got their apartments at the same time during their military service, and Ilya lived three floors below us in Northern Butovo. If I had the right to make only one phone call, Ilya Potapov would be at the top of my list of memorized numbers. He'd never not come. He's been Bingley to HRH's Darcy since their military school days and has loyally followed HRH into private business, weathering the ups and downs of the roller-coaster economy. They're solid, the Potapovs. Solid and funny, and as truly Russian as birch trees.

Svetlana and Ilya put a lot of time and effort into being great parents, and that includes having a dacha, which for them is nonnegotiable. Petya and Xenia must spend their summers in the fresh air. Sveta, particularly, believes in dachas and in the moral imperative that all well-brought-up children spend summers at a dacha. I often wonder about this, because most of the city kids I know come home after a summer of playing with the locals at the dacha with a spicy vocabulary that would make your hair curl.

When Petya was born, Svetlana shanghaied Ilya into purchasing a postage-stamp-size plot of scorched earth on which they erected a shack, right next door to the slightly larger shack her chum from school had built on his plot of scorched earth—

all an arduous eighty miles from Moscow on largely unpaved roads. Before there was even a theoretical discussion about the proportion of the shack's foundations, an impressive two-story, full-service banya, or sauna, was constructed over the property line. The Potapovs' fate was sealed. They are *dachniki*.

Every disposable kopek in the Potapov family budget has been, is, and will continue to be poured into the big black hole that is their dacha. Limited, and never very reliable, electricity was hooked up in 2005, fueling a lackluster fridge the size of a Rollaboard that takes a week to make one tray of perfunctory ice cubes. Sveta works hard on her flower garden, and in a generation or three it will be lovely, but today it provides absolutely no shade. The boards with splinters and nails that used to litter the garden, ever a source of fascination to two-year-old Velvet, morphed eventually into a narrow porch: a good idea in theory but on the wrong side of the house to catch any breeze.

No expense, however, has been spared on the *banya*. A third story was added in 2003, providing additional sleeping space for six, steaming room for ten, and in pride of place a state-of-the-art eucalyptus-oil diffuser imported from Sweden. The walls of the *banya's* sleeping area are decorated with thirteen completed ten-thousand-piece jigsaw puzzles. Svetlana assembles one puzzle each summer, a distraction that keeps insanity at bay.

Sveta keeps Ilya on a very short leash, so he doesn't get much opportunity to comparison-shop aphrodisiacal food festivals. There is certainly no Super Stop & Shop just up the road. Each Friday afternoon he loads his Ford Focus to the brim with groceries, drinking water, badly dubbed copies of recent DVDs, and that week's Russian *Good Housekeeping* and heads off to his dacha to join Svetlana and the kids. If Ilya leaves by 3:00 p.m. he can make the eighty-mile journey in just under six hours. If it isn't raining, that is. Rain can turn the last twenty miles of unpaved dirt road into an impassible quagmire. Arriving from a hard week at the office, exhausted from battling snail-paced traffic jams, and nearly asphyxiated from diesel fumes, Ilya can be forgiven for wanting to pop a cold—well, tepid—beer and chill out.

Nothing doing.

Svetlana, who has spent the week making sure her kids don't drown in the river, polishing the Swedish eucalyptus infuser to a high gloss, and walking two miles to the only retail establishment within a twenty-mile radius for cigarettes (she takes up smoking each May 1 and gives it up each September 1), is always ready for a little "me" time. She certainly was that Saturday when we arrived as late afternoon faded into early evening. We had gotten terribly lost twice, and I experienced a wild hope we might have to turn back, but HRH called Ilya, who drove forty miles to meet us and lead us down the unpaved roads, with no signs, to the dacha. Sveta could not believe it had taken Ilya that long to find us, and without drawing breath resumed her rant of all the dacha's current faults and foibles.

"Eeeeeeeeeeee-ll-eeeee-ya!" she upbraided him, hands on her hips. "Look at this door! It is practically hanging off the hinges! It's no wonder Petya is literally covered with mosquito bites!"

Ilya sheepishly promised to get the screwdriver out and fix the door.

HRH and Ilya began to unload the groceries. Svetlana greeted each item with horror.

"Eeeeeeeeeeee-ll-eeeee-ya!" she moaned. "I told you to bring Granny's Country Cottage Mixed Fruit Juice individual boxes! This is store-brand apple juice in bulk! You know Xenia won't drink anything but Granny's Country Cottage Mixed Fruit!"

Ilya attempted to explain that the cash-and-carry had been out of Granny's Country Cottage Mixed Fruit Juice individual boxes, as indeed it is out of most things by Friday morning from May to September.

"Is it so very much to ask, Eeeeeeeeeeee-ll-eeeee-ya," exploded Svetlana, throwing up her hands, "for you to just get what I put on the list? It's not like you do much up in town during the week. What the hell is this? How many times have I told you that I need Ariel Liquid Gentle, not Persil powder?"

It's in moments like these that I picture Vladimir Lenin turning over in his tomb.

Ilya, chastised, promised to run the gauntlet of the unpaved twenty miles at sunrise to source Granny's Country Cottage Mixed Fruit Juice in individual boxes and Ariel Liquid Gentle, putting paid to any thoughts he might have had about sleeping in.

"Oy!" Sveta heaved. "You are useless. See if you can get the barbecue lit without screwing that up." She beckoned me to follow her into the house.

I hope I have made it clear that I have a lot of time for Svetlana Potapova, especially from October to April. During these months she is engaging and interesting. She reads and goes to all the latest shows and has some interesting thoughts on politics. She is also literally the only Russian who has ever written me a thank-you note. The minute she hits the dacha, however, she morphs into Dacha Hag, becoming that lethal combination of bored and exhausted, with only a ten-thousand-piece jigsaw (this year a detailed rendition of the entire Sistine Chapel with the Sibyls and *The Last Judgment*) to bolster her sanity. When I imagine the Dacha Hag pandemic from the Arctic Circle to the Black Sea, across all nine time zones, I shiver. I reminded myself that there, but for the grace of God, go I. I dialed up my female solidarity to the maximum and made what I hoped were appropriately sympathetic noises as Svetlana gave me a privately guided tour of everything that was wrong with the dacha. This took about two hours.

Which was just as well, really, because that is how long it took the menfolk to get the barbecue going. Russian men, as a rule, do not cook. Cooking is considered a bit effeminate and lacking in scope, as well as time consuming. It may also involve multitasking and long-range strategic planning, which are rarely found in the Russian male tool kit. The big exception is *shashlik*, or shish kebab. Like men all over the world, Russian men do barbecue. *Shashlik*, they assert, "cannot tolerate a woman's touch." I've noticed that the *shashlik* seems able to tolerate a woman's touch well enough during prep and cleanup. Everything in between, that's what the guys do. As this is their sole culinary contribution, they throw themselves into it with abandon. Heated debates take place over the exact chemistry of the supersecret ancestral marinade (vinegar, oil, salt, and pepper) and the arrangement of kindling in the special metal, boxlike *mangal*. Arguments last enough time to consume several beers. *Shashlik* meat is handled far more tenderly than a firstborn child ever is: lovingly impaled onto lethal, three-foot *shashlik* spears. Once the meat is on the fire, the men relax slightly but hover worriedly over the transformation from cold, clammy, unresponsive flesh to sizzling, hot, juicy, and tender meat, displaying a single-minded concentration their wives despair of ever experiencing.

If you are a devotee of the low-carb lifestyle, then dacha life

*

is for you, with its unchanging *table d'hôte* of pork *shashlik*, whole tomatoes, cucumbers, and green onions. If you are a not-too-fussy dipsomaniac, then dacha life, where tepid alcohol flows like mercury, is also for you. If you like to get drunk and make a total jackass of yourself, then dacha life chez Potapov is just the ticket. As the last hunk of *shashlik* is gnawed between exhausted jaws, out comes the karaoke machine! Call me a killjoy, but if I were Svetlana Potapova, I think I'd have invested in a dishwasher or, god forbid, a space heater (since by this point we usually have our snow pants on) or some other mod con that might mitigate the abject misery of dacha life before I considered something like a karaoke machine. What does it say about a society, I asked myself, where you can plug in and use a karaoke machine but not flush the toilet?

I like a good session with the karaoke machine as much as the next person, but the Potapovs' collection of discs is limited to rock music of the former Soviet Union from 1985–1991, which is not Russia's golden or even silver age of music. The accompanying visuals are strange: Asian women in sherbet-colored bikinis, relaxing on the sands of a beach against a generic Asian slumscape. It doesn't quite mesh with the lyrics of the Russian songs, all of which are rather mournful numbers about leaving the Soviet Union and never coming back—a notion that always strikes me as very sensible at this particular point in the evening.

After half a case of beer and a few vodkas, HRH fancies himself very musical. He's mistaken.

"Play 'Simona'!" he cries, like Victor Laszlo ordering up "The Marseillaise" in *Casablanca*.

"Simona" is HRH's signature karaoke number and about the cheesiest Russian song there is, the refrain of which requires the singer to wail "Seeeeeeeeeeeeeeeeeee-mon-ahhhhhhhhhhhhh" in ascending thirds. Sadly, the amount of booze HRH consumes combines lethally with the fact that, really, he is totally tone deaf. Poor HRH—an alpha male in everything else he does— never achieves a very high score on "Simona."

He does marginally better with the more upbeat homage to "The Stewardess Called Zhanna."

Picture us, then, oversize chunks of pork solidifying in our bowels and low-grade Chenin Blanc from Moldova—*vino ordinarnoyoe*—already making itself felt in our temples, listening to a grown man wailing off-key about his Ukrainian lady love, singing to an Asian hottie in a lime-green thong who is sprawled on one of the less attractive oceanfronts of Pusan, South Korea.

"Shall I check on the children?" I asked Svetlana, desperate for an escape.

"Oh, they went to bed about two hours ago," she responded, lighting another slender, pink Vogue menthol.

"On their own?" I asked, amazed.

"Oh, yes!" She poured another hefty tote of tepid *vino ordinarnoyoe* for us both. I sipped mine, ruminating that children going to bed of their own accord are rather like rats deserting a sinking ship or a city on the brink of famine: a highly accurate barometer of just how desperate a situation is. I had to get out of there.

"Darling," I cooed to HRH, taking his arm. "Why don't we head up as well? We will need to make an early start tomorrow," I said in English, so no one else would understand.

"Huh?" he slurred in Russian. "Whadda you mean? The *banya* is getting warmed up. We are going to steam a little."

Steaming myself, I faded into the shadows and padded up the treacherously steep stairs in the pitch-black. I stubbed my toe, then swore loudly—in Russian, so that everyone could understand. Hopping on one foot, I delved into my tote bag for a duvet and my iPod. I rummaged around HRH's for the bug repellent and Advil, then realized that the bag was still out on the porch. I swore again—in both languages—then curled up on my side of the world's most uncomfortable sofa bed (which the morning light revealed as our divan from the Northern Butovo days), my head on a musty, scratchy pillowcase. I stuffed my earphones into my ears; they almost, but not quite, drowned out the shouts of encouragement as HRH performed a spirited encore of "Simona."

In what seemed like thirty seconds, I blinked in a hazy gray light and became conscious that my left arm was fast asleep. It was pinned down, used as a pillow by a comatose HRH. He's not musical, but HRH does sleep for Russia. Following the rigors of a night at the Potapovs' dacha, he usually sleeps for a very long time. He also tends not to shave for two days, making pillow duty scratchy work. I heaved him off of me, sure that it would take the Red Army Chorus at full blast to wake him, and peered

★

at my watch. It was 7:13 a.m. I groaned. This was an obscenely early start to a day that seemed unlikely to ever end. Everything hurt. My neck was stiff from the world's most uncomfortable sofa bed, my legs were covered with mosquito bites, my temples were pounding from all that *vino ordinarnoyoe,* my tongue felt like proverbial sandpaper, and my lower bowels felt as if I'd swallowed a blacksmith's anvil. I groaned. I needed a bathroom, a hot shower, and an iced beverage. Bitter experience suggested that I was likely to strike out on all three.

This kind of scenario is so funny when Kingsley Amis writes it or Hugh Laurie performs it and yet so seriously unfunny when it happens to me. I couldn't find one funny aspect about not being able to find socks—not one of the fifteen pairs I'd packed neatly in the L.L. Bean bag for just this eventuality. I reluctantly admitted to myself that they, along with the Alka-Seltzer and bug spray, must be in the car. There was nothing for it. I eased my bare feet into my dank Wellington boots and braved the steep stairs, even more treacherous going down than they were going up.

The cold and clear front from the previous evening had moved on, giving way to oppressive low-hanging clouds and muggy, clammy air. I picked my way through the previous evening's debris to the outdoor toilet. I took a deep breath, held it in, and then yanked the door open. I sat down gingerly and was reminded of a Canadian woman I knew briefly in Russia. Although she spoke no Russian, she married a Russian guy who spoke no English. They seemed to really care for each other, but after about three months she disappeared back to Canada and never appeared again. Which was odd, but what I chiefly remember about her was that she hated dachas even more than I do. She refused to ever spend a night at one because she could not face the toilet facilities. Maybe that's why she disappeared? She used to eat six hard-boiled eggs before leaving to spend a day at a dacha. She drank no liquid until she left, which sort of defeats the purpose, but she claimed it did the trick—she never had to use the outdoor facilities. At that particular moment, as I crouched over the wooden seat, I wished I'd done something similar. What does it say about a setup where you have a luxurious, state-of-the-art birchwood *banya* that can sweat ten and sleep six, complete with imported Swedish aromatic eucalyptus oil diffuser, yet has eleventh-century toilet arrangements?

I attempted a sketchy wash in cold water at the outside tap, slapping the first of a zillion mosquitoes away from my grimy neck, then picked my way back across the garden, knocking a stack of empty vodka bottles over onto the cement path with a deafening din. I scrambled after them as they clattered and clanked, then stumbled into the kitchen in search of liquid anything.

It was like one of those post-apocalypse films: I appeared to be the sole inhabitant of an abandoned planet. I rummaged around the tiny fridge and found half a box of lukewarm, sticky, sweet peach juice, which I truly loathe, but I downed it gratefully in one gulp, the viscous liquid running like a balm down my parched throat. I heaved a five-liter bottle of mineral water over to the tiny gas stove and filled the kettle. I went back to the garden and rooted around the table to find Sveta's Bic lighter. Holding my breath, and sending up a prayer to whatever deity might be listening, I turned the gas dial slightly to the right, flipped the lighter, and jumped back as a blue flame flared up, then died.

"Fucking hell!" I moaned. "Can someone just cut me some slack?"

"Will I help you?" asked a polite voice in careful English. I wheeled around to find Petya standing behind me.

"Petya," I said, blushing—I was sure a well-brought-up young man like Petya had never heard an adult use such awful words in any language. "You frightened me. I was just trying to light the stove, but . . ."

"She is tricky," acknowledged Petya. "I will make it for you."

Chip off the old block, I thought, as the kettle simmered slowly and Petya produced mug, spoon, sugar, coffee, and, miraculously, milk that hadn't gone sour. He politely declined a cup of coffee in favor of some far healthier kefir, then excused himself and disappeared behind the hedge. I wondered if he had been a hallucination. I took my cup of coffee out to the narrow porch and perched on the top step.

The hot coffee gradually did its work, and I began to feel more human. It was still eerily quiet in the garden, with only birdsong and the occasional distant whine of a drill or rattle of a broken muffler to puncture the early morning silence. I toyed with the idea of pinching the keys, leaving a note, jumping in the car, and heading back to civilization on my own, but dismissed the idea as ill-conceived. Even if I could get the heavy metal gate to the dacha compound open, which was unlikely, I'd probably get lost in about two seconds on the unmarked, unpaved roads. If I stopped to ask for directions from a traffic policeman in my accented Russian, I'd be detained, Breathalyzed, fined a whopping large sum, and possibly have the car impounded until HRH could come and get me, and that, I knew, would seriously piss him off.

I began to feel very trapped and surly and, as always, focused on Russia as the primary culprit. Was it any wonder the Russians couldn't move their civil, economic, or any other part of their society forward, I fumed, when only a small percentage of the population (all of them male) felt comfortable moving from one part of the country to another while the rest (female, old people, and children) were stuck in the countryside with those eleventh-century toilet facilities? The kids seemed to do nothing at all: no summer jobs, summer camps, or summer schools. Large enterprises still ran Soviet-style pioneer camps for employees' children, but most of Russia's youth seemed to while their summers away under the exhausted eyes of their grandmothers and mothers at dachas, where all the fun was reserved for adults, particularly those who controlled the transportation.

I sighed, placed my mug on the step beside me, then stood up to relieve the backs of my legs. I wondered what I could possibly do. There was no comfortable place to sit down, so the idea of curling up with those back issues of the *New Yorker* was a bust. I toyed with the idea of taking notes for a piece on just how much I thought the entire dacha scene was designed to keep women barefoot and pregnant, but that seemed rude. This got me wondering if Hemingway ever worried about being rude, and I came to the conclusion that this was unlikely. I rudely slapped down a midge mid-bite. There was no scope for going somewhere and reading or writing, and I'd feel too guilty to sit still while Sveta heated water on the stove to make a stab at washing last night's dinner plates and *shashlik* spears, by now coated with an impenetrable veneer of grease that would only be reinforced by the application of cold water. Once the dishes were out of the way, I knew, we would probably move right on to the prep work for lunch, our conversational topics exhausted. I decided to start on the cleanup. Sveta emerged later, urged me loudly to put everything down, brewed up another pot of coffee, lit a cigarette, and toyed with her jigsaw, keeping up a running commentary on the general uselessness of all men, and Ilya in particular.

Around 11:00 a.m. Ilya eased himself gingerly down the stairs of the *banya's* sleeping story dressed in the standard *dachnick* uniform: synthetic tracksuit bottoms, a grubby blue-and-white-striped Russian Navy tank top, and plastic flip-flops. Svetlana clicked her tongue against the roof of her mouth, then indicated Ilya's abandoned toolbox and the tipsy door with an eloquent tilt of her head and lift of her eyebrows. Suitably chastised, Ilya opened his toolbox and squinted to focus his bloodshot eyes on the chaotic collection of screws and washers. It was time to attempt an escape.

I hazarded the treacherous stairs with a mug of Alka-Seltzer as a bribe for HRH. I always hope someone will bring me a gently fizzing restorative when I've had a rough night, but no one ever does. I was underwhelmed, therefore, by HRH's lack of appreciation as he groaned and burrowed deeper under the covers.

"Darling," I wheedled in dulcet tones, "listen, I'd really like to go home this evening. Do you think you could get up, help me pull stuff together, then maybe help Ilya with the barbecue, and then after lunch we could take off?"

HRH rolled over, squinted at me uncomprehendingly, grunted, then hid his head under the musty pillow. I pulled it off of him.

"I'll drive," I said, although in what universe would that ever happen? "You can have some beers at lunch and then sleep all the way home . . . please?"

He sat up, and I reeled back to avoid a blast of eucalyptus-infused vodka. He accepted the mug of Alka-Seltzer and downed it in one swallow.

"Petrovna," he said, hiccupping slightly, "you don't get it. This is my relaxation . . . we're going to steam a little bit more before lunch, and then lunch, and then, well . . . we'll see."

I knew what that meant. We were so staying another night. It was no good offering to take a train back to Moscow; he'd never let me get on one. Far too dangerous, he'd say, and he'd be right. HRH rolled over and was instantly snoring peacefully.

I don't know how he does it. I eased my way over to the small window and looked out over the yard. Sveta was weeding the flowerbeds, Ilya was still scouring his toolbox for an elusive something. Xenia and her friend Olga were splashing in a plastic pool, and Petya the Paragon was laboriously running a rusty manual lawn mower over the prized patch of emerald Canadian grass Ilya had planted the year before.

It was all such a slog. I wondered why they went to all the trouble. They were such nice people, and they worked so hard, and I wished I could wave a magic wand and make it all instantly perfect for them with hammocks, iced drinks, and shade.

I let my imagination linger there a minute, and suddenly, in my mind, Martha Stewart drove up the unpaved road in a yellow Hummer to the strains of *The Magnificent Seven* theme, equipped with the mother of all staple guns, rolls of screening, monochrome linen napkins in subtle taupe tones, waterproof cushion covers, tasteful and comfortable garden furniture, and a large Weber gas grill. In the passenger seat sat celebrity guest blogger and grillmaster Emeril Lagasse, clad in immaculate chef's whites, who would gather up the boys and teach them to brine. Martha would magic up peonies and shade, gravel walks, and an indoor bathroom . . . possibly with potpourri. She would replace the karaoke machine with tasteful storm lanterns. She would banish (to next door, no doubt) all of the moldy furniture the Potapovs' friends and relations had gifted them because it no longer worked in their house, regardless of the fact that it totally didn't work in the dacha. Martha would plug an ice machine into the outlet formerly reserved for the eucalyptus oil infuser and thereby solve the tepid wine issue with ice and a cooler tastefully encased in a teak bench. She'd introduce seasonal side dishes like quinoa and minted cucumbers. Martha would keep Sveta so busy spray-painting and harvesting the rosemary crop that Sveta would give up the cigarettes and the jigsaws. As for the *banya* . . . well, even Martha might not be able to completely banish the *banya*, but hey, even the Tatar Mongols had to give up eventually.

"Zhen-eef-eer?"

My reverie was interrupted by Sveta urgently calling my name. I scurried downstairs, banishing my sanitized vision of the Martha-ized dacha. Who was I to tell the Potapovs how they should live? I scolded myself silently. It was time to get with the program—these were my friends, my good friends who would do anything for me. They'd never not come if I needed them. Suck it up, I told myself sternly. If Svetlana needed me, I'd never not come either.

It seemed that she did need me.

"Have you ever been to the Vatican?" she asked desperately.

"Sure. Sure I have," I said, confused.

"Thank god," said Sveta, grabbing my arm. "I need your help."

In the excitement of the previous evening, it seemed the box top of the ten-thousand-piece jigsaw puzzle depicting the Sistine Chapel with the Sibyls and *The Last Judgment* had somehow ended up in the *mangal* and been burned to a crisp. Sveta was incandescent with rage, hurling abuse at poor Ilya, who hung his head in shame and silently re-counted the washers and screws in his toolbox. And those would be the only screws poor Ilya could count on for a very long time if I couldn't put Michelangelo's masterpiece back together again.

"Don't worry," I said, channeling my inner Martha Stewart. "I minored in art history. We'll have this sorted in no time." I beckoned to Xenia and Olya and put them to work sorting the terra-cotta pieces from the turquoise pieces. Sveta calmed down enough to piece together the iconic face of the Libyan Sibyl. We made good progress: as the sun broke through the clammy cloud cover, Sveta unearthed a bottle of South African Chardonnay from the back of the freezer that had reached a vaguely chilled state. She poured it into two tumblers, and it tasted like the nectar of the gods. HRH appeared to help Ilya finish his repairs, and as their hammers rang out, Petya dug a large hole in the garden into which Sveta lowered an iron cauldron with an Uzbek rice pilaf that I'm sure Martha would be more than happy to feature on her next picnic show. At sunset a gentle breeze cleared the air, and we sat up stargazing until late in the night, talking about the American election and Petya's upcoming trip to the United States. Ilya Potapov, finally forgiven for all his many transgressions, looked around with pride. HRH, his pores immaculately clean, eschewed the karaoke and sat next to me holding my hand, not making one Obama joke.

"Do you ever think about doing something else in the summer?" I asked Svetlana as we headed for bed.

"Not really," she said, surprised by the question. "Well, it's a lot of work, but nights like tonight make it all worth it, and I enjoy imagining what this might be like in twelve years. I have an idea to plant those really fluffy pink flowers . . . what are they called?"

"Peonies," I answered, concealing a smile.

CHAPTER 8

TSARINA
OF THE
ROAD

"I'D LIKE TO do a piece on LGBT issues in Russia," I said to the editor who oversaw the monthly column I wrote for an English-language paper.

"That's interesting, but possibly not right for this exact moment," she hedged. "And besides, you are doing so well as a humor columnist. LGBT doesn't seem very funny."

I wasn't shocked. Disappointed, but not shocked. I'd promised Jesus I'd try.

"Well, I was going to do it as a send-up," I countered. "Sort of talk about the potential revenue drain to travel agencies, good restaurants, and interior designers."

"Hmmm . . ." She pretended to consider it.

"And," I continued, in for a penny, in for a pound, "I thought I could talk about how if we drive the gay population from Russia, who will ever point out to the Russian hetero population how ghastly those pointy-toed, white snakeskin shoes are?"

"That's funny," she conceded. "But let's shelve it for the moment, okay? We're going for informative and entertaining but not controversial. What else you got?"

I had my Plan B to hand.

"Traffic jams?" I suggested.

"There you go," she said, with palpable relief.

The morning after Barack Obama was elected president for the first time, HRH carefully peeled the Obama '08 sticker off the back of our car.

"What do you think you're doing?" I whimpered. I was feeling slightly woozy from biting my nails all night long, a champagne breakfast, and the general sense of relief and elation.

"The election is over," said HRH. "Don't we take it off now?"

"Certainly not!" I said indignantly. "We keep it on as a badge of honor."

"It will be misunderstood," warned HRH.

"Not by me," I retorted.

"Well, it's too late now," said HRH with a certain amount of satisfaction as he crumpled up the sticky strips that were once my bright spot of color in the endless gray of Moscow gridlock.

"You realize, don't you, that we—or rather you—will never be able to look Emily and Charlotte in the face again?" I warned. HRH shrugged, unfazed.

Back home in the United States, my sister Grace and her family are everything Al Gore would have them be: they stride the green stride. My niece Emily, age seven, has been a committed vegetarian since birth for a number of moral reasons she'll be happy to outline for you. In detail. Charlotte, age five, who does sneak the occasional Chicken McNugget, is nevertheless a passionate advocate of recycling and can correctly sort the six different kinds of paper they bundle up in their blue bins each week. It would be impossible to keep up with them even if we lived next door, but living as we do in the brown capital of the galaxy, I don't even try. The green rules seem to change so quickly and so arbitrarily. No sooner do I kit HRH out with Nalgene sports bottles, in a sincere effort to cut down on our personal intake of plastic, than Emily chides me gently but firmly about the amount of energy it takes to make and manufacture Nalgene bottles. This apparently is far more harmful to the planet than just plowing through a case of Evian every week. On my last visit Charlotte helpfully suggested that the best thing I could do was to invest in stainless-steel bottles. I did, but HRH refuses for some reason to use them, saying they "will be misunderstood."

Needless to say, they drive a hybrid. A righteous and worthy Prius bearing all the appropriate liberal credentials: a faded Kerry-Edwards bumper sticker to the right, a swanky Obama '08 sticker to the left, and the one in the middle, which I truly covet: Come the Rapture, Can I Have Your Car?

"I'm just going to pull in here and fill the car up," said my brother-in-law Paul during our summer holiday in Massachusetts. "Do you mind?"

"What kind of car do you have in Moscow, Aunt Jennifer?" Charlotte piped up from her booster seat.

"A dark blue one, sweetie," I responded quickly.

"But it's a hybrid, right?" demanded the more strident Emily.

"Well," I said carefully, "it's British."

I know, I know, I shouldn't lie to children. Even to Emily, who, if you ask me (and no one ever, ever does), knows way too much about carbon emissions for a child of not yet eight.

"It's a Land Rover Discovery 3," said Velvet, who had reached the limit of her patience, uncomfortably squashed between Charlotte's booster seat and Emily's stainless-steel water bottle. "It's totally cool: it has air-conditioning, and it's huge, and there is, like, tons more space than this stupid car. And it has a white leather interior, which doesn't make me carsick, like yours does."

A profound silence ensued. I checked my nieces in the rearview mirror nervously. For once in her life Emily was struck dumb. Charlotte's eyes grew as big as saucers, as if she'd just encountered a real live Republican. Paul, who has a great sense of humor, studiously kept his eyes on the road to avoid bursting into laughter. I tried desperately to think of something that could possibly redeem me in Emily's and Charlotte's eyes. I took a deep breath, turned around, and smiled brightly.

"It does have an Obama '08 sticker on it," I offered up lamely.

HRH and I don't exactly agree on bumper decorations, but we do agree that our high, sturdy, safe, and powerful car is perfect for Moscow's challenging driving conditions. It can also go at a clip, though this is less of an issue in Moscow, where you almost never get a chance to do fast. The traffic is usually at a total standstill from dawn until midnight, Monday through Saturday. Still, as the Russians say, it's a sin to complain. At least sitting in traffic jams affords the increasingly rare opportunity to have HRH all to myself.

"Darling, shouldn't you pull over? There is an ambulance behind us," I said to HRH from the passenger seat as we inched down a packed Kutuzovsky Prospekt. Behind us wailed an insistent siren as an ambulance prodded and probed the traffic for an opening. No one appeared to be in any way inclined to make way for a medical emergency.

"I'm not moving over for some clowns on a beer run," said HRH. No Russian man will tolerate being told how to drive by anyone, let alone a girl. I thought his reaction was very cynical until the white and red ambulance came alongside us. HRH, as usual, was right: tucked behind the ambulance was a brand-new silver Lexus, and you could see that the ambulance had been hired to plow the traffic just like a snowplow clears a path in a blizzard. I reflected that it was sort of comforting to know that the outrageous number of ambulances you see in Moscow these days is not, after all, a sign of an imminent pandemic.

We crested a small hill that led down to a busy intersection, and HRH and I let out identical wails of frustration. Our side of the street was a solid block of cars, but a telltale swath of empty street stretched, as far as the eye could see, down the opposite side of Kutuzovsky Prospekt. In front of each line of backed-up traffic stood a stocky traffic policeman, legs apart, head held high, swinging his signature black-and-white-striped stick.

"Someone is on the move," HRH said. He eased the car into park and pulled out his mobile phone, determined not to waste time during the inevitable delay created whenever one of Russia's ruling elite moves from A to B. For about twenty minutes, all traffic in the vicinity sat still until the motorcade of sedans and SUV chase cars finally sped by, flashes of shiny black going so fast they seemed blurred.

"I have to pee, darling," I whispered. "Badly."

HRH responded with a Slavic shrug, which enraged me. The Slavic shrug is a three-second gesture (blink and you'll miss it): shoulders rise toward the ears and forward toward the nose, arms flex out akimbo, four fingers curl into the palms of both hands with thumbs flexed away from the knuckles, and the head shakes back and forth. A slight bounce on the balls of the feet adds emphasis. Only a Russian can do it. Tiny gesture; speaks volumes. Since we have nothing like it in English, the translation is rough: "Well, don't look at me—it's not my fault, and it isn't my responsibility. I'm not touching this one. I didn't cause this problem, so I don't see why I should have to make any kind of effort to help you solve it . . . and in general, are you looking for someone to blame? Well, the devil take it, blame X over there. Of course he's responsible! But it isn't much good blaming him either, because he will tell you that this is the way it has always been and how it will always be."

And now here was HRH employing it maddeningly to indicate that there is nothing he can do about my urgent need for a bathroom.

"Don't you Slavic shrug me!" I cried. He smiled indulgently and continued to bark orders into his mobile phone.

I propped my elbow on the window, crossed my legs tighter, and tried to ignore my straining bladder. I gazed out into Moscow's immovable traffic, reflecting that I've spent far too much of my life sitting in it.

When I worked for the The Firm, my commute by car was anywhere from twenty minutes to two hours. Thank god for audiobooks! One month I listened to an entire unabridged reading of Gibbon's *Decline and Fall of the Roman Empire,* all sixty-three hours of it! This worked out to a weekday average of three hours in the car, and all for a round-trip journey of nine miles per day.

Some driving days are worse than others. Tuesdays, for example, I try to limit my travel to destinations I can reach on foot because it is solid gridlock, all day long. Each season of the year also has its own driving challenges. I never complain when the temperature dips down below minus-thirty degrees Celsius— the roads are deserted, since not every car can start when it's that cold. (Do we think the Prius would?) In general, winter is better because, as a Russian would say, "the teakettles have put their snowdrops away." This means that the less-experienced drivers (the teakettles), who own cars that don't do well in the ice and snow (the snowdrops), put them away for the winter. Come the summertime, however, the roads are absolutely impassible from 4:00 p.m. to midnight on Fridays and Mondays as all the lunatics perform their biweekly crawl out to their dachas.

Driving in Russia is traditionally a boy's bailiwick, and you can understand why. Driving really is the ideal outlet for the Russian alpha male to channel his own inner Peter the Great. The disturbing fusion of alpha-male Russians with way too much horsepower turns driving into a primeval contact sport in Moscow, with its own very specific playbook.

Woe betide the neophyte who ignores the unwritten highway hierarchy! Brand and size rule Russia's roads. By universal unspoken agreement, a Mercedes enjoys the inherent moral right to rudely cut off a Ford or a Skoda which, in turn, is entitled to nose into an adjacent lane, without the hint of a blinker, and cut off a box-shaped Russian-made Lada. The poor Lada driver asserts his dominance over cars with license plates that don't sport the enviable 77 code for Moscow. How did I absorb this information? I have no idea, but I know it is so. My ozone-slashing Land Rover Discovery beats a Volvo SUV or Subaru Forester, but I always deferentially cede the road to a BMW stretch sedan or Porsche Cayenne.

The Hummer will never go out of fashion in Russia.

Some drivers are more equal than others. We are all supposed to get out of the way of anyone sporting a blue siren on the top of their vehicle. This siren, called a *meegalka*, emits a noise I've never heard anywhere else but Russia. I've thought long and hard about how to describe this sound, and the best I can come up with is a nuclear submarine with a bad sinus infection: *mbuhooooooooiiiiiigggggghhhhhhhh*. It's the fanfare for an uncommon hegemony. In total gridlock, the elite fire up the *meegalka* and attempt to forge a path through solid blocks of cars. If in a greater hurry than usual, or if the *meegalka* fails to dislodge total gridlock, the privileged ease their way onto the double yellow line. This, the theory goes, separates northbound and southbound traffic. As if! Into this too-narrow channel they switch on the sinus infection and *mbuhooooooooiiiiiigggggghhhhhhhh!*—their German car speeds away at 250 kilometers per hour.

It used to be that any tin-pot minigarch wannabe with five thousand US dollars and an ego the size of Kazakhstan could bribe his way to a blue light, but times seem to be changing. The current Kremlin crowd places an emphasis on quality, rather than quantity, when doling out these perks. So today, in theory, you must be one of the "Ps" (president, prime minister, or patriarch) to get the blue light and the nuclear submarine sinus infection. In reality, there are a lot of blue lights still out there throwing their weight around, but Moscow drivers have started to fight back by affixing light-blue children's sand buckets to the tops of their cars and dash cams to their windshields. These modern-day crusaders use social media and YouTube to track and document the abuse of power on the Moscow roads. They haven't gotten much done, but they make everyone smile, and that's rare enough in a Moscow traffic jam.

No one smiles in a Moscow traffic jam when they spot a traffic policeman, a *gaishnik* (plural *gaishniki*), standing at an intersection, arms casually folded, propped up against a telephone pole. He watches the traffic snarl up with a profoundly disinterested expression as he enjoys a smoke, hawks and spits, or indulges in an unhurried chat on the phone. Christ, you think, that's my tax rubles at work. The *gaishnik* will leap to action quickly enough, however, if the call comes through that someone is "on the move." He straightens his spine, hurls his half-smoked cigarette into an oncoming windshield, pockets his mobile, and wades bravely into the tangle of cars, blocking off all access at the intersection by bravely taking up a defensive stance in the middle of the five lanes: legs spread, hands on hips, ready to salute smartly as the motorcade whizzes by.

If corrupt minor officialdom has a face in Russia, it is the *gaishnik*. They all look alike: ruddy complexions, squinty-eyed, stocky build, and medium height, and they exude a combination of smug self-satisfaction and menacing demeanor. They aren't there to help, and it never occurs to anyone to ask them how to turn left on Alabianaya Street. *Gaishniki* wear dull, slate-gray uniforms and, in the winter, padded snow pants and heavy parkas with matching fur hats, thick gloves, and storm-trooper boots. In the summer they look slightly less menacing in their military tunics and peaked police caps. They are always instantly recognizable by their emblematic *pozhaluysta* (please) sticks—as in "please pull over." It's meant to be facetious. *Pozhaluysta* sticks are twenty inches long, painted in white and black stripes, and hang from a well-worn leather strap. At the *gaishnik* academy, I'm guessing, the mandatory curriculum includes complicated majorette-type twirling routines with the sticks. They really are very accomplished at these intricate swings, twirls, and twists, since *gaishniki* don't lack for practice: they spend most of the day in training for the national *gaishnik* semiannual baton-twirling jamboree. *Pozhaluysta* sticks are meant to direct traffic, but the true purpose is to act like one massive index finger. A *gaishnik* seeks out his victim—a hapless transgressor of some obscure traffic rule—swings his *pozhaluysta* stick up, executes a quick flip, and then plunges it down like a dagger right in the direction of your windshield. He then swings it around 180 degrees and snaps his wrist adroitly to point to the side of the road, motion-

★

ing you to pull out of traffic and prepare for battle.

I'm a pretty careful and defensive driver, so this does not happen to me as often as it happens to, for example, Joe Kelly, who is pulled over two or three times a week. When it happens to me, my heart plummets to my accelerator foot, and as I roll down the window of my expensive, planet-punishing SUV with the Obama '08 sticker, it does not ever occur to me that I can get off without a fine. This is why I keep a stash of crisp thousand-ruble notes hidden between the pages of my copy of *Rules of Automotive Conduct of the Russian Federation* in the glove compartment.

The *gaishnik* runs through his compulsory polite routine. He makes a curt salute, then rattles off his name and rank at lightning speed in a tone that doesn't make you confident that he sees himself as a servant of the public. He asks for, and I hand over, the car's registration card, certificate of roadworthiness, HRH's power of attorney giving me permission to drive the car, my license, and what will earn me a further increase in whatever fee is surely heading my way: my blue American passport. Failure to produce any of these documents is not an option; it's not like trying to get out of gym by forgetting your shorts. Not having the full set of documents gets your car instantly confiscated, the assumption being that you must have stolen it. In Russia you are always presumed guilty until well past the point that you have been proven innocent. The *gaishnik* does a thorough investigation of the documents, checking them once, checking them twice, because there might well be a juicy little bonus stream if any of them is outdated, incorrectly stamped, or in any way defective. He takes even more time with the American passport because, let's be honest, he can't read anything but certificates of roadworthiness in Cyrillic. He flips through the pages to find something written in Cyrillic he can understand. Finally he looks up and greets me. "Citizen Dzhineefeyr?" I attempt a charming smile. Charm is Plan A. Tears are Plan B, and calling HRH is the strategy of last resort.

"Citizen Dzhineefeyr, you have broken law number blitherblather of the rules of automotive conduct of the Russian Federation." (This is said at lightning speed, and I catch nothing, making me unlikely to refer to my really-not-all-that-well-thumbed copy of *Rules of Automotive Conduct of the Russian Federation*.)

I've been with Joe when he gets in this kind of situation. At this point in the proceedings, Joe launches into a complicated and eloquent argument in his appalling Russian. Joe might actually exit the vehicle (which is enough to scare anyone who doesn't know him well) and start to reenact the scenario. Joe often tries (and fails) to prove that he's in the right. Men like HRH and Joe often exit the vehicle to discuss their transgressions with the *gaishniki*, sort of as a male-bonding experiment. Girls tend to stay in the car, and this suits me just fine.

"Oh, dear," I say. "How shall we proceed?"

Here's a confession: I've lived for two decades in an emerging market, and I still have no clue how to bribe. Joe might argue, haggle, or negotiate at this point, but I never do. The *gaishnik* pretends to be about to write me up a summons, so I pretend to be very frightened and ponder, out loud, what my husband will say when he finds out. Or I bite my lip and say I'm running late for picking my three children up at kindergarten, and could there possibly be a way to settle this thing quickly and simply? I think psychologists call this mirroring: sensing what the *gaishnik* wants and becoming it. I become a helpless female.

The *gaishnik*, in turn, makes a production of sighing deeply, glancing surreptitiously to the left and to the right, as if checking to see if a nonexistent senior officer is looking on, then tells me it is a massive exception, because he is an incredibly nice guy, but he'll let me streamline my penalty by paying him directly. He quotes an (outrageous) figure, which I pay promptly, using the crisp notes lying ready between the pages of *Rules of Automotive Conduct of the Russian Federation.*

They may be capable of reading only Cyrillic Sovietese, but the *gaishniki* are not stupid. They are incredibly resourceful and practical, constantly coming up with new and different ways to increase the bottom line. I learned not long ago that their latest stunt involves random Breathalyzer checks on motorists. If caught (and people who had not had a drink for seven years have been deemed "within the margin of error"), negotiation starts at five thousand US dollars. The many and varied stakeout sites all have one thing in common: each is directly opposite an ATM. The *gaishniki* don't yet have iPads with the credit card swipe device, but give them a year or so. They'll get there.

I wasn't always Tsarina of the Road. Once upon a time I was an inveterate cab rider, but I had to give it up. I feared imminent death or severe bodily harm either from bad road conditions or criminally minded taxi drivers. I felt as though I were constantly trapped in a vehicle whose certificate of roadworthiness had lapsed about two decades previously, driven by someone who was more at home on either a combine harvester or a Wii controller. What really drove me round the bend, however, was having that template conversation you have to have with every single goddamn cab driver in Moscow. I hit my Road to Damascus on the road to Leningrad one Tuesday night in February of 2003. The weather was wet, cold, and windy with a pulpy sleet that instantly hardened into glare ice on the sidewalks. I'd been shopping after work, and the handles of my three plastic bags of groceries dug sharply into one palm as I tried to hail a cab with the other.

Moscow isn't like New York or London. It isn't the kind of city where a highly regulated municipal organization ensures that a cab is never far away. There are some private cab companies in Moscow, but they cost a lot. You also have to phone them to come and then wait for them, which isn't always convenient. And you'd better know how to get where you are going, because the first thing the driver usually asks you is "Can you show me the way?"

Happily, however, in Moscow there is another option. To hail a cab, you stick your arm out at a right angle to your body (not up, but out) and waggle your hand slightly. This is an indication to any motorist on the road—not just a taxi driver but also any old Ivan in a Zhiguli—to pull up alongside you and offer to swap a ride for money. Visitors to Russia call these "gypsy cabs," which would outrage the Russian drivers if they knew. They don't want to be confused with the non-Slavic crowd.

Many ordinary motorists moonlight as gypsy cabs to supplement their income. Off-duty firemen have been known to do it, ambulance drivers do it, as do the full-time drivers of multinational companies in their company cars. Stick out your hand, and you just never know who will pull up. When they do, there is none of this sugarcoated "Where to, luv?" you get from London cabbies and certainly not the deferential Parisian "*Bonjour, madame!*" I'm not saying that a cheerful Russian driver with rosy cheeks and a twinkle in his eye, looking for all the world like Sam Gamgee before he set out for Mordor, won't ever pull up curbside on

Tverskaya Street and chirp "Where we off to, *krasavitsa*?" But, like, don't hold your breath.

The more likely scenario is the following: the driver pulls up alongside you, spraying you with about five gallons of Moscow street muck. You open the passenger door, often with a certain amount of tugging, and the driver barks, "Where to?" You respond in kind, with a matching air of irritation and a distinct wrinkle of your nose, implying that you could not be more inconvenienced by this exchange. Then you engage in a vigorous haggle. If you have a foreign accent, try to conceal it so that you don't have to take out a second mortgage to pay for your ride. While you are haggling, run through a quick visual spot check:

- Is the driver's Ossetian accomplice lurking in the backseat, poised to whisk you off to white slavery and the opium dens of North Omsk?

- Sniff the air. Can you stand the unique fusion of Eau de Not Bathed in This Calendar Year and Essence of Three Decades of Cigarette Smoke?

- Is the vehicle roadworthy? Does it have all the essential elements of a working car, including a gearbox and part of the steering wheel?

- Does the passenger door have a handle on the inside? No = automatic deal breaker.

- Is your driver, in fact, sober? Remember that cheap vodka is the most common form of windshield wiper fluid in Russia.

Go with your gut. If you don't like what you see, slam the door, stick your arm out again, and lather, rinse, and repeat until the conditions suit you. When they do, get in the passenger seat, not the backseat, of the car.

Don't let your guard down. There are other challenges on the horizon. Do not count on the driver being able to make change. Most gypsy cabbies claim to be operating on nothing smaller than a five-thousand-ruble note. Be supremely confident about how to reach your destination, ready to produce an atlas to back up your hypothesis. They don't care if you can navigate your way like a honing device through the confusing rabbit warren of streets behind the Ministry of Foreign Affairs; they don't want to hear it from a foreigner, or a woman, and definitely not from someone who combines both of these handicaps.

Riding the gypsies eventually becomes second nature, so much so that you may find yourself in the ludicrous position of trying to force open the passenger door of a New York City or London cab only to have the startled driver throw up his hands or pull a knife on you. This happened to me recently in Manhattan, but I was lucky. My driver that day was from Irkutsk and understood immediately what I was trying to do.

Careening around Moscow in gypsy cabs—particularly after dark—added a certain frisson of excitement to my life when I was in my twenties, but as I trudged through my thirties it got a little old. On the sleety, slushy Tuesday in question, I was reaching a tipping point as I gingerly climbed into a rust-encrusted Zhiguli that proceeded to cough, lurch, and sputter up Leningradski Prospekt. Each change of gear hurled me dangerously forward toward the cracked windshield. There was no seat belt. The driver peered at the road through three-inch-thick Russian national health glasses, chain-smoking unfiltered Russian cigarettes, as if he were being paid by the piece. The toxic fug, exacerbated by the heating fan going full blast, would normally be a deal breaker for me because I do like to be able to breathe during my taxi rides. In this particular case, however, more than enough air was circulating from below through a gaping hole in the battered chassis, which forced chilly blasts of air, and the petrol-infused wet filth from the Moscow streets, right up between my legs.

Physical discomfort is tolerable. The tedium of having exactly the same conversation with every single taxi driver in Moscow over a period of ten years is not.

Driver: Where are you from?
Me: America.
Driver: Ohhhhhhhhh . . . America.
Me: Yep.
Driver: You speak good Russian.

Me: Thank you.
Driver: Where is better—here or America?
Me: Here is certainly never dull.
Driver: I have a cousin who went to Chicago.
Me: You don't say.
Driver: He has a house with five bathrooms.
Me: Why don't you just drop me right here?

That evening clinched it. It was time to take control and get behind the wheel myself. There was a perfectly good car at home with luxury safety features that included a chassis running from the front of the car to the back in one uninterrupted panel. There was climate control and a CD player and, for a few months, the tattered remains of a Kerry-Edwards sticker, which HRH later removed because, of course, they lost. If I could learn to drive, I reasoned, my life expectancy would soar and my dry-cleaning bills would plummet. I'd be left alone with a good audiobook as I crawled through traffic, free at last from demurely declining to list all the reasons why America might, after all, have the slightest edge on Russia.

One small hurdle remained before I could become Tsarina of the Road. I had to learn to drive. Properly, that is. In Moscow. I knew how to operate a car, but in my late teens and early twenties I lived in New York City, where it costs more to keep a car than it does a baby. Then I went to work in the guide seat of a tour bus. I didn't have a lot of tenure behind the wheel. HRH produced a well-connected colonel who allowed me (and countless others, if the driving standards in Moscow are anything to go by) to get a Russian driver's license in exchange for a sealed envelope and a large bottle of expensive French cognac. Like so many other Moscow drivers, I had the document before I'd completely mastered the skill.

Moscow is not the optimal venue to perfect the automotive arts. In 1992 traffic was as volatile as the economy. Driver's licenses were bought and sold on street corners, used cars appeared from Western Europe under highly suspicious circumstances, and all the traffic lights sputtered like last year's Christmas tree lights. Cars were protected with huge steering wheel clamps, and they were stolen, despite these, if left unattended. Low-level criminals chased one another in creaky Ladas through streets pitted with potholes and devoid of yellow lane indicators. It wasn't the ideal time or place to perfect on-ramp mergers or parallel parking. I still can't parallel park.

HRH, on the other hand, had no hang-ups and can parallel park on a one-kopek coin (which is microscopically small). Unlike my high school in Connecticut, his military academy in Leningrad did not consider learning to drive optional. Sustained world domination, their educational theory ran, relied heavily on the ability to pilot many and varied vehicles. HRH learned to drive in a large Gazelle truck, after which almost anything handles like a Formula One race car.

You aren't supposed to learn to drive from a close relative or spouse, but HRH blew that theory right out of the water. So I forgive him when he forgets all three of our wedding anniversaries or refuses to wash the dishes, because teaching me to drive in Moscow turned him into Heroic Russian Husband. He sat next to me in the passenger seat until I could confidently merge out of our side street into oncoming traffic on Leningradski Prospekt, move five lanes to the right in the space of twenty feet, execute a tricky U-turn, and finally join the ranks of rush-hour commuters. He showed me how to overtake, swerve on that one-kopek piece, and brake hard if I needed to. He tried to teach me to parallel park. We'll get there. Someday. He doled out expert advice:

"A man who wears a hat inside a car is a teakettle," he informed me. "Just give him a wide berth."

"Ignore that asshole in the BMW behind you—no, it's his problem if you are going too slowly, not yours."

"Stay in the middle lane here and the *gaishnik* won't see you."

"Don't worry about the gas station. That's not a job for women."

The day came when he handed me a travel mug of coffee and the keys and waved me off for my first solo crawl down Leningradski Prospekt.

The power! The liberation! It felt amazing. For the first time, I felt as if I could conquer Moscow! Like Napoleon!

Napoleon, of course, had the good sense to do his conquering in a Moscow abandoned by all the Muscovites and all of their vehicles. No sooner did I master the ability to pilot my vehicle than it was driven home to me that this was a skill set that could only ever be practiced between 6:00 and 9:00 a.m. on Sunday mornings. I could join the gridlock for as long as the gas held out, but there was simply no place to park, at all, anywhere.

Cars, bumper to bumper, lined streets that should have been easy two-way thoroughfares but became the locale for numerous games of chicken, or "stand down, my car is bigger than yours," with fellow motorists, many of whom were not in game-playing moods. On some streets a second line of cars was parked in front of the real parking spaces, effectively blocking the first row. Cars were shoved into spaces too small for them, and some cars were deliberately parked horizontally across two vertical lines. In the winter there were even fewer parking spaces to be had; large mounds of dirty gray snow took up most of them. There were cars on the sidewalks and cars parked in playgrounds, as well as cars perched on pedestals outside casinos.

The obvious parking spaces, the ones indicated by painted lines at the side of wide streets, were all taken up all the time or zealously guarded by representatives of a paramilitary group of fake law enforcement types with rubber pylons who would sell you a spot for a small fortune. My best friend during this time was a charming parking attendant at an upscale supermarket called The Alphabet of Taste, whom I shamelessly overtipped on a highly regular basis so that he would not only let me drive up onto the sidewalk and park, but would also very gallantly load my groceries as well as help me back out.

The worst situation, however, was in our own courtyard, where parking spaces supposedly designated for homeowners were being gradually illegally annexed by an annoying tribe of local policemen. Their beat was the Moscow Metro, which meant they were about as low on the food chain as cops can get, but their precinct was housed in the basement of our building, so we were stuck with them.

I couldn't see that the Metro cops ever accomplished much law enforcement. They seemed to spend all of their time lining up—all forty of them—to be inspected by their superior officer right there in our parking lot. This usually coincided with my needing to move my vehicle through the very space they occupied. When they weren't being inspected or checking out the slot-machine kiosks on our block, they kept very busy kicking the tires of each other's new cars. One of those clowns had a new Ford or Mazda every week, which makes me think that they were taking more than just a casual interest in those thriving slot-machine kiosks.

We homeowners left for work and returned to find that the Fords and Mazdas occupied every single space. I'd wheel into the courtyard, panting for a glass of Chardonnay, eager to catch the beginning of *EastEnders,* and there would be no place to park at all. Moscow Metro's finest would all be standing around smoking, spitting, and scratching their crotches the way Russian men without a viable to-do list do, primed for the main event of the evening: watching the foreign chick in the Discovery attempt to back into a tight parking spot without running one of them over. Sometimes I would start backing in, get halfway there, and then get stuck. They loved this. They would surround my Land Rover and smoke, spit, scratch, and laugh. More than once I burst into tears, cradled my head in my arms on the steering wheel, and just howled. The cautious Tadzhik janitors and groundskeepers threw me the occasional sympathetic glance of solidarity, but they were not going to risk the ire of the crotch-scratching uniformed Russians by coming to my assistance. It was a miserable situation.

I know what you're thinking. Public transportation: it's cheap, efficient, eco-friendly, and free of parking hassles, the *gaishniki,* and four-hour traffic jams. Yes, Moscow does boast one of the most extensive and efficient metro systems in the world, and I do nip on to it if I need to get somewhere fast and it's a straight shot. I also like that you can drink—a benefit many of the Metro's five million daily passengers clearly also appreciate. And unlike HRH, I do know how much it costs. HRH hasn't ridden the Metro since the last century. He feels that our life should be all about why we don't have to take the Metro. HRH counters the fast-cheap-efficient argument with the crowded-boring-overheated excuse, and I have to admit that there is a pungency to the air down there that I could do without. The Metro is a whole lot of Russia right in your face, and a little of that can go a long way.

HRH believes in the chauffeur-driven car.

If you aspire to be Someone in Moscow in business or government, eventually you have to employ a driver. If you aspire to be Someone Special, then you must have more than one driver. Working in shifts, your team of drivers ensures that there is a sedan purring gently outside wherever you are at any time of the night or day. During the first-ever national road safety week, the chief *gaishnik* was filmed driving his own car around Moscow with the Russian Tom Brokaw. HRH and I were literally rolling on the floor at the idea that this über-apparatchik (right out of central casting) had even touched a steering wheel in the last two decades. So likely.

When you feel you are approaching the state of being Someone Very Special Indeed (and remember that the Russian male ego stretches from Kaliningrad to Vladivostok), you are obliged to move around in a convoy: you and your telephone in the roomy backseat of your Mercedes stretch sedan with a Toyota Land Cruiser chase car behind you, its front bumper touching your back bumper. Color of the vehicles is mandatory: black. Number of bodyguards: flexible.

HRH is currently at sort of a halfway point between being Someone and Someone Special, so thankfully we don't have all of the hassle of a chase car, though I suspect HRH secretly yearns for a *meegalka*. We do now have his and hers drivers, which everyone we know outside Russia thinks is very glamorous. HRH has Vitaly, who shaves daily and wears a tie. He drives HRH around in the You Can Tell I'm on the Verge of Becoming Someone Very Special Indeed silver stretch sedan (the only car in the family fleet that has never sported an Obama '08 or Obama-Biden 2012 sticker and never will). Then there's Tolya the Driver, who doesn't always shave every day and wears Polartec and nylon. Tolya is basically in charge of driving Velvet from school to sports and back home. I sometimes co-opt him to drive me places where I'm sure I won't be able to park or if I have to buy a ton of stuff at IKEA or the cash-and-carry. In addition to ferrying around the females, Tolya is also in charge of being the man about the house, handling all of the guy stuff that men who ride around in You Can Tell I'm on the Verge of Becoming Someone Very Special Indeed silver stretch sedans are too busy to take care of. It's a question of "from each according to his ability, to each according to her needs" in our family, and a typical weekly to-do list for Tolya could look like this:

✳

- Pick up dry cleaning

- Look at the broken DVD player in a certain way that always makes it work again

- Schedule, confirm, wait for, and supervise repairs to stove, dishwasher, and refrigerator

- Reverse climate-challenging Land Rover into the (woefully too small) underground garage space to face out, ensuring that I don't back out and crash into our menacing neighbor's new Bentley

- Disassemble and reassemble (correctly this time) Tancy's IKEA bookcase, incorrectly assembled by Joe and Holt

- Bribe the *gaishniki* to fake an accident report to account for the dent I put in the Land Rover when I tried—and failed—to get into the (woefully too small) underground garage parking space

- Take me to any of my three book-club evenings, wait around much longer than the 10:45 p.m. departure time, and then bring me home

- Buy wine

The buying wine thing is fairly recent. Tolya the Driver was not, let's put it this way, brought up taking part in an annual vendange. He doesn't lie awake at night pondering the subtle differences between Pinot Noir and Shiraz. Until recently. Left to himself, his approach to wine would have been best described as cheaper equals better. The dilemma was this: good wine for cut-rate prices involves a schlep out to the cash-and-carry on the outskirts of Moscow, and in gridlock this can often be an all-day event. The wine selection there is rather like the clothes selection at T.J.Maxx—you just never know what you'll find. Tolya wasn't going to pounce on the case of hard-to-get Lindeman's Bin 65 or think, "*Bozhe moi,* that new Orvieto looks like a steal!" and snap up five bottles.

But you have to be creative and resourceful in Russia, like the *gaishniki*. So I steamed the labels off my favorite bottles and then glued them into a student's exercise book. Thus was born the Label Book, which I intend to patent in expat communities across the BRICs and retire on the proceeds. To help Tolya, I added Russian footnotes to each, providing helpful hints like "white" or "red," as well as geographic indications such as "Spain" or "Australia." Armed with these clues, Tolya can now accurately locate the appropriate section in the cash-and-carry and keep the wine flowing at our house. It's freed me up to no end, and I have high hopes for Tolya, who called me from the store last week to announce that, although they were all out of our favorite cheap and cheerful South African Sauvignon Blanc, he thought there was a suitable substitute to be had in the similarly priced New Zealand Chenin Blanc, and what did I think?

I think teach a man to fish, and you feed him for life. It only remains for me to persuade HRH to find three like-minded fellow minigarchs to form a car pool, and we will all be able to face Emily and Charlotte at Christmas with a clear conscience.

CHAPTER 9

IN SICKNESS
AND IN
HEALTH

"I'M DYING," LUCY rasped over the telephone.

"Well, you're in luck," I said. "I've just made a fresh batch of chicken noodle soup. What else do you need?"

"Something to watch?"

"*West Wing?*"

"I don't have the energy for *West Wing*," Lucy croaked. "I tell you, I'm dying."

She certainly looked weak and pasty when I arrived at her apartment an hour later laden with plastic containers of chicken soup, a bag of oranges, lemons, a bottle of whisky, a head of garlic, a jar of honey, and a big bottle of jealously hoarded Advil. I took in the unpacked suitcase, the abandoned laptop, and the sink full of unwashed dishes and put the clues together.

"You look like hell," I said bluntly. "What happened, did you catch something on your last trip . . . you don't have leprosy, do you?"

"Ha-ha," Lucy managed to say, as she sneezed into a soggy Kleenex. "No, I think I picked this up at the office. Of course the staff says I got it because I had the window open."

"They would," I said shortly. "Go take a hot shower, Lucy. You'll feel much better if you do. Then you can have some soup and orange juice. I've brought *Big Love* over. That should see you through this thing."

While she showered I changed the sheets, and heedless of the universal belief in Russia that breezes cause cancer, I opened the windows in the bedroom wide to clear the stale air. I warmed the soup on the stove, then sliced cloves of garlic into thin slivers and floated them on the surface. I made some fresh orange juice, sorted her laundry, put a load in, and washed the dishes. I got Lucy into a clean nightgown, into bed, and brought her some soup and toast on a tray.

"Do you want some ice?" I asked, as I poured her a glass of juice.

"I do, but don't tell anyone; you'll be done for manslaughter."

"Well, you're already dying," I said, plopping ice cubes into her juice.

"You are an angel," she murmured, sipping the juice. "How do you do it?"

"Comes with the instructions in the mom kit," I said, handing her two Advil. She washed them down with orange juice.

"I've brought you some honey and whisky. I'll make you a hot toddy; then you can sleep. You'll live, Lucy." She closed her eyes and sank back against the pillows.

"Thank you," she whispered.

Lucy was an ideal patient, certainly a much easier one than HRH, whose health issues have more than once brought us to the brink of divorce.

"My kidneys caught a cold again," HRH announced the previous winter.

I didn't laugh. Out loud, that is. "Catching a cold" is standard phrasing in Russia to describe any inflammation, infection, or minor ache and pain. Your neck can catch a cold. Your toe. And, it seems, your kidneys.

For a few years now, HRH has had some kidney issues. They caused him a lot of discomfort and took up an inordinate amount of my time. Apart from trying to convince him to buy comprehensive international medical insurance, I researched preventive measures on the Internet. I became, I suppose, a bit pedantic about it, and HRH didn't like being told to stop drinking mineral water and taking a sauna every day: both were flagged as bad for the condition in general. HRH, who has no medical training and is afraid of the sight of blood, went all alpha-male Russian and started to grandstand. He informed me in an annoying know-it-all voice that the mineral water and sauna were essential to purging his system of impurities.

"It says on Webmed.com that you should be drinking a lot more plain filtered water than you are," I suggested.

"I'm drinking cranberry juice," he said.

"Yes, but it says here that cranberry juice is one of the things that will make things worse. You are supposed to drink grapefruit juice."

"I don't like grapefruit juice."

"Well, okay, but what you should really be cutting out completely is beer. I can't help seeing a connection between your latest flare-up and that three-day beer festival in Sochi," I suggested nonchalantly.

He gave me A Look.

"Well, I give up," I said, as I had said a million times before.

Nowhere are the cultural gaps between Russians and Westerners wider than in attitudes toward sickness and health. A Grand Canyon of misunderstanding yawns between our differing ideas about health, preventive measures, treatment, and cures. Westerners find Russian attitudes outdated and superstitious; Russians find Westerners haphazard and wont to take really shocking risks.

Like so many other things, the Russian health-care system has a feast or famine theme to it. Russia is a country that pioneered laser eye surgery but still uses jam where Western physicians would prescribe penicillin. You can get a first-rate boob job in Moscow, but blood pressure medication is usually sold out. I still don't understand where they sell the vitamins, if indeed they sell them at all, which I am beginning to doubt. Health, however, is a huge big deal in Russia. Each birthday, I spend the entire day on the phone with earnest Russian well-wishers who insist on bestowing on me their fervent and sincere enjoinments for my good health in the coming year: "First, I wish you good health," they rattle off, "because health is the most important thing!" For some reason, I find this very embarrassing. I never know how to respond. It's like that thing at Orthodox Easter when Russians hail me with the traditional greeting "Christ is risen!" I feel deeply foolish when I let rip with the appropriate response: "He is risen indeed!"

Every foreigner knows the Russian toast "*Nazdarovya!*" This literally means "to your health." Spend just a few weeks in Russia and you begin to understand why. Ill health lurks around every corner in Russia, and the causes are many and manifest. I don't understand half of what they are talking about, so I just tune out and start to make a mental grocery list whenever a Russian starts to talk about being sick. I've never been able to sort out the incomprehensible vocabulary, and I've never been much good at matching the illnesses Russians describe to the ones that exist in the rest of the known world.

I never seem able to register the appropriate response. Young, fairly hale and hearty Russians used to shock the hell out of me when they announced they had "angina" and yet seemed not at all nervous about a major gateway symptom to coronary heart disease. Someone finally explained that what the Russians call "ahn-GEE-nah" actually means strep throat. So I cleared that up, but there are still a gazillion illnesses in Russia that don't seem to exist elsewhere. For example, can you make head or tail of this conversation overheard in an elevator?

Russian Middle-Aged Woman 1: "My heart hurts!" [That's right: "heart," not "head."]

Russian Middle-Aged Woman 2: "It's the weather. It is pressing."

Russian Middle-Aged Woman 1: "Yes, it's the pressure."

The pressure thing eludes me completely, though it seems to just shellac my cleaning lady, Raisa, two days out of five each week—more in the shoulder seasons of spring and autumn. It could be the barometric pressure, which would explain why they always mention it on the weather report. It might also have something to do with blood pressure. There are times when I am assured it is neither; it's just . . . well, it's just the pressure. But is the pressure high or low? A conversation often heard in a workplace canteen:

Katya: "My head hurts so much!"

Anya (nodding in agreement): "The pressure is very low."

Galina (with sympathy): "It's the magnetic field."

The magnetic field is my red line. I will never, ever understand the magnetic field. It must exist on some level, because the weather people spend a lot of the forecast on it. Of course, Russia does have a fairly impressive track record of pulling the wool over its own national eyes, but why invent a magnetic field that causes headaches? This seems a bit much even for them. What's it in aid of? Not to increase productivity, that's for sure. I tell

Russians, "We don't have magnetic fields in America," and their reaction is as though I've just suggested we don't have Coca-Cola. This is very unfair of the Russians, really, since I long ago accepted that they don't have cholesterol in Russia. Joe Kelly's girlfriend, Tanya, who is no fool, also told me that they don't have ADD or Asperger's syndrome in Russia.

"You mean you don't diagnose or treat them," I qualified.

"No," she said in her scariest no-nonsense voice, "we don't have such illnesses in Russia."

So there you go.

Right up there with the pressure are drafts and breezes. These do exist. They are caused by opening a window of a house or, say, a car and allowing a cleansing, refreshing breeze to flow into the invariably stuffy hothouse fug that is the interior climate in Russia. It's what I tried to create by opening the windows in Lucy's stale, fuggy bedroom, and I'm guessing it is what she tried to do in her stuffy office before the toxic fresh air felled her with the flu. As soon as you create a draft, any Russian in the vicinity will yelp and dive out of the path of terminal illness. This is one of those things that will forever divide Russians from Westerners.

On a random day in early September the radiators begin to sputter, hiss, and clank all over Russia as the central heating is switched on from one very evil central command center regardless of the relatively mild temperatures outside. Come the moment, on they go, from Kaliningrad to Khabarovsk: *putt . . . sputtt . . . hisssss . . . clank.* Full throttle for the next eight months. In two days the apartment is stifling. Foreigners who live in Russia don't put their summer clothes away in September—they put them front and center in the closet, as apartments and offices become saunas. We break out the La Prairie as our skin begins to pucker. We put the cotton sheets on our beds and sleep with fans oscillating. We loathe Russian central heating.

"Open the window!" I hear you cry. We do! We do! The few Russians who actually believe in climate change and global warming lay the blame for it firmly at the feet of expats who leave their windows wide open throughout the long Russian winters. HRH and Raisa refuse to put up with that kind of death wish. They shut the windows with moral fortitude whenever they find them open.

"Just turn down the radiator!" is another naive suggestion.

For so many years I tried, with various implements of destruction, including the heel of a boot, a hammer, and a hardback copy of *Das Kapital,* all to no avail. The knobs, into which the German prisoners of war who built the house clearly poured all of their resentment, remained unyielding. Finally we had the grim Nazi radiators replaced with flashier perestroika models from Yugoslavia. They had shiny red knobs that . . . moved.

HRH warned me. He made it clear to me that, though the radiators were new, the heating system was not. Our Soviet heating, he explained, remained something I had no business tinkering with. He hinted at grave consequences, then set off for work. I tried to ignore them, but those shiny red knobs kept calling me from across the steamy room. I rationalized that no one had died and made HRH executive producer of *This Old House.* So I went through the apartment and turned all the shiny red knobs to zero.

The results, while they lasted, were amazing. It was cool in the apartment. It was like the sweet relief of a desert night after the sun has gone down or the rush of fresh air when you step out of a transatlantic flight onto the jetway of your destination. I put the summer clothes away and brought out the flannel sheets. I issued a stern admonishment to Velvet—"Get something on your feet!"—a constant refrain in my childhood, one seldom ever heard in hers. Wild fantasies bubbled into my consciousness, most of them culinary: dinner parties in February that didn't feature gazpacho, iced gin and tonics, and sorbet.

The Big Chill lasted about a week. Then one mid-morning, as I relaxed with a neon-blue seaweed mask slathered an inch thick on my face, it ended abruptly and unpleasantly. One thing I've noticed about Russia is that the minute you get into this kind of comfort zone, something invariably comes along to ruin it. That day, persistent and impatient rings at the doorbell shattered my peace. Another thing I've learned in Russia is that nothing good ever comes from unexpected rings at the doorbell or telephone. So of course I ignored them. The rings abated only to be replaced, about forty minutes later, by loud thumps on the door and shouts to open up for the ZHEK, the custodians of the building complex.

Another thing I've learned in Russia? When you need the ZHEK, they are always and ever on a lunch break. But here they were: three short, stocky men, easily recognizable as the guys who hung around the courtyard, who spat, smoked, shouted into mobile phones, and watched the Tadzhiks do all the heavy lifting.

They thrust official-looking permits up to the peephole.

"Open up, woman," they ordered. That's how they talk all the time.

"I'm not really dressed for it," I responded through the metal door.

"Woman, there is a problem with your heating. We need to see your radiator."

"The radiator is fine," I assured them. "It works beautifully."

"Woman, it is not fine. Your neighbors are complaining. Open the door or we will return with the police."

These way-down-the-totem-pole officials are, of course, deeply capable of bringing the police around. They love to flex a bit of official muscle and play a minor, if not responsible, part in a local drama, and they get huge bonus points for doing it to a foreigner. The Russian police have ways—to say nothing of the authority—to break the door down. So I opened up, resplendent in my mask. The ZHEK seemed completely unfazed by my neon-blue face.

"You are not allowed to turn off your radiator," said one.

"But it is so hot in here," I protested.

"That makes no difference," he said, and then made an expansive gesture toward the ceiling. "You have turned off the heat for the entire building. Your neighbors have complained to the police, and it will go very badly for you if you turn the radiator off again."

"But how can I make it cooler here?" I pleaded. "You must be able to do something!"

They looked at one another and sighed deeply.

"This isn't Paris, you know," the other guy finally said.

And on that, at least, we could all agree.

When we moved to our new apartment, HRH agreed to a heating system we could regulate. A guy came to install it, and I asked him to set a steady year-round temperature of nineteen degrees Celsius (sixty-six degrees Fahrenheit). When I was a child growing up in a series of drafty New England houses, this temperature was considered a wild extravagance, permissible only when my octogenarian grandmother was visiting from below the Mason-Dixon line. The Russian guy looked at me as if I had asked for a syringe of bubonic plague.

I repeated my question, enunciating the numbers as clearly as I could: "Nineteen. One-nine. Comes after eighteen? Precedes twenty." He squinted at me.

"In Celsius?" he asked after a moment.

"Yes," I said firmly.

The workman backed away slowly and then asked Tolya the Driver (who supervises this kind of visit from service providers for just this reason) to call the "master of the house" to check that he really wanted it That Cold. Turns out that if you want it colder than the standard twenty-three degrees Celsius, you have to sign additional paperwork, including a general indemnity signed by the master of the house. They eventually set the thermostat at twenty degrees and warned us that it was not going to be their fault if we fell fatally ill.

Once you do fall ill in Russia, either from the igloolike conditions in your bedroom or the breezes or the magnetic fields, you have a number of options for your treatment. You have to hand it to them: Russians are super inventive. Their first line of defense against illness is to stay at home and employ the folk remedies handed down to them by their peasant grandmothers. These admirable women, operating in conditions of war, famine, and revolution, understandably used what they had on hand, and with impressive success. Many of these remedies, like mustard plasters, do work, as does vodka, used both topically and internally. They are disgusting, but they work. So does vodka, which was first brought to Russia by the Poles as a medicament. I personally don't care to have my three-year-old smell like the inside of Kazansky railway station, but vodka does bring a fever down if rubbed on the stomach and limbs. Taken with a heaping tablespoon of sea salt, vodka is also the cure for both diarrhea and constipation. Vodka, needless to say, is usually on hand in the average Russian household.

"How are you feeling?" I asked Lucy four days into her breeze-related illness. "Do you need anything?"

"Much better," she said. "Lyudmila Petrovna, the cook at our office canteen, sent me some jam. I've been mainlining that."

"You could cut the calories and just buy some soluble

vitamin C tablets. Same effect," I sniffed.

"Jam tastes better."

"Watch out, Lucy, you're going native."

"When in Rome," she croaked.

"I'll go put the kettle on," I said. "But you've given me a great idea for a new column."

"About what?" asked Lucy.

"Asinine Russian medical folklore," I said pointedly.

When a Russian falls sick, he usually puts on the kettle for tea, then reaches for jam, preferably homemade by someone over the age of forty-five at a dacha. He spoons the jam directly into his mouth and takes sips of the tea. And that's it. The jam makes sense. In the nineteenth century, jam and preserves were the only reliable sources of vitamin C during the long Russian winters. The older generation still regards jam as far more reliable than the soluble tablets available in just about every pharmacy.

Chicken soup, oddly enough, is not in the vanguard of the remedy lineup. Russian chicken soup leaves a lot to be desired: greasy stock with stodgy, halfhearted noodles floating apologetically around. Of course, most of the chicken-soup experts were persuaded to leave Russia en masse around 1905, and again in the 1970s, so it is hardly surprising that this is a lost art. I always suggest it when HRH has a cold, and he always looks at me with blank incomprehension.

The companion to chicken soup in my childhood was iced ginger ale, but I've stopped even mentioning this as an option for fear my mother-in-law will swoop over from Lviv like an avenging angel and have me arrested for attempted murder. Russians consider ice on a par with arsenic in the bad-for-you category. A Russian visitor once refused to eat oysters not because he didn't love them but because they were served on a bed of ice. I kid you not. It was one of those moments when it was hard to remain a gracious hostess. I'd have more respect for the ice-as-toxin concept as a serious proposition if Russians didn't consume ice cream on the street in February.

Seeking professional medical advice—such as that dispensed by someone who has had medical training—is never immediately considered. Why? The jam-tea-vodka trinity, preferably administered by a mother or grandmother, can usually be relied upon to solve the problem. HRH tried it for three days but found no immediate relief for his kidneys.

"Petrovna!" he bellowed. "This is not funny. I am in a lot of pain."

"Go to the doctor, sweetheart," I begged him. "The doctor will know what to do. This is just beyond me and the tea. You go see the doctor. I'm telling you, they have these lasers that just zap that thing into a million pieces."

HRH looked almost ready to agree.

"You can go to the International Medical Centre," I continued patiently. "It's around the corner . . . appointments available after work. I went to a really nice urologist last year—Dr. Shevchenko—he trained in Canada, and he speaks fluent Russian."

HRH was still skeptical, and I knew why. Every Russian knows that finding the right doctor to deal with your particular complaint should be much, much harder than one phone call and a pleasant five-minute stroll through picturesque Patriarchy Ponds. No, doctors need to be run to ground by a lot of time on the phone, sorting through the many degrees of separation between your close friends and a suitable health care provider. You then have to bribe the health care provider to give you the right diagnosis and prescribe an appropriate treatment, which may or may not include producing some almost-impossible-to-obtain medicine. There appears to be no such thing as a primary health care physician in Russia nor the concept of an annual physical.

"Will the insurance cover it?" he asked cautiously.

I tried not to lose it. HRH still considered medical insurance a needless extravagance.

"How many times do I have to tell you? The insurance covers everything, at any licensed medical facility, with any doctor, in any country except North Korea," I rattled off.

HRH's lower lip slid out in a pout, and he threw me a pleading glance from behind furrowed brows. "Will you call them?" he whined. This from a grown man who refers to his years at a Soviet military school as "character building."

So I called the clinic around the corner, with its French specialists and Russian doctors trained in the West. HRH returned after the appointment with a worrying swagger in his step.

"What did Dr. Shevchenko say?" I asked with an upbeat in-flection. As always in these problem-solving situations, I naively imagined we were coming into the home stretch only to discover that Hurricane Hill looms just ahead.

"*Doctor*," snarled HRH, as he bent the index and middle fingers of each hand twice to indicate quotation marks—a potent gesture of just how useless he finds the staff at the IMC—"*Doctor* Shevchenko suggested that I go to Carlsbad and take the waters for two weeks, which is, by the way, exactly what my mother suggested a week ago, and I didn't need to pay her a thousand euros. You have to fill out this stupid form." He thrust an insurance claim form at me. Despite his discomfort I could see that HRH was on a roll. Here was proof positive that Western service providers and international medical insurance companies were one big Ponzi scheme.

"You are giving up on the quick, easy, and noninvasive laser treatment?" Had I suggested a radical vasectomy he could not have been more dismissive.

"Carlsbad," he stated.

"But darling," I protested, "that is, like, a nineteenth-century solution. I think the last person to take that kind of thing seriously was King Edward VII."

"Carlsbad, and until I can get there, no more beer. San Sanich Stepanov is going to put me in touch with a really good urologist the general knows at the Ministry of Defense clinic. We need to take this seriously."

The next level of treatment, as suggested by the unfortunate Dr. Shevchenko, is a therapeutic stay in a quasi-medical facility called a sanatorium for "observation." This lasts a minimum of three weeks, and as far as I can see, nothing very much medical or conclusive happens except that you eat really heinous food, drink incredibly sulfurous water, and maybe take a sauna or six a day. But Russians adore this! They puff up like pigeons and announce that they are headed for a sanatorium that their cousin's boss's sister runs on the outskirts of Tula as if they'd just been invited by the queen to dine at Windsor Castle.

I wasn't really clear what HRH expected from Carlsbad or, when it appeared Carlsbad was all booked up, the Caucasus resort alternative a friend of Sasha Stepanov's cousin's wife's father ran. I immediately christened it "Kidneykavkaz" and expected

✦

very little. HRH and I did achieve a solidarity of sorts about the very expensive lab on the outskirts of Moscow (laboratories are always a gazillion miles away from where your primary care takes place) to which Dr. Shevchenko suggested HRH submit a sample. It was a total waste of time and money. Tolya the Driver chauffeured the sample out and returned the findings, which the lab had burned onto the blank DVD they made us send with the sample. Classy, right? The lab found the tests inconclusive. They certainly weren't conclusive enough for our international health-insurance provider, who lobbed back a resounding *nyet* to underwriting three weeks at Kidneykavkaz. HRH went for one week. As I predicted, nothing very conclusive happened.

As much as stays at sanatoria are notches in the belt, stints in hospitals are vaguely humiliating experiences to which a Russian succumbs extremely reluctantly and only as a last resort. Mention that you are going into a hospital, and Russians look at you with a mixture of pity and disgust; it's as if you couldn't assemble the resources necessary to dodge this particular bullet. No one likes to stay in a hospital anywhere in the world, but I'm willing to bet that there are more cases of Munchausen syndrome reported per year in just one of the Federated States of Micronesia than in all of Russia. As my friend Claudia said recently when her Russian mother-in-law was hospitalized with a minor heart condition, "Well, being in a Russian hospital is an excellent incentive to get well." It certainly is!

Apart from the need to bribe the medical staff to do things like run labs, change IV drips, and all that stuff the *Grey's Anatomy* crowd are always doing, friends and relatives have to provide essentials like fresh sheets, food, toothpaste, clean syringes, and new bandages. Nothing is included, and you pay through the nose for luxuries such as private rooms, flushing toilets, and a sober surgical team, which looks nothing like the *Grey's Anatomy* cast.

"Hey," said Lucy on the telephone, "can you send Tolya over with a few more seasons of *Big Love*? It's actually great, once you get past the Mormon thing, but you only gave me seasons one through three. I'm getting very bored here in bed."

"Are you still on sick leave?" I was surprised. It had been six days, and Lucy sounded perfectly healthy.

"Yeah, well, I got a note from the doctor for eight days, and I figure I need to rest up for this trip to the Hindu Kush."

"Lucy, you can't take a strategic illness—it makes no sense. You own the company!"

"I'm working from home!" she protested. "Can you send over *West Wing* too? I'm feeling a lot better."

It must be all that jam, I thought, putting the phone down.

The only time a Russian might willingly sign on for a stay in a hospital is for what I call "the strategic illness," like the chief lawyer associated with the Red Handshake—the one who called in sick for fifteen months and all the chief accountant could say, with a classic Slavic shrug, was, "She is a lawyer, after all. She knows exactly how long she can be sick." If you are strategically ill, which you can always arrange by giving a doctor a small envelope of cash, you enjoy the medical equivalent of diplomatic immunity. You can't be fired, and you can't be arrested.

The "strategic illness" issue featured in the news in connection with a particularly lugubrious and arrogant Russian minigarch called Andrei Lugovoi. He rocketed to fame as a major suspect in the infamous "Alexander Litvinenko death by polonium in a sushi bar" case. Officials from Scotland Yard battled for months through red tape before they were finally given visas to come to Russia to investigate. When they arrived, however, it turned out that Lugovoi had been hospitalized with a vague illness that was proving difficult to diagnose. The Scotland Yard team was unable to visit him in hospital or question him, and they ultimately left Russia empty-handed. Shortly thereafter Lugovoi sauntered out of hospital, joined the ultra-right LDPR party, and is now enjoying parliamentary immunity. Now that's a note from the doctor!

Poor lifestyle choices are sometimes seen as a cause of Russia's shocking life expectancy, especially by those killjoys at the World Health Organization. A few years ago the health and social development minister announced that the thirteen-year gap in life expectancy between men and women in Russia could be attributed to the fact that men consume six times as much alcohol as women and smoke twice as much. This may well be true, but I think there is more to it. What I've observed is that Russian women are obsessed with health issues, while Russian men would much rather resign themselves to the inevitability of shuffling off the mortal coil than attempt to run the gauntlet of seeking medical advice.

★

Russian women will try all the folk remedies and dubious faith healers available, whereas Russian men feel that if they ignore them, health problems will just go away. So of course the women live far beyond anyone's expectations. Think about it: whenever you hear about the oldest person in the world, isn't she always some woman from the foothills of the Caucasus?

Neither group is very good at preventive medicine. We still don't know where they keep the vitamins. They don't dash off for mammograms at forty or colonoscopies at fifty. And yes, they smoke and drink a bit, but Russians have a saying: "The one who doesn't drink or smoke is the one who dies healthy."

Like most expatriates in Russia, I suffer from the occasional blues. In the winter of my thirty-ninth year I began to be very SAD (seasonal-affectively disordered). A general lethargy in October developed into a full-blown, chronic, can't-get-out-of-bed malaise by February. I had no energy, I couldn't sleep, and I only left home to crawl over to Volkhonsky's bakery to feed my curious new addiction to carbohydrates or to collect Velvet from the bus. I was not getting a lot done. Desperate for a cure, I doubled my intake of (imported) vitamins, which made me gag; I tried a vegan diet, which made everything much worse; and I tried rooibos tea, which didn't do anything at all. I tried yoga, gently easing myself into supta baddha konasana, only to have Raisa, bang on cue, burst in on me saying, "I'm not bothering you, am I?"

"*Querida*, try the colonics," urged Jesus. "They will change djour life!"

"Can you get to bed earlier?" my mother emailed.

"Go see Dr. X," dictated Posey Farquarshon in her "empire-building" British expat voice. "You need pharmaceuticals," she continued, with all the authority of one who has accompanied an ambitious oilman husband for two decades to hellholes like Jeddah, Lagos, and Houston.

I'll call him Dr. X, but of course anyone who spent more than three weeks in Moscow in the 1990s will understand immediately to whom I refer. They will also no doubt agree with me that it is high time we raised sufficient funds to have a small but tasteful bronze bust of his familiar Gallic/successful-rock-star features erected on a certain leafy side street in central Moscow.

I knew all about Dr. X. Everyone did. I first heard about him from my friend Gail, who runs an American pro-democracy NGO that on any given day is the subject of six separate investigations by the Russian tax police. She maintained that if you went to Dr. X's office and burst into tears, he would wordlessly pull out his prescription pad, scrawl you a "recipe" (as the Russians so aptly put it) for legal mood enhancers, and/or pen the official note you needed to pull a strategic illness. Most doctors gave you a note for forty-eight hours, but Dr. X had given Gail one for sixteen days. This enabled her to do a reverse Lugovoi the time she was summoned to a rather scary meeting with the Interior Ministry. A two-pack-a-day smoker, Dr. X famously didn't give you a hard time about lifestyle issues the way the stuffy crowd over at the American Diplomatic Clinic did, and he always maintained it was fine to combine alcohol with antibiotics.

"If," he qualified, "it is a good French Bordeaux."

Russians, of course, don't believe in mental illness, unless it is related to politics. I feel this is a real shame, because quite a few Russians I know personally, and all of the ones I see on television, might benefit hugely from getting off the universal drug for unhappiness (alcohol) and experimenting with some form of mood-enhancing drugs. Certainly the crowd at Volkhonsky's bakery, which pushes, shoves, and cuts into the line during rush hour, could use a major Xanax hit.

Dr. X informed me, in a direct manner you just don't get for your thirty-dollar co-pay in the USA, that what I needed was sleep, and the only way to get that was a major pharma-forklift.

"You, madame," he said, "are laike a computer."

I tried very hard to look like a Mac, not a PC.

"We must reboot your sees-tyem!" Dr. X cried, pulling out the legendary prescription pad. I sat in awe as he wrote, without a glance down at the pad, a "recipe" for a six-day carpet bomb of Lexapro, "Zee CD to upgrade zee softwaire," and a three-month chaser of Prozac. This eventually got me off the sofa, off the carbs, and back to work.

"Can a computaire work wizzout zee battery, eh?" asked Dr. X rhetorically, moving right along to my insomnia. I shook my head. "Of course not," he said, tearing off another sheet from the pad with practiced flourish. "So for sleep, you will take one pill: not 'abit forming—not at all! Each evening then you will bruss your teez, read a chapitaire of *Brozzers Karamatsoff,* zen taike the pill—an 'alf or an 'ole, whichever. Et voila, it arrives zee morning, and what we 'ave? We 'ave madame two point oh."

"Could I get a two-month supply of those?" I asked breathlessly. Posey was right—the guy was a godsend!

"One on-lee," he said, suddenly stern. "I am your friend . . . not your dee-leur."

I knew Lucy was out of danger when she and Tancy appeared at a yoga class on the Arbat. After sixty minutes of doing something good for our health, we repaired to a nearby wine bar to do some damage.

"You look much better," I observed.

"I'm feeling much better," Lucy agreed. "We went out to my friend Katya's dacha and spent the weekend there. I think the fresh air helped. One sad thing, though."

"What?"

"Tance is sterile," she announced.

"How awful," I responded calmly, signaling for another glass of wine. "Are you sure?"

"Yep," said Tancy, sanguinely firing up a Parliament Light. "Katya's grandmother yelled at me for sitting on the grass— said it would rot my women's bits. When I moved to the stone steps, she said that was worse."

"Oh, dear," I said.

"But she said it really didn't matter, because my women's bits are already fried anyway from all the plane trips I take," Tancy sighed. "Fried and rotted . . . things look pretty bad."

"Well, Tancy, I have news for you—you are too old to have babies anyway," I informed her.

"I'm forty—plenty of people have babies at forty," she yelped, outraged.

"Any pregnant woman over the age of twenty-nine is considered high risk in Russia."

"Seriously?" asked Tancy, inhaling smoke.

"Katya's granny felt that a *tselitely* could be the answer," said Lucy. "So that's encouraging."

Lucy really does have the most amazing Russian vocabulary. So much more interesting than mine, which is dominated by words like "plumber" and "Hefty two-ply garbage bag." Lucy knows how to say "rhinoceros hide" and "private-jet airstrip" in Russian. She also enjoys an enviable command of the entire dirty-word lexicon, which HRH doesn't let me use.

I took a stab. "Fortune-teller?"

"Medium," corrected Lucy.

"I don't want to have a baby," cried Tancy. "I want to have an IPO!"

"It's people like you, Tancy," I said sternly, "who are keeping the birthrate down in Russia."

The declining birthrate and general downward slide of population numbers in Russia are much in the news. My chums in the liberal opposition, or "creative class," assure me that each year, somewhere in the region of a hundred thousand Russians quietly, but steadily, do something called "stealth emigration." It works like this: if you are a Russian dental hygienist or a nurse and you speak a bit of English, you simply pretend you are going on vacation to the United Arab Emirates. Once there, you get a job, and you never go back. If you are a computer programmer and you speak a fair amount of English, well, you're probably already working in Silicon Valley, aren't you?

Russian authorities are doing what they can to tackle stealth emigration, which they claim isn't really happening or isn't happening on the scale that a random walk down Fifth Avenue suggests it is. Dmitry Medvedev, who was president for a while, suggested a solution that involves issuing an invitation to all the Silicon Valley programmers to come back to Russia, get Russian passports, and go to work at a Potemkin village in Skolkovo called Moscow School of Management. This, they feel, should do the trick, but just in case, they are padding the repatriate numbers with a few new Russian citizens. The French actor Gérard Depardieu recently signed on, and Brigitte Bardot and Diana Ross are said to be seriously considering taking advantage of the low tax rate to swap their passports for one of the spanking-new ones the Russian government is handing out like candy.

Really, though, the demographic thing is simple. Fewer Russians are having fewer kids, and they aren't having them in Russia. Anyone who can sends their kids abroad to school. So the government has introduced a number of measures designed to kick-start mass-scale childbearing. This isn't new. After World War II women who had more than nine children were given a medal of "maternal glory" and called "heroine mothers." They got their electric bills paid, which was no big deal, and they

★

didn't ever have to stand in line, which was. This was phased out during the cynical Yeltsin era (when absolutely no one was having babies). It was rebranded in 2008 as the medal of "parental glory" and is awarded to any couple, married or in a civil union, who raises more than seven citizens of the Russian Federation—either biological or adopted. You can get it if you are a single parent but not if you are a single-sex couple.

Medals are all very well, but the government also realized that times are hard, and the burden of raising a large family needs to be mitigated in some monetary way. With rising costs of food, heat, and housing, even those who might hanker after a large family have to do some serious thinking before committing to the financial responsibility of one. A couple of years ago the government decided to take the plunge and introduce cash inducements to raise the population. They put out a massive, countrywide campaign: a patriotic call to all Russian citizens to consider having a second, and possibly third, child. In exchange the government offered what was widely understood at the time to be a ten-thousand-US-dollar cash bonus.

Initial euphoria among the fecund turned very quickly to suspicion. The rumor mill rumbled: Was it ten thousand dollars per family or per child? In other words, if you had four kids, did you get forty thousand dollars or just ten thousand dollars? Was it taxable? Was it paid in one lump sum or installments, and if in installments, how was the government going to deal with inflation? When would it be paid, upon birth or conception? What if birth and conception happened in different fiscal years? What about twins or triplets?

The fine print, when finally released, explained that the then thousand dollars wasn't going to be a suitcase of crisp one-hundred-dollar bills but rather credits for government subsidies for boring things like housing, health care, and education. Not hard cash, then, but another nebulous promise of something intangible for an unclear future. This wasn't a winning marketing strategy for this particular Russian target market.

Sales of condoms among the urban creative class soared. They decided it was better to postpone parenthood and focus on their careers. In this way, they reasoned, they could earn their own money and make up their own minds about how to spend ten thousand US dollars. As for the *narod*, those stalwart, not-so-bright types who pull the stuff from the ground, plow the fields, and hurl themselves in front of the oncoming enemy, they paused a bit longer to consider the deal. Everyone knows you can't spend a government subsidy on essentials like mother-of-pearl nail polish, trips to the Red Sea, and a flashy car, but the *narod* doesn't read the fine print at the best of times, and it makes it more complex when said fine print is not widely disseminated or even released. So they started to go at it like rabbits until it became clear that Dmitry Medvedev was not, after all, going to appear at their humble abodes with a briefcase full of crisp one-hundred-dollar bills. So they stopped doing it like rabbits and started buying condoms and having abortions again. In a few years this blip may cause a small uptick in the demographics, so perhaps the government plan worked after all. Maybe it has ensured that, for a time anyway, there may still be enough of the *narod* to drill the oil, forge the steel, and dig the coal out of the ground. There may still be enough of them to drive the buses, serve in the army, load and unload the trucks, and perform repetitive tasks on the assembly lines. And when they get sick, there may still be enough of them to beg their friends and relations to find them a good doctor to bribe, a sanatorium to visit, or a hospital to hide in.

HRH, meanwhile, is scheduled to see a Harley Street specialist, which will cost about three times the amount that his stay in Kidneykavkaz did. He is skeptical, but we are forging ahead anyway now that the international insurance agent has given us the green light.

Nazdarovya!

CHAPTER 10

DEFENDERS
OF THE
FATHERLAND

THE MORE THINGS change in Russia, the more they stay the same, and nowhere is that more true than in the celebration of Russia's staggering number of public and professional holidays. Imagine that the Russian calendar is a huge body of water with a series of stepping-stones across which Russians navigate their year. Some are huge rocks, representing the major public holidays known as the "Red Days" in the calendar. New Year's Day is one, as is May 9, or Victory Day, which celebrates the USSR's single-handed total and irreversible victory over the Nazis in 1945. Public holidays like these are significant and call for serious fireworks, televised speeches from the president, and often a large parade of military might in Red Square. From Rurik on down, Russia's rulers have always subscribed enthusiastically to the "circus," if not the "bread," part of the "bread and circus" school of government, and Red Days offer the perfect opportunity to put this in play. If good weather is called for, rain clouds are herded by special planes; this produces a curiously flat kind of heat that lingers for the next three weeks. Major public holidays are always good for at least two days off, which everyone appreciates, but in vintage Russian fashion, how and when these days off occur is always confusing.

"If Wednesday is the actual holiday, what does that mean? Do we get Thursday off as well?"

"No, I think Monday is a working day, but Tuesday and Wednesday are days off."

★

"Actually, what's going to happen is that we work the previous Saturday and then get Monday, Tuesday, and Wednesday off."

"Are you sure?"

"Not really, no."

In January and May Russians enjoy the convenient phenomenon of not one but two big holidays, spaced some eight to ten days apart. Naturally, the goal of Warped Calendar Dude is to smush them into one long holiday. Russians celebrate New Year's on January 1 and 2, followed by Old New Year's on January 13.

"Old New Year? What the hell is Old New Year?" asked DeeDee.

"A big fat excuse for the goddamn stock market to recover," said Tancy through gritted teeth. She gets restless when the markets aren't open.

"It's actually the Orthodox Christian New Year," I explained in my geeky historian/tour-guide voice. "The Orthodox Church is thirteen days behind the rest of the world."

"Because . . . ?" DeeDee queried.

"Because they stayed on the Julian calendar when the rest of the world went to the Gregorian calendar in the fifteenth century." I continued. "The Julian calendar is not as precise as the Gregorian calendar, and so a thirteen-day discrepancy developed. Russia only went on the Gregorian calendar after the revolution, so if you traveled to imperial Russia there was a date change as well as a time change."

"*Querida*," marveled Jesus. "I am impressed. How djou keep all this *majaderías* in djour head?"

"Or a better question might be, *why* the fuck do you?" said Joe.

You'd think getting the first two weeks in January off would be enough for holiday-obsessed Russians, but not six months goes by and they do it all over again in the first two weeks in May, during the interval between May 1, Labor Day, and May 9, Victory Day. Again, nothing is open during the lengthy break, and anyone with the means to do so leaves the country. All business hangs in limbo; the refrain "after the holidays" echoes all over Russia.

HRH once had a nightmare job as the deputy to a very old-fashioned, Soviet-style Red Director. The Red Director was mean and he was also crazy, which isn't a great combination. He somehow always got advance notice each year of the exact number of days off in May and January. He would then block off his own vacation days in sync with the public days off and thereby automatically double the number of his own vacation days, at the expense of HRH and the rest of his "team." Nice, right? Because one of them had to be in the country all the time, HRH got stuck in Moscow during the long breaks in January and May, and we got stuck with him. We don't miss the Red Director.

I am fascinated by the holidays, particularly the awkward Soviet ones that are no longer relevant, nor indeed appropriate, in our post-perestroika era, though they remain significant stepping-stones in the progress through the year. November 7 is a good example. Once the reddest of all Red Days, November 7 marks the anniversary of the Great October Socialist Revolution.

"Okay, wait a minute . . . why do they call it the October Revolution if it is in November?" asked DeeDee.

"If you remember," I said patiently, "the Russian empire was thirteen days behind——"

"Oh, right," said DeeDee. "This is so confusing!"

In the Soviet era, November 7 was celebrated with two days off, massive parades in Red Square, and the annual showcase of Kremlin leaders on top of Lenin's tomb. These days, socialist revolution is not currently in vogue in Russia, but the inhabitants of the world's largest country have come to expect a long weekend in early November. So the warped individuals who sit in windowless rooms in the Kremlin figuring this stuff out came up with the "Day of Unity and Accord," which commemorates Russia's victory over the Roman Catholic Polish-Lithuanians in 1618, which, if you ask me (and no one ever, ever does), is pushing it just a bit.

Some Communist holidays have remained calendar fixtures, but the mode of celebration has radically changed. Labor Day, on May 1, once celebrated with tumultuous parades through Red Square, mass demonstrations of volunteerism, and a general postwinter cleanup, is still a two-day holiday, but nowadays Russians celebrate May 1 by boarding rump-sprung Soviet-era planes to jet off to three-star all-inclusive resorts in

Antalya, Turkey. After all, what could be more proletarian than that? International Women's Day, first celebrated in Russia on March 8, 1913, by the female firebrands of the Russian Revolution, Rosa Luxemburg and Clara Zetkin, focused on the need to liberate women from their traditional domestic shackles. Today in Russia, International Women's Day is celebrated by a general emptying of all the greenhouses of the Netherlands and Kenya, mass purchases of perfume, overbooked five-star restaurants, and a run on upscale chocolate stores.

Nice round numbers, like the 850th anniversary of the founding of Moscow, or any year ending in five or zero since the beginning or end of World War II, considerably up the ante. Milestones of this magnitude call for massive public partying: fireworks in Red Square, folk-dancing demos on the main streets, and fun runs around the Garden Ring. Nice ideas in theory, but in practice, the execution leaves a lot to be desired. The total inability to move through the city's streets or use public transportation somewhat takes the shine off this kind of event, as do the battalions of riot police that line the venues. I always have a disquieting sense that any minute one of the riot policemen will break into a spirited rendition of "Tomorrow Belongs to Me" as the camera pans down his face.

For his most recent inauguration, Vladimir Putin drove through a totally deserted capital, which was eerie. All of the streets around the Kremlin had been blocked off twenty-four hours before the ceremony, and no one showed any inclination to go out of doors and cheer him on. There was no fun run that day.

Some 250 smaller stepping-stones across the calendar year mark the plethora of Soviet professional holidays. Each day celebrates a different profession or branch of the military, and each year more holidays get added to the list. Some professions have turned their holidays into national events, such as my particular favorites, the border guards (May 28) and parachutists (August 2), who vie with one another for the most raucous public partying by featuring epic booze-ups and swimming in public fountains. Other holidays, such as that of the furniture-makers, pass relatively quietly, noted and feted only among the members of that particular guild. The present-day calendar still celebrates each major branch of the military (the navy alone has nine separate holidays) and traditional professions such as doctors, teachers, surveyors, construction workers, and farmers. Recently minted holidays have given IT workers, headhunters, and banking specialists the opportunity to clink glasses. When I first came to Russia this seemed excessive to me until I began to do a little research and unearthed their historical development. The professional holidays simply replaced the existing Orthodox saints' days. The Bolshevik effort to eradicate the influence of the Orthodox Church from the lives of the Russians left an uneducated agrarian population rudderless in purely practical, as well as spiritual, terms. Illiterate nineteenth-century Russian peasants had no idea how to read a calendar, but they knew to plant crops on one saint's day and harvest them on another. Secular public and professional holidays were simply substitutions for the saints' days, creating new iconic heroes for the masses. Those Bolsheviks never had one single original thought.

All this holiday-making can be confusing for the uninitiated expat, as Jesus discovered the first time he found himself in Moscow during late February.

"*Querida*, what djou know about this Man's day?" he shouted to me from an adjacent pedicure chair over the techno rap that ricocheted around the walls of our favorite nail bar.

"The what?" I shouted back.

"The Man's day," Jesus whined. "What eet ees? What I have to do?"

I groped for clarification.

"*Mantsday?*" It sounded like a character in *Game of Thrones.*

"Jes," said Jesus impatiently, "the Man's day—next Tuesday, so Monday is the day off."

The fog lifted.

"You mean Men's Day?" I said. "February 23?"

"Jes . . . this is what I say, *querida*," said Jesus impatiently, "the Men's Day."

"How is it you have lived in Russia for what, two years, and you don't know about Men's Day?"

"We usually in Zermatt," said Jesus impatiently, "but Alexei has the merger, so here we are." He sighed with resignation, pulled out a little silver notebook, and clicked his glittering pink Swarovski pen to the ready. "So what eet ees and what I have to do? Tell me everything."

"Men's Day—February 23—is Defenders of the Fatherland

★

Day," I told him. "It's the anniversary of the founding of the Red Army, in 1918."

"Why the army is red?" Jesus's understanding of Russian history screeches to a halt at Fabergé.

"The army that was reorganized after the Russian Revolution. I think they also had some kind of mini-skirmish with the dregs of the German army on that day."

"Oh . . . ," said Jesus, more relaxed, "so thees ees a military holiday; she not like the Valentine's Day."

"Well," I cautioned, "remember, pretty much every Russian man has to serve in the army, so this has come to be like a one-way Valentine's Day for men, at least those men who have done their military service."

And, I added silently, as both HRH and Alexei Soloviev would tell you, anyone who hadn't done military service in Russia does not deserve to be called a man. Alexei, always elitist, had done his military service in the prestigious officers' training program of Leningrad State University, where they taught him to do something incredibly grown-up and important in the event of war.

"Women—sorry, darling—*partners* really try to do this holiday up big," I continued, "because it comes about two weeks before International Women's Day on March 8. We want to set the bar very high so that the men will go all out on our holiday. There's even a saying: 'As you spend the twenty-third, so shall you meet the eighth.'"

"Ees this how djou got your Cartier watch?" asked Jesus, perking up a bit.

"No, I gave that to myself after HRH's relatives came and stayed with us for a month. I felt I'd earned it. But Men's Day, you know, it is more of a 'sit around the table with your family and the guys you served with.'"

"Ai!" wailed Jesus. "I know what ees thees; thees ees the mayonnaise and the dill?"

I burst out laughing. "Mayonnaise and dill" is expat code for the stodgy Russian salads that dominate Russian home cooking and make relentless appearances at most weddings, all funerals, and far too many official banquets. They are full of processed mayonnaise and often topped with dill, and to anyone who knows about food they are truly awful. To anyone brought up on them, however, they are an essential part of a celebration, and any attempt to update them, replace them, or make them slightly more healthy or palatable meets with granite Soviet resistance.

"Oh, I don't think you have to go that far," I said, knowing that Jesus would much rather shop than chop, "but do get him something nice—a present that kind of underscores his masculinity."

"*Querida*!" said Jesus in a much brighter tone. "This is perfect, because I try to get him into that new Hugo Boss black silk T-shirt since the forever. He resists—I don't know why. He works so hard on the . . . 'ow djou say, no, I know . . . the pecs, and no one—no one ever sees them in those suits . . . *aburrido*! So boring! So I go right now and I see Andrei at the Tverskaya shop and maybe I buy two, and then we will be the matching!" He leaned down and blew on his toenails to hasten the drying process.

"*Querida*, what djou think—maybe Alexei, ee will propose on thees Man's Day? Eet would be very romantic."

I felt a twinge of sadness.

"Getting engaged is not a traditional part of the Men's Day celebrations," I began as tactfully as I could. "You seem very focused on marriage lately, but you know that a lot will have to change here before—"

"I know!" cried Jesus, sticking out his lower lip. "I know, I know, I know, but I can' help eet! I want a wedding! How many weddings djou have, *querida*?"

"I had three," I said sheepishly. "But all to the same guy."

"Well, I only want one, but I want eet! I know exactly where we go: a leetle town on the beach in France. I already plan the wedding ceremony and the food and then where we go for X-rated honeymoon—oh!" Jesus reared up again from the pedicure chair with a new thought.

"*Querida*, what djou think—maybe I stop by the EuroIntime for something a leetle . . . anyway, thank djou, *querida*! Djou always know! What djou get djour HRH, anyway?"

"Nothing from the EuroIntime," I said regretfully. "Ours is very much a family celebration, and in fact this year we have to go to a multigenerational thing at the Stepanovs, which, trust me, will be the mayonnaise and dill to end all mayonnaise and dills. Velvet and I got him some funny cuff links, and he gets a serious amount of stuff at work."

HRH arrived home from the office with a lot of very impressive loot from Men's Day. One of the perks of his steady upward climb through the corporate hierarchy is that over the years the swag has improved exponentially, both in quality as well as quantity. He used to get a bottle or two of the kind of vodka we keep aside as windshield wiper fluid (cheaper and more effective than the real stuff), but this year there was an impressive array of single-malt whiskys in classy wooden ceremonial boxes, many of which were embellished with the coat of arms of imperial Russia or something equally pretentious. As a former PR manager (professional holiday on July 28), I was charmed with one company's creative efforts: a standard army-issue burlap rucksack with HRH's surname stenciled on the back. Inside were tins of what looked like army rations but turned out to be caviar and smoked fish. I gave them full marks for a rare fusion of good taste, good humor, and the spirit of the holiday.

Velvet's favorite gift was a large leather box, which at first glance seemed like an oversize book, but once opened appeared to be a set of everything needed to open a mini casino. There were several decks of cards, poker chips of all sizes and denominations, dice, and even fake money. Velvet is a mean poker player, so she was thrilled.

"Let's play!" she squealed, tearing the cellophane off a pack of cards. I started to tidy up the shiny wrapping paper and ribbon.

"Mommy," said Velvet after a moment, "something is wrong with this pack of cards."

"What?" I asked, marshaling the whisky bottles.

"They are made out of chocolate."

"No way," I said, abandoning the whisky bottles and coming over to take a closer look.

Everything in the mini casino was, indeed, made of chocolate, from Russia's leading candy maker, Kournikov. I couldn't quite believe it, but a sniff of the chips confirmed that they too were edible, and what seemed like bootlegger bricks of ten-thousand-ruble notes were actually solid blocks of white chocolate.

"Well," I said cheerfully, "we know what's for dessert!" I surreptitiously reached for the camera.

"Don't photograph this," said HRH sternly, with his uncanny ability to read my mind, "and for god's sake don't write a blog about it, and don't forget, we are going to the Stepanovs tomorrow."

I tried in a sort of halfhearted way to cut a deal with HRH to get out of going to the Stepanovs. Velvet had wisely decamped to Bald Hills for the long weekend, so I tried to lure HRH away from the Stepanovs with a number of attractive offers designed to appeal to his masculinity. I offered to cash in a jealously hoarded voucher for an overnight at the Kempinski with brunch in bed the next day. I rattled off the staggering number of European sports channels on the hotel's cable. I hinted subtly at a visit to EuroIntime, but that went right over his head. HRH would not budge. "Officer's duty," he insisted. "You like the Stepanovs, and don't forget, Volodia introduced us!"

So we set sail for what I secretly call the "Alexander Palace," since it is home to a total of four people with the name Alexander. The nominal head of the household is my buddy Volodia Stepanov's younger brother, Alexander, who is nicknamed Sasha. Sasha and HRH were schoolmates in East Berlin, smoked their first cigarettes together, and sold black-market comic books to their Soviet embassy schoolmates. With Sasha lives his wife, who is confusingly also called Sasha, being Alexandra to his Alexander, and this gives rise to the names we know them by: Sasha the Husband and Sasha the Wife. They have sixteen-year-old twins—Andrei, known as Andriusha, and another Alexander, who for the sake of everyone's sanity they call Shurik. Sasha the Husband and Volodia's father is also Alexander, but as his patronymic is Alexandrovich (of course it is), he is always referred to by the traditional slurring of "Alexander Alexandrovich" into a truncated hiss: "San Sanich." This is an archetype in Soviet life. I have encountered a number of San Saniches during my time in Russia, mostly in a professional capacity, and to a man they all play the role of a spider at the center of a complex web of Byzantine transactions, ever the source of something elusive, like your visa support letter. Their connections are always hinted at but never completely explained. They have a kind of edgy, slightly reptilian charm, but San Saniches aren't anyone you want to get on the wrong side of.

San Sanich Stepanov runs to type. I'll just come out and say it—he is a retired KGB hotshot. If I were with Russians, I would be more discreet and just tap the palm of my hand onto my shoulder, and this would impart the same information in a less vulgar way. But that's what he did, San Sanich, and in fact, legend has it that a young Vladimir Putin used to wait outside his office for hours to get stuff signed. I see no reason to doubt it.

These days San Sanich is retired and has acquired the requisite beet-red face and three-inch eyebrows of Soviet-era power brokers who have been put out to pasture. He wears a battered tracksuit and spends a lot of time mushroom hunting out at his dacha. San Sanich has made a separate peace with post-perestroika Russia, her waning geopolitical power, and the end of what must have been his very pleasant and privileged existence. He remains mildly influential, since he's connected to a number of people in the KGB's successor organization, the FSB. These rising stars, like Vladimir Putin, were young whipper-snappers during the Cold War. Memory and loyalty are a big deal with this crowd, so while a phone call from San Sanich may not get the tax police completely off your back, it could very well get you into a meeting with someone who could get the ball rolling. San Sanich's primary regret in life is that his sons have not been able to follow in the path he so carefully laid out for them. He worries less about Sasha, who parlayed his initial success hawking Turkish refrigerators to Syrians into a solid and fairly transparent business selling construction materials.

Volodia, however, with his talent for languages, was the one destined to follow his father into the service, until a Yeltsin-era decree aimed at attacking rank nepotism in government service put the kibosh on Volodia's application to the KGB academy. Volodia ended up on the state tourism committee's couch instead, sleeping off long nights of drinking while his Syrian clients shopped for refrigerators. I suppose, as an American, I shouldn't be sorry that the KGB missed out on a really good brain, but I'm fond of Volodia, who did after all introduce me to HRH, and it seems a shame, all that talent wasted. Volodia quit the state tourism committee in the early 2000s and went to work for Sasha the Husband. Sasha the Husband drinks less than Volodia, enjoys a good marriage with Sasha the Wife, and has the twins and this very large apartment in respectable Yugo-Zapadnaya. The apartment is actually an amalgamation of three separate dwellings and the triumphant culmination of one of the most complicated real estate deals ever in a world where toddlers cut their teeth on complicated real estate deals.

"It was like this," Sasha the Wife explained to me once. "I had my two-room apartment, which I shared with my grandmother, on Leninsky Prospekt. When I married Sasha, we traded my two-room for a one-room for Granny and a room in a communal flat in the center. Then we traded Sasha's one-room apartment and my room in the communal for a two-room out in Fili. Then Granny died and I inherited her one-room. So right about that time San Sanich and Valentina Andrievna got their three-room apartment with Volodia on Begovaya. So Sasha took the three-room and Granny's one-room and our two-room, and we got the first four-room apartment here in Yugo-Zapadnaya. San Sanich was friendly with a major who had the one-room apartment to the left of us; when he found out he was moving to Tver to be with his daughter, Sasha bought that apartment. Then we waited about four years, and the guy on the right-hand side—well, we think he was arrested or something, but his wife was willing to cash out, so we traded her Volodia's one-room and gave her something like eight thousand dollars, and she gave us the other apartment."

"No," said HRH, negating the way he always does when emphasizing a fact. "No, it's really something of a tour de force—I don't know anyone else who did that much with so little cash."

The result is an enormous apartment that laps one side of the building, curiously much wider than it is deep. There is one long corridor connecting the various rooms where the Sashas, their two children, and his parents live, along with a few semi-permanent guests, such as Volodia, who is currently between wives, and Sasha the Wife's uncle Vladimir, who is currently between jobs. There is only one fly in Sasha the Husband's domestic arrangements, and she now made her dramatic appearance.

"Ahhhhhhhhhh, you are heeeeeeeeeeeeeere," a shriek went up from deep inside the apartment as we shrugged off our coats. A flash of dark green sateen and a huge, cranberry-colored beehive updo, and Valentina Andrievna, Stepanova mère, hurled herself at HRH and smothered him with tangerine-lipstick kisses. She has known him since he was a baby and is loud and vocal, as she is about everything, about the fact that she massively prefers him to either of her own sons. This, of course, is poppycock: Sasha is her clear favorite. As Volodia says, the youngest child in Russia is always spoilt putrid.

Unlike San Sanich, Valentina Andrievna has not gone gentle into the Soviet Götterdämmerung. She has burned and raged—mostly at Sasha the Wife—but really what she has done is energetically work the pyramid schemes. Sasha the Husband's entrepreneurial instincts, honed in East Berlin with the comic-book racket, come entirely from his mother. When San Sanich retired and they returned from Germany to what was for them a barely recognizable country, San Sanich resigned himself to his tracksuit, the dacha, and his mushroom hunting. Valentina Andrievna, on the other hand, rolled up her sleeves and began to sell things. She started out as a representative for the diet supplement company Herbal Life (in Russia pronounced "Gerbal Laif"), wearing a large button on which was printed in bold red letters, "Want to Lose Weight? Ask Me How!" Wearing this, she accosted perfect strangers in the Metro, which horrified San Sanich. From there she went on to New Ways, a remarkably similar product to Herbal Life except for the packaging. She branched out to Mary Kay and managed to sell me over two hundred dollars' worth of base and powder that made me look like a ghoul. She shunted into the Avon game for a while and did well with that too, but then she really got the bit between her teeth with a special kind of German metal cooking pot (manufactured in China) that, according to Valentina Andrievna, is nothing short of miraculous.

"It cures cancer," she told me enthusiastically over the phone.

"Really?" I said, vowing never, ever again to pick up the receiver.

"This is the god's truth—I'm crossing myself as I tell you this—a man in Austria was dying of stomach cancer, and the doctors told him he had only four weeks to live. He got the three-in-one pot (the steamer, the fryer, and the stock pot) and started to cook for himself, and six years—yes, six years now—he is cancer-free! Can you argue with that?"

"I think I'm all set with kitchen equipment," I said, edging around the question. "Storage is sort of an issue in our apartment."

"Well, you should throw everything out," insisted Valentina

Andrievna. "All that enamel and stainless steel—it's killing you!"

"I don't think I can afford to throw everything out," I said tentatively.

"Nonsense," she guffawed, "how can you afford not to? And anyway, Sasha tells me your husband just got a new job—how much does he make a month? I'll show you how you can pay this off in very manageable monthly increments of just—"

"Really," I pleaded, "I don't think we can."

"Well, what about all your rich foreign friends? Foreigners are always concerned about health. I'll tell you what—you invite them all over, and I'll come and do a free cooking demonstration. We're supposed to charge for it, but forget about that. And if your friends buy, and I can assure you they will buy, I will give you—no, Jennifer, no arguments—I will give you 8 percent of what we make. It will kill almost all the profit I make, but in this business it's volume that counts. What do you say?"

I pictured Bees Rees and her court of princesses and ladies-in-waiting watching a German cookware demo by Valentina Andrievna out at Bald Hills. It was a tempting proposition, if only as one-upmanship with Holt. Handled correctly, it could be an excellent stunt.

"The thing is," I said when Valentina Andrievna eventually paused for breath but not before upping her offer to a final and profit-decimating 10.3 percent, "everyone I know really prefers the French cast-iron cookware—Le Creuset. I find it really cooks very evenly—"

"Evenly?" shrieked Valentina Andrievna. "You haven't experienced *evenly* until you've tried the centrifugal casserole attachment! It sends the heat waves so evenly that it lowers your cooking time by almost half."

"But the point is to cook a casserole on low heat for a long time," I argued, getting into the contact-sport aspect of debating Valentina Andrievna.

"Well," she said impatiently, "if you want your family to die from toxic digestive enzymes, I suppose that's your own business. What is your mother-in-law's number in Lviv? I think she'd want to know about this; we have a distributor down there, but it's no trouble for me—I can just hop on a train and bring a sample down. After Chernobyl, you know, everyone down

★

there has to take extra special care of how they prepare food. Do you think your husband could arrange a ticket for me?"

"Valentina Andrievna," I said through gritted teeth, "he hasn't done that in about fifteen years."

"Well," she said dismissively, "don't tell me his people still aren't at the railway station. Do you have their number? I'm supposed to collect six referral numbers from everyone I call."

I had a brain wave and gave her Dragana Galveston's number.

Valentina Andrievna always says that Volodia should never have introduced me to HRH but married me himself, and that I should be her daughter-in-law. Sasha the Wife informs me that I've had a very lucky escape. She and Valentina Andrievna famously do not get on. Sasha the Wife does not use the miraculous German cookware. She did take the Herbal Life for four months to shed some of her post-pregnancy weight, but then, as she recounted it to me, Valentina Andrievna tried to gouge her over the unit price, which was not their first, and certainly will not be their last, clash.

Valentina Andrievna tells anyone willing to listen that Sasha the Wife is a slattern, a bad mother, and a terrible cook who is driving golden boy Sasha the Husband to financial ruin. It's true that Sasha the Wife is a little overfond of deep décolletage, animal prints, and lurid nail polish, but she's a very competent mother and an okay cook, and slattern seems harsh. Sasha the Wife tells everyone that Valentina Andrievna is a harpy, and the whole idea in the first place with the apartment project was that Valentina Andrievna and San Sanich were supposed to live most of the time at their winterized dacha. Sasha the Wife, hand on heart, tells me she never signed on to live with her in-laws. She complains that Valentina Andrievna's incessant clanking of her inventory and the twelve hours a day she ties up the telephone working her pyramid schemes make it impossible for Sasha the Wife to get anything done around the house.

Mother-in-law and daughter-in-law called a momentary and legendary three-month truce when Volodia married his first wife, Dasha. HRH and I liked Dasha, who seemed harmless enough, but Valentina Andrievna and Sasha the Wife were in total agreement: the slut was just using Volodia to get in on the Alexander Palace apartment legacy. United, Sasha the Wife and Valentina Andrievna were truly formidable. They ganged up on poor Dasha, which seemed unfair after Dasha had sunk so much cash into Mary Kay products—so much, in fact, that Dasha eventually fled back home to her parents and divorced Volodia. Their common enemy vanquished, the two allies promptly resumed normal hostilities. Things are a little easier during the summer, when Valentina Andrievna moves the base of her operation to ensnare the summer residents of their dacha community, but from September to May a state of icy cold war exists between them.

Russian hospitality is legendary; everyone knows that. The fact that they were not speaking to one another did not hinder Valentina Andrievna's and Sasha the Wife's efforts to produce an epic mayonnaise and dill in honor of the many Defenders of the Fatherland currently in residence at the Alexander Palace. We were ushered into the longest of the many long rooms in that apartment, and I felt my eyes go glassy as I surveyed the table: it was going to be a very long and very boozy night. It was a good thing Tuesday was also a day off.

When entertaining at home, Russians never let spatial issues limit them. A sit-down dinner more often than not becomes a buffet in my home when the number of guests invariably exceeds the number of chairs in the dining room. No such qualms for Russian hosts. The only firm rule is that everyone must sit around one very large (but never quite large enough) and very long (but never quite long enough) table, which is pushed up against a huge, slippery, overstuffed leather sofa. Around the other side of the table are assembled anything that looks like, or can potentially be used as, a chair. I remember a legendary evening in St. Petersburg when I sat on a defunct television from the 1970s.

True to form, the Stepanovs were a fusion of the old and the new: traditional enough to have the large, squishy leather sofa but modern enough to augment it with a set of eight chairs from some upscale Italian furniture company. Each place was set with one teeny tiny plate: something between a bread plate and a salad plate. The paucity of porcelain, however, was more than adequately compensated for by an overabundance of crystal: each place was set with at least six glasses; Sasha the Wife's Turkish smoked-glass imports with extensive faux-gold filigree edging were teamed up with Valentina Andrievna's heavy, leaded Bohemian crystal from the Stepanovs' tenure in Prague.

I made a beeline for one of the chairs, knowing from bitter experience that sitting on the slippery leather sofa would put the table approximately at my shoulders: an awkward reach to eat and an increased possibility of spillage. The sofa also offered very little back support, important for an evening that is a marathon and not a sprint and in which alcohol plays a major role. I was foiled immediately by Volodia, who was encamped at one end of the sofa and motioned me to join him.

"Happy Men's Day," I congratulated Volodia, who did his requisite three years as a reservist Arabic- and English-speaking interrogator. We exchanged the traditional three kisses, and I was enveloped in a powerful vodka embrace.

"Volodia," I said reprovingly, "it's two o'clock in the afternoon. What time did you start drinking?"

Volodia grinned his charming drunk smile that reminded me of our misspent youth in the tourism biz.

"I waited until lunch," he assured me.

"Lunch when? Last Thursday?" I countered.

"Get off my back," he said, shooing me away with his hand. "You are in no position to give me a hard time today . . . I'm a Defender! In fact," he said in English, squinting at me, "what is your name, rank, and serial number?"

"Piss off," I said cheerfully, punching him in the arm.

"What can I get you to drink?" asked Volodia, squinting at the groups of bottles on the table, ranged at regular intervals for easy access. Each cluster contained separate beverage options for each gender. For the men, who always make out much better at this kind of gathering than the women do, there were bottles of French cognac, bottles of very good vodka, and a disgusting Georgian mineral water called Borjomi, which remains one of the many unsolved mysteries about Russia. How can anyone like something that, quite frankly, tastes like someone has farted in it? There were two boxes of juice, orange and tomato, both tepid, which were for both sexes. For the women the options were headache-inducing Sladkoye, a sweet champagne, as well as Baileys Irish Cream. There was no ice, nor would it be politic to ask for any. Ice is the devil to Russians like the Stepanovs.

"Hmmm?" asked Volodia. "Let's see, there is champagne and . . . hmmm, and, well, I guess for you there is champagne and champagne?" He let out a giggle as I grimaced.

I know I am a very annoying and high-maintenance guest for the Russian hostess. "Oh, god!" I can hear her moan at 5:00 p.m., after she has polished and set out some seventy-eight glasses and is more than ready to move into her boudoir for a welcome drop-down before the festivities commence. "The weird American wife who likes wine . . . Dima, do we have any wine? No? Perhaps you should pop out." I would never dream of bugging the Stepanovs about an alternative to the choices on offer. Sladkoye champagne, when you cut it with tepid, viscous boxed orange juice, is actually okay.

Sasha the Wife brought out a plate of smoked fish and added it to the already groaning table, then shrieked for her twin sons to join the table.

"What a spread, Sasha," I said encouragingly. She looked exhausted and cast her eyes furtively out toward the balcony, where Sasha the Husband was showing HRH something. I could tell she was longing for a Vogue menthol.

"Valentina Andrievna did the *zakuski*," she said pointedly. "I did the main course."

That figured. It was typical of Valentina Andrievna to grab the culinary showstopper and relegate Sasha the Wife to the second tier. I wondered for the umpteenth time if perestroika (reconstruction) would ever make it to the Russian dining table. Pull up a chair at the Stepanovs' board, and you sit down to a table in the Brezhnev era. There exists an admirable culinary tradition in Russia. Check out Levin and Stiva's lunch in *Anna Karenina* or Meriel Buchanan's real-life account of the coronation of Nicholas II. The roots are there, but the stalks have withered in a seventy-year frost. When I first came to Russia, twenty years ago, entrée choices were limited to "meat in a pot," salted fish, beets *à la maison,* and maybe chicken Kiev for a gala dinner (if you were really in with the chef). Today, restaurants serve all kinds of international dishes: sushi any way you like it, pasta with pesto sauce, barbecued ribs, truffle-and-potato soup, tiramisu, and sea bass with a rock-salt crust. These welcome innovations, however, have not yet permeated the home-entertainment lineup. Not at the Stepanovs' home, in any case. They don't stray far from the way things have always been done, and this means that the majority of any meal is the first course:

a groaning board of labor-intensive *zakuski*. *Zakuski* is set out on the table when you arrive, and you chip away at it for most of the evening. The *zakuski* is the main event. Sometimes it goes on all night, and you never even see the second course.

I looked up *zakuski* in the *Larousse Gastronomique* recently and let out a big belly laugh when I discovered it was translated as "hors d'oeuvres." Hors d'oeuvres to me conjure up something light, possibly frothy, a tidbit cleverly nestled in layers of *pâte feuille-tée*: something to whet the appetite. *Zakuski* is designed more to bludgeon than to whet.

Valentina Andrievna had really gone to town, with a reckless disregard to everyone's digestive enzymes. Every spare millimeter of the table was covered with mother-of-pearl, golden filigreed plates draped with thin yellow tissue on which were painstakingly arranged (and this is bog standard from Kaliningrad to Vladivostok) glistening, greasy Russian salami sliced in meticulous ellipses, with the rind left on; delicately arranged fillets of smoked fish, treacherous bones still lurking in their flesh; bunches of dill, tarragon, purple basil, flat Italian parsley, wedges of cucumber, pickled garlic cloves, pickled scallions, pickled red lettuce, pickled cucumbers, and pickled tomatoes; mounds of carefully sliced black bread, which over the evening would be largely ignored, then curl and harden into blocks.

There were sardines topped with thick curls of butter and sprigs of dill. There were store-bought tartlets filled with Russia's favorite mayonnaise salad: *salat Oliviye,* a viscid substance composed of peas, potatoes, pickles, and a lot of mayonnaise, topped with yet more dill. In the middle of the table, glistening with self-importance, was the signature dish of any Russian hostess worth her salted cucumbers: *selyodka pod shuboy,* or "herring under a fur coat."

"Valentina Andrievna," said HRH, as he slid into one of the comfortable chairs next to her, "just look at that herring under fur coat! My favorite!" HRH is almost never a brown-noser, but Valentina Andrievna really brings out the eight-year-old in him. She beamed and immediately reached for his teeny tiny plate. I quickly filled mine with smoked salmon. I cannot stand herring under fur coat. To me it's a culinary crime, and what's more, it's a metaphor for everything that is wrong with Russia.

"Herring under fur coat" takes counterintuitive to new

heights. With the exception of fruitcake, I can't think of a dish that contains so many incongruent ingredients and requires so much nitpicking preparation, yet produces such a universally unappealing result. It consists of layers of salted herring, diced beets, pickled cucumbers, sliced hard-boiled eggs, and diced potatoes, which are mortared together with gluey synthetic Russian mayonnaise. The top layer of mayonnaise is crowned with a liberal helping of grated egg, cheese, or both. It's a toss-up whether the salt or the cholesterol is more damaging, but this Russian dinner party staple is right up there with cigarettes and vodka as a major contributing factor to the less-than-stellar life expectancy in Russia today.

Sasha the Husband took his place at the foot of the table, within reach of the huge television. When we had gathered, the TV had been mercifully muted, but now Sasha the Husband flipped a few channels until he found the cheesy military concert that goes on all day during Men's Day and Victory Day, then cranked up the volume just loud enough to make your fillings rattle. Live from the Kremlin Palace of Congresses, Soviet-era crooners in way too much glitter belted out patriotic songs. San Sanich took up his place at the head of the table.

"Please help yourselves," boomed Valentina Andrievna. "The boys are still watching some kind of video game. I thought they might come to the table out of respect for the Defenders of the Fatherland, but," and here she sniffed pointedly, "I'm not their mother, so——"

"Okay, Mama, okay," soothed Sasha the Husband, "let's just make sure everyone has something to drink." Sasha the Wife poured a hefty tote of Baileys Irish Cream into the largest of the glasses and slugged it back in one efficient swallow.

I dug into my salmon with relish. Someone recently asked me what the best thing about living in Russia for the last twenty years had been. I did not hesitate for a moment. "Plentiful and affordable smoked salmon," I responded promptly.

Food, however, though the battlefield on which Valentina Andrievna and Sasha the Wife had fought today's skirmish, was really only a sideshow compared to the main event of the evening: alcohol and the intricate Russian mores of its consumption. As the eldest male at the table, San Sanich kicked off the afternoon. Hauling himself to his feet and clearing his throat, he poured himself a full shot glass of vodka, then cast a commanding look from under his three-inch eyebrows. A hush fell over the room. We all stopped what we were doing and lowered our forks mid–herring under fur coat. The men around the table bustled about to fill everyone's glasses, which we then all held the requisite seven or eight inches above our plate while San Sanich held forth.

"Comrades, friends," he began, and then launched into a complicated, and to me incomprehensible, story about some quality time he had spent with Comrade Andropov back in the good old days. Valentina Andrievna butted in a number of times with corrections about the who, what, where, and when, but he managed to silence her each time with a brushing-off motion and continued his toast. I say "toast," but at twelve minutes, perhaps "speech" is more appropriate. The arm holding my glass of tepid Sladkoye champagne went to sleep. On the television, orange-faced Josef Kobzon, the Soviet Dean Martin, prefaced a lengthy patriotic song by quoting a famous line from the hit war movie *Officers*, which runs in a continuous loop for the entire day each February 23 and May 9.

"There is a certain profession," he said, pointing his finger for emphasis, "to defend your motherland."

I let my mind linger on the interesting contrast between "motherland" and "fatherland," which were used interchangeably. I wondered why and resolved to ask Volodia before he had too much more to drink.

"By the way," interjected San Sanich, who then went off on another tangent about how Comrade Andropov had loved *Officers* (which, for this crowd, is synonymous with loving fresh air). I switched my glass surreptitiously from my left hand to my right and hoped we'd be in the home stretch soon. After a few more twists and turns, San Sanich grabbed a piece of the curling black bread and took a deep sniff. "To the fatherland!" he declared. The men at the table all followed suit. They then all exhaled sharply and knocked back their vodka shots. They sniffed the bread again, then sat back down. We took ladylike sips of our sweet champagne, and gradually conversation resumed.

This is how it always is. Each male guest gets up in turn to make an interminable toast to the reason why everyone has gathered, be it the Defenders of the Fatherland, a new flat-screen

TV, a single-handed total and irreversible victory over the Nazis in 1945 with no help from any other country, or—god forbid— a birthday. With birthdays you have to bring your PJs and your toothbrush, as they go on all night.

Toasts are designed to ensure that everyone around the table is fully aware that the thing or event in question is undoubtedly the very best Defender of the Fatherland, flat-screen, or total victory over the Nazi hordes with no help at all from any other country in the whole wide world. If it is a birthday, you have to drink to the parents of the birthday boy or girl at least four times. And at some point in the evening all of the men stagger to their feet and drink a general toast to the ladies in the room because what, questions the toaster, would they do without us?

We do not have to wait long to find out.

Promises elicited from HRH on these occasions that he won't abandon me are useless. Whether he wants to leave me or not, forty minutes into the evening he is always sucked into the vortex of the Russian-guy thing and ushered into an adjacent room or out to the balcony with the other men to talk about business, drink all the good cognac, and smoke cigarettes. So it was on this February 23. After the second toast Sasha the Husband, right on cue, ushered all of the men onto the balcony for a smoke. Volodia wasn't with them because he had fallen asleep, and gravity had propelled him down the slippery leather couch into an awkward slump, his head lolling back and forth. He snored gently.

Valentina Andrievna took advantage of a lull in the proceedings and made for the telephone so that she could continue to congratulate all of her client base on Defenders of the Fatherland Day. This left me with Sasha the Wife. Dinners at the Stepanovs are not designed for long-term mingling of the sexes. I don't mind it so much when we are at their house, since I'm fond of Sasha the Wife and she has known me long enough to get over the typical xenophobic hump that usually renders most Russians completely silent when they encounter foreigners in close proximity.

HRH and I were once out to dinner with a number of his colleagues from the regions, and a couple of them simply refused to take any of the conversational bait I lobbed at them. They even refused to clink glasses with me, which seems churlish, really, in this day and age. Their wives were the same. I smiled encouragingly, and they slid their eyes away quickly. All attempts to converse were futile. Direct translations of reliable English-language opening gambits such as "And what do you do in Chelyabinsk, Oksana?" always failed. The next attempt—"Where in Russia do you originally come from?"—was clearly perceived as an insult. In desperation I said to no one in particular, "How 'bout that Kiev Dynamo?" I eventually retreated to the safer confines of the weather, that eternal font of safe, neutral topics—but even my irreproachable "very icy today" was met with suspicious consideration, as if it might contain some anti-Russian smear or Western conspiratorial double meaning. I surreptitiously checked my armpits. Did I smell? Did I have something hanging out of my nose? I knew my handbag was from two seasons ago, but there was nothing I could do about that.

This is never a problem with the Stepanovs, whom I have known for two decades. They are used to me, and I am used to them. We are comfortable with each other, so I felt no panic when Sasha the Wife clicked the TV's mute button and relative silence descended on the room, punctuated only by Volodia's occasional snores. She plucked several nearly empty bottles from the table, scrutinized their contents, then removed the empty ones to the floor, where they could not tempt fate. An empty bottle on the table meant financial ruin, and contrary to what Valentina Andrievna thinks, Sasha the Wife is fairly prudent about money. She began to stack the teeny tiny plates, sticky with mayonnaise. I rose to help her and heard the pop and crackle of machine guns from inside the house and recognized it as a video game.

"How are the boys?" I asked, as we moved into the long, narrow galley kitchen.

Sasha the Wife dumped the stack of dishes into the sink, then groped for her cigarettes. She motioned me to the kitchen table and sat herself down with a thump. She rubbed her upper arms for a few seconds, then lit a thin, mint-green cigarette, drew in sharply, and exhaled.

"Shurik is fine," she began, "but Andriusha is going to be the death of me."

I was not surprised. I've heard this report about the Stepanov twins since they were a week old. Shurik, HRH's godson, from birth had been no trouble—a happy and attractive child with chubby cheeks and a propensity to eat and sleep at comfortingly regular intervals. He potty trained at two with no difficulty and trotted off to kindergarten cheerfully at six. He was popular, smart, and universally adored. At ten he discovered computers and was showing a marked aptitude for programming. He had taken the exams needed to get into the prestigious Bauman Institute and was set to matriculate a full year earlier than most students.

Andriusha, however, had been a bad seed from the get-go. As a child he was sneaky and stubborn. He refused to eat what was put in front of him and delighted in making big messes in his diapers long after Shurik had shed his for proper underpants. When he was eight Andriusha terrorized his grandparents' elderly dacha neighbors by putting snakes on their front steps and letting off stink bombs in the driveway. Valentina Andrievna would not hear a word against him and often placed her considerable bulk in front of his diminutive frame when punishment was meted out. She plied him with candy and money, even after Sasha the Husband begged her not to.

When Andriusha was ten, the teachers at the Yugo-Zapadnaya neighborhood school asked Sasha the Husband and Sasha the Wife to find another alternative for him. He was constantly in fights in the playground, he spat at a teacher, and when he was bored, which was almost all of the time, he delighted in acts of sabotage, such as blocking the toilets or leaving the tops off all the paints and markers. In despair, and over the high-decibel protests of Valentina Andrievna, San Sanich made a few calls and got Andriusha into the Suvorov military academy for young boys, and they packed him off to the provincial campus in Tver. This prestigious military preparatory school churned out the elite officer class, and it was hoped the rigorous discipline would whip Andriusha into shape.

Hopes were dashed when Andriusha was thrown out six weeks into his tenure for running an illicit pornographic magazine racket. This brought more than a glimmer of a smile to Sasha the Husband's lips when he recounted it to HRH, who guffawed and said the Russian equivalent of "boys will be boys," as they recalled their own black-market comic book ring. Sasha the Wife, however, among whose relatives numbered at least five Suvorov graduates, was mortified. She read Andriusha the riot act, then, for reasons no one understood, packed him off to Davos, Switzerland, to an alpine climbing program, then to the balmy island of Malta to learn English.

"That's a punishment?" I asked HRH incredulously. He shrugged.

Eventually home again, with a good tan and passable English, Andriusha was enrolled in a private high school designed for kids like him, where it was possible to pay for the supervision and assistance needed to finish Russia's secondary-school requirements. Sasha the Wife brought me up to speed on the current debate raging among the Stepanovs as to what should happen next.

"The army seems to be the only thing for it," said Sasha the Wife, stubbing out her cigarette.

"The real army?" I asked, aghast. Things had to be pretty horrible if the Stepanovs were looking at the real army as a serious option. I didn't know anyone who wanted their sons to do the mandatory year of military service required by law for all men who were not university students or medically unfit. Everyone I knew mortgaged their homes to come up with the necessary funds to either buy off the military recruiters or obtain a medical certificate. This could be anything between four and six thousand dollars. Seeing the army as a measure to knock your kid into shape was a desperate move for desperate parents. The army was a notorious hotbed of hazing, abuse, bad food, awful living conditions, and alcoholism. Suicides were not unheard of, and though many in the government called for radical reform, the only change to date was that the two years had been reduced to one, which slightly mitigated the hell.

"Shhhh . . . ," hissed Sasha the Wife. "Don't let Valentina Andrievna hear you! She's dead set against it."

"What about Sasha?"

Sasha the Wife shrugged. "He's fed up with trying to come up with something that will keep Andriusha out of trouble. San Sanich thinks it's a good idea."

On the way home in the car, I ran this by HRH.

"Can you believe it?" I said. "Thank god we don't have any sons. I seriously don't think I could cope with the whole army thing."

"I'm sure Sasha will do what's best," said HRH. "I'm just glad it's Shurik who is my godson and not Andriusha. Valentina Andrievna would never get off my back—call this general, call that major, every time that piece of work breaks a toenail."

"Don't think she won't try," I warned, as my phone began to vibrate and play "Mambo No. 5," indicating an incoming text from Jesus.

"No, it'll be fine," said HRH dismissively. "It'll make a man of him."

The text contained a link to a photo of two red leather boxes that could only have come from Cartier. These were tastefully arranged on a silver tray with two champagne flutes, a plate of oysters on the half shell, and some Maison du Chocolat truffles. The shot was candlelit, but I could tell that the tray was perched on top of Jesus and Alexei's best Pratesi sheets.

"*Querida*," it read, "Man's Day fantastic! I propose :))))) Alexei already did have the rings! Very happy! U B my best person?"

I didn't show it to HRH.

"It's Jesus and Alexei—sending you congratulations on Men's Day," I paraphrased.

"That's nice," said HRH. "They having a good day?"

"Oh, yeah," I said. "They sure are."

I decided to sit on the momentous news for a few days. I had a feeling that, for my Defender of the Fatherland, anyway, it might prove more digestible on International Women's Day.

CHAPTER 11

THE BALCONY SCENE

"OKAY," I SAID to HRH and Velvet one Saturday morning over breakfast, "you know what would be great to do today? If we put in about four hours together, I think we could clear out that space under the stairs."

"I have a birthday party at Deytski Arlecchino," said Velvet quickly.

"Really? I don't remember anything about that," I said. "Is it in my diary?"

Velvet fished around in her schoolbag, untouched since she'd slung it carelessly over a dining room chair the previous evening. She pulled out a large pink card and waved it triumphantly in my direction.

"Katya Lavrientieva," I read. "When did she give you this?"

"Yesterday," said Velvet.

Classic, I thought. This is how the weekend gets splintered. I passed it over to HRH, who shrugged.

"I have a VIP room reserved at the Sanduny baths," he said matter-of-factly. "And before you ask me if it is in the diary, it's work. The guys from the Ukrainian tractor factory are in town, and I have to spend some quality *banya* time with them. God knows what they got up to last night, but an afternoon at the *banya* is the perfect time to get them primed for the next round of discussions."

"Are we ever going to clear out that space under the stairs?" I moaned.

"Not this weekend, but hey, I can take Velvet to the party and you can pick her up."

That was something. Birthday parties in Russia for the nine-year-old set are dangerous time suckers. They take place in large clubs called "children's amusement centers" and are elaborately choreographed affairs with clowns, thumping music, and a designated area where parents are held hostage, fed watery cappuccino and greasy crab salad, and forced to attempt casual chat drowned out by the thumping music. You never want to take your coat off at a children's amusement center or you'll get trapped as another four hours of precious weekend time drains away. HRH is quite good at keeping the engine running during birthday party drop-offs.

"Still," I said to HRH, as Velvet trotted away to get ready for her party, "we've been talking about getting all that stuff organized since we moved in here. It's going on two years now. I'm sure those rugs I bought in Morocco are in there somewhere, and your cross-country skis really can't be anywhere else, can they? What about this evening? Could you blow off hockey practice just this once?"

HRH let out a sound that was half snort and half laugh.

"It's peak ice time," he said.

Like the cluttered storage area, HRH's company hockey league was a serious bone of contention. Practice took place on Saturday nights from 8:00 to 10:00 p.m., which made it awkward to accept invitations to dinner parties or really do much of anything as a couple on Saturdays.

"Can we put a date to do this in the diary?" I begged.

"I don't see why Raisa can't do it," said HRH, referring to our housekeeper.

"Darling, Raisa is incapable of throwing anything away. In fact, it would be seriously counterproductive to even get Raisa involved. She'll take everything out, mop the floor, possibly dust a bit, then pile everything back in. That storage area could be great, but it's totally full of junk we don't need and a lot of nice stuff we can't get at."

"Well, this is all your fault, you know," argued HRH. "If we had glassed in a few balconies, at least the one off the bedroom, we could—"

"I'm not having this discussion again," I said firmly, "absolutely not. Not up for negotiation." I stacked the breakfast dishes and made my way into the kitchen.

"Listen," he said, "everyone does it. We could do it this summer, when you and Velvet go to the US."

"Let me be very clear: if you do that thing where you wait until I'm out of the country to glass in anything, I'll divorce you from here to Vladivostok," I warned. "I still remember that crappy Korean car you bought without asking me. We made a deal: neither of us can spend more than five hundred dollars without asking the other."

"Sasha Stepanov says——"

"I don't give a damn what Sasha Stepanov says!" I exploded. "And I don't care what Ivanov, Petrov, and Siderov think is acceptable either. We're not glassing in anything, period."

HRH retaliated by passively aggressively refusing to help clear the table. I banged cutlery into a pot of sudsy water and fumed. There was no way I was going to agree to glassing in any of our little balconies, and I was prepared to go to the cross about the large roof terrace that ran the length of our living room.

The balcony issue in Russia is a big deal. In the Soviet era, housing was always in short supply, and space constantly at a premium. A balcony tacked on to a tiny, two-room apartment inhabited by three adults and two children was, therefore, a lot more than just an appendage to one wall of the apartment. It was A Feature: a few extra square meters to do everything from drying underwear to pickling cucumbers. For many Russians, it still is. Since no one ever throws anything out in Russia, the balconies provide vital storage for all the flotsam and jetsam of old furniture, broken appliances, and banjaxed musical instruments.

To expand and prolong the balcony's usefulness throughout the year, Russians go to great lengths and expense to enclose the balconies in glass paneling, what the Brits call "double glazing." In theory, this protects the laundry, the pickles, and the broken furniture and appliances from the elements. Since Russians waited for years during the Brezhnev era for hard-to-find materials and highly unmotivated glaziers, a glassed-in balcony was as much a status symbol as a Lada car, a trip to Prague, or a dacha. The cachet still lingers. Neighbors vie with one another to use the most up-to-date technology, colors, and materials on

★

their balconies, so there is no uniformity to the facade of any residential building in Moscow.

To my unappreciative eyes, the balconies are all eyesores. From the outside of the apartment buildings they look like warts on a decaying corpse. From the inside, covered with Moscow's gritty, diesel-infused dust and piled to the very top with junk, they block the light and make already cramped quarters feel even more cluttered. Balconies reek of a million unfiltered cigarettes smoked on them by men banished outside to indulge this habit. I've never visited a pre-perestroika apartment where my fingers didn't itch to tear the balconies down and throw the entire contents, lock, stock, and barrel, into a nearby Dumpster.

We had too much junk in our own storage space because our move to the new apartment had spiraled out of control—a fairly typical experience for any move in Russia. We were ready to move from our old apartment. Neatly packed boxes, color-coded to indicate the room they were destined for, were stacked in the corridor, and The Delicate Move removal company was booked and rebooked three times. The problem was that the construction and renovation teams weren't quite finished with the new apartment. It looked pretty much done to us, but no, they kept honing and polishing, one more go with the grout in the guest bedroom, they insisted, and another layer of paint in the kitchen. The electricity needed to be . . . the water pressure still wasn't . . . We couldn't move until they were really finished, because they were all living there. The teams hailed from the Near Abroad. There were female painters and plasterers over from Belarus, carpenters up from Eastern Ukraine, and a cheerful plumbing-electrical team in from deepest Siberia. Each team set up camp in a different room of the apartment. It was always done along proper gender lines with small camp beds and electric stoves. The occupant of each bed decorated the plain sheetrock walls around his space with pictures that ran the gamut from pretty flowers to pretty naked women.

They ate in whatever room lent itself best to communal dining, and no matter what time we visited to check on their progress it was always lunchtime. A large pot of glutinous meat and chicken bubbled on the camp stove, and the workers hunched around it, looking very put out that we had interrupted their dinner hour. As the apartment neared completion, in late April, I began to understand their reluctance to give up what was becoming a comfortable residence right in the center of Moscow. Who wouldn't want to live there?

"We have to get them out next week," I said to HRH. "I only have a week's vacation to do the move, and I can't change it. If you want us to be remotely settled, we are going to have to crack the whip. Their next gig is some hideous mansion out on Rublyevka, where the nearest shop is, like, a forty-minute walk. They are going to drag our job out until May, then they'll all go home for the holidays, and god knows we won't get them back here until midsummer."

"Who told you that?" he asked, amazed. HRH only ever dealt with Igor—the super-slimy overseer of the whole project.

"Liuba, the painter," I said.

"What on earth do you talk about?" asked HRH.

"She was telling me how they apply gold leaf. Apparently there is a whole bunch of gold leaf out at the mansion on Rublyevka. I'm telling you, they are not in any hurry to get out of our apartment."

HRH called Sasha Stepanov, who had extensive experience with renovation and moving. Sasha's advice was to present the builders with a fait accompli: announce a date, book The Delicate Move team, and simply arrive one early morning with all the color-coded boxes and firmly take up residence.

"They'll shift themselves soon enough, Sasha says," HRH reported.

"Okay," I said, cracking open a new package of colored tape, "it seems extreme, but let's go for it. You have to be the one to tell Igor, though. I can't face that."

Seventy-two hours later abject chaos reigned.

HRH promptly disappeared into one of his alpha-male ethers, leaving me to deal with the unspoken, but palpable, tension created between the regional workers and the slightly more skilled Muscovite team who came to put the German kitchen together. Any idea that they might cooperate was left with their outdoor shoes on the threshold, and all the clashes were run through me.

"I don't care," sniffed the snooty Muscovite kitchen guy. "But this kitchen is top of the line, and your . . . your *people* here haven't properly prepared the workspace."

★

Igor sucked on his teeth and scowled, motioning us out of earshot.

"We are not responsible for the kitchen assembly," he hissed menacingly. "But we need to get to the ceiling to install the light fixtures, and we can't do that with your . . . your *people* assembling the kitchen."

I brokered an uneasy truce just as the female painters and plasterers gathered for lunch in their accustomed locale of the guest bathroom. They unearthed Sebastian the cat, trapped inside a large cardboard box and weeping piteously. I rummaged through a few boxes with orange tape on them and finally found a tin of cat food. I opened the tin, and the snooty Muscovite kitchen guy sniffed pointedly. I scooped up cat, dish, tin, and fork and fled to Velvet's room for what I hoped would be a soothing hour of listening to English-language podcasts while I unpacked her books.

Fat chance.

A fiftysomething woman who looked, I kid you not, exactly like Cruella de Vil from *101 Dalmatians,* complete with one white streak in her hair and scary, blood-red lipstick bleeding into the cracks around her mouth, strode into the apartment like she owned it but was prepared to flip it quickly to a fairly low bidder. She looked around her with barely disguised disgust, which is how most service-provider negotiations begin in Russia. She was one of those psychological vampires you encounter a lot in Eastern Europe. I don't know how they do it, but with her entry, *poof!* There went all of the oxygen in the entire apartment. My head began to throb, and a hush fell over the tilers, plumbers, and plasterers. I sensed their heads were throbbing as well.

"I'm here to talk about glassing in the balconies," she announced to the assembled masses. Everyone looked at me. I felt my hackles rise.

"Get the fuck out," I said in English.

Everyone looked deeply shocked. Up until then I had definitely been the beta half of the couple. Although they didn't always understand what I was trying to say, "fuck" needs little interpretation.

"Seriously," I continued in Russian, "I'm fed up with you people. This is my house, and I am so sick of you all barging in here without a by-your-leave, eating in the goddamn bathroom, and I don't know what! We are not glassing in any balcony. Enough!" The Belarusians looked dead impressed, and I basked in their admiration.

Cruella didn't blink a false eyelash.

"Your neighbors—"

"Go and sell your double glazing to the neighbors!" I screamed. Cruella raised one heavily penciled eyebrow. Igor grabbed my arm and force-marched me into the laundry room.

"She's from the city government," he spat out. "She's the one who is in charge of your inspection."

"She's not selling balcony glass?"

Igor sucked in his teeth, then shook his head. It occurred to me that he was just as fed up with me as I was with him. I apologized. He sucked in his teeth again.

HRH was upset that I had been so rude to the inspector, but in a rare admission of guilt he acknowledged that in both neglecting to tell me she was coming and disappearing into the alpha-male ether, he'd been asking for trouble. Since we were already criminally over budget, we shelved the idea of glassing in any of the balconies. Two years later HRH still brought up the balcony idea, though, referring to his plans at regular intervals as he did that Saturday morning while I hastily wrapped up a nearly new Barbie doll for Katya Lavrientieva.

"Think of all the storage space!" he said.

"We have a perfectly good storage area under the stairs," I retorted, "or we would if you would help me clean it up."

"Can we still play The Boy in the Cupboard under the Stairs?" Velvet nervously sought reassurance. The success of her many sleepovers hinged on the ability to reenact scenes from *Harry Potter* around the house.

"Of course you can. In fact, you'll have more room to play if we cleaned that space." I handed Velvet the wrapped present and asked HRH, "What else do you think you need to store anyway that needs a balcony?"

"My hockey equipment, for example."

"Bringing up your hockey is not a great strategy," I warned.

"A glass balcony is well known to keep the heat in," HRH continued.

"Fantastic. It's already a tropical rain forest here from September to May," I spat. "If you glass in that balcony we won't be able to open the window at night. But that won't matter, will it, because we'll be dead of asphyxiation."

"It will cut down on the dirt," hypothesized HRH.

"It will be a dust magnet," I countered, "and we'll have to take out a second mortgage to pay to have those glass panels cleaned from the outside—"

"No, except—"

"Which we will have to do about once every two days," I shouted to drown him out. "Look at those balconies!" I gestured toward the neighbors' windows. "They are disgusting! There is dirt in every single shade, from light bilge to toxic-waste gray!"

"I think you still have a lot to learn about our culture," HRH said as a parting shot.

Everyone was tired that evening. Velvet plummeted down to earth from an epic sugar high and was dead to the world by 8:00 p.m. HRH came home from hockey practice in need of a long, hot soak in the tub. I climbed wearily into bed with a book. My eyes were drooping when my mobile phone jangled "Mambo No. 5." I checked the clock on the phone; it was 10:30. This, I knew, was the beginning of the day for Jesus and Alexei during the weekend. Our nine-year-old's birthday party circuit didn't often intersect with their nightclubbing scene.

"*Querida*," texted Jesus. "What U Monday?"

"Nothing that can't be CXL'D," I texted back. I waited two minutes before "La Cucaracha" pealed from the phone and Jesus's picture flashed on the screen.

"Hello there," I said. I could hear the thumping pulse of techno rap and the clink of glasses, indicating that Jesus was already ensconced at Party Boy, 3 Monkeys, or whatever was this week's hottest hotspot of Moscow's thriving gay nightclub scene. I always found it mildly depressing that just as I swallowed my "'alf" an Ambien and coaxed body lotion into my sandpaper elbows, somewhere not too far as the crow flies Jesus was just beginning his evening's revels.

"*Querida*, what about the Monday?" repeated Jesus over the din.

"I thought I'd go to IKEA for some candles," I said in a desultory fashion, then sat up with more enthusiasm. "You aren't free, are you? Come with me! We can stock up on coffee at the Starbucks and go to the cash-and-carry for some wine."

"Djou have Tolya?" Jesus craftily dodged the question by

substituting one of his own.

"I do," I said. "I can't manage IKEA on my own."

"Keep Tolya, but we no going to IKEA," instructed Jesus. "We go to . . . Novoyoe Zavidovo."

I caught my breath. "Really?" I asked.

"Really," said Jesus. "The *Seventh Day* or whatever it ees, she come for the photos. Polina wants me to . . . 'ow you say, *querida*, to put onstage, the house."

As always, it took a moment to decipher what Jesus was trying to say.

"Do you mean *7 Days*—the super cheesy TV magazine?" I asked. "Are they coming to shoot the Bichiyuks' house?"

"Jes, this is what I say," said Jesus impatiently. "My leetle Igor who drives me and helps with the measuring tape, ee ees sick, so *querida*, djou will come with me to talk eef we have to talk to somebody. Probably we don't see anyone, but djou weel see the house. You will laugh. But djou can't write about it on your theeng."

"Oh, don't worry about that," I assured him. "I never use real names, and I always change a huge amount of personal stuff so that, really, it's more fiction than nonfiction. They are calling it creative nonfiction these days, but I—"

"Who am I in the theeng?" asked Jesus excitedly. "*Querida*, maybe you make me the Norwegian in the story, jes? Thees is very sexy."

"That might take too big a leap of the imagination," I said, having trouble imagining such a radical change of skin tone. "And I can't think what a Norwegian would be doing in a minigarch mansion."

"Hmmm . . . well, maybe you make me the chef, no? I can be French like Jean-Luc. What about Alexei? What you make eem?"

"Oh, he's dead easy," I said. "I'll just give him a different alpha-male job, like a corporate lawyer or one of those assholes from Gazprom. I'll make him brunette instead of blond, and he'll come from Siberia instead of Karelia."

"Make eem twenty extra pounds," begged Jesus.

"No way," I said staunchly, recalling all of those congenial Friday evenings with the single-malt whisky.

"Ever since we agree to get married ee lets the gym slip," Jesus grumbled. "But I'm thin in the theeng, right, *querida*?"

"Not if you are the French chef you're not."

"Okay, we discuss thees on the way to Novoye Zavidovo," said Jesus.

This was exciting. We all knew that Jesus was working on the interior design of a suburban house for Sergei Bichiyuk, HRH's business *banya* buddy. Jesus had recently become quite tight-lipped about it, making a number of unexplained trips to St. Petersburg. These unexplained absences, and the towering stack of Russia's leading tacky design glossy, *Salon-IDEA*, in Jesus's living room, had heightened my curiosity.

"Jesus," I crooned, "you are such a mensch."

"What is mensch?" he asked.

"It's the opposite of schmuck."

"Schmuck, of course, I know . . . everyone here to djou ees the super schmuck."

"Well, you are a super mensch . . . I can't believe I'm going to finally see this monstrosity."

"*Querida*," drawled Jesus, "nothing I make ees monstrosity. Djou just remember that thees . . . 'ow djou say, *querida*, thees triumph, she go the long way to paying for our new guest cottage at the house in France, which—"

"Which you are going to lend to me as a thank-you for the introduction to Sergei, so I can finish my book," I finished for him.

"Alexei say djou will never finish your book," said Jesus. "'Ow much you write today, *querida*?"

I gritted my teeth and refrained from calling Alexei a super schmuck, then launched into a rant about HRH's renewed interest in glassing in our balconies, but Jesus had lost interest.

"*Querida*, I go now," he said hurriedly. "Just now they put that Algerian in the fish tank. Pick me up at ten. Kiss kiss."

HRH climbed into bed next to me.

"You will never in a million years guess where I am going on Monday!" I said, bursting with anticipation, as he switched the TV on.

"The International Space Station?" he guessed, shaking the remote to make it work.

"Better than that! Jesus is taking me for a sneak peek of Sergei Bichiyuk's new house in Novoyoe Zavidovo!"

"Oh my god . . . ," groaned HRH.

"*7 Days* is coming to photograph it for a shoot!"

"Seriously? Sergei agreed to that?"

"I know, right?"

Russia's *7 Days* is what would happen if *TV Guide, Us Weekly,* and *Salon-IDEA* had a baby. Each week it features the TV schedule, which is just an excuse for the true purpose of the magazine: sixteen glossy pages on some C-list Russian celebrity I've never heard of but who is clearly a minor big deal in Russia. The spreads are set in truly tasteless houses, all located outside Moscow, and the C-list celebrity poses in a number of skimpy outfits in the house's various rooms, including the obligatory shot sprawled all over a large rug made from a large dead animal. Sometimes, but not always, he or she is wrapped around a spouse. We buy it religiously every week because HRH has a touching faith in their surprisingly accurate horoscopes.

"Well," said HRH, "whatever you do, just don't write about it," then turned over and fell instantly asleep in that annoying way he has.

I tossed and turned for a while, deeply annoyed that everyone seemed determined to prevent me from writing about the Bichiyuks. They were such a mother lode of perfect material. I had helped Jesus reel them in more than a year and a half ago at HRH's birthday party. Normally HRH does his entertaining—almost always male only and business related—off home ground. I think he stresses about the food I serve and the fact that my favorite entertainment setup is buffet. For HRH's acquaintances, the lack of a table to squeeze around, the absence of mayonnaise-based salads, and what they would consider a paucity of glassware constitute a major deal breaker. For this spring birthday, however, we agreed to showcase the outdoor terrace with an urban picnic. I made pesto and tabbouleh, and we grilled sausages on the brand-new Weber grill Joe had lugged back from Berlin for me.

"You know," warned Tancy, "the Moscow city government came out with a pamphlet telling foreigners how to behave if they want to reside in the capital. They specifically mentioned that you can't roast a goat on a balcony."

"Oh, puh-leeze," I responded, arranging sausages on a platter. "This is a terrace, not a balcony, and these are from Sausage Man—they're pork and sage, not goat."

"Those instructions are for Tadzhiks," added HRH, "not for people like us." We carried the food out to the terrace. The weather was perfect. The urban family all rallied round to help me keep things moving. Tancy and Jesus came early to help set up—Tancy to make sure I ran and unloaded the dishwasher before the festivities began and Jesus just because he liked to be in the thick of things. I set him to arranging wineglasses on a large table, next to a cooler.

"Who come tonight, *querida*?" he asked, expertly polishing a smeared glass.

"Well, Holt said he'd come, and Joe, of course; Tanya if she can get out of a meeting. HRH has invited the Bichiyuks, and I am just going to be very patient about that."

"Sergei?" asked Jesus, grabbing my arm. "Sergei is coming? *Querida*, this is fantastic!"

Tancy and I exchanged glances. Sergei Bichiyuk was nobody's idea of a "get" at any social gathering, and that went double for his latest marital upgrade, Polina, a.k.a "Mrs. Bichiyuk 3.0." She started out life in some depressing Russian city like Omsk, where she worked as a "promo *dyev*"—you know, the kind of leggy blonde who stalks trade shows in glittery short shorts squirting something cloying at you. Sergei took her away from all that and installed her in a small sex nest near Kurskaya metro station.

Polina is no fool, and she quickly became pregnant, which forced Sergei to divorce Mrs. Bichiyuk 2.0, by whom he had three children. This brought the total of his ex-wives to two. Mrs. Bichiyuk 1.0 was born the daughter of a high-ranking Moscow city official who did something important with the electrical grid. She bore Sergei two sons but then blotted her copybook by having a torrid, taboo, and embarrassing public affair with her driver-bodyguard. As a result, Sergei now had six children ranging in age from two to seventeen. This kind of large, polyparental family is currently very much in vogue in minigarch circles. I'm not sure why, but I suppose if you do the math, the cost of eight first-class tickets makes a private jet seem like cost savings. It's also seen as dead patriotic, until of course the minigarch sends them all to school in "Laaaandon," from whence, surprisingly, they never want to return to Russia.

Polina took to life in Moscow with gusto. After having her

baby, she disappeared for a while to have what I suspect was a lot of plastic surgery. Then, with a lot of help from a few hired guns, she opened a wildly successful designer lingerie boutique catering only to sizes 0 to 4.

"I think Sergei Bichiyuk has bought an enormous house out in Novoye Zavidovo," said Jesus, fluttering his hands. "This house, she ees huge! *Querida*, I want that contract!"

Tancy and I once again exchanged dubious looks.

"Jesus," said Tancy evenly. "Sergei Bichiyuk is an alpha-male Russian; he isn't going to get within three feet of a gay man, much less one dressed in leather pants and a silk shirt and that Rock of Gibraltar you have in your left ear."

"She's right," I concurred. "Yes, they did just buy a house, but I'm guessing Sergei doesn't know his ass from his elbow about decor or design. He's not going to go in for that shabby chic Upper East Side pink-carpet-and-chintz look Roland taught you. And have you seen her? No? Well, she is totally the type who goes in for ostrich-leather furniture and cheetah pillows. They won't get the chic of you at all, Jesus, I'm telling you. Do you know Sergei once offered me a glass of wine from something he called the 'Island of Burgundy'?"

"He never did," said Tancy.

"Hand to heart," I said, placing my palm over my chest. "It was a few years ago, but still."

"Djou don't get eet," said Jesus, stamping his foot. "Ees exactly why I want the contract—Giancarlo has a warehouse full of stuff! 'Ow you say *cursi* in English—no, I know! Pre-tent-tee-ous! Right? Ee 'as the pretend marble, the really shiny, shiny brocade, and, 'ow you say, the fake Ghent tapestries with the unicorns, and, *querida*, ee 'as an enormous bronze nymph! Djou can't imagine!"

"What happened to the person who ordered it?" asked Tancy.

"Oh, ee 'ad to run away to London because of something, and poor Giancarlo going to have to pay a fortune een export duty eef we can't use thees on somebody. Sergei and the Barbie doll, they weel love it."

"Jesus, I'm not sure HRH—" I began warily.

"No, no, *querida*, trust me. I make eet work. Russians like the Sergei, they love this. Eet what Roland called all the rage. Djou would know that eef you ever left this"—he waved his arm to encompass my apartment—"this . . . what djou call this style, *querida*?"

"Scandinavian sparse," suggested Tancy, with a wicked grin.

"How about 'busy family with active nine-year-old who thinks she's a horse'?" I mused, plunging bottles of wine into a cooler. "What the hell else were we supposed to do with this place, anyway? The woman who sold us the shell and core of this apartment gave me the plans her architect had drawn up, and you never saw anything in your life like it. It was a French tart's boudoir as interpreted by a Turkish designer. Or maybe a Turkish tart's boudoir as interpreted by a Russian designer. It was all disgusting layers of sheer curtains, urns, and faux Louis XV furniture with cherubim and seraphim blowing trumpets." Jesus shuddered involuntarily, and Tancy broke out into her deep, tobacco-honed laugh.

Right on cue, HRH ushered the Bichiyuks in. Sergei, in classic Russian fashion, carried a large, stiff bouquet of flowers wrapped in three layers of colored plastic and affixed with a huge gold silk bow. He presented this to me with a sweeping flourish even though it wasn't my birthday.

"How lovely! Aren't you thoughtful?" I breathed. I never know what to do with these enormous floral tributes. It is lovely to have them, of course, but it takes about thirty minutes to liberate them from the two pounds of stiff colored plastic paper and chicken wire they are engulfed in. Setting them down seems rude, and yet it is impossible to pour drinks, take coats, and make people feel welcome while holding a five-pound beach ball of a bouquet. "Polina, how nice to see you again!" I said, exchanging tepid air kisses with Sergei's willowy third wife.

Sergei and Polina look exactly like the most famous Russian stereotypes of my childhood, and probably yours too: Boris Badenov and his charming wife, Natasha. Like their cartoon counterparts, the height difference between them is a good foot, made all the more acute by Polina's ever-present four-inch Jimmy Choos. Sergei is a classic square-shaped Slav: short, thickset, broad shoulders, barrel chest, short stocky legs, and a heavy jaw. Polina has the enviable silhouette of a Barbie doll. This evening, however, she seemed to be channeling her inner Eva Perón: blonde hair scraped back in a bun, her plump collagen-injected Slavic lips painted bright red and stretching all the way from one perfectly chiseled cheekbone to the other.

For her eye makeup she'd taken Elizabeth Taylor in *Cleopatra* as her cue, then expanded and enhanced. Polina always made me feel that I hadn't put on enough eye makeup. What I couldn't tear my eyes away from, however, were the long diamond-and-emerald chandelier earrings glittering from her ears down to her shoulders. I'm no jewelry expert, but I'd have hazarded a guess they were worth at least six figures if they were real, and knowing both Polina and Sergei, real seemed the only likely possibility.

I think I'd heard Polina say about four sentences in the two years I'd known her. This might have been learned behavior, since Sergei, like most Russian men of a certain net worth, almost never drew breath, declaiming loudly on a wide range of topics about which he felt he was an absolute authority. His voice was deep and guttural, and I often had trouble understanding what he said, although I always knew when he was addressing me, since he prefaced each sentence with an annoying little preamble to be sure of his captive audience: "Eyeh . . . Zhen-eef-eer, eyeh-ah Zhen, ah?" Like most Russians of their ilk, neither was completely comfortable with foreigners, foreign customs, or foreign food and drink. At large gatherings of this sort, they stuck closely to themselves and other Russians. I looked around for the Potapovs or the Stepanovs, but Jesus deftly moved from the periphery to the center of the conversation.

"Sergei, Polina," I said, stretching out my arm to draw him further into the conversation, "I don't think you've met my good friend from Venezuela, Jesus Arismendi. He lives in Moscow now, and he is a fantastic interior designer!"

"How do djou do?" gushed Jesus in his enthusiastic, if heavily accented, Russian. "So nice to meet you—oh! Djour earrings! *Qué hermosos!*" he said to Polina. "I am from a diamond-producing nation," he added by way of explanation.

"Sergei and Polina have just purchased a house in the country outside Moscow," I said to Jesus.

"Really?" gushed Jesus, flashing his dazzlingly white teeth in a huge smile that would melt any frozen Slavic heart.

"You know, Sergei," I said as if I'd just thought of it, "you should talk to Jesus about doing your house."

"Oh!" gasped Jesus, clasping his hands to his heart. "*Fantástica!*

I would love to look at eet . . . ees always apartments, apartments, apartments here in Moscow. So boring! Where eet ees, djour house?"

Sergei squinted at Jesus suspiciously. I groaned inwardly. You never ask a Russian where he lives: the Stalin years . . . too soon. I could see that Sergei was on the verge of bolting, taking in the purple silk blouse, the butter-yellow leather pants, and the diamond stud, counterbalanced by the fact that HRH seemed completely at ease with Jesus.

"Jesus did Dmitry Lobovsky's apartment," I said, desperately throwing out the name of a publicity-mad multigazillionaire owner of a chain of mobile-phone stores. Lobovsky went to university with Alexei and did a certain amount of work with The Firm. He had a nuclear-powered publicist and a statuesque TV-show-host girlfriend. Their finished apartment had been photographed by *7 Days,* and this launched Jesus on the road to fame in the Moscow decor world.

"Really?" asked Sergei, looking as if he was willing to overlook the diamond stud earring, if not the silk blouse. "Who else, *eyeh*?"

Jesus looked pointedly at me. The truth was that Jesus's Moscow clientele, apart from Lobovsky, consisted primarily of the gay demimonde: Tihon, who was famous for his massive installations in ironic venues; Slava, the tortured shoe designer; and Jorge, the nightclub owner. They were all famous enough in their own circles, but these did not intersect with Sergei's. I tried to buy some time.

"Of course, Jesus used to be based in New York, right?" I lobbed tentatively over the conversational net.

Polina arched a perfectly threaded eyebrow, and I could read her mind. Importing a designer has distinct cachet for the *7 Days* crowd.

Jesus volleyed the ball back.

"Jes," he sighed, "I deed. But eet much more interesting here, I find."

"Eyeh . . . Zhen-eef-eer, eyeh-ah Zhen, ah," Sergei inserted. "Anyone we know?"

I paused. Here was a real dilemma. Sergei, I was pretty sure, had a central line to insider information on the Russian end, but did those tentacles stretch as far as East 86th Street? We couldn't make up American clients Sergei had actually heard of, like Bruce Willis (whose face graced bank advertisements on billboards all over town). But if we mentioned other famous New Yorkers Jesus had worked for, such as Calvin Trillin, would it have the same impact? I was 400-percent sure that Sergei had heard of Calvin Trillin.

I looked from Sergei, looking at me expectantly, to HRH, who might intervene if things got out of hand, and to Jesus, for once out of his depth. They stood grouped in front of the floor-to-ceiling bookshelves. And suddenly I knew exactly what to say.

"Don't be so modest, Jesus," I waded in. "There was the summer house you did out in East Egg for the Buchanans: Daisy and Tom." I looked to Sergei, who nodded appreciatively.

"Jes . . . ," said Jesus tentatively, and I gave him an imperceptible nod to continue. "Eet very large house." I scanned the shelves behind Sergei again. "And the Bingleys' country home . . . Jane and her very nice husband. What's his name?"

"I don' remember . . . ," said Jesus slowly. "I only ever call heem Mr. Bingley."

"*Da*," said Sergei, anxious not to be left out. "Bingley . . . *da da*. I've heard something." My eyes slid down and to the right.

"Of course, the little flat you did for Brett—Brett Ashley . . . you said she was very difficult."

"Deeficult, jes," Jesus agreed, getting into it.

"But great taste she had—very modern, right?" I added, getting into the swing of things.

"Modern?" asked Sergei. "Eyeh . . . Zhen-eef-eer, eyeh-ah Zhen, ah . . . we are traditional, aren't we Polina . . . eyeh, Polin?"

Polina gave an imperceptible shrug.

"Oh, Jesus does traditional!" I cried, as my eyes scanned back up the shelves. "Remember that enormous country house you did for Edward Rochester and his second wife . . . now, what was her name? Janet? No, Jane—that's it."

"I prefer Italian," said Jesus, wrenching the conversational reins out of my grasp just in time. "The marble and the brocade . . . very rich, very . . . *querida*, 'ow you say in Russian 'plush'?"

"Plush?" asked Sergei.

"*Plusheviy*," I supplied.

"*Da, da*," said Sergei, nodding his head. "Something like that, eh Polin?"

"No one does plush quite like Jesus," I said.

Polina shrugged her shoulders, setting her diamond-and-emerald earrings dancing.

"Well, I will love to come and see djour house," said Jesus, whipping a card out of his seemingly too-tight leather trousers. "Djou can call me, and I weel come with my leetle Vanya, ee ees the translator. I bring my measuring tape and we go from there, okay?"

"Ok-eh," said Sergei, squinting at the card, then shoving it into his jacket pocket.

"Would anyone like a drink?" I asked, panting for one.

"I show djou," said Jesus. "Polina, I make you a cosmopolitan, djes? I make it just like in *Sex in the City*. Djou know *Sex in the City*? Of course djou do!"

A shadow of a smile cracked Polina's otherwise perfectly smooth features. The two sashayed toward the bar. Jesus was amazing: he could land on Pluto and be mixing up Negronis by sundown for the locals. HRH said something to Sergei about a cigar and steered him toward the terrace. I took a large slug of my white wine and let my shoulders relax down about a foot.

Jesus was signed up for the job within two weeks, and for a long time after that we never saw him because he was always out at Novoyoe Zavidovo or up in St. Petersburg.

"Tolya," I said to Tolya the Driver on Monday, "we are going to Novoyoe Zavidovo . . . here is a map, and Jesus knows what to do once we get to the compound." Tolya bobbed his head and revved up the engine. He cast a wary glance in the rearview mirror, as Jesus settled himself in the back of the car. It's not every day Tolya encounters members of his own gender dressed in leather pants, a mink overcoat, a pale coral cashmere scarf, and a diamond-stud earring, all wrapped in a cloud of Jo Malone's Lime, Basil & Mandarin. I think it makes him a little uncomfortable, although being, like Jesus, one of nature's born gentlemen, Tolya conceals it well. He took a sip of his caramel latte; he clearly appreciated being included in Jesus's Starbucks run, which is not a detail all of the expats I know would remember. We headed out into the gridlocked Monday morning traffic.

"Do you actually know what 'Novoyoe Zavidovo' means?" I asked Jesus, as we cozied up in the back of the car and settled in for a nice long gossip in the midmorning traffic.

"Large bizarre gated compound built yesterday?" he hazarded.

"Close. It actually means, literally, 'new envy.'"

"No!"

"It does," I said, nodding my head. "It's from the verb *zavidit*, meaning 'to envy.'"

"*Dios*," said Jesus, delicately wiping the milk foam from the corner of his mouth and winking at Tolya in the rearview mirror.

"Jesus, stop making goo-goo eyes at the man who conducts the vehicle!" I said, deliberately using complicated words and sentence structure so that there would be no chance that Tolya would understand what we were talking about. "He does not share your orientation."

"Beeg pity," sighed Jesus. "Ee ees cute, thees one."

"How long have you been working on this house?" I asked to change the subject.

"Forever," moaned Jesus. "Foo, *querida*, eet doing me in. Last week, I wait all day for Sergei's very scary . . . ees driver or bodyguard or something, and ee come back from the customs with the howdah."

"The what?" I asked.

"The howdah," he said. "Eet is . . ." He pursed his lips, looking for the right words. "Howdah, she a thing on which . . . the thing on top of the, 'ow djou say, the *elefante* . . . that thing. Djou ride on eet."

"Get out of town," I said.

"No, no, eet ees a howdah, and they buy eet when they were on a crazy trip to India. Lucy, she make for them. Eet was hell to get inside the customs. Antique ivory."

"Isn't ivory an endangered species?"

Jesus gave me A Look.

"Lucy, she—well, she know someone at that end."

"Lucy," I interjected, "has someone at every end."

Jesus got the joke and cackled for a moment. "Sergei knows everyone thees end . . . but eet take six boys to bring it in, and I don't really know what we are going to do with it. Djou can't sit on eet, and eet clash with the flooring. . . ."

"Which is?"

Jesus let out a groan. "Eet impossible to describe," he said. "Djou wait and see."

Tolya inched the car through a bottleneck at the end of

Volokolamskoye Shosse made even narrower by the dirty gray snow piled high on either side. We grimaced as Tolya turned off the main road onto an access road full of potholes and dirt-encrusted ice ruts. The car rocked back and forth, and Jesus narrowly missed getting a large splash of tall skinny latte all over his fur coat.

"Oy, sorry," said Tolya, exhausting his English-language reserves.

"No problem," Jesus smiled angelically in the mirror.

We off-roaded across the potholes for about three more miles, then came to a large clearing in the woods. A ten-foot-high iron-and-concrete wall stretched hundreds of yards in each direction, studded on top with an additional foot of twisted barbed wire and shards of glass jutting up menacingly. Two feet before the wall, the road abruptly became silky smooth and neatly plowed. It led to a large, gunmetal electronic gate guarded by two men in standard-issue private security guard kit: black fascist flak jackets with GUARD embroidered on the back in large yellow letters (just in case you were in any doubt what they did), tight black pants tucked into black commando boots, and Kalashnikov rifles slung around their torsos. They paced up and down, more, I suspected, to keep warm than to rehearse a quasi-military drill.

They motioned for us to brake, and one strode manfully over to the car. Tolya slid the window down, as Jesus passed him a sheaf of papers encased in plastic document protectors, each stamped and signed. The guard regarded them for a few moments, then leaned back to Tolya and said, "Passports."

Tolya handed them over, then switched off the engine and checked his mobile phone. Jesus nestled deeper into the mink coat, pulled his deep shawl collar up around his cheekbones, and sighed. I took a final slug of coffee, praying that we would reach a working toilet before too much time elapsed.

After ten minutes the guard strode manfully back, clutching our passports and paperwork, which he silently passed to Tolya. The iron rungs slid to one side, sort of like the Black Gate of Mordor, as Tolya eased the car forward.

The layout of Novoyoe Zavidovo was like any gated community: houses sat on uniform plots of land on either side of aggressively landscaped winding streets and cul de sacs. In Novoyoe Zavidovo, however, each house had its own version of the iron-and-concrete wall with the barbed wire and the shards of glass. There were no mailboxes, which made sense since the Russian postal service is a national disgrace that no one in his right mind would ever use. And anyway, it didn't strike me as the kind of neighborhood where soccer moms gathered to gossip in the morning while they waited for the school bus. This hunch was confirmed when we turned a corner and saw a man, a woman, and small child all wrapped up well against the cold. As our car came into view, the family was suddenly surrounded by four hefty men with buzz cuts and earpieces. With practiced efficiency they formed a human cordon around the family, who paid absolutely no attention to them or to us.

The houses of Novoyoe Zavidovo were all rectangular McMansions of a uniform size got up to look like cut-rate Cotswold manor houses. Jesus told me that Novoyoe Zavidovo limited its residents to three color choices, none of them, in his opinion, a good version of that particular hue. There was a blue that was perhaps meant to be robin's egg but had ended up like the baby-boy section of a South American maternity ward. I thought the yellow might have taken its inspiration from early-nineteenth-century neoclassical architecture, but it veered too close to lemon drop. Then there was a color that was neither pink nor beige but sort of a lurid combination of both. If I had been in the paint-naming business (if only!), I'd have christened it "phlegm."

Jesus directed Tolya up a small hill that led to a fresh set of iron gates, guard huts, and another intimidating-looking tollgate. Tolya cut the engine as an even more burly security guard strode out of an even larger hut toting an even bigger semiautomatic rifle.

"How djou say in English?" asked Jesus, pointing to the tollgate. "In Russian, of course, I know—it is *schlak-baum*. I like thees word so much. What eet ees in English?"

"Something like tollgate or barrier," I said. "*Schlagbaum* is German, I'm guessing, originally. Probably one of those Peter the Great imports."

"Russians, they don' have a word for eet? I thought they invented thees *schlagbaum*. Ees such a Russian thing." Jesus shrugged his shoulders. "Anyway, *querida*, thees ees the last *schlagbaum* we go through: here ees the VIP section."

"Thank god," I said. "If I don't get to a bathroom soon, I'm going to burst. Sorry, did you just say the VIP section? That's a thing? A VIP section of an already-gated community?"

"*Querida*," said Jesus patiently, "how long djou live in Russia already? Of course there ees VIP section. What the point eef there isn't? There ees VIP everything: VIP restaurant, VIP parking, VIP massage——"

"HRH had a VIP room at the Sanduny baths yesterday," I mused. "I'm not sure what goes on there."

"Djou don't want to know, *querida*." Jesus squirmed a bit in his seat, and in a rare moment for him, he looked uncomfortable.

"Huh?"

"I see a sign for a VIP sushi once," he said, hastily changing the subject.

The burly security guard waved us on, and the *schlagbaum* rose majestically. Tolya revved up the engine and eased it over the speed bumps, evenly placed every six feet. The VIP section of Novoyoe Zavidovo was special in that the plots of land were larger, the wrought-iron fences more elaborate, and the barbed wire and shards of glass higher up and much more menacing. Every tree branch seemed bowed down with the weight of large security cameras. There also seemed to be a much broader artistic license permitted: I could see turrets, and was that a replica of Big Ben peeping up from behind the gates?

Jesus leaped gracefully out of the car, picked his way to a discreet key pad, and punched in several numbers. The aggressively gilded gates shuddered, then majestically opened inward, like the beginning of a Disneyland commercial, revealing another faux Cotswold mansion, only this one was on steroids. It was longer and had two additional floors. The proportions were off, like a photograph stretched too far by someone who has not completely mastered Photoshop. The house was Pepto-Bismol pink and topped with a large bronze imperial double-headed eagle.

Jesus bustled to the front door and fiddled with another key pad and a ring of large skeleton keys, each as long as my hand.

"Do you want to come and have a look?" I asked Tolya, who smiled and shook his head. He plugged his portable DVD player into the cigarette lighter and fired up the next episode of *Lost*.

Tolya was obsessed with *Lost* and *Modern Family.*

Jesus rattled the keys, then turned the door handles, which were huge bronze rings threaded through the nostrils of two enormous lions. He flung the doors open and strode inside.

"Djou can leave your boots on, *querida*," he called over his shoulder. "We are done, but I have the drop clothings down still because the naughty workers still finish the fur safe upstairs. They are so untidy!"

"The fur safe——" I began, then fell completely silent as I stepped into the house.

I've seen a lot of outrageous interiors in Russia. I've seen a dining room got up to look like the inner chamber of an Egyptian pyramid, complete with gold-and-lapis-lazuli statuary and floor-to-ceiling reproductions from the *Book of the Dead.* I've seen the inside of cupolas, where there were never domes on the top, decorated with pictures of the seven wonders of the ancient world on something truly scary called "photo wallpaper." I've seen a kitchen deliberately designed from illustrations in *Hansel and Gretel,* but the Bichiyuk domicile took the cake. I looked at Jesus, speechless. He shrugged his shoulders and smiled.

"Have they seen it?" I asked.

"Of course they see eet!" Jesus retorted. "They looooooove it. Eet ees exactly what they want. Roland, ee always say to me, geeve people exactly what they want and never judge. I never forget thees."

"Do they have a Stewart Granger fetish?" I asked. "Because that is exactly what you've given them: the set of *The Prisoner of Zenda!*"

"Who?" asked Jesus.

"Never mind," I muttered, and let my eyes wander around the room again. The doors to the outside opened directly into the house; there was no hallway or receiving area. A Cotswold mansion normally opens onto a central staircase with receiving rooms ranged on either side. You got the sense that the original architects of the Novoyoe Zavidovo houses had created a layout with that template in mind. The Bichiyuks, however, having purchased more height and breadth with their VIP upgrade, had clearly felt no obligation to adhere to any traditional architectural tenets. The casing of their house was knock-off Georgian, but the inside was pure Ruritania.

To the left of the big room, slightly off center to accommodate its bulk, was an immense staircase designed with one thought in mind: that minor Eastern European royalty should descend from it. It curved in an aggressive trajectory up to the second floor from its anchor: a ten-foot-high bronze nymph holding aloft a torch. Jesus extracted a gold-plated remote control from its Baroque niche on the wall and clicked a button. The torch's top burst into neon lime-green, orange, and purple flame. He pressed another switch, and I was nearly blinded by a massive Bohemian-crystal-and-gold chandelier that hung from the third floor all the way down to the second. Jesus pressed again and the chandelier began a slow descent down to the main level. I bent to shield my eyes and caught sight of a corner of the drop cloth. I pulled it to one side, revealing a thick red velvet carpet and brassy stair rails, gleaming dully through their plastic wrap, on top of shiny white stone.

"This is never solid marble," I asserted hopefully.

"No," admitted Jesus. "Beeg fight over thees. Sergei wants the solid jasper from . . . where that place, *querida*, where they shoot the tsar? No, I know: Yekaterinburg. But frankly, *querida*, thees house ees not so good constructed—eet don't support the marble. Solid anything, she collapse the entire first floor. Thees ees actually tile casing from Turkey, but djou didn't hear eet from me. We sign a paper saying we don't tell."

I pulled myself to my feet and moved to the other side of the room, which was dominated by a titanic fireplace that I could stand up in. It was faced with pinkish stone and flanked by rows of carved fleurs-de-lis and what looked a lot like the coat of arms of the House of Windsor running up each side. There was something funny about it though. I stepped back to get the full perspective, then moved closer to inspect it.

"Now that ees marble," said Jesus. "Marble facing, anyway."

"Yes," I acknowledged, squinting at the wall next to the fireplace. "But I don't quite see how this can be a working fireplace; it isn't set into the wall or anything. Where is the chimney?" I swung one leg and then the other over the tooled-leather-and-bronze fire rail and hunched down to peer up into the chimney. My nose banged up against cold metal. I turned around to face Jesus, who smiled and flipped another switch. The logs in the grate I had straddled burst into electric flames. Another switch, and the sound of crackling. There was no heat.

"It's not even gas?" I cried.

"That," said Jesus, with a dismissive gesture, "that nothing I deed. First theeng I say, let's do a proper fireplace and djou can use thees as a mantelpiece, but no . . . they like eet like eet ees."

"Well, they do have five children under the age of twelve," I said.

Jesus pursed his lips disapprovingly. "What djou theenk three nannies ees for?" he asked, and beckoned me up the stairs. We picked our way over the drop cloths, climbing up and up the grand staircase until we got to the first-floor landing. Jesus paused, then silently pointed up like that picture of John the Baptist. I followed his index finger and gasped. Above the staircase was the interior of the house's central dome. The perimeter was painted in heavy, classical detail in dark-red-and-gold leaf. Inside the dome, in a style that owed a little to Tiepolo and a lot to *HELLO!* magazine, was a full-size portrait of Sergei seated on a golden throne in the classical robes and gilded laurel wreath of an emperor from the "decline" era of the Roman Empire. Polina stood next to him wrapped in a diaphanous gown and wearing an enormous tiara, her emerald-and-diamond earrings glinting down to her shoulders. One post-plastic-surgery breast was bared, her nails were painted purple, and she had on her silver Jimmy Choos. Their Chihuahua, Chappie, sported a matching emerald-and-diamond collar. The four youngest children were arranged around them portrayed as putti; the two eldest boys wore medieval armor and held spears.

"I almost love that," said Jesus.

"It certainly is what it is," I agreed. We gazed for a moment.

"Come see the master bedroom," said Jesus, breaking the spell.

The master bedroom was immense. The walls were papered in very busy gold-relief paper, and the windows were smothered in complex layers of drapery: bright red velvet with gold tassels, lace sheers, and a shimmering layer of gold base cloth. In the middle of the room was an enormous round bed covered in a red sateen quilt and something stitched together from a lot of white fur pelts. Like the windows, the bed was festooned with red-and-gold velvet curtains. These were gathered at the top into a canopy topped with a gold crown.

"Where do you find round bedsheets?" I wondered aloud.

"Amsterdam," Jesus said matter-of-factly.

A pair of red brocade fur-lined mules were placed strategically next to the round bed. I noticed that there were no bedside tables, no sticky, half-used tubes of Eucerin, no reading lamps, no bottles of Advil, no waterlogged copies of the *New Yorker*. I made a mental note to myself to stage my own bedroom a bit more, or at least clear some of the clutter from my own bedside.

Jesus pointed to the seventy-two-inch flat-screen television anchored to the ceiling.

"That double as a mirror," said Jesus. "Eet very good, actually. Djou tell Alexei I don't mind to have one for Christmas."

The oval-shaped master bath was cavernous. The ceiling was painted with a mural of the night sky, all of the stars of the zodiac signs picked out with glow-in-the-dark crystals. The more lifelike attributes of the bull, crab, ram, and so on were fleshed out in thin silver lines. Jesus flipped the lights on and off so I could appreciate the effect. A huge black marble sunken bathtub that could easily fit four dominated the middle of the room.

"Are those solid gold?" I asked, pointing to the faucets.

"Are djou keeding?" scoffed Jesus. "Do djou know what solid gold faucets cost, *querida*? These are gold plated."

"Why are there two bidets?" I asked, and Jesus did a really good imitation of a Slavic shrug.

There were more dead-white-animal rugs around the toilet, which to me seemed impractical; and again, in readiness for the *7 Days* team, there were no signs of any habitation or regular daily use, such as a toothbrush or a neti pot. Another pair of brocade slippers were lined up in front of the massive walk-in shower, which was a nod to the Orient: it had bronze dragon-head handles and spouts and plum blossoms etched into the glass with a vaguely gold paint. One of the dragons had ruby red eyes, which peered at me suspiciously.

"This is a little creepy," I said. "Let's go back downstairs." I was suddenly reminded of a Victory Day party we had when Valentina Andrievna Stepanova gave a few people an unsanctioned tour of my bedroom and closet, where, I was sorry to say, there had been not only signs of habitation but seriously untidy habitation at that.

Jesus took me downstairs to Sergei's study. The walls were

lined with panels of a lovely seasoned wood, made much less lovely by mother-of-pearl inlaid designs of military insignia covering every inch of each panel. There was a massive, highly polished wood desk with a marble top, on which was a huge malachite-and-bronze sculpture of the imperial double-headed eagle. Behind the desk were rows and rows of new-looking leather-bound volumes behind glass doors.

"This is a surprise," I said, pointing. "I've never been sure that Sergei can actually read."

"He buy these by the meter," Jesus explained. "There comes from St. Petersburg a nice leetle man—Roland, ee always used to call people like that, 'nice leetle man'—and he measures, then goes back to order the books to fit the shelves. But now, *querida*, djou will see the real triumph. Come!"

If the main hall was Ruritania, the central dome ancient Rome, and the master bedroom Las Vegas, in the dining room the Bichiyuks had channeled their own inner eighteenth-century Russian aristocrat. One of these lurks inside every ambitious post-perestroika minigarch. The dining room was painted white with elaborate gold-leaf designs around each of the windows and floor-to-ceiling mirrors evenly spaced around the room. The ceiling was decorated with more oil paintings, this time not of Sergei and Polina but of very lifelike, in-your-face dead animals. A large blue-and-white-tiled Dutch stove dominated one corner of the room. The long, oval table was set for twelve with delicate pink and blue plates. White brocade chairs were placed slightly away from the table, which was heavily draped in a shiny white damask cloth and festooned with a heavy garland of plastic pink and white roses. Elaborate pyramids of fruit and flowers flanked each end of the table. These also looked fake.

"This looks seriously familiar," I said, probing the back of my memory for why.

Jesus's naughty eyes sparkled.

"Do eet? I 'ope so!"

"I've seen this before, I know I have. But I can't have. I've never been here—yes I have, though! I totally recognize these paintings. What is this?"

"Theenk, *querida*." Jesus clapped his hands with delight.

I leaned in to scrutinize the heavy centerpiece. From a circle of mirrored glass rose a ceramic pavilion atop a ceramic knoll. I knew it as well as I knew the icon screen in the Assumption Cathedral: a familiarity born of hundreds of visits. It was a miniature of the folly at Catherine Palace, the summer residence of the Romanovs. My head snapped up. I whirled around and looked again at the dead animals, the brocade chairs, the delicate china, the regular squares of the parquet floor, and Jesus's barely concealed excitement.

"It can't be?"

"Oh, jes eet can!" shouted Jesus, triumphantly.

"This is . . . what do they call it? I know! This is the White State Dining Room from the Catherine Palace at Tsarskoye Selo?"

"*Exactamente*! They tell me they want exact copy! Sergei, he go to some party up there with some minister of the Metro or something. Ee come back with a book, and ee say to me I have to make thees just like the pictures."

"Are you serious?" I said, walking around the table, marveling at the reproduction Meissen china. "I remember these butter dishes—they were a big talking piece. But this is insane! What kind of wack job copies an eighteenth-century royal palace dining room down to the last teaspoon for his own house?"

"The wack job with me working for heem," confirmed Jesus. "Thees is why I go to Petersburg so much, *querida*! I go to that damn palace four hundred times. Sergei, ee hire one of the palace restoration guys to do the gold leaf. We have to bring him 'ere blindfolded, can djou imagine? Giancarlo, ee find the china reproductions and the fabric. Eet take forever. Djou can't tell anyone, *querida*. I know you won't write about thees because eef you do, I weel be killed by the scary bodyguard. We all sign the paper."

"Will they actually eat in it?"

"Djou see her—djou theenk she ever eat?"

"Well, I know he does, and he certainly drinks for Russia."

"He eat from the tins," said Jesus dismissively. "His favorite meal ees the buckwheat porridge."

I opened a pair of French doors leading out to a good-size balcony. The balcony looked directly onto the garden, and as I stepped forward to admire the view my toe hit a stack of steel girders.

"What are these?" I asked.

"Oh," said Jesus with a dismissive gesture, clucking with disapproval. "What you theenk, *querida*? They both say we must put horrible glass on thees balcony. *Están completamente locos!*"

"Are you sure I can't write about this?" I asked.

"Okay, but djou change the details, okay? And *querida*, djou make sure I'm thin and sexy."

RUSSIANS
EN
ROUTE

"BABYCAKES, WHY DON'T we run away together?" Joe asked one gloomy March afternoon.

"Okay," I agreed. "Can you get away on Thursday?"

March is hands down the longest month in Russia. After International Women's Day, it is a long, slow slog to spring. Our friend Posey Farquarshon, who had left Moscow the previous year, was having a big birthday party in London, so Joe and I decided to go and recharge our batteries.

"I've never been to London except to change planes," Joe confessed. "Can we go a few days early and play tourist?"

"Lovely," I agreed. It seemed like a good time to go. HRH's mother came to look after Velvet, and with a first draft of my book complete, I felt like a little toot.

To make the most of our time, we boarded the early morning British Airways flight, settled in to our "aisles across" seats in the middle of the plane, and waited to take off in the pre-dawn gloom, lulled by the gentle hum of the airline's engines into something that was not quite sleep, but not wakefulness either. It was the sweet doze that comes after you've been up all night. All was quiet calm until the silence was shattered by a high-decibel, upper-range Eastern European battle cry. The first discernible word caused Russian yuppies, bilingual bankers, and smooth-haired wannabe models to open their eyes in horror.

"Tovvvaaaaaaaaaaaaaaarishi!" came a voice—half wail, part howl—racing down the length of the aircraft and hurtling us back

through time to the late 1970s. "Comrades, who here is flying to San Francisco?" No one answered; everyone seemed frozen in horror at the apparition coming down the aisle right out of the late Brezhnev era.

"Comrades, please! Who will help this babushka find her connecting flight to San Francisco? I appeal to you!"

Even Gavin, the louche and effeminate British Airways flight attendant, who looked like someone who had seen it all, appeared visibly shaken as a bulky woman with an abundance of peroxide-blonde hair (some her own, some possibly not even human) hoisted up in a bouffant poof over her sweaty forehead and gathered in back in a jaunty and completely age-inappropriate ponytail appeared in the economy-class cabin. Determinedly, she stomped down the aisle, her feet crammed into spiky kitten heels. Her operatic, mottled cleavage was barely encased in a skintight, hot pink, zebra-striped V-neck top riding up over capri pants that looked like they might not make it to London, let alone all the way to San Francisco. In one hand she held a cheap, frayed, Turkish knockoff designer bag; behind her she dragged a bulging, scuffed, snakeskin-patterned Rolla-board, which was too wide for the aisle and kept getting noisily caught in the arm rests as she impatiently yanked it behind her.

I stared, fascinated. You don't see this kind of thing in Moscow much anymore; you have to head deep into the regions to get this level of pure unadulterated Stagnation Era getup. Or Moldova. Her thick and theatrical makeup, possibly applied in another time zone on the previous day, was beginning to run down her face. Her bloodshot eyes were ringed in shiny turquoise eye shadow and purple mascara, and her mouth, smeared with gummy cotton-candy-pink lipstick, opened up once again to disgorge her passionate appeal.

"Good people," she keened, flinging off Gavin's restraining arm, "I'm changing planes in London to fly to my daughter in San Francisco. I don't know what to do . . . who can help this babushka?" Her peroxide head darted about the cabin, releasing an acrid odor: one part cloyingly sweet perfume from South Korea, one part Armenian cognac, and three parts Aqua Net hairspray.

I raised my eyebrows at Joe and at the empty seat next to him. He surreptitiously closed his copy of that morning's Russian business daily, *Vedomosti*, and slid it into the seat pocket in front of him, then crossed his arms, closed his eyes, and feigned sound sleep.

The Ukrainian diva jammed her hands on her hips and surveyed an entire planeload of people, all refusing to meet her eyes. Her voice transitioned from the upper-register desperate wail to the lower, more strident and bellicose tones of the fruit and vegetable market: "So! Not one single person on this entire plane speaks Russian! Strange."

She shook her head and continued to make pithy comments about the sad state of the world as she crawled over Joe and somehow squeezed herself into the middle seat. Then she turned her attention to the hapless Rollaboard, too big to go under the seat in front of her no matter how much she pushed and prodded.

Gavin, anxious no doubt to achieve pushback, asked if he could assist in stowing it for her, a kind offer she totally misunderstood. She let out a new howl of protest, clutching the handle of the Rollaboard and looking like she was going to sock Gavin in the nose if he came one millimeter closer, until Joe snapped open his eyes and explained to her that Gavin would certainly give her the suitcase back. The diva experienced an immediate mood shift, affixed the broad, fake smile Slavs reserve for foreigners, and intoned what had to be the only four words of English she actually knew: "Zank you . . . zank you verry mach." She beamed at Gavin, who sashayed away, rolling his eyes to heaven, to find a place for the bag. She patted Joe's knee and repeated, "Zank you . . . zank you verry mach." I giggled. The diva placed a ring-studded hand on her heaving chest, sighed deeply, crossed herself three times, fastened her seat belt after a few aborted attempts, and finally we were prepared for takeoff.

My own seat companion was far less trouble. He boarded the aircraft, immediately fell asleep, and spent the entire trip snoring. He was dressed in the universal traveling outfit of middle-agedmen from Russia: a white nylon tracksuit with red and gold scrolls and the words SOCHI 2014! printed in enormous letters on both the front and back.

"The town with the next Olympics . . . how do you pronounce that? Sock-ee?" one of Posey's friends asked me at her party.

"No, it's *sew*, as in a needle pulling thread," I recited my well-

★

rehearsed response. "Then *chee*, which rhymes with *knee*. Sochi."

"But where on earth is it? Is it near Moscow?"

"No, it's way down south. It's a seaside resort town on the Black Sea. It backs up on the Caucasus Mountain range. They've turned it into a winter recreation center."

"How do you do the Winter Games in a seaside resort?" he asked, drawing his eyebrows together.

"I'm not sure," I confessed.

"Funny sort of Olympics," he said in that very understated British way they have. "No one seems to have heard of it or have any idea where it is."

Russians have always known about Sochi, which is their version of Florida. It was developed in the early twentieth century by the Bolsheviks as a proletarian answer to nearby, and far more aristocratic, Yalta. Since then, the Soviet leadership has summered and autumned in overblown villas. You can imagine how cheesy it is.

No one is quite sure where the idea to hold the Winter Olympics there came from. Depending on who you talk to, the Olympics in Sochi, or as the PR-*schiki* like to say, "Sochi 2014," is gearing up to be either an unprecedented triumph or the biggest national embarrassment since the Russo-Japanese War of 1905.

The jury is out, but skeptics agree: Sochi is impossible to get to, even if you wanted to, and who on earth does? If you want to ski, well, that is why God invented Austria. For average Russians, though, who have never visited Sochi and are even more unlikely to after it gets tarted up for the Olympics, Sochi 2014 is a point of pride. "It's high time we had the Olympics," they say.

Joe and I saw a lot more SOCHI 2014! tracksuits as we explored London on the top of red buses. London was heaving with Russian tourists.

"We could have stayed in Moscow and dealt with this," muttered Joe, as we stood in line to see the Crown Jewels. Three teenage Russians tried to cut in line ahead of us. The British pursed their lips and looked pained, but Joe barked at them in Russian: "This is Britain, you little shits—go to the back of the line!" They scurried away.

"Nicely done," I congratulated him.

"They should bring back that thing," said Joe.

"What thing?"

LENIN LIVES NEXT DOOR

"That thing when they didn't let the Russians out of Russia."

"That wasn't a super-fun time for the Russians, Joe," I reminded him.

"More fun for the rest of us," he humphed.

For large swaths of Russian history, including the recent Soviet period, Russian rulers have felt, for various reasons, that the world was best served if its citizens stayed inside its own borders. Foreign travel until the eighteenth century was limited to diplomatic missions, one of the most famous being that of Peter the Great, who set off to explore Western Europe in 1697 and ended up trashing the place. The military mission of 1812 witnessed the Russian army chasing Napoleon's forces all the way back to Paris. Once there, they hung out at small eateries, demanding quicker service by pounding on the tables and yelling "*Bistro! Bistro!*" ("Faster! Faster!") The name stuck.

Images of Cold War Russians venturing into the West featured tortured dissidents and sexy ballet stars as well as a memorable performance in *Moscow on the Hudson* by Robin Williams as a Brezhnev-era Russian going berserk at the sight of all of the food on the shelves in a New York supermarket.

Then came perestroika and glasnost and in their wake a group referred to wryly as the "economic refugees." Apolitical and motivated by their desire to escape the downsides of perestroika—criminal gangs, no food, uncertain prospects— this new wave of émigrés began to colonize the United States, Britain, and Western European countries. Russian women married foreign-passport holders twice their age whom they'd never met, would never love, and planned to abandon as soon as they got their own passports. People squeezed into cargo containers bound for Europe or went on tourist jaunts and simply disappeared into the growing Russian diaspora communities around the world. These communities absorbed them, hid them, and then regurgitated them with legitimate documents. Russians abroad became masters of immigration-finagling and benefit-scamming, and they morphed into lukewarm citizens of their adopted countries, as I learned when I made phone calls to Russian-speaking voters in swing states on behalf of Barack Obama.

When HRH and I were married, in 1994, the United States wasn't encouraging much tourist traffic from Russia, having found that, in its case, the risks did outweigh the rewards.

Oppressed Jews and political dissidents during the Cold War were one thing, America reasoned, but half of the former Soviet Union trying to treat the USA "like a goddamn Candy Land board," as one counselor officer put it to me succinctly, was quite another. So it came as a surprise during our honeymoon in the Caribbean to hear a Russian call to her husband to bring their umbrella: "Llyonia, *vozmi soboi* UMBRRRRELLLA!" HRH and I giggled. We loved the way the English word had been dropped into the Russian sentence, and umbrella is a perfect word to showcase what became known as a Brighton Beach accent: a heavy emphasis on the rolling *R* native to Odessa.

"Umbrella" became our family code for the Russian émigrés who suddenly seemed to be everywhere: in T.J. Maxx picking through the underwear bin, at the A&P buying up huge jars of mayonnaise, ahead of us in line at the VAT return desk at Heathrow with a fistful of receipts, and, much to our chagrin, table-nabbing at our slightly shabby and much loved resort in St. Croix.

A family of Russian émigrés, cashing in on the Cruzan natives' inability to distinguish one Slavic name from the other, pinched our carefully reserved table overlooking the ocean and the twinkling lights of Christiansted, forcing us to take a vastly inferior table right behind them. The romance of the evening was completely squelched by having to listen to them complain loudly in Russian about the food, the service, the heat, and general shabby infrastructure of our favorite holiday resort. They let up only to loudly, and in frank violation of the prominently displayed visual symbol of a mobile phone with a line drawn through it, telephone their children in Chicago, all of whom, for some inexplicable reason, seemed to be named for American rock stars: Jackson, Mick, and "Dee-Anna."

By unspoken agreement, at our table Velvet and I executed the conversation in English, and HRH, well camouflaged in the monochromatic polo shirt and khakis any self-respecting Russian would consider dull, confined his responses to soft, monosyllabic grunts to our prompts. I don't know that we fooled the "umbrellas," but we certainly staved off any kind of acknowledgment of one another. Because that kind of thing can lead to big trouble.

"Get this," I said to Joe, as we clamored back onto the top

deck of our sightseeing bus, "Lucy says that she had a Russian family in her office buying a really upscale trip to some wacky place like Bahrain or something. They told her she would get a ten-thousand-dollar bonus if she booked them into a hotel where there were no Russians."

"You shitting me?" said Joe.

"No, and here's the thing—they paid it," I said. "But only because she booked them into a dry hotel. No alcohol allowed. They had to go out to get a G&T."

"I love it," Joe cackled.

"This is totally a trend," I said. "Last year I took the Potapovs' kid Petya over to the US for summer camp. They are about as patriotic as it gets, but they were adamant about finding a place for him that didn't have any Russians."

I'd never seen Sveta Potapova so worked up.

The dacha, she explained, was getting a little cramped for Petya, who had shot up to six feet; there was kind of a rough crowd in the next-door compound. The general feeling was that it was time for him to expand his horizons. There was also the added element of Keeping Up with the Stepanovs or, once Andriusha came home from his time in Malta, even more a question of Doing It Differently from the Stepanovs. It was important for Petya to beef up his English and "acquire some new impressions," as the Russians say, but, Sveta stressed, Petya's time needed rigorous supervision and structure—a camp or summer school, it didn't matter; they would leave those details to me. There was one stipulation, however, and they felt strongly about it. "Under no circumstances," insisted Svetlana firmly, "do I want Petya mixing with any other Russians."

"Absolutely not," agreed Ilya, who never disagrees with Sveta about anything. "A completely Russian-free environment. That's why we are not sending him to Malta like Andriusha Stepanov! We've heard awful things about what goes on there: kids drunk at lunchtime, coming back knowing less English but more Russian swear words than when they left."

Sveta and Ilya were particularly grateful to have Petya safely stowed for the summer, because it meant they were able to get away themselves for a few weeks. They sent Xenia to Siberia to visit her grandparents and grabbed a reduced-for-quick-sale "Burning Trip" to Turkey. They were really, really lucky because

★

nothing went wrong. They didn't get held hostage by Turkish hoteliers, they didn't have to spend four nights at the airport, and they had a great time.

Like so many things in Russia, leisure travel is vastly polarized. At the top end you have Lucy's outfit—high-end VIP (pronounced in Russian as it is spelled: "vip," rhymes with "sip") travel for the crowd that graces the front pages of the financial press and the smaller group that is rich and powerful enough to stay off the front pages. On the opposite end of the travel spectrum are the massive migrations from all over Russia to the crowded beaches of Egypt, Tunis, and Turkey. From thence all the sun-worshiping Germans, Dutch, and Scandinavians have long since fled, shaking their heads and waving the white beach towel of defeat against the Russian onslaught toward the all-inclusive breakfast buffet and the strategic occupation of every deck chair by 9:00 a.m. This kind of travel is referred to as "charter."

Everyone really needs to experience this kind of thing at least once. Preferably early on in their travel career. I saw a great deal of this kind of thing during my happy time working for that large blue-chip Russian company you've heard of. The murky charter business and the truly unattractive people who work in it were great reasons to leave the travel business and go into banking. Anything for a quiet life.

Charter travel in Russia can be purchased, per person, for much less than the average Russian woman spends in a year on nail polish. The price doesn't suggest you are getting a lot of value for money. Burning Trips has offices in each major town in Russia, with sidewalk signs pointing the way to dingy second-floor offices. There, gray-faced sales clerks reluctantly surrender documents and plane tickets about five hours before you are scheduled to depart. But that's actually okay, because charter travel usually kicks off with an eight-to-ten-hour delay in an un-air-conditioned airport due to circumstances that might include any or all of the reasons listed below, none of which will be disclosed by the airline, the airport, or the tour operator:

- The airport runway's asphalt, which dates back to the 1980 Olympics, has buckled in the 100°F heat. All planes have therefore been grounded until evening, when the tarmac cools, at which point, because some airlines are more equal than others, the charter flights are bumped to the very back of the runway slots, behind Delta and Air France, who in turn are forced to wait behind their "strategic partner," the Russian national carrier.

- The Russian tour operator who created the air-hotel package has neglected to pay for a block of Turkish hotel rooms it used two seasons ago. The Turks, not known for their *sangfroid*, are protesting by holding Russian tourists hostage in the hotel ballroom. The Russian tourists/hostages are scheduled to return on the incoming charter aircraft, which is sitting on the tarmac in Antalya. This is grist for the current regime's xenophobia mill.

- Various mid-level Russian politicians race to express their outrage on live TV. They are all dressed in casual sport shirts bearing the logo SOCHI 2014! and standing against the waving palm trees and emerald waters of that elite Black Sea resort. The angry tourists who are stuck in Moscow, all dressed in the signature Russian travel uniform of SOCHI 2014! tracksuits and plastic sandals (men) and tight jeans, animal-patterned halter tops, mirrored sunglasses, and stiletto boots (women), begin to make snarky comments on TV that of course it's fine for the Russian tourists being held hostage in a Turkish ballroom, because (sniff) they are all being fed fresh fruit in the ballroom, which, unlike the airport, is air-conditioned. Probably, the Russian tourists muse, the Russian tourists/hostages don't have to wait for forty-five minutes to go to the bathroom, which in the Moscow airport is now a stinking cesspool, toilet paper being only a dim memory from several hours ago.

- The charter company, which has leased its battered, smelly, and dilapidated Illyushin Il-86 aircraft from the national carrier, has either (A) not paid for the gas or (B) the national carrier has discovered that it needs one or two more battered, smelly, dilapidated Illyushin Il-86 aircraft to execute its regularly scheduled flight to Sochi. So it has commandeered the aircraft meant for the charter.

★

Just as things reach fever peak there is generally an expediently timed and extremely well-publicized intervention from a very odd duck called Dr. Roichal. He is a curiously famous pediatrician who, for reasons I don't exactly get, always turns up during these regularly scheduled travel emergencies. His timing is impeccable. He arrives at the very moment when dog-tired mothers from Rostov-on-Don, crouching on their sagging nylon duffle bags bearing the logo SOCHI 2014!, have run out of patience.

Dr. Roichal immediately restores order, produces bottled water stamped with the logo SOCHI 2014!, and gravely accepts the handwritten *zayevleniya*, or petition, that is always got up by some outraged passenger demanding reimbursement not only for the entire cost of the trip but also for the *moralnaya usherp,* or moral outrage, suffered by the passengers. This money will never, ever be paid, Lucy assures me, despite the fact that all tour operators have to contribute to a fund "to bail out the idiots who create the problems in the first place," as Lucy explains it.

The tour operator representatives are always unavailable for comment and rarely ever seen again. A spokesman from the national carrier, on the other hand, dressed in a casual sport shirt bearing the logo SOCHI 2014!, is usually available for a super-smug comment about how the national carrier executed all of its regularly scheduled flights in the last months and is prepared to execute its obligations toward all its paying passengers in the months going forward.

Sometimes crises of this sort are averted, and the charter flight actually takes off on time and without incident. In these cases, there are only the regularly scheduled unpleasant hurdles associated with this level of service. As there are no actual seat assignments, adult males are dispatched in the vanguard to participate in the human stampede that is "the boarding process." They secure seats by literally blocking them with their bodies, arms and legs outstretched. This can take up to three hours and lead to at least five fistfights. Fainting spells are not uncommon. Eventually a semblance of order is achieved; generally there is a bum in every seat, including the jump seat and all of the toilet seats. Those who have working seat belts have fastened them. Finally the plane can take off.

Takeoff is the signal to bring out the duty-free purchases.

Despite the extreme heat of the airport, the aircraft, and the destination, the universal drink of choice is cognac. Messages printed on duty-free bags bearing the logo SOCHI 2014! that alcohol consumption on the aircraft is positively prohibited are ignored as passengers unscrew bottle tops and use them as shot glasses. Despite recent attempts by the Russian authorities to introduce nonsmoking regulations to Russian aircraft, a group of die-hards gather at the back of the aircraft to indulge. After forty-five minutes, the flight attendants give up trying to stop them and start bumming cigarettes from them. Turkey, they advise the passengers between drags, is an awfully dirty country, full of black people. Sochi, on the other hand . . .

Joe and I took the overnight flight back to Moscow, which always just fells me, but it gives you more time at the destination, and neither Joe nor I had to be in an office the next day.

Flying back to Russia is always hectic and a little bittersweet. Before email and mobile phones and everything, which today keep the border porous, I used to feel like Reepicheep at the end of *The Voyage of the Dawn Treader*: heading into the utter East. And although these days you can get everything except vanilla extract and Ziploc bags in Russia, I still feel a visceral need to stock up on everything before I head back.

Ours was one of the last flights out, so we heard a lot of Russian in the duty-free shops. I loaded up a basket with tea, face cream, and gin. Joe manfully worked through a long list Tanya had sent him via text message.

"What is 'Touche Éclat,' for chrissakes?" he called over to where I was comparing Bobbi Brown lip glosses.

"Yves Saint Laurent," I called back. "It's that gold wand thing."

"And 'Diorshow'?"

"That's mascara. No, Joe, you aren't going to find it in Chanel, obviously."

"What's the difference?" he cried.

"Huge difference," I said.

A few minutes passed.

"Okay, what the fuck is 'Lime, Basil & Mandarin'? This is the duty-free, not the freakin' fruit stand."

"Give me your list," I said, laughing and propelling him toward the Jo Malone counter.

We sat down for a last glass of wine, and Joe watched with barely concealed admiration as I swiftly released the purchases from their bulky packaging and stowed them in a big hold-all I produced from the pouch of my Rollaboard.

"You've done this before," he said.

"Yep," I agreed. "Now let's get on board fairly soon or there won't be any room for this stuff in the overhead thingy." This is absolutely essential when you are traveling back to Russia. Everyone is loaded down with purchases. Back in our "aisles across" seats, we watched other passengers boarding with large glossy carrier bags from Harrods, Harvey Nichols, and Hamleys toy store. No one—including the flight attendants—paid the slightest attention to the hand-luggage allowance.

"It's like Russia doesn't have any stores," said Joe, leaning across the aisle.

"Well, everything is three times as expensive," I countered. "And it's more fun to shop here, for some reason."

"You ever been on a plane back from Asia or the Middle East?" asked Joe. "That is something. Everyone comes loaded down with the most amazing crap. I'm surprised the plane can even take off!"

"I'll tell you a funny story about Russians in the Middle East," I said as the plane began to taxi out to the runway.

"Is it in the book?" asked Joe, who was almost as eager to meet his fictional avatar as Jesus was. "Am I in it?"

"It is in the book," I said. "But no, you aren't in this particular story. I think it will be toward the end, maybe even the last thing in the book."

The memory of one Russian abroad will always be with me. He stands out for a number of reasons, but primarily because the object of his travel seemed to be to bring a massive amount of baggage from home to his travel destination and leave it there.

For my birthday that year HRH allowed me to choose the annual May holiday destination, and I chose Jordan, somewhat to his dismay. HRH's idea of a good holiday is to find a beach with an adjacent bar and divide his day between running, sleeping, and consuming the local beer. He eats sparingly of local fruits and fish and falls into an exhausted heap at the end of the day. In ten days his batteries are recharged, and I'm bored out of my skull. I don't mind this kind of thing, but I'm with Bilbo Baggins that "still there are so many things that I have never seen." Jordan was high up on my list. Velvet, who is always up for an adventure, was all for Jordan as soon as she saw that most of the sites could be—and in her opinion should be—explored astride either a donkey or a horse. Most nine-year-olds might find a four-day trek through Petra tedious, but not Velvet. She was in love with a spindly donkey called Abdul who drank Coca-Cola straight from the can.

We happily explored Petra for four days, then exchanged the horses for camels and headed into Wadi Rum, where *Lawrence of Arabia* was filmed, and finally, like Lawrence, we proceeded down to Aqaba for some much-needed beach time.

It was on the way to Aqaba that we first encountered the couple. We stopped at an observation platform overlooking a Crusaders' castle, complete with complimentary toilet facilities and obligatory oversize portraits of King Abdullah and Queen Rania. As our guide was explaining the history of the Crusaders in Jordan, which I found interesting (HRH and Velvet, well trained by me to be nice to the guides, were listening politely enough), our attention was diverted by a couple instructing their guide in broken English how to use a complicated digital camera. There, literally in the middle of nowhere, we were confronted with *Homo novus Russicanus.*

This couple looked to be on the low end of this high-end species—possibly regional, rather than Muscovite, but with all the trappings. The man was right out of central casting: stocky, balding, intense turquoise-blue eyes that exactly matched his wife's finger and toenail polish. Jordan is pretty tolerant as Muslim countries go, but the wife seemed prepared to test that tolerance to its utter limit. She wore a sheer pearl-pink silk tunic over a lacy black bra that left little of her impressive cleavage to the imagination. Her skintight white jeans and gold lamé sandals did not, to me, seem the ideal ensemble for trekking through Wadi Rum, and I wondered how on earth she ever mounted a camel got up like that.

She struck a red-carpet pose and pouted prettily against the backdrop of the oversize portrait of Queen Rania (which no woman in her right mind should ever, ever do because even if you are Angelina Jolie, the contrast is impossible). But that's a New Russian for you: lots of expensive camera equipment, which they use exclusively to take pictures of themselves in front of famous monuments. Russians never seem to think that it would be nice to have pictures of just the monuments or the natural beauty on its own. Tancy and I once went to Asia with a bunch of people from Dragana's reading circle while I was still a member. While Tancy spent the whole time buying carpets, I tried to capture artistic shots of tortured-looking Tibetan pilgrims at a temple. The Russian members of our group spent the whole time hamming it up in front of any fire hydrant they could find, just like the couple at the Crusaders' castle in Jordan.

"Oh, wow," I said. "Do you think they are on their way to Aqaba as well?"

It turned out that they were and even staying at our hotel. We were somewhat thrown onto the same side of the beach when, come the Islamic weekend afternoon of Thursday, a group of Saudi women arrived, swathed from head to toe in black abayas, with a passel of children. The women took one look at Blue Fingernails and scurried as far away from her as they could. Velvet, on the other hand, was riveted. Blue Fingernails had a blue bikini the exact color of her nail polish and a blue dragon tramp stamp hovering strategically north of her bikini bottom. The dragon was breathing fire due south.

We watched, transfixed, as Blue Fingernails pulled a dog-eared Russian-language Harlequin romance from her beach bag and settled herself on a lounge chair. She flagged a passing waiter and asked for a Coke without ice, which was brought promptly and placed on the table next to her. As the waiter turned to attend to other patrons, Blue Fingernails, in a swift and clearly practiced gesture, pulled a fifth of Canadian Club out of her bag, deftly added about a third of it into her Coke, then quickly deep-sixed the bottle back into her bag.

It was 10:30 a.m.

Blue Fingernails was soon joined by her husband, whom I instantly christened "Pectoral Cross." His poolside ensemble consisted of the Russian swimsuit of choice: a teeny tiny Speedo leaving absolutely nothing to the imagination. Happily, I have convinced HRH that, despite his impressive physique, teeny tiny Speedos are not suitable beach attire. On his feet, Pectoral Cross wore black flip-flops and not a blessed thing else except for a massive gold cross, hung around his thick neck with a heavy chain, featuring an intensely Baroque treatment of Jesus Christ. Christ also wore a teeny tiny Speedo and had been captured during a particularly agonizing stage of his Passion. The cross was the size of my outstretched palm, and it remains the largest piece of religious jewelry I have ever seen on a member of the laity.

Pectoral Cross lay down next to Blue Fingernails and turned his face up to the heavens for some sun worship. I wondered what kind of a tan line the cross created. Did he, I mused, carefully replace it in one established position at each session to ensure a crisp line? Russians, including HRH, believe that the sun contains vital nutrients and vitamins, so they never use SPF of any level, and I could tell from their ruddy complexions that Blue Fingernails and Pectoral Cross had spent several weeks enthusiastically cultivating the vitamin D.

Velvet gets her enthusiasm for people-watching from me. HRH doesn't care for the pastime—he's never gripped by the latest gossip and remains frustratingly indifferent when I greet him with, "You will not believe what X just told me about Y." So it is probably just as well he missed the main Pectoral Cross and Blue Fingernails event, and who knows—had he still been with us, might we have missed it entirely?

After our respite in Aqaba, HRH flew back a day early to Moscow, because real alpha males in Russia always interrupt their vacation to fly back and put out some corporate fire. This left Velvet and me to finish up our holiday at the Dead Sea. Again, Blue Fingernails and Pectoral Cross turned up at the same hotel. Fate handed us a chatty Jordanian driver who discovered that we had not done much of the Biblical sightseeing around Madaba and insisted he take us to the baptism-of-Christ site. Well worth the trip, he advised. HRH's mother is dead religious, and I thought we might score some brownie points by picking up something meaningful for her at the gift shop.

I was intrigued to see the Jordan River, so we agreed, thinking it would be a "quick stop/photo op/potty hop/must shop" kind of visit. I should have known better. I once led a tour called "Walking in the Footsteps of St. Paul," during which I learned that anything to do with that early-Christian crew is always uphill, hot, and crowded, with challenging and uneven footing. The Baptism of Christ Center was all of those things. It was also ecumenical and multilingual. We were placed in a group with a couple from Seattle who had arrived the night before, two Albanian nuns who spoke not one word, and to our surprise, Blue Fingernails and Pectoral Cross.

Blue Fingernails was dressed more demurely for the baptism of Christ excursion—it was her first appearance in sleeves, which were attached to a filmy sort of tunic over a long pair of skinny jeans. She carried a plastic laundry bag, purloined from the Aqaba Kempinski, that clanked. I wondered if she had brought along her Canadian Club. She also had a weird kind of kerchief on her head that was too flimsy to provide any real protection from the sun and certainly not in keeping with her usual wardrobe choices.

Pectoral Cross was also wearing jeans and a close-fitting T-shirt made of a very shiny black material against which his enormous cross writhed in the Middle Eastern glare, making the Jesus figure dance about as if actually squirming in pain. We smiled the awkward smile of people who have been traveling in tandem for several days but who have not actually met.

The baptism site—like the footsteps of St. Paul—covered a lot of ground, most of it downhill toward the riverbed along a slippery set of stone staircases. As we picked our way down, the guide drew our attention to a small stone platform some twenty-five feet below and to the right of our path. This, he explained, was where Jesus had stopped to pray before being baptized.

"I go down there to pray," said Pectoral Cross in a matter-of-fact kind of way.

Heavens, I thought. Whatever for? I looked again at Blue Fingernails' weird kerchief and suddenly realized that, fancy Nikon, Canadian Club, and Harlequin romance aside, Blue Fingernails and Pectoral Cross were in Jordan primarily for religious reasons! The kerchief suddenly made sense: like any observant Orthodox Christian woman, Blue Fingernails covered her head to visit a site of religious significance. I listened hard to the exchange between the guide and Pectoral Cross.

"It is not permitted to descend," said the guide in a weary manner that suggested that Pectoral Cross was not the first person he'd encountered who wanted to literally walk in the way of the Lord.

Pectoral Cross gave the guide a nasty Slavic smirk that com-

★

municated, "Listen, you inferior brown towelhead, I know that you know that I know this is a rule, but you know that I know that you will look the other way, because you know that I know that if you do look the other way, I will tip you enormously when—and only when—this thing that I want that you know and I know is against the rules is accomplished to my satisfaction."

"What's going on?" asked the girl from Seattle, leaning over to tighten the toggles of her KEEN trekking sandals.

"He wants to pray down there," said Velvet helpfully, as calmly as if she were announcing that Pectoral Cross wanted to make a potty stop.

"Really?" asked the guy from Seattle in wonderment. He, like me, had not immediately pegged Pectoral Cross as the religious type.

"It seems so," I said, and we all leaned over the railing to watch the drama unfold.

The Albanian nuns crossed themselves and the Jordanian guide looked around guiltily while Blue Fingernails handed Pectoral Cross the Aqaba Kempinski laundry bag, and Pectoral Cross scurried down the slope to the stone platform. He knelt down and drew a small church candle in a glass holder from the laundry bag, then tugged a gold Zippo lighter out of his back pocket. He lit the candle, carefully returned the Zippo, then crossed himself using three fingers in the ultra-Orthodox manner and intoned prayers we couldn't hear.

I took a swig of tepid mineral water and handed the bottle to Velvet. Time passed. From somewhere nearby, a muezzin crackled and then moaned out "*Alllllaaaaaahhhhhhhhh akbarrrrrrrrrrrrrrr!*" calling for noonday prayers. Pectoral Cross finally lifted his head, extinguished the candle, hiked up the slope, and rejoined the party without a word. We continued on.

Our next stop, the guide informed us (casting a nervous look at Pectoral Cross), was the place where Jesus disrobed prior to getting baptized by John in the waters of the Jordan. There was a little grotto just to the side of the path. Without a word, Blue Fingernails handed Pectoral Cross the Aqaba Kempinski laundry bag, and he went into the grotto. The Albanian nuns crossed themselves again and the Seattle couple looked on with growing fascination, as Pectoral Cross, once again down on his

★

knees, relit the candle with the gold Zippo and then removed the shiny, skintight black T-shirt, carefully readjusted the Savior of Mankind on his hairless chest (did he wax? I wondered), and crossed himself a few more times. Rising, he placed the folded T-shirt into the laundry bag and, shirtless, rejoined the party.

"He's not wearing sun block, Mommy," Velvet observed. I was always trying to make Velvet wear more sun block.

"Very naughty," I agreed.

We continued downhill along the shady walkway until it abruptly stopped and we were once again in the bright sunshine. To our left was a gaudy Russian Orthodox church that looked as if it had been completed last week (it had) and beyond that, the River Jordan.

I don't know what you think of when you think of the River Jordan, if indeed you think about it at all, but my image of it had always been of a wide, majestic sort of waterway with a slow, but steady and stately, current—nothing so unbridled or inelegant as a torrent or anything but a commanding flow like the Hudson River or the Thames.

If I'd thought about the color at all I would have assigned it a blue in the marine hues with subtle hints of green, flecked with the occasional silver highlight of foam. As for its depth, wasn't there a song that went something like "Jordan's River is deep and wide"? Or was it "chilly and wide"? I did, however, imagine a shallow end, possibly with convenient steps leading down into it for Jesus to kneel on while John dipped a gourdlike thing into the river and poured the crystal-clear water droplets over Jesus's head.

Today, Jesus and John would have had to tote their water bottles to hold a baptism here. Time, and the diversion of water by neighboring countries, have have taken a toll on the once-mighty Jordan. You can see where the river might have been both deep and wide, and possibly even somewhat chilly, but today it is a putty-gray silt bed baking in the sun. At the bottom of the riverbed is a five- or six-foot-wide trough of cloudy, opaque water that looks like dishwater. It's just sort of lying there, stagnant. It smells awful, sort of rank and rotten.

The thing about traveling in the Arab parts of the Middle East is that you sometimes forget about Israel. But there, on the opposite side of the hugely disappointing River Jordan, was a whole bunch of barbed wire, taking itself very seriously indeed. About forty oversize Israeli flags, flapping majestically in the breeze, left nothing to the imagination. There it was—Israel. You could reach out your hand, if you dared, and you'd almost be there. At regular checkpoints, impossibly good-looking Israeli soldiers, both men and women, in pristine military garb and mirrored sunglasses, stood at attention, semiautomatic weapons raised skyward, their unblinking gazes trained on the opposite bank: the site of the baptism of Christ.

Pectoral Cross wasted no time. He eased off his lizard-skin loafers. Then unbuckled his belt.

"Oh my god," said the girl from Seattle. "You don't think he's going in . . ."

"Mommy, can I—" started Velvet.

"Don't even think about it," I said.

The Jordanian guide shook his head, started to intervene, clocked the Israeli soldiers, who were fingering the triggers of their semiautomatics, thought better of it, and slowly backed away, motioning us to come with him.

Blue Fingernails was now all purpose and action. She adjusted her kerchief and stood like a handmaiden, accepting the chunky Rolex Pectoral Cross carefully removed from his wrist. She waited patiently while he eased off his jeans, revealing the teeny tiny Speedo.

"Jesus Christ, I hope that guy has had a tetanus shot," breathed the guy from Seattle, as Pectoral Cross strode purposefully, without any hesitation, into the cloudy and rank River Jordan.

An Israeli guard yelled something in Hebrew and made a shooing gesture with his hand. We watched, rooted to the spot, while Pectoral Cross submerged himself completely into the stagnant, cloudy dishwater of the River Jordan not once, but thrice. He then rose, resplendent in his teeny tiny Speedo and his cross, everything covered with a fine film of gray silt, yet somehow he glowed with a new sense of something. He ignored the shouts of the Israelis and turned his face toward the sky for a moment. Then, cleansed of his sin or whatever it was (and I imagined it was epic, that sin), he languidly strode out of the River Jordan and joined Blue Fingernails, who had been busy shaking out a white silk shirt fresh from the Aqaba Kempinski's overnight dry-cleaning service.

Solemnly, Pectoral Cross donned the shirt, then less solemnly struggled to get his tight jeans back on over his silty wet legs. Blue Fingernails took the empty Canadian Club bottle and filled it up with opaque water from the River Jordan, oblivious to the Israelis, now grouped together and using a megaphone to express their desire that we get as far away from the River Jordan as possible. And so, even though it was uphill all the way, we scurried up that hill as fast as we could go.

"Come on, babycakes. You made that up," said Joe, as our plane hit the tarmac in Moscow. Even as the crew delivered a strict message to refrain from using any electronic device until the aircraft had come to a complete standstill, everyone on board pulled out their mobile phones and started to use them. People in the back rows, where they stash the unimportant and inexperienced travelers, leaped up and began to tug at their belongings in the overhead compartment.

"Come on, Joe," I remonstrated. "No one can make this shit up."

ABOUT THE AUTHOR

JENNIFER EREMEEVA is an American writer based in Moscow, Russia. Eremeeva received a BA in Russian Area Studies from Columbia University and studied at the Moscow Academy of Photography. She has lived in Moscow for two decades and speaks fluent Russian (so helpful for eavesdropping on conversations). Eremeeva is the author of an award-winning humor blog "Russia Lite: The Funnier Side of Life in the World's Largest Country," and creator and curator of the popular food blog "The Moscovore: Culinary Adventures in the Russian Capital." Eremeeva is the regular humor and cooking columnist for *Russia Beyond the Headlines*. Her work has appeared in *The Moscow Times, Russian Life*, and the BBC's *Russian Service*. She divides her time between Russia and the United States. This is her first book.*

---

*To receive a free digital copy of Jennifer Eremeeva's *second* book, *Have Personality Disorder, Will Rule Russia*, a condensed history of Russia and companion piece to *Lenin Lives Next Door*, email: jennifer.eremeeva@gmail.com.

jennifereremeeva.com

CPSIA information can be obtained at www.ICGtesting.com
Printed in the USA
BVOW04*2046300114

343535BV00001B/1/P